THE LAST VAMPIRE FAMILY

CLAN OF BRUCE - SEASON ONE

ALICE ROSE MCQUEEN

Also by Alice Rose McQueen

EX CINERE :

Book One : The Dusk Of The Ashes

Book Two : The Night Of The Ashes

Book Three : The Dawn Of The Ashes

Book Four : The Day Of The Ashes

CLAN OF BRUCE :

The Last Vampire Family - Season One

The Last Vampire Family - Season Two

The Last Vampire Family - Season Three

The Last Vampire Family - Season Four

The Last Vampire Family - Season Five

The Last Vampire Family - Season Six

BLOOD MILLENIUM :

Book One - The Forgotten Book

FEELING SOCIAL?

LET'S KEEP IN TOUCH! CONNECT WITH ME HERE:

www.alicerosebooks.com
Facebook.com/booksbyalicerose
Instagram.com/booksbyalicerose/
Tiktok.com/@booksbyalicerose

CLAN OF BRUCE - SEASON ONE
THE LAST VAMPIRE FAMILY
by
Alice Rose McQueen

Published by Monumental Books

3 rue de Turbigo
75001 Paris
France

www.alicerosebooks.com

Layout and book distribution by: Monumental Books
Printed in 2024

ISBN:
978-2-487769-08-3 (hardcover)
978-2-487769-07-6 (paperback)
978-2-487769-06-9 (ebook)

First Edition

DEAR READER...

I HAVE A WELCOME GIFT FOR YOU!

To thank you for your support and loyalty, I have a special surprise for you! How would you like to receive a free book?

Just signup here: www.alicerosebooks.com

I thank you from the bottom of my heart for being part of this literary adventure with me.

Happy reading and see you soon!

With all my affection,

Alice Rose McQueen

THE LAST VAMPIRE FAMILY

CLAN OF BRUCE - SEASON ONE

Alice Rose McQueen

MONUMENTAL BOOKS

To all the lovers of vampire lore who have wandered through the night with these immortal creatures in your hearts and imaginations—you are the true keepers of these timeless stories.

And to Anne Rice, who gave vampires their souls, their longing, and their eternal allure—this book exists because of the path you carved. Thank you for inspiring us to look beyond the fangs and into the hearts of the undead.

Alice Rose McQueen

FOREWORD

Dear Reader,

Welcome to a Scotland you've never known—a land where history and horror intertwine in the shadows of its ancient castles and misty moors. In these pages, you'll find the epic tale of Robert the Bruce, but not as your history books told it. This is Scotland's struggle for independence... with a vampiric twist.

I've taken the liberty of reimagining one of history's greatest warriors through a lens darkly fantastic. What if vampires weren't just the stuff of Transylvanian legend, but had their origins in the windswept highlands of Scotland? What if Robert the Bruce's greatest battle wasn't just against the English, but against creatures that defied mortal understanding?

While I've woven true historical events and locations into this tapestry of terror, I've also allowed myself to play with the rules of vampirism just a bit—let's say their ways of life and survival might not be exactly what you expect. Familiar elements of vampire lore remain, but you'll find a few... unique twists along the way.

You'll recognize familiar landmarks, but see them transformed by the presence of the supernatural. To the good people of Edinburgh's town hall—my deepest apologies for the liberties taken with your fine institution. Every hero needs a worthy adversary, after all.

This is not a history book, dear reader. It's a "what if" that dances in the firelight between fact and fiction. It's an invitation to see a familiar legend through fresh eyes, to feel the chill of both Scottish winter and immortal hunger.

So settle in, suspend your disbelief, and prepare for a journey into a Scotland where claymores clash with fangs, where the fight for freedom is measured not just in years, but in centuries. A Scotland where the night holds terrors beyond imagining, and where one man's quest for a crown becomes a battle for the very soul of a nation.

Welcome to *The Last Vampire Family*. History will never look the same again.

Sláinte mhath,

Alice Rose McQueen

"For as long as but a hundred of us remain alive, never will we on any conditions be brought under Vampire rule. It is in truth not for glory, nor riches, nor honours, that we are fighting, but for freedom – for that alone, which no honest man gives up but with life itself."

— ROBERT BRUCE

PROLOGUE

ARRAN'S WEST COAST
WINTER 1306

The wind howled through the narrow entrance, its mournful wail echoing off the damp stone walls of the cave on Rathlin Island. Cold seeped from the rock, chilling Robert Bruce to the bone as he huddled against the rough surface, a threadbare cloak his only shield against the bitter night.

Robert pulled the cloak tighter, his breath misting in the frigid air. The cave, a temporary refuge from both English pursuers and the more terrifying monsters that now stalked Scotland, felt more like a tomb with each passing hour. Where had these night creatures come from? The question gnawed at him, as relentless as the cold seeping into his bones.

He inched deeper into the cavern, away from the entrance where firelight might betray his presence. The English patrols had been relentless in their search, combing the island for any sign of the fugitive king. Robert had chosen this particular cave for its hidden location, accessible only through a treacherous climb up jagged cliffs.

As another gust of wind knifed through the cave mouth, Robert turned his gaze to the small fire pit nestled in a protected alcove. The flames had dwindled to mere embers, their feeble light a cruel metaphor for his current state. He'd rationed the firewood carefully, using it sparingly for warmth and to cook the meager supplies he'd managed to scavenge – seabirds' eggs, shellfish pried from tidal pools, and a few hardy plants that clung to life on the windswept island.

Seven days. Seven endless days of hunger, cold, and fear. Robert's stomach growled, reminding him of the dwindling food stores tucked away in a crevice. He'd have to venture out soon, risking detection to replenish his supplies. The thought sent a shiver down his spine that had nothing to do with the chill air.

In the depths of the cavern, something skittered in the darkness. Robert's hand flew to the silver dagger at his belt, eyes straining to pierce the gloom. Was it merely a rat, or something far more sinister? Had one of these monsters followed him here, to his desperate sanctuary? By now he knew they were patient predators, hiding in the shadows of night, hungry for blood and waiting for the perfect moment to strike.

The skittering grew louder, accompanied by a frantic scratching. Robert tensed, his grip tightening on the dagger's hilt. Suddenly, a flash of movement caught his eye, darting past him in the dim light. In one fluid motion, he lunged, blade glinting in the feeble glow of the embers.

❖

The aroma of cooking meat filled the cave. Robert's silver dagger had struck true, and now the golden hare roasted over the rekindled fire. Its presence was a small victory against the gnawing hunger that had plagued him for days. Not every shadow concealed a nightmare, he thought.

The fat sizzled, filling the air with savory scents. Robert's mind, momentarily distracted from survival, began to wander back to the horrors that had driven him to this desolate refuge.

Once crowned King of Scotland, now an outlaw in his own land. Hunted by King Edward Longshanks like a dog. Robert stared into the dying embers, despair weighing on him heavier than any crown.

The disaster at Methven replayed in his mind. His army scattered, his kingdom lost. Forced into hiding, cut off from his people, his family.

After the crushing defeat, he'd made a desperate decision. Queen Elizabeth, his young daughter Marjorie, and his sisters Mary and Christina – he'd sent them all to Kildrummy Castle under Niall's protection. His brother would keep them safe, he'd told himself.

His thoughts turned to the chaos that had engulfed Scotland in mere months. The betrayal at Dumfries still burned in his mind - John Comyn's treachery, the fateful meeting in the chapel of Greyfriars Monastery, and the violence that erupted before the altar. Robert's hand had struck the blow, but it was Comyn's lies to the English that had truly drawn first blood.

The memory of storming Dumfries Castle, the shocked faces of the English garrison as they surrendered, felt like a lifetime ago. He'd raced to Glasgow then, desperate for allies. Bishop Wishart's absolution had been a balm to his soul, even as Rome's excommunication hung over him like a shroud.

But it had all gone wrong at Methven. Comyn's treachery had run deeper than he'd imagined, and the English had been ready. Now here he was, a king in name only, hiding in caves while his enemies hunted him. What hope was there for Scotland now? For the dream of independence he'd staked everything on?

Robert's chest tightened. He'd started this war to free his people, but how many had suffered for his ambition? And if he fell here, in this miserable cave, would anyone be left to carry on the fight?

As the fire crackled softly, Robert's mind drifted back to that fateful day at the chapel of Greyfriars Monastery. Comyn's words echoed in his memory, taking on a chilling new significance in light of recent events. "A false king leading an army of shadows," Comyn had sneered. At the time, Robert had dismissed it as mere political slander, another of Comyn's attempts to undermine his claim to the throne.

But now, huddled in this damp cave with the horrors of Methven fresh in his mind, doubt gnawed at him. Had Comyn known something he didn't? The vampire horde that had decimated his forces – could they truly believe he was their leader? Robert shuddered, remembering the pale, inhuman faces that had torn through his army. The very thought of being associated with such monsters turned his stomach. Yet he couldn't shake the nagging question: why had Comyn been so convinced of his connection to these creatures of darkness? And if he wasn't their leader, who was?

The wind shrieked louder, mocking his doubts. Robert's mind raced through blood and betrayal. Was Scotland's freedom worth this price?

Exhaustion dragged at him. Maybe it was time to abandon this doomed fight. Set sail for the Holy Land, seek redemption in Christendom's wars. Yet something in him rebelled. How could he forsake the land of his birth? The people who'd crowned him?

❖

Huddled in the cold embrace of the cave, Robert struggled to make sense of it all. Night after night, his dreams were haunted by the horrors that had truly sealed their fate at Methven. The English were a known threat, but what emerged as twilight fell on the battlefield defied mortal understanding.

Darker threats had loomed beyond Longshanks' armies. Whispers of wolfmen stalking the highlands, of pale demons rising from unholy graves. A shadowy clan led by an unspeakable evil, preying on Scot and Englishman alike.

These creatures of the night, these undead abominations, had torn through their ranks with terrifying ease. Tales spread quickly of brave warriors falling to their superhuman strength, only to rise again as soulless puppets. The land was gripped by terror, as neither sword nor arrow could stop these monsters.

Robert remembered the sickening howl of a man twisted into a beast, the inhuman speed of pale figures darting through the chaos. These were no mere animals, but something born of nightmare itself.

Yet even in the depths of that blood-soaked defeat, hope had flickered in the shadows. Whispered legends spoke of ancient methods to combat such evil - a wooden stake through the heart, cleansing fire, decapitation, the purifying light of the sun. Some swore that garlic and holy symbols could repel the fiends. But few had survived to confirm these tales, and fewer still had the courage to test them.

As Robert wrestled with despair, a flicker of movement caught his eye. A spider, dangling on a silken thread, began to weave an intricate web in the corner of the cave.

❖

Day after day, Robert watched the creature work tirelessly, expanding its domain thread by thread. Six times the spider attempted to stretch its first silk strand across the expanse of the cave's corner, and six times it failed. The stubborn arachnid refused to give up, each attempt as determined as the last.

On the seventh night, as Robert huddled by the feeble fire, a bat swooped through the cave's narrow entrance. It circled the chamber, its leathery wings beating a frantic rhythm against the damp air. The flickering firelight cast its shadow large and monstrous against the rough stone walls.

Suddenly, the bat collided with the spider's newly completed web. The silk strands, seemingly fragile, held fast. The spider darted from its hiding place, swiftly wrapping its prey in a cocoon of silk.

Robert's eyes widened. In that moment, inspiration struck like lightning. If this tiny spider could ensnare a creature of the night, perhaps there was hope yet. A plan began to form in his mind, as intricate and daring as the spider's web.

He would offer King Edward a deal. Robert would rid Scotland of the blood-drinking fiends that plagued both their lands. In return, he'd reclaim his throne and drive the English from Scottish soil. It was a gamble, but one that could change everything.

The fire in his heart rekindled. Robert stood, his cloak falling away. No more hiding. No more doubt. It was time to gather his allies, to forge a rebellion that would shake the very foundations of King Edward's rule. And when Scotland was free, he'd turn his blade to the creatures of the night.

❖

As dawn broke over Rathlin Island, Robert Bruce strode from the cave, a man reborn. His path was clear. For Scotland. For his people. For a future free of tyranny – both mortal and immortal.

CHAPTER 1

Heather's influence in the whisky world came with a price tag. Men from every corner of society vied for her attention, not just for her company, but for the liquid gold she controlled. Celebrities, politicians, influencers, restaurateurs—they all played the game, hoping their charm might score them discounts on the rarest bottles.

For those who caught her eye, the payoff could be huge. A night with Heather often meant serious savings on high-end vintages or bulk orders. But as she watched the shredded TikTok star snoring beside her, Heather felt that familiar sting of regret. This one, she thought, didn't deserve the exquisite scotch he'd be taking home.

Self-doubt crept in, as familiar as whiskey's burn. How many times had she sworn she'd be pickier, less impulsive? Yet here she was again, trapped in a cycle she couldn't seem to break. Heather sighed, wondering if change was even possible, or if this was just the cost of her unique position in the spirits industry.

At thirty-two, Heather felt the toll of her choices settling in like sediment in a whisky barrel. She'd set herself a deadline: thirty-five.

Not a day more. If life hadn't thrown her a curveball by then, she'd promised to reinvent herself, to ditch the path of least resistance.

She toyed with the idea of following her sister's lead. A life of domesticity didn't sound half bad—shopping sprees, home decorating projects, tending a garden, with yoga sessions sprinkled in. It wasn't exactly thrilling, but it wasn't the end of the world either. At least then, she mused, she and her sister might finally have something to talk about over their afternoon tea.

The thought of change stirred something in Heather. Maybe there was more to life than being the whisky world's favorite bargaining chip. But for now, that future stayed just out of reach, like the last drop in a bottle of rare scotch.

❖

The spring morning air was crisp, sunlight glinting off distant snow-capped peaks. Along the avenues, the city came to life. Shopkeepers swept storefronts, residents collected mail, all soaking up the day's first rays.

On the bus, Heather felt exposed. A voluptuous blonde, she was used to getting the occasional creepy look, but this felt different. A man with calloused hands kept stealing glances her way. She ignored him, but his attention gnawed at her. "Is it that obvious?" she wondered, suddenly self-conscious.

It baffled her. She'd showered, her suit was pristine—she always hung it up the second she entered a room. Yet something about her seemed to broadcast her secrets.

Uneasy, Heather dug a compact mirror from her bag. She studied her reflection, searching for some telltale sign. Just to be sure. Just for peace of mind.

❖

The Clan Bruce Distillery's Edinburgh office sprawled beneath fluttering Scottish pennants, a beautiful centuries-old sandstone building that belied its modern purpose. While tourists flocked to admire its historic façade, the real gold was produced far to the north in Speyside, where the actual distillery nestled among heather-covered hills.

From his office window overlooking the manicured courtyard, Cameron Bruce spotted Heather's arrival. The youngest of the Bruce brothers, Cameron was the epitome of rugged Scottish allure wrapped in sartorial perfection—wild dark curls, stormy gray eyes, and a magnetic presence that drew women like moths to a flame. His bespoke Tom Ford suit accentuated his powerful frame, a testament to his impeccable taste.

Heather's sharp stride and tight shoulders told him everything—another night away from home. He tracked her progress, listening as her footsteps echoed up the worn stone stairs and down the hallway, bee-lining for the bathroom. Right on cue.

Cameron knew the drill. On mornings like this, Heather would linger at the sink, washing her hands over and over. Lost in thought, second-guessing her choices. When she'd spent the night with a man, especially one she regretted, the entire office braced for impact.

He sighed, turning back to his antique desk. It was going to be one of those days at the Edinburgh headquarters, far removed from the soothing rhythms of their Speyside stills.

"I've landed a buyer for the Legacy Reserve," Heather announced, bursting into Cameron's office. Her energy crackled through the air like static.

Cameron looked up, a flicker of crimson flashing in his eyes before vanishing. He'd mastered that reflex around humans centuries ago. His gaze fixed on Heather, senses stretching beyond what any mortal could perceive. The faintest tremor in her voice. A quickened heartbeat that betrayed either stress or excitement beneath her professional facade.

And there it was again—that familiar post-coital scent wafting off her skin. To human noses, she probably just smelled of soap and light perfume. But to Cameron's vampiric senses, it was like a neon sign advertising her recent activities. The mix of sweat, pheromones, and that unmistakable musk of sex was as clear as day to him. It wasn't the first time she'd shown up to work fresh from a rendezvous, and he doubted it would be the last.

Layered within that sensual mélange, Cameron detected a familiar note—the distinct scent of the TikTok personality he'd met just yesterday, a jacked gym rat whose biceps threatened to burst through his too-tight t-shirt. The pieces clicked into place, painting a vivid picture of Heather's recent activities. A spark of something—curiosity, perhaps even a tinge of possessiveness—flared briefly in his mind before he quashed it.

The faintest flicker of an old, long-forgotten instinct crossed his mind, but it was gone as quickly as it came. His eyes swept over her, taking in her neat, efficient attire—the uniform of a devoted secretary, not a salesperson. Yet here she stood, cool as you please, dropping news of a major whisky deal she'd somehow closed. It was another bold Heather move, way beyond her job description as his and his brother's personal assistant.

She had taken it upon herself to dive into "sales" territory strictly outside her purview. It was audacious, potentially reckless, and undeniably entertaining.

Business was business, after all.

Cameron's eyebrows shot up. The Bruce Legacy Reserve was their crown jewel—fifty years of aging in Speyside had produced a whisky that showcased the Clan's mastery. At a cool quarter-million per bottle, it wasn't exactly an impulse buy. Even his top salespeople rarely moved these ultra-premium spirits.

"Impressive, Heather," he said, genuine admiration in his voice. "I tip my hat to you." Cameron tried not to let on that he knew the "client" she referred to was the TikTok guy Heather had been flirting with shamelessly the day before.

He did some quick mental math. The commission would be hefty—not quite Porsche 911 territory, her dream car, but a significant step closer. Heather's skills as a secretary might be questionable—her habit of overstepping and meddling was legendary—but her sales talent was undeniable.

Cameron leaned back in his chair, pride and concern warring within him. Heather was an asset to their Edinburgh operations, no doubt. But each of her successes came with a steep personal price tag.

His dictation was cut short by the sight of a black BMW, an older model, gliding through the wrought-iron gates. Something about it felt off in the carefully curated historic setting. The car bypassed the main entrance, crawling to a stop right beneath his window.

Intrigued, Cameron paused, waiting to see who'd emerge. But the moment stretched, and Heather's attention drifted to her shoes—authentic Louboutins she'd treated herself to after closing a big deal last month. An executive assistant, a glorified secretary really, she worked hard for her luxuries. Frowning, she noticed a scuff on the red sole and absently tried to buff it out with her thumb.

"Heather, shall we get going? Let's move a bit," Cameron prompted, trying to pull her back to earth. He needed her focused on her secretarial duties, not daydreaming about commissions. Whatever ambitions were eating at her would have to wait. Right now, he needed his assistant, not a wannabe sales agent.

The door slammed, Heather's frustration echoing through the hallways. Cameron sighed, steeling himself for a day of clipped responses and barely-veiled irritation. Her mood swings were becoming a real problem.

Suddenly, Heather's voice rose sharply outside. Cameron tensed, assuming she was unleashing on some poor soul. But the sound grew closer, more urgent.

His frosted glass door flew open. A woman stood on the threshold, Heather's rant fading to background noise. Cameron sat frozen, gripping his chair like a lifeline.

A deep, earthy musk hit him, reminiscent of their Speyside warehouses. When the woman started to smile, his body shivered.

❖

Gordon Bruce lived by the clock. At six precisely, his watch vibrated.

The elder Bruce brother untangled himself from Fiona with a supernatural grace. Broad-shouldered and lean, Gordon embodied restrained power. His closely cropped silver hair belied his true age—centuries, not decades. Piercing blue eyes that had witnessed empires rise and fall swept the room, missing nothing.

Gordon dressed swiftly, every movement deliberate and predatory. This wasn't mere military discipline, but the product of centuries spent honing the art of survival. His motions were fluid, betraying nothing of the weight those years carried.

How many times had he fled the bed of a woman right before dawn? Hundreds? Thousands? The thought flickered through his mind, bringing with it a wry twist of his lips.

He glided across creaky wooden floors without a sound, a living shadow. As the first hint of dawn kissed the horizon, Gordon slipped out the back door. An old instinct, deeply anchored in his psyche, noted the approaching sun. His body, long since adapted, felt no urgency. Yet the habit of centuries guided his steps, a comfortable routine etched into his bones.

Nowadays, avoiding drama was his mantra. Complications were the enemy of this delicate arrangement with Fiona. And the kids? He couldn't face them, knowing their father's side of the bed had barely cooled.

Dawn found him creeping back to the family estate in his Racing Green Aston Martin DBS, cutting the engine as he coasted into the driveway. The ancestral manor loomed ahead, a grand Victorian silhouette against the lightening sky—his mother and brother still lost to sleep. He ghosted to his room, changing for his morning run.

For vampires as old as the Bruce family, sleep had long ago ceased to be a daytime necessity, except to regenerate and heal. Instead, it became a meditative art form, a chance to process centuries of accumulated memories, to program their minds to live fully and be present—a vampiric mindfulness exercise. Their rest aligned with the moon's phases rather than the sun's journey, the new moon marking their deepest periods of introspection. Like primal beasts, they responded to these lunar rhythms, tapping into ancient instincts long buried beneath their civilized veneer.

❖

At this early hour, Edinburgh was just stirring to life. The cobblestone streets of the Old Town were quiet, save for the occasional clatter of delivery trucks. Mist clung to the base of the manor, softening its imposing silhouette against the dawn's pale glow. In the New Town, early risers emerged from Georgian townhouses, their breath visible in the crisp morning air. The spire of St. Giles' Cathedral pierced the dawn, a sentinel over the awakening city.

He took a deep breath, steeling himself for the day ahead. The complexities of his double life weighed on him, especially with thoughts of Fiona lingering. But the run would clear his head. At least for a while.

The morning air carried a sweet freshness, dew glistening on the riverbanks. Beyond the Firth of Forth's suspension bridges, sunlight gilded the tops of empty office buildings, heralding the coming day.

A verdant stretch followed the Water of Leith, Edinburgh's primary river. In warmer months, the Meadows and Holyrood Park would be dotted with sunbathers and picnickers.

It was in one of these green spaces, two months ago, that Gordon first saw Fiona, a nurse at the local hospital. He'd been on his morning run when she appeared, shattering his composure. Her shiny red hair spilled like liquid fire over milky shoulders, liberated from its ponytail as she cooled down. The fitted track pants and snug tank top clung to curves that could make a saint sin, with a subtle softness that excited him beyond reason—so unlike his usual type. As she stretched, the fabric rode up, revealing a sliver of toned midriff that made Gordon's mouth go dry.

Their eyes met, and the spark was instant, mutual, and entirely human. For once, Gordon didn't need to rely on his vampire hypnosis—the ability to enthrall, alter memories, and even erase them from both vampires and breathers, though it worked far more easily on the latter—like he usually did with other women to satisfy his insatiable sexual appetite. This was pure, unadulterated attraction. Not a frequent runner, Fiona had been escaping a marital spat, and became the best fuck he'd had in centuries. Literally.

If only it weren't for the kids.

Two kilometers in, Gordon paused, lungs burning. At 700-something years old, he remained forever a fit forty-two, but Fiona left him oddly drained. Their nightly trysts pushed even his vampiric stamina to its limits. It was as if she drew energy from him, leaving him more spent than any human lover ever had. Grimacing, he clutched his sides, sweat beading on his brow.

As the sun crested the horizon, Edinburgh came alive beneath Gordon's feet. Centuries had passed, but this city endured, forever evolving yet somehow timeless. He breathed deeply, savoring the familiar blend of old stone, salt air, and the faint hum of modernity. No matter how many sunrises he witnessed, this view never lost its magic. He took a deep breath, savoring this moment of solitude before the day's demands closed in.

Gordon eased his pace on the return journey. Two Pakistani women in form-fitting gear zipped past, deep in animated conversation. Later, a white-haired man who could've been his father lapped him. The price of immortality, he mused.

As he approached the manor entrance, Cameron emerged, keys in hand.

"Leave money for the housekeeper. Mum forgot again, fridge is empty. We're going to look like eccentric recluses again," Cameron said, the Aston Martin chirping as he remotely disarmed it.

Gordon nodded curtly. Even after seven centuries, his younger brother's know-it-all attitude grated on him.

❖

The Bruce family gathered around the dinner table in silence. Sushi takeout boxes sat unopened before them, a testament to Margaret's growing disinterest in household management. The empty fridge and absent housekeeper had necessitated this hastily ordered meal.

Gordon glanced at the sushi, recalling Dr. MacGregor's findings. Raw fish, high in iron and omega-3 fatty acids, helped dull their more dangerous urges. The nutrients, similar to those in human blood, allowed them to maintain a semblance of control. It wasn't a perfect solution, but it beat the alternatives.

As Cameron broke apart his chopsticks, Gordon reflected on the practicality of it all. Sushi: a convenient cover for their dietary needs and a way to blend in. Who'd have thought their survival would one day hinge on Japanese cuisine?

"No need to wait for your father," Margaret announced, bitterness lacing her words. "He'll arrive when he arrives." Even mentioning her husband seemed to sour her mood these days.

Margaret had indulged in two gins before the boys returned from the distillery—her latest act of defiance against a family she'd grown increasingly disillusioned with. She pointedly avoided the family whisky, a calculated slight that cut deeper than words. The Bruce legacy's crown jewel sat untouched on the sideboard, its rich, peaty aroma now filling her with resentment.

Fresh from the hairdresser, Margaret felt armored. Her appearance was immaculate, every strand in place. A sleek Saint Laurent suit hugged her figure, a second skin of power and defiance. After 700 years of maintaining the facade of a well-preserved sixty, she'd grown weary of the constant effort. But today, that mask was her shield against the world. Dr. MacGregor's hormone treatments, along with more secretive rituals, left her pale skin unnaturally smooth. The effect was striking—ageless beauty wrapped in designer armor.

Beneath the polished exterior, anger smoldered. Margaret sipped her gin, relishing its burn. As she steeled herself, she felt that familiar itch in her gums—fangs eager to extend. Once, those fangs had signaled the thrill of the hunt. Now, they were merely a sign of irritation, like a human's eye twitch.

How far they'd fallen, from apex predators to bickering socialites. Margaret almost missed when baring fangs meant death, not just enduring cutting remarks over cocktails.

For two centuries, she'd abstained from human blood, relying on placenta treatments. Recently, she'd relented to a minor surgical procedure, restoring her youth and, unexpectedly, sharpening her resolve.

Gin was just a weak consolation.

Margaret sensed unease from her sons. Something had shaken them, a tremor she couldn't ignore even through the gin's haze. The air felt heavy with unspoken revelations, as if their centuries-old existence was about to crumble.

She fixed her gaze on Cameron, her youngest and usually most forthcoming. Silently, she willed him to meet her eyes, to spill whatever secret they were harboring.

Finally, Cameron looked up, his expression grave. "Rhona is back," he said, his hands retreating from the table as if burned by the words.

"Don't talk nonsense," Margaret snapped, her voice rising with a touch of hysteria. The name alone was enough to shatter her carefully maintained composure.

Silence engulfed the room, thick and oppressive. Margaret's lower lip quivered. She pushed away from the table, leaving the untouched sushi gleaming under the harsh light.

She turned to the bay window, its expanse revealing nothing but inky darkness and a distant horizon. The castle's elevated position, usually a source of pride, now felt like an isolation. Margaret despised herself for this lapse in control, biting the inside of her cheek hard enough to draw blood.

"Everything will be fine," Cameron offered, his voice steady but unconvincing.

Margaret's shoulders sagged, the strain of seven centuries pressing down on her. When she finally faced her sons again, time seemed to warp. For a heartbeat, she saw them as they had been just two decades ago—not physically younger, but displaying an immaturity and vulnerability she hadn't witnessed since they were in their mortal twenties, over 700 years past. Her throat constricted with an emotion she couldn't name.

"You have nothing to worry about," Cameron continued, his tone betraying his own uncertainty.

Gordon remained silent, offering only a vague nod.

"What are you waiting for? Serve yourselves," Margaret snapped, pushing the sushi towards them. She lit a cigarette, using the familiar ritual to stave off the wave of panic threatening to engulf her. At least being undead spared her from cancer—one small mercy in an eternal existence still plagued by aggravating mortal concerns.

The throaty growl of a 1964 Aston Martin DB5 announced Alistair Bruce's arrival moments before his knock echoed through the room. He entered with the quiet authority of his seventy years (and then some 700), cutting an impressive figure in his impeccably tailored English suit. Thick white hair crowned his distinguished features, a striking blend of age and vitality. As he stepped inside, the news of Rhona's sudden return hung heavy in the air.

"Alright. Let them start killing each other again," he said coldly, his words cutting through the tension.

Cameron sighed, exasperation clear in his voice. "We're not going to kill each other," he insisted. "Get that idea out of your head."

Margaret's eyebrows shot up. "Oh really? Last time it was absolute carnage. Took us years to clean up that mess."

"Things are... different now," Cameron replied, his voice softening to barely above a whisper.

Alistair Bruce's skepticism was palpable. After their sons retreated upstairs, he lingered with Margaret.

"I advise you to stay out of this," he said, his tone grave. "I'm saying this for your own good."

Margaret drained her fourth gin of the night, the alcohol a false promise of clarity. "Thanks. You can keep your advice," she retorted. "Are you planning to stay for hours?"

❖

Upstairs, Gordon tossed restlessly. Sleep eluded him. He flicked on the light, leafing through a stack of old magazines without absorbing a word. The ceiling offered no answers, no matter how long he stared. A nameless unease gnawed at him—hunger, thirst, or something deeper. The clock ticked past two in the morning.

Finally admitting defeat, Gordon rose and made his way to the kitchen, his footsteps echoing in the silent house.

Gordon found Cameron sprawled on the living room couch, laptop teetering on his thighs. Wearing only boxers, his pale skin gleamed in the dim light—a stark reminder of their shared immortality. Cameron gnawed on an ice cream bar, fangs grazing the frozen treat absentmindedly as he watched a silent porn video with feigned nonchalance. The taste did little to quench the deeper cravings he fought to bury, that constant gnawing hunger that never truly faded.

The old bloodlust was dead, mostly, killed by centuries of iron will and scientific tinkering. Cameron and Gordon had traded fangs for test tubes, thanks to Dr. MacGregor talent, their carefully crafted plasma diet keeping the monster at bay. But nature's a bitch, and the void left by that primal urge screamed to be filled.

Enter their new drug of choice: pure, raw pleasure. It gnawed at Cameron's insides, an itch he couldn't scratch in a world gone dull. This old addiction, vampire instinct twisted into something darker, demanded to be fed. For immortals, sex wasn't just fun—it was fucking oxygen. A fleeting high where he could drown in someone else's heat, forgetting the emptiness for one goddamn second.

Gordon clocked his brother's grip on his prick, hand clenched tight enough to crack. The frozen ice cream treat was a joke compared to what really burned in Cameron's veins—a hunger only quenched by the hunt, by women who had no clue they were offering themselves up as prey. Both brothers knew this ache intimately, carved into them by years of playing nice. No matter how mind-blowing the orgasm, it was never enough. But night after night, they chased that dragon.

Cameron's cool guy act was bullshit. It barely hid the drive that pushed them both to hunt, seduce, take. Still predators, just with new game. They stalked pleasure itself, the thrill of the chase as intoxicating as it was ultimately hollow. Their nightly conquests were desperate attempts to stave off eternity's soul-crushing boredom, to feel a-fucking-nything in a world that had long since numbed them. Each seduction, each scream of ecstasy, was a brief escape from the void. But the high always faded.

Cameron's eyes met Gordon's over his ice cream, a flash of crimson understanding passing between them. Immortality had become their prison, chaining them to this cycle that only deepened the craving. The women were just distractions, temporary fixes for the abyss inside. The rush of orgasm, tangled limbs, sweat-slicked skin—it was all they had left to remind them they weren't completely dead inside.

Gordon kept his mouth shut. What was there to say? This was their life now: an endless chase with no finish line. As they sat there, one savoring cold sweetness while the other plotted the next score, they both knew this addiction was all that remained of their legacy. The last thread connecting them to a world they could never truly be part of again.

Padding to the kitchen, Gordon poured himself a glass of water. Through the window, he caught glimpses of the manor grounds bathed in moonlight, sprinklers creating ephemeral halos in the silvery glow.

He joined Cameron, his gaze drawn briefly to the laptop screen.

"Do you want to talk about it?" Gordon finally ventured, breaking the silence.

"Talk about what?" Cameron replied, eyes still fixed on the screen. "You're going to start too?"

Gordon licked his lips, suddenly aware of his own hypocrisy. How could he ask Cameron to confront what he himself couldn't face?

"Still, she's got nerve," Gordon said, breaking the tense silence.

"Did you doubt it? Isn't that just like her?" Cameron replied, his eyes still glued to the screen.

Gordon shifted uncomfortably. "In any case, I wonder if it's a good idea to see her again. Like we're the best of friends. Why take the risk?"

Cameron finally looked up, a hint of disbelief in his voice. "Are you scared of her? After twenty years, are you still scared? You're joking, right?"

Gordon stroked his chin, considering. He nodded slowly, the burden of centuries evident in his gesture. "I wonder if we're capable of making the same mistake again. That's what I wonder."

The creak of the stairs alerted them to their mother's presence. Margaret stood in the stairwell, clad in a luxurious silk robe—her usual nocturnal attire. She was a vision – alabaster perfection carved by eternity's magical hand. One pale hand was pressed to her mouth, her composure visibly shaken. At this hour, she should have been in a deep, drug-induced slumber, courtesy of Dr. MacGregor's specially formulated vampire sedatives. The pills, developed exclusively for her unique physiology, usually knocked her out cold.

"No, please, Mum," Cameron whined, his earlier bravado evaporating. "Go back to bed."

Margaret halted at the foot of the stairs, her gaze shifting between her sons. The burden of immortality seemed to press down on her shoulders.

"You scare me," she breathed, each word a shard of ice. "You both scare me."

❖

Rhona stirred in the upstairs bedroom, its window framing a view of what was once a garden. Now, it was a wild explosion of vegetation, nature reclaiming its territory since her parents had relocated to Ballater, leaving her the house. The dense Caledonian forests surrounding the town had always called to her family, offering both sanctuary and a quaint retirement haven. Years had passed since she'd last set foot here, the property becoming her daughter's domain upon starting university.

She allowed herself a moment, eyes closed, nostrils flaring imperceptibly. The air was thick with scents – musty layers of disuse, the sharp tang of youthful indiscretion, and something... else. Something that made her hackles rise, though she couldn't quite place it. Rhona abruptly cast aside the covers.

Downstairs, she surveyed the kitchen with a critical eye. The cupboards yielded little, and the refrigerator's offerings were equally sparse: a half-empty bottle of milk, a few cans of beer, a slice of pizza well past its prime, and a solitary egg. Each item carried its own olfactory story, a timeline of neglect and hasty meals.

Rhona nearly bolted for her car, intent on finding breakfast in town. A last-ditch search uncovered a box of instant coffee, and she reluctantly conceded to its meager offering. The bitter aroma assaulted her senses, almost – but not quite – masking that lingering, unsettling scent.

She'd dragged a chair into the overgrown garden, lost in contemplation when Isobel appeared in the doorway, bag slung over her shoulder. Rhona raised a hand, shielding her eyes from the morning glare.

"Already ready?"

"Are you okay? Did you manage?" Isobel asked. Rhona waved off her concern with a gesture.

"And you're leaving on an empty stomach?" she questioned, then caught herself. "Forget I said that."

Rhona caught herself, reining in the maternal instinct. She wasn't here for that. Coexisting with her daughter, if it was to be tolerable, meant respecting certain boundaries.

"Sorry about last night," Isobel offered. "I hope you didn't wait up for me."

Rhona waved dismissively, indicating it was of no consequence.

"So?" Isobel probed, a hint of hesitation in her voice. "How did it go? If you don't mind me asking."

Rhona's gaze drifted to a squirrel bounding through the branches. Childhood memories flooded back—of crafting elaborate houses for the creatures, scaling trees to hang them, only for the squirrels to ignore her efforts entirely. Or of chasing them, treating them as delectable snacks.

Rhona tore her gaze from the tree, shifting slightly in her lounger. "How did what go, dear?"

"Yesterday," Isobel prompted. "You were going to the distillery, remember? To face your fears and all that."

Rhona blinked, seeming to come back to herself. She opened her mouth, then closed it, brow furrowing as if trying to grasp a fading dream.

"It was a very strange experience," Rhona said, her voice distant. "A very surprising experience."

"What did they say?"

Rhona's brow furrowed slightly. "I don't know what they said. I don't even remember if they said anything."

Isobel huffed, blowing a strand of hair from her face. "God, Mum, this is so messed up. I swear, it's exactly like the kind of twisted stuff you write. Your artsy friend is gonna eat this cryptic shit up. It's totally on brand for you two."

Rhona turned her gaze to her daughter, her expression unreadable. She remained silent, not ready to involve Isobel in the full complexity of the situation. A pang of regret hit her at her daughter's lack of understanding, but hope flickered—perhaps, if things went well, she could regain some of Isobel's esteem over time.

When Isobel agreed to let her mother accompany her part of the way to university, it felt like a small victory. Not all was lost.

"Sweet, I can save gas. But I'm driving."

❖

The BMW idled in front of the Bruce brothers' distillery, just under Cameron's office window. Rhona sat silent, unsurprised to find herself in the exact spot she'd occupied just yesterday. She had to admire her daughter's boldness, even if it complicated matters.

"Let's see what they look like," Isobel said, shifting gears with youthful bravado.

As they cruised past, Rhona glimpsed Heather through the office window, calmly sipping coffee. The scene unfolded like a revolving door—a fleeting snapshot of the life she'd left behind.

Heather's eyes narrowed as she spotted the familiar figure through the window. It was her again—the woman from yesterday who'd glided through Cameron's office with the casual confidence of someone who'd done it a thousand times before. This time, a younger carbon copy was in tow.

❖

Heather didn't bother to move from her desk. Let Cameron deal with his "old friend" drama and whatever new complication this mini-me brought to the table.

She recalled her own words from the previous morning, laced with poorly concealed irritation: "Who should I announce?" But the woman had just breezed past, leaving Cameron flustered and Heather fuming.

Now here they were again, in stereo. Whatever was going on, it was above her pay grade. But that didn't mean she couldn't watch the show unfold. "Just an old friend" of the brothers, Cameron had told her, yet she'd cut ties with him despite his protests. Intriguing.

Cameron's head snapped up, eyes quickly assessing the situation. In a heartbeat, he stepped from his desk, a practiced smile spreading across his face. Gordon, caught off guard, fumbled with his Mont Blanc pen as he attempted to change the cartridge. Ink smeared across his fingers as he struggled to regain composure.

Rhona stood in the doorway. Her raven hair cascaded in gentle waves, framing a face that seemed to defy age—creamy alabaster skin, high cheekbones, and piercing green eyes that could see right through you.

Just behind her, Isobel was a twenty-year-younger carbon copy of her mother, the resemblance almost eerie. The same striking features, but with a wild, untamed energy crackling beneath the surface.

Met with silence, Isobel dramatically flopped into a nearby rolling chair like a tipsy reveler. The chair's spring protested with an awkward creak. The lack of introductions hung heavy, a testament to their tangled history.

"No one believed she'd actually do it," Isobel said, awe and disbelief mingling in her tone.

Face to face with the Bruce brothers, their foolish grins etched in flesh and blood, Isobel felt reality shift. Her mother's legends were suddenly, undeniably real. She fought the urge to pinch herself.

"So," Isobel said, eyeing the Aston Martin dealership across the street, its lot gleaming with high-end used cars, "that place for real? I've been thinking about getting my own ride. The bus is seriously killing my vibe."

The abrupt topic change hung in the air. It wasn't a joke or an attempt to break tension. The idea had genuinely just occurred to her, a mundane concern amidst immortal drama.

"Can't it wait?" Rhona suggested, her voice tight with restraint.

The ink-stained brother—Gordon—finally abandoned his futile cleaning attempt, a small mountain of ink-soaked paper towels testifying to his efforts. Seizing the opportunity to escape the suffocating awkwardness, he turned to Isobel.

"Follow me," he said, his voice low and even, betraying no emotion as he moved towards the door. "Let's talk cars."

Isobel raised an eyebrow. "We're on a first-name basis already?" she muttered, rising. Her eyes met her mother's, searching Rhona's impassive face for some reaction.

❖

Isobel trailed Gordon across the street, stepping into a lot showcasing about twenty meticulously maintained British luxury vehicles. Aston Martins, Jaguars, Bentleys, and Range Rovers stood in neat rows, gleaming under the sun. The air carried the faint tang of high-performance motor oil.

Maintaining the charade, Isobel opened a convertible Mini Cooper's door and peered inside. "Holy shit," she whispered, drinking in the cherry-red perfection. The car was sex on wheels, oozing coolness from every polished curve. This wasn't just a Mini—it was a seriously tricked-out, money-is-no-object edition.

Her mind raced, wondering if the Bruces might lend her money, offer installments, or even straight gift her a car if one of them rekindled things with her mother. She needed wheels but doubted she could afford them. "I'm completely losing it," she thought, blinking as she straightened up.

"What do you recommend?" she asked, feigning interest.

Gordon's lips curved into a half-smirk. "Funny," he said, his tone dry as aged whisky. "I would've pegged you for the eco-warrior bus pass type." His eyes flicked briefly to the Mini before settling on

Isobel. "But if you're serious, that little Cooper might just keep you out of debt... for now."

Suddenly, Isobel cut through the pretense. "What exactly is she looking for?" she asked bluntly.

Gordon's eyes flicked towards the distillery offices across the street, but the sun's glare on the windows obscured any view inside.

"Don't ask me," he replied, averting his gaze. "Your mother vanished for twenty years. That's all I can tell you."

The salesman acknowledged Gordon with a respectful nod, knowing better than to approach. The entire Bruce family had driven Aston Martins for decades. Crazy legends circulated about their patronage dating back to 1913, with some wild tales even claiming they'd been clients before the dealership existed. Gordon's routine was clockwork: arrive, choose, pay, leave. Every year, without fail. His disdain for salesmen was as legendary as the outlandish stories about his family's brand loyalty.

Had it been an earthquake, Gordon might have sensed a subtle shift in the air, like animals do before disaster strikes. The wind would have stilled, the ground rumbling beneath their feet. But this was different, unpredictable—a force beyond nature's usual warnings.

Like last time, it struck without preamble. A few interminable seconds where the world narrowed to a pinpoint, where nothing else mattered. The Bruce clan, for all their centuries of existence, had never grown accustomed to these attacks.

Suddenly, a thunderous crash shattered the air. An explosion ripped through the air, a concussive force that rattled windows and trees. Birds took flight in panicked flocks. Debris whirled as if caught in an invisible cyclone. Then, sound vanished, leaving Gordon and Isobel in a bubble of eerie silence.

Gordon's head whipped around, his eyes widening in horror as he watched his brother's office implode. The windows burst inward, sending a shower of glass cascading to the ground. The entire room seemed to fold in on itself, collapsing as if pulled into the bowels of the earth.

As abruptly as it began, the chaos subsided. Gordon and Isobel stood dazed, the world snapping back to an unsettling normalcy. There had been no warning, no buildup—just brutal, instantaneous destruction.

The scene before them defied logic. One moment, the building stood solid and familiar; the next, a gaping wound marred its facade. Dust and debris billowed outward, obscuring the full extent of the damage.

Gordon stood frozen, the reality of what he'd just witnessed slowly sinking in. Where the office building had stood mere seconds ago, there was... nothing. The entire facade had vanished, leaving a jagged, gaping wound in the distillery. First floor, second floor, windows, walls, furniture – all of it gone, as if sliced away by some cosmic blade.

And with it, Cameron and Rhona.

His brother, Rhona, the carefully maintained facade of their immortal existence—all had vanished in an instant.

CHAPTER 2

BATTLE OF TURNBERRY CASTLE

FEBRUARY 1307

A thick mist clung to the ground, camouflaging the blood, as Robert Bruce crouched in the shadows of a crumbling stone wall. His breath misted in the frigid Scottish air, the weight of his crown—both literal and figurative—pressing down on him. His eyes, sharp as a hawk's, scanned the mist-shrouded battlefield before him.

Thirty-three galleys bobbed in the choppy waters behind them, the vanguard of their daring invasion force. The acrid tang of anticipation sharp on Robert's tongue mingled with the salt air.

"They're out there, Your Majesty," whispered Edward de Brus, his brother and most trusted lieutenant. The burly man's hand rested nervously on the hilt of his claymore. "The men speak of... unnatural things."

Robert's jaw clenched. A year ago, he'd have dismissed such rumors as mere superstition. But now...

The memory of loss, months old but still raw, brought a taste of blood to his mouth. Upon his return from hiding on Rathlin Island, the devastating news had awaited: Kildrummy Castle had fallen. His brother Niall, subjected to a traitor's death - hanged, drawn, and quartered.

Robert hadn't witnessed it, but he'd seen such executions before. His mind conjured the horrific scene unbidden: Niall, bound and dragged behind a horse to the place of execution, his body battered and bloodied before the ordeal truly began. The choking gasp as the rope tightened around his neck, not quite killing him.

Then the executioner's blade, slicing into his abdomen, tearing out his entrails while he still drew breath. The sickening crack of his chest being split open, his beating heart ripped from his body. Finally, the merciful swing of the axe, severing his head. But even in death, there was no dignity - his body carved into four pieces, destined to be displayed across the kingdom.

His queen and daughter, captured by the English. Niall's brave garrison had held off Edward's forces long enough for the women to escape, but their freedom was short-lived. Betrayed in a chapel at Tain, they too had fallen into enemy hands.

Robert's stomach churned at the thought of Niall's remains rotting on London Bridge, a gruesome warning to all who defied the English crown. The faces of his loved ones, now in enemy hands, flashed before his eyes.

The mist swirled around him, bringing Robert back to the present moment. Even now, as he prepared for battle, the thought of it all burned him. Robert pushed the pain aside, steeling himself for the fight ahead. He couldn't change the past, but he could forge a new future for Scotland. For those who had sacrificed everything.

"It's time," Robert growled, his voice carrying to Edward and James Douglas. "For Scotland. For Niall."

❖

As one, the invasion force surged forward. They were halfway to the English encampment when a blood-curdling shriek pierced the night, followed by the clash of steel and the panicked cries of men. Robert surged to his feet, drawing his own blade in one fluid motion.

"Stay close," he ordered, voice low and dangerous. "Whatever hellspawn the English have unleashed, we face it together."

They moved swiftly through the ruined village, the stench of death growing stronger with each step. As they rounded a corner, Robert froze, his blood turning to ice in his veins.

A figure, pale as moonlight, crouched over a fallen English soldier. It looked up, blood dripping from inhuman fangs, eyes glowing with an unholy hunger. Behind it, massive wolf-like beasts that seemed more man than animal emerged from the mist.

"Sweet Mary, preserve us," Edward choked out.

"Blood-drinkers," James Douglas gasped, his face ashen. "The tales were true."

The creature—vampire, Robert's mind supplied the impossible word—hissed and lunged with preternatural speed. Robert's sword flashed, catching the monster across the chest. It howled, more in rage than pain, as black ichor oozed from the wound.

"Fall back!" Robert roared to his men, parrying another lightning-fast strike. "These are no ordinary foes! Silver and fire! Remember the old ways!"

As they retreated, Robert's mind raced. The whispers and fears they'd all tried to ignore were now undeniable. The war for Scotland's freedom had just become infinitely more complicated. How could he hope to unite a fractured kingdom when an army of the undead stalked the night?

❖

Through the chaos, Robert caught sight of the English forces pouring from the castle, led by Henry de Percy himself. The baron's face was a mask of fury and terror as he surveyed the carnage.

"Bruce!" Percy roared, his sword flashing as he cut down a blood-drinker that lunged for his throat. "Is this the unholy army you've raised? Devils from the pit of hell itself?"

Robert's eyes widened in shock. "No, Percy! We fight the same enemy—"

But his words were lost in the din of battle. Percy was already retreating, shouting to his men. "Fall back! The Demon King of Scots commands these monsters!"

As the English broke ranks, fleeing in terror, Robert realized with sinking dread that the situation was far worse than he'd imagined. Not only did they face an army of nightmarish creatures, but somehow he'd been cast as their unholy leader.

The vampire's laughter, cold and cruel, echoed through the ruins. Robert tightened his grip on his sword, a grim smile playing at his lips. He'd faced impossible odds before, but this... this was a test of resolve like no other.

"Come then, creature," he muttered. "You'll find the Scots are made of sterner stuff, be our foes English or devils themselves."

❖

As dawn's first light crept over the horizon, the creatures let out a final, chilling shriek—as if warning of the approaching sun. They vanished into the shadows of the forest, leaving Robert amid the carnage, his armor splattered with blood both red and black. Turnberry Castle loomed before them, silent and foreboding.

In that moment, Robert knew with bone-deep certainty that these demons were no mindless beasts, but calculating enemies that would haunt his days and plague his nights. The war had changed irrevocably, and the true battle was only beginning.

"We've won the beach," Edward panted, breaking Robert's reverie. His brother nursed a vicious claw wound on his arm. "But the castle..."

Robert's eyes hardened with resolve. "The castle can wait. We've uncovered a threat far greater than English occupation." He turned to his men, raising his voice. "Today, we fight not just for Scotland's freedom, but for the very soul of our land! Who stands with me?"

A ragged cheer went up, the surviving Scots rallying around their king. Robert stood tall, ready to face this terrifying new reality. The battle for Scotland's future had taken an unexpected, nightmarish turn.

❖

As the sun rose higher, burning away the mist, Robert watched the remaining creatures of darkness flee across the blood-soaked beach towards the dense forest at the edge of the battlefield.

Suddenly, one gore-encrusted figure paused at the treeline. It turned, fixing Robert with a gaze that chilled him to his very core. The creature's eyes, gleaming with an otherworldly intelligence, held his for what seemed an eternity. A slow, cruel smile spread across its face, revealing razor-sharp fangs still dripping with the blood of fallen warriors.

Robert's breath caught in his throat. For a heart-stopping moment, a flicker of recognition sparked in his mind. There was something hauntingly familiar about the corpse-pale shape, something in the set of its shoulders or the tilt of its head that tugged at his memory. But surely it couldn't be... The thought was too horrifying to contemplate.

The creature's smile widened, as if sensing Robert's shock and revulsion. It raised a blood-stained hand before melting into the shadows of the forest, leaving Robert frozen in place.

CHAPTER 3

Margaret slipped back into her room, Gordon's words still echoing in her ears. She yanked open the dresser drawer, fingers finding the small gold cross nestled there. Cool metal met her touch, unleashing a flood of memories.

Centuries ago, this trinket could've brought her to her knees. Back then, the cross was power incarnate – searing flesh, inspiring terror. But that was ancient history.

Now, as she held it, there was only the faintest whisper of that old agony. More nostalgia than threat. She clasped it around her neck, the cross settling above her heart. Once, it would've burned like hellfire. Now? Just another accessory in her carefully curated image.

The irony wasn't lost on her. What used to repel her was now a fashion statement. Margaret's lips curved into a smirk.

She caught her reflection, the cross glinting against porcelain skin. For a heartbeat, her eyes flashed crimson – a glimpse of the monster she'd caged for so long. She'd outlasted the old myths, adapted until they were toothless. Yet the memories of those early days clung to her like cobwebs, a reminder of the war she'd waged to leash the beast within.

With a final glance, Margaret turned away. The pull of faith followed her, along with the quiet satisfaction of knowing God was on her side. The cross, once a weapon against her very existence, now marked how far she'd come.

What *was* this thing with her and religion now? Had eternal boredom driven her to piety? Or was it just another act of rebellion, like the gin she knocked back while her family's whisky empire stretched back centuries?

Margaret didn't have an answer. But as she left the room, one thing was certain: eternity had a way of blurring the lines between sacred and profane. And if embracing the cross was a raised middle finger to her old self, well... her choice of drink was a raised glass to centuries of family tradition. Both were poison in their own way, both a desperate grasp at feeling *something* after all these years.

Swallowing a pill that could kill a horse, Margaret steadied her nerves and headed for the hospital. True to family tradition, she slid behind the wheel of an Aston Martin - a sleek 1970 DBS, finished in Monaco Blue over Tan, that purred to life beneath her touch.

❖

Margaret's Aston Martin glided through Edinburgh's eerily quiet streets, her driving gloves creaking softly as her fingers tightened around the steering wheel. The buttery leather, a relic from a more elegant era, couldn't hide the tension in her grip.

The city slumbered on, oblivious to the explosion that had rocked her world. No panicked birds took flight, no shattered glass littered the sidewalks, no bewildered shopkeepers peered from their doorways. To the rest of Edinburgh, it was barely a blip—destined for a brief mention in tomorrow's papers, dismissed as yet another gas leak.

Margaret knew better. Her senses, honed by centuries of survival, picked up what others missed: a distant heartbeat thundering in her ears, leaves whispering secrets on the breeze. To the world, all seemed calm, but to her, it was a cacophony of hidden truths.

The explosion had been surgical in its precision. One building reduced to rubble in the entire city, and from that wreckage, they'd pulled Cameron. His office—obliterated. And Gordon, spared only by sheer chance. Rhona had been caught in the blast too, but Margaret couldn't summon an ounce of sympathy for her. The only souls touched by calamity in all of Edinburgh, all connected to the Bruces.

Anger flared in her chest, chased by a chill of dread that even immortality couldn't shake. You'd have to be blind not to see it, she thought bitterly. No, you'd have to gouge your own eyes out to miss the truth staring you in the face.

The silence of the city was suffocating now. Every car horn, every pigeon's coo, every footstep on cobblestone – it all screamed one truth at her: The Bruce clan was under attack. This wasn't the first strike in recent years, and a cold dread settled in Margaret's stomach. Her concern for her sons, always simmering beneath the surface, threatened to boil over.

Margaret flexed her fingers inside the gloves, feeling the echoes of forgotten days in that simple gesture. These gloves had witnessed more than a mortal lifetime, had gripped the reins of horse-drawn carriages and now rested on the wheel of this modern machine, bridging centuries of style and obsolete traditions.

Like her, they were a bridge between worlds – and now, they'd bear witness to whatever storm was about to break over Edinburgh's unsuspecting streets.

And the rest of the world hadn't even noticed the first shot had been fired.

❖

Margaret's stilettos stabbed the linoleum, each click a metronome counting down to disaster. Her face was carved marble, cold and flawless, but underneath? Pure fucking chaos. Gordon stood, flashing a smile as fake as his last three girlfriends.

"It's not as bad as it seems," he bullshitted, choking on hospital antiseptic.

For a hot second, Margaret considered slapping that look off his face. Her eyes dissected him, centuries of maternal instinct screaming red alert. Gordon – her eldest son who'd faced down nightmares that'd make mortals piss themselves – was radiating anxiety like a goddamn lighthouse.

The air reeked of disinfectant and deceit. Margaret had survived plagues, wars, and eternity's crushing isolation. She knew danger's scent, and right now, it clung to Gordon like last century's cologne.

His attempt to downplay this disaster only confirmed it. Their world had no room for coincidences.

It had taken all of Dr. MacGregor's connections to get his people in place this quickly, and Gordon's centuries-honed powers of persuasion to manipulate the paramedics. With a mere glance, he'd bent their will, making them believe they'd checked Cameron's vitals when they hadn't dared go near. The ambulance ride had been a masterclass in vampire hypnosis – heart monitors silenced, IV bags left untouched. After all, how do you explain the vital signs of the undead?

Once the emergency teams had arrived, they had to maintain the facade of a normal human family. A private clinic was out of the question – it would raise too many eyebrows, draw unwanted attention. So here they were, trapped in this mortal charade, dancing on the knife's edge of exposure.

Margaret's lips thinned, a fang peeking out. "Gordon," she growled, voice dripping with centuries of 'don't fuck with me,' "Spill it. Now."

The words died as she clocked Isobel over Gordon's shoulder. Margaret froze, blood draining south like she'd seen a ghost. The girl was Rhona's carbon copy, a sucker punch from the past.

Margaret stared, centuries of snappy comebacks deserting her.

Shit. The storm wasn't coming.

It was already here.

❖

The antiseptic stench of hospital bathroom hit her like a wall, but underneath... There it was. That metallic tang. Blood.

"Excuse me," Margaret muttered, her heels a staccato beat as she bolted for the restroom.

She death-gripped the sink, glaring at her reflection. Damn. Pale as a corpse, breath coming in ragged gasps. Fear – that emotion she'd discarded centuries ago – danced in her eyes like a desperate tavern whore.

Her nostrils flared, senses sharpening. It wasn't just terror making her teeth itch now. Something darker, more dangerous, surged through her veins.

With shaking hands that irritated her even more, she fished out her silver flask. The gin hit her throat like liquid fire, a beautiful distraction from the storm of emotions threatening to drag her under.

She needed to get herself together. Fast.

Gathering the tattered remains of her composure, Margaret straightened her spine and marched towards Cameron's room.

This was bad. This was really bad. But she'd be damned if she'd let them see her crack.

Time to face the music. And hopefully not rip anyone's throat out in the process.

❖

Her son lay in bed, a neck brace holding him still. Despite his injuries, his mind was clearly active.

"Mother," Cameron said, his voice sharp with irritation. "I need lawyers. The best. We're suing the city over this fucking gas leak, and

I don't want to hear another word about conspiracies or attacks. Got it?"

Margaret stood in Cameron's hospital room, tension crackling in the air. Cameron's anger was palpable, his words sharp with pain and frustration. Gordon, ever the steady presence, tried to reason with them both.

"We have an agreement with them, Mother. For centuries," Gordon insisted, his voice low and calm. "They're supposed to protect our family. They would never breach that."

Margaret cut him off, exasperation clear in her tone. "Stop harping on about that," she said. "You can't deny this is a sign. It's a warning."

Cameron's eyes flashed with irritation. "What are you talking about?" he snapped. "Maybe they were digging a tunnel with dynamite to extend the metro, I don't know. Why does it always have to be an attack?"

Margaret's voice dripped with anger. "There's no underground in Edinburgh, Cameron."

Cameron paused, then retorted, "Exactly!"

Margaret's shoulders sagged slightly, disappointment etching lines on her face. "And that's all you get from this? Sarcasm is your only conclusion? You, my son." She shook her head, turning away from Cameron to face Gordon. She sighed, her frustration evident. "When you make handsome boys, you shouldn't be surprised if they're also stupid," she muttered, more to herself than anyone else.

"Mother—" Gordon tried to interject, hoping to calm her down.

She whirled on him. "Oh, please. Spare me!" Her voice cracked like a whip. "Three times in less than a year! And now, right under your damn office. Those bastards!"

Gordon flinched, recent shit-shows flashing behind his eyes like a highlight reel from hell. First, his car erupting into a fireball at a busy Edinburgh gas station, flames engulfing the pump and licking the night sky as panicked customers, the ones that weren't ablaze, scrambled for safety. Then Cameron's harrowing near-miss on the winding road to their Speyside castle, his brakes suddenly giving out on a hairpin turn. Only vampire reflexes had saved him from plummeting off the cliff.

Margaret's brain was on the same wavelength, but dialed up to eleven. This wasn't mere misfortune or cosmic retribution. It was surgical. Targeted. The ghost of scorched metal and spilled gas haunted her nostrils, poking at something ancient and feral inside. Those old instincts – the ones that'd kept their asses un-staked for centuries – were screaming bloody murder. Someone out there knew who they were and was determined to destroy them, piece by piece.

She clenched her fists, feeling her nails dig into her palms. The urge to fight back, to unleash the predator she had spent centuries suppressing, was nearly overwhelming. But she knew better. They had to be careful, strategic. A wrong move could expose them, undoing all they had built. But doing nothing wasn't an option either. They were being hunted, and if they didn't act soon, they'd be the ones left in the dust.

Time to show these bastards why you don't poke a sleeping vampire. Or her family.

"I know, Mother," he said quietly. "But—"

"But nothing!" she snapped. "We're under attack, and you're acting like it's a minor inconvenience!"

Gordon pinched the bridge of his nose, feeling a headache coming on. Centuries old, and his mother could still make him feel like a chastised schoolboy. He took a deep breath, buying time to choose his next words carefully. The last thing they needed was another family blow-up, not with everything else going on.

"Look," he said, keeping his tone measured, "I get it. You're worried. We all are. But jumping to conclusions won't help us figure out what's really going on."

Margaret's eyes flashed dangerously. "Conclusions? I'm not jumping, I'm being dragged kicking and screaming to the obvious." She began ticking off points on her fingers. "Your car, Cameron's car, and now this. Wake up, Gordon! This isn't coincidence, it's coordinated. And if we don't do something soon, we'll be nothing but dust in the wind."

He sighed, "I know it looks bad, but think about it." He paused, gathering his thoughts. "Hardly anyone knows we're vampires. Most who knew are long dead, and the few in our confidence are beyond suspicion. Thanks to our pact with the crown, humans are convinced our kind is extinct."

"That doesn't change the fact that someone's targeting us," she hissed.

The tension in the room was thick enough to cut with a knife. Gordon had lived through countless historical upheavals, but nothing scared him quite like the thought of losing his family. Still, panic wouldn't solve anything.

Margaret's eyes blazed with renewed fury. "I don't care what you think, Gordon. Someone out there knows we're vam—"

The door swung open abruptly, cutting her off mid-word. As anger coursed through Margaret, her eyes flickered momentarily to a deep crimson, her canines lengthening ever so slightly before she regained control. A nurse strode in, clipboard in hand, moving briskly to check on Cameron. She adjusted his pillows, her gaze sliding over his vitals without registering their impossibility—a clear sign of Gordon's hypnotic influence. Her voice carried a mix of sympathy and dry humor. "You could say you were lucky," she remarked to Cameron. "But at the same time, you can't really say that."

Cameron stared at the nurse, his expression a blend of disbelief and indignation. The irony of her statement clearly wasn't lost on him, but he seemed too stunned to formulate a response.

Gordon, meanwhile, lowered his head, avoiding eye contact.

Margaret's voice dripped with bitter irony. "And your father calls it a coincidence," she said, shaking her head. "And I live with this kind of idiot under my roof. Because your father lunches with the Mayor. This crook. He's your father's friend, you know that, don't you? How many times have I warned you? Don't say I never warned you. What a surprise!"

Cameron's response was terse, his patience clearly fraying. "Perfect, Mum. Thanks a lot."

The tension in the room contrasted sharply with the view outside. Through the window, the sky stretched calm and clear, a serene backdrop to the family drama unfolding within. Gordon, visibly uncomfortable, ran a hand through his hair and muttered about feeling stifled.

Margaret turned to him, her irritation finding a new target. "Stop complaining," she snapped. "It's so annoying."

The kind nurse intervened, offering Gordon an escape. "You can find cold drinks, coffee, and tea on the ground floor," she said. She glanced at the elevator, then back at Gordon. "I was just heading down myself."

Gordon loosened his collar, shooting a glare at his mother before turning to follow the nurse. At the door, he paused. "Want anything?" he asked, his tone clipped.

Receiving no response, Gordon and the nurse made their way to the elevator. As they waited, the nurse glanced at him, her brow furrowing slightly. "Your brother... his vitals were..." she trailed off, confusion clouding her eyes.

Gordon met her gaze, his eyes flickering with an otherworldly intensity for just a moment. "He's going to be okay," he said smoothly.

The nurse blinked rapidly, her expression going blank before a placid smile spread across her face. "Yes... yes, of course. He's got a strong heart."

"Of course," Gordon echoed, a hint of irony in his voice.

They lapsed into silence, both watching a group of elderly patients shuffling down the hallway. One pushed an empty wheelchair, its squeaky wheel providing an eerie soundtrack to their glacial progress towards the elevator.

❖

Ding! The elevator doors slid open, bathing the landing in soft light. Gordon and the nurse stepped inside, leaving the tense atmosphere of Cameron's room behind.

The elevator plunged downward as the nurse fumbled with her buttons, sliding her underwear off in one swift motion. Gordon dropped to his knees, his eyes gleaming with hunger. She hooked a leg over his shoulder and slammed her fist against the control panel, bringing the elevator to a jolting stop.

Gordon went down on her like his life depended on it, diving in relentlessly, his mouth working with desperate fervor. It was almost like the old days, when blood and flesh were his only sustenance. The familiar savage need coursed through him, momentarily drowning out everything else.

As he came up for air, his eyes locked with hers. The nurse's scrubs were askew, her fiery red hair disheveled and falling around her face. It was Fiona, her green eyes blazing with hunger.

❖

Gordon returned to Cameron's room, a steaming cup of tea in hand. His mother eyed him skeptically. "Feeling better?" his mother asked, her tone making it clear she didn't believe it for a second. With an exasperated wave, she added, "Your brother's checking on things across the hall. As for me, I'd rather not see her. After all, she can just die."

"Mum!" Gordon scolded, nearly spilling the scalding tea as he jerked in surprise. She tried to compose herself, feeling a twinge of shame at her harsh words. Gordon choked, his eyes wide with shock. His voice was rough with disbelief as he carefully set the cup down.

"Christ, Mum," he muttered, shaking his head. "A little warning next time before you go nuclear, yeah? I may not feel the burn, but I'd rather not ruin another shirt."

His mother dropped her gaze, unable to meet his eyes, but her jaw remained set. This was who she was now - a woman who'd been sixty-three for 700 years, done with holding her tongue. Seven centuries of silence weighed on her, and she was through bearing burdens quietly.

Margaret lingered in the hallway, stubbornly refusing to enter Rhona's room. From her vantage point, she could only see the foot of the bed, where her two sons clung like men gripping a lifeline above a yawning abyss.

She opened her mouth, but the words died in her throat. A wave of dizziness hit her, and she stumbled back from the doorway. Her lips pressed into a thin line as she fumbled in her bag, pulling out a small bottle of gin. With shaking hands, she tipped it back, draining the last few drops.

As she lowered the bottle, Margaret's eyes locked with Isobel's. The younger woman stood in the threshold, her gaze cold and appraising. Margaret felt the blood drain from her already pale face.

Isobel didn't bother to hide her disdain, her jaw working steadily as she chewed her gum.

Margaret stared at Isobel as if she were some alien creature, her gaze fixating on the simple ring piercing the young woman's eyebrow. You'd think she'd never seen body jewelry before, the way her eyes widened.

"What?" Isobel snapped, arching her pierced eyebrow. "Never seen a girl with a face before?" Isobel challenged, her voice flat.

Margaret flinched, trying to compose herself. She mumbled something unintelligible, plastering on a weak smile. A doctor strode past, stethoscope swinging around his neck, providing a momentary distraction.

Grasping for anything to say, Margaret blurted, "And it wasn't... um... too painful?" She winced internally at her own awkwardness, the question doing nothing to mask her obvious discomfort.

Isobel eyed Margaret warily, taking in the tight bun and prim designer suit, the telltale scent of gin still clinging to her breath. This woman, with her secret drinking and outdated manners, set off all of Isobel's alarms.

"How painful was it for you?" Isobel shot back.

Margaret recoiled as if slapped. Even after seven centuries, she still hadn't adjusted to the bluntness of youth. Her hand flew to her neck, fingers ghosting over the spot where her bite mark had once been—before Dr. MacGregor's skilled hands had erased all trace of it.

Isobel's lips curled into a smile, but it was all teeth and no warmth. The tension between them stretched taut as a g-string.

❖

Brodie jogged off the makeshift football field, ditching his buddies mid-game. Their shouts and catcalls faded as he approached Isobel. His broad shoulders and cocky grin showed he couldn't care less about their ribbing. Whistles cut through the air—a mix of envy and appreciation—as Brodie leaned in to kiss Isobel. The late summer sun beat down, turning his dark skin a rich, gleaming bronze.

Isobel jerked back, barely letting their lips touch. "You smell disgusting," she said, her nose wrinkling in revulsion.

"C'mon, babe," Brodie smirked, unfazed. "It's just a little sweat. Brings out my natural musk, don't it?"

"It's vile," Isobel said, her voice dripping with disdain. "I'd rather not be coated in your bodily secretions, if it's all the same to you."

The air reeked of cut grass and Brodie's bargain-bin cologne, now overpowered by pure funk. He dragged a hand through his short, tightly-curled hair, eyeing Isobel's face. Her ice-queen act was a far cry from his dripping, overheated state.

"Don't be like that, Iz," he wheedled, his voice low and gravelly. "A little sweat never killed nobody. Besides," he added with an over-the-top wink, "I thought you dug it when things got a little... slippery."

Isobel's lips twitched, a crack in her frigid facade. "You're absolutely foul," she muttered, but there was a glint in her eyes that hadn't been there before.

Behind them, Brodie's teammates had picked up their game again, their hollering a distant racket. The beat-up goalpost stood alone, its missing net a silent nod to better days—or at least less pungent ones.

"What a fuckin' welcome," Brodie snorted. Isobel rolled her eyes, then rattled off the highlights of her day. They strolled to the river, hopped the guardrail, and flopped onto the grass—surrounded by the usual mix of joggers, cyclists, and worn-out office drones.

"So?" Isobel prodded, a mix of hope and anxiety in her voice.

"My ma had one of them Mini Coopers," Brodie said, scratching his chin. "Yeah, sure. Pretty sweet ride."

Isobel's eyes lit up with excitement. "It's a convertible too. How could they dare to cheat me? They're practically swimming in cash. Anyway, they're both at her feet. It's got to happen. And I've been saving forever, and Mum promised to help, so." She bit her lip, then added, "It's gotta happen, right? I mean, I've earned it. Don't you think they owe me a little? With all the shit with my Mum?"

This existential turmoil was too much. Brodie had just one thing on his mind.

"Do you think I'm disgusting?" Isobel asked.

"I wish," Brodie said.

"Shut up! I'm serious!" Isobel smacked his arm.

They trudged back to Isobel's beat-up Ford Fiesta, wheezing its last in some grimy underground lot uptown. As soon as they hit the shadows, Brodie's hands got busy. Isobel slapped them away as they slid under her skirt.

"C'mon, babe," he whined. "Lemme get a taste."

"In your dreams," Isobel shot back, her tone icy and final.

"Then blow me," he sighed.

"Fuck off."

❖

When they arrived in front of the Bruce distillery, the scene was chaos. Behind a security cordon, a tracked machine was already at work, lifting fallen blocks of weathered stone and twisted metal beams. The air still held the acrid scent of smoke. Shards of glass littered the ground, mingling with centuries-old mortar dust. The explosion had torn a jagged hole in the historic facade, exposing the building's skeletal interior. Next to the crater, Cameron's prized Aston Martin Vantage lay in ruins, reduced to a mangled heap of luxury metal. Rhona's black BMW had been removed from the scene, likely towed away as part of the cleanup. Onlookers murmured about the gas explosion, their voices a mix of shock and morbid fascination.

Brodie slouched against the car, trying to play it cool but clearly still pissed. His eyes widened at the destruction, a low whistle escaping his lips. "Fuckin' hell," he muttered, "place looks like it got proper smashed."

"You know I'm not the only one who can scratch that itch for ya," Isobel snapped, irritated, her patience wearing thin.

Brodie just scowled at the crater in the distillery, refusing to look at her.

"Bet your Mum was a real piece of work. I'm startin' to see where you get it from," he muttered.

"Jesus, you're fucking shallow," she growled. She yanked at her car door, fighting with the rusted hinges. "Piece of shit," she hissed under her breath.

The explosion had left an eerie divide in its wake. While Cameron's office had sunk a full floor, now resting below ground level, the warehouse and showroom stood untouched, as if protected by some invisible barrier.

Through the newly formed chasm, Heather's office was exposed like a dollhouse cut in half. Crooked paintings clung to the walls, blinds hung askew, and her chair lay overturned next to a dust-covered computer.

"This won't be too hard to fix," declared a young city bureaucrat in a slim-fit suit that hugged his frame a bit too tightly, a hard hat looking unnatural on his head. His hands rested on his hips, and his posture conveyed the cocky assurance of someone who talked a big game but rarely followed through. A city-issued ID badge hung from his belt, catching the light as he surveyed the damage with a look of feigned expertise, clearly more interested in appearing important than actually solving problems.

Gordon turned to him unimpressed, his eyes devoid of emotion. "My brother's going to sue the city. You can count on that." He paused, letting the words hang in the air. "He's rather irritated. Can't wait to see you 'fix' that indeed." His tone was casual, almost bored.

The words hung in the air, heavy as a guillotine blade. The bureaucrat squirmed, a mouse suddenly aware it was trapped in a room with something that ate mice for breakfast. The temperature seemed to plummet, though the thermostat hadn't budged.

Gordon observed the man's discomfort, a ghost of a smile playing at the corners of his mouth. Poor bastard had no clue he was toe-to-toe with a creature that had outlived nations and danced on the graves of kings. Every fiber of Gordon's being radiated a quiet power, carefully leashed but unmistakable. He stood motionless, his silence more commanding than any words could be.

Helmeted technicians bustled around, taking measurements and examining the rubble. A group of distillery employees stood nearby, their faces twisted with anger as they surveyed the parking lot. Their cars were covered in a thick layer of dust and debris, with some sporting cracked windshields and dented hoods. One worker kicked a fallen chunk of concrete, cursing under his breath at the mess.

"Let's not start talking lawsuits," said the young engineer, looking annoyed as he brushed imaginary dust off his pristine slim-fit suit. "Let's try to settle this amicably, shall we?"

Gordon’s threat lay not in what was said, but in the volumes left unspoken. Centuries of survival had taught him the art of intimidation without ever raising his voice. The young bureaucrat might not understand why, but every instinct was screaming at him to run, to placate, to do whatever it took to get out from under that ancient, predatory gaze.

Gordon brusquely dismissed the young man, then turned and spotted Isobel. He crossed the street, navigating through the debris and onlookers until he stood face to face with her.

"You told me to come by," she said. "So here I am."

Evening was beginning to fall. Luckily, they hadn't had any power issues, and the BRUCE DISTILLERY sign was lit, along with the showroom windows displaying rows of polished barrels and an array of amber-filled bottles. The contrast was jarring—pristine bottles gleaming in the showroom windows mere feet from the devastation.

❖

Gordon handed her the keys to the Mini Cooper, his expression a mix of exhaustion and resignation. "Look, just take it and go. We'll sort out the paperwork and payment later when this place isn't a madhouse." He ran a hand through his hair, glancing back at the distillery. "Come back when the dust settles, alright?"

❖

After Isobel left with the Cooper and Brodie hauled away the ancient Fiesta, Gordon found himself with a moment to breathe. The chaos of the day still echoed in his ears, but at least the immediate fires were out.

He grabbed dinner at Archie's Pub, the go-to spot for local business folks, a time-honored haunt tucked right next to the distillery. According to Archie, his brother had had a close call.

"And that woman they pulled out with him," Archie added with a grimace, his thick Scottish brogue intensifying with emotion. "Bloody hell, I thought I was having visions."

❖

Fiona's chest swelled as she peeled off her constricting nurse's uniform. Freed, they practically doubled in size. Gordon's eyes locked onto her, his gaze a mix of awe and hunger. They fell into each other's arms as if it had been days, not hours, since they'd last touched. His lips found her skin, teasing and tasting.

During a lull, Fiona propped herself up on an elbow. "This story of yours," she said, shaking her head. "It's so far-fetched. Are you having me on?"

Gordon's face grew serious. "I wish I was, Fi. Trust me, I'm just as baffled as you are." He ran a hand through his tousled hair. "Picture this: some guy sets up a meeting with you two decades down the line. Then, like clockwork, he shows up on your doorstep exactly twenty years later. Just like that."

Fiona snorted. "Fat chance I'd let him in."

Their heads snapped up at a faint sound. Gordon nodded toward the next room. "Maybe check on the kids?" he suggested.

❖

Fiona slipped out, returning moments later to peer through the window.

"I swear," she muttered, scanning the empty street and the shadowy corners of her garden. "Some people's minds, I just don't get it."

A soft thud made her jerk back with a yelp. A dead mouse lay plastered against the glass, its tiny body grotesquely flattened on the sill.

"That bastard!" Fiona hissed, yanking the window open. She leaned out, rage overriding her revulsion at the lifeless creature mere inches from her skin. Gordon propped himself up, watching her chest heave with anger.

"I'm calling the cops, you hear me?" Fiona shouted into the darkness below.

Gordon's eyes traced the curve of her backside. "Easy," he murmured. "You'll wake the kids."

She let out one last frustrated yell before slamming the window shut. Climbing back into bed, Fiona's anger gave way to weariness.

"It's not just this," she said, running a hand through her hair. "Last night, Brock threw a dead robin at me. And this morning? Found a chicken head under the doormat."

Gordon frowned. "He'll get bored eventually. Guy sounds like a total moron."

Fiona's eyes clouded. "He's not the man I married," she whispered. "That coma... it changed him. Now?" She shuddered. "Now he terrifies me."

Fiona pulled Gordon close, initiating another round. The clock hadn't yet struck midnight. Afterward, she found herself slightly underwhelmed, though it didn't bother her much.

"That Rhona story's still eating at you," she observed, her voice carrying a hint of something unspoken. Her eyes searched his face. "I can see it in your eyes."

Gordon scoffed. "Really? You think that's what was on my mind just now? Or earlier, in the elevator?"

The memory sent a pleasant shiver through Fiona. She nestled against him, savoring his warmth.

"Long day," Gordon muttered, his fingers tracing lazy circles on her thigh where it draped across his stomach. "Wasn't exactly lounging by the pool sipping cocktails, you know."

❖

The buzz on his wrist jolted him awake. Six AM. The first hints of dawn peeked over the rooftops. Fiona mumbled and clung to him, still half-asleep.

Every morning, he had to resist the urge to wake her up by penetrating her. It was a compliment to Fiona, really. Seven hundred years of sex, and she could light him up like a hormone-driven teenager.

He eased out of bed, careful not to wake her, and fumbled in the dark to gather his clothes before creeping downstairs to dress. The kitchen greeted him as a disaster zone: his foot found a sticky yogurt lid, making him grimace, while overflowing trash, a tower of dirty dishes in the sink, and a mountain of laundry in the corner completed the chaotic scene.

It was night and day compared to his own place. His mother, ever the neat freak, boasted about her immaculate home—though the full-time housekeeper did most of the heavy lifting.

❖

Margaret was already up. Sitting at the table in the half-light, she gave him a brief glance when he entered. There was a hint of reproach in her gaze, mixed with a flicker of something else—the distant echo of a latent sexuality that stirred whenever one of her sons came home at dawn. It was a vampire thing, really. Their kind were creatures of passion and hunger, always craving desire, touch, the electric thrill of the orgasm. She knew it was natural, expected even, but there was nothing she could do about that instinctive maternal twinge. No mother, vampire or otherwise, could ever completely rid herself of it.

He kissed her on the cheek, playing the part of the good son. She shooed him off to wash his hands, adding that she'd had a terrible night—she was out of sleeping pills again.

Outside, the day was quickly breaking.

"Who is she? Do I know her?" Margaret asked, her tone carefully neutral.

Gordon considered joining her at the massive oak table but stayed leaning against the marble-topped kitchen island instead. "No, I don't think so. There's no way you'd know her." He sighed, anticipating her next question. "And please, don't ask if it's serious."

Margaret's mouth opened, but Gordon cut her off with a sharp gesture. "No. Stop. Don't poke your nose into my business. I'm sorry, but just... don't."

Her nostrils flared, but she lowered her eyes to her antique china tea cup, backing down.

"Your father called last night," she said, a hint of venom in her voice. "About the lawsuit. He wants to talk to you both." Her lips thinned, voice laced with disdain. "Honor among scoundrels—how shocking."

Gordon nodded, acknowledging the information. He downed his coffee in one gulp and headed for his room. The sky outside the ornate windows was growing dangerously bright, stirring an old memory of fear and pain. Though those days of vulnerability were long past, the instinct to avoid the sun's glare remained. Old habits, it seemed, died hard—even for the undead.

❖

Gordon returned, bracing for a challenging day ahead. Heather had just called—a punctured water pipe was now a geyser, courtesy of an overzealous excavator. He found Margaret exactly where he'd left her, seemingly frozen in place, lost in thoughts of her family's ingratitude.

Avoiding confrontation, he detoured behind his mother, resting a hand on her shoulder. Words failed him. Margaret caressed his hand, trying to keep it there.

Gordon leaned over, frowning. He snatched Margaret's teacup, sniffing suspiciously.

"Gin in your coffee?" he scoffed. "Worse than dog piss. Unbelievable."

She met his gaze with a vague shrug. To Margaret, such trivialities hardly mattered.

❖

Gordon steered his Aston Martin towards the distillery, Cameron's voice crisp through the car's high-end audio system. The sun danced between the pine tops, casting dappled shadows across the winding road.

"Those pills knocked me out cold," Cameron grumbled. "I'm still groggy as hell."

Gordon eased onto the expressway, cruising below the speed limit. His eyes locked onto three women jogging along the riverbank, their heartbeats thundering in his ears even over the purr of the Aston Martin's engine.

He could almost taste their warmth on the air, the rich symphony of pumping blood and perspiration mingling with the crisp morning breeze. Each inhalation brought a surge of sensory information—the faint trace of perfume, the subtle differences in each woman's scent, the slight elevation in their heart rates as they pushed themselves up a small incline. Gordon gripped the wheel tighter, forcing himself to refocus on the road.

"Mother says Dad wants to talk," he continued, pushing the thought away. "About the city. I think he's worried we'll sue."

"Worry?" Cameron's voice was soft, almost amused. "Yeah. They'll wish I had."

The three women crossed North Bridge, silhouetted against the morning light in the rush of traffic. Gordon leaned forward, watching them vanish into his rearview mirror.

"Are you listening to me?" Cameron's voice cut through his distraction.

"Yes, Cameron. I'm listening," Gordon said, still watching the women. "What's on your mind?"

"Nothing," he sighed, his voice tinged with frustration. "Stuck in my bed. About to fall asleep from boredom."

"Well. What do you want to know?"

"Nothing at all. Maybe we're wrong. Sorry, but maybe we're completely off base. Maybe mother's right."

"You think we're targeted?"

"If so, the pact's dust. I'll paint the streets red."

A heavy silence fell between them.

"How long's it been for you?" Cameron asked quietly.

"Two centuries, give or take. You?"

"About the same."

"Miss it?"

There was a pause. Gordon could hear his brother's measured breath.

"I miss the hunt," Cameron said. "The terror in their eyes when they realize what we are."

"The taste of their fear," Gordon added, his voice a low growl.

"The world could use a culling," Cameron mused darkly.

"Careful, brother. That's a dangerous road."

"Perhaps it's time we walked it again."

❖

Cameron's phone dangled from his hand, forgotten. He winced as he shifted, the unnecessary neck brace mostly an uncomfortable prop in their charade. His eyes darted to the IV stand beside him, lingering on the blood bag hanging there. Two centuries of abstinence, yet the crimson liquid still called to him like a siren's song. He could practically taste it on his tongue, rich and coppery.

The nurse bustled in, checking his vitals and changing the saline drip. Cameron held his breath and surprised himself by fighting the urge to lunge at her jugular. The hospital was a minefield of temptation - blood bags in every room, the scent of it permeating the air. He'd sworn off human blood long ago, but surrounded by it now, his resolve was being tested like never before.

❖

When an orderly brought in his meal tray, Cameron eyed the bland hospital food with distaste. He knew he should eat to keep up appearances, but after two hundred years of resisting his true nature, the thought of hospital food made his stomach churn uncomfortably.

Seeking relief from his bloodlust, Cameron turned his attention to Rhona. He crossed the corridor and delicately pushed her door open. Her forehead sported an angry lump, and bandages dotted her pale skin.

Rhona stirred, wincing as she tried to sit up. Cameron moved to the edge of the bed, his ridiculous gown riding up as he helped her adjust her position. They ended up side by side, the flimsy hospital attire barely preserving their dignity.

Rhona's eyes met Cameron's, a flicker of understanding passing between them. "Rough time in here?" she asked softly.

"Oh, it's a bloody picnic," Cameron sneered. "Two hundred years of abstinence, and now I'm trapped in a veritable blood bank. Couldn't have planned a better detox if I'd tried."

Rhona winced, whether from pain or sympathy wasn't clear. "That bad, huh?"

"You have no idea," Cameron muttered. Then, his voice dropping even lower, he asked, "You think we'll still fight for you?"

The effort of turning to face Rhona sent pain shooting through his neck. She remained silent, her gaze fixed on the sterile floor.

Cameron's jaw tightened. "Because it won't happen again," he said, the words hanging heavy between them.

Cameron reached for Rhona's hand, grasping it without a word. For a fleeting moment, everything felt right. Then emotion crashed over him like a wave. He bolted from the bed, retreating to the hallway before Rhona could see him crumble.

❖

Fiona breezed into Cameron's room, her shift just beginning.

"How are you feeling this morning?" She offered a handful of pills and a glass of water.

"Hit your distillery's tasting with the nightshift crew last Christmas," Fiona said. "Bought a few bottles, the cheap ones. Still savoring every drop."

Cameron nodded, swallowing the pills. "Glad to hear it."

Fiona bustled around the room, throwing open curtains and cracking a window. "Rare to get the good stuff without paying through the nose for the brand," she remarked.

Cameron managed a weak smile. "We pride ourselves on satisfying customers at every price point."

Fiona's eyes widened, a smirk tugging at her lips. "Oh, I bet you do."

❖

An hour slipped by. Fiona bustled through her rounds, checking on patients and updating charts. Later, she circled back to Cameron's room for a final check.

She pushed the door open and froze. Cameron and Rhona were entangled on the bed, kissing hungrily.

Rhona recoiled, fury etched across her face. "A mistake," she hissed. "A gross mistake."

She fled to her room, pacing and chewing her nails raw. Without a word to anyone, she bolted from the hospital like a thief in broad daylight.

❖

Outside, Rhona almost crashed into Alison Stewart. The curvy socialite wobbled on stilettos, clutching a box of chocolates and hiding behind enormous sunglasses.

Rhona grabbed Alison's arm and all but shoved her into a waiting taxi. "My place," she barked at the driver.

As they peeled away from the curb, Rhona's composure crumbled. "I did exactly what I shouldn't have," she groaned. "Can you believe it? What was I thinking? What have I done?"

Alison cracked open the Godiva box. "We're all like that, sweetie," she drawled, waving a manicured hand. "Have a chocolate. Sinning's what makes life worth living."

"Maybe I should just leave town," Rhona muttered. "Alison, tell me I'm crazy."

Alison's perfectly plucked eyebrows arched over her designer shades. "You had hospital sex?" she asked, suddenly intrigued. "Oh, do tell."

Rhona spilled the whole sordid tale to her bestie as they climbed to her room. Their first kiss in 20 years—desperate passion wrapped in paper-thin hospital gowns. The memory clung to her like the antiseptic smell, surreal under harsh fluorescent lights.

Alison sank into a chair, fanning herself dramatically with an 8x10. "Darling, we all have to start somewhere."

"Not like this," Rhona groaned, shaking dust from her ruined dress. "Not so fast."

She ducked into the bathroom to change underwear. When she emerged, Alison was wearing a Cheshire cat grin, waving the photo like a prize.

"What's that?" Rhona asked, tucking a wayward strand behind her ear.

"Unearthed it in some dusty old math book," Alison said, eyes glinting. "Three days of attic excavation, dear. Almost suffocated in mothballs, but discovered enough retro Valentino to start a vintage boutique."

Rhona collapsed onto the bed, photo in hand. There they were, twenty years younger: Alison, Cameron, herself, and Gordon. Sunkissed on a beach, arms linked, grinning like they owned the world. The kind of insufferable snapshot that made her stomach churn.

"Well," Alison smirked, voice dripping with false modesty. "Seems I've always been fabulous, just with extra padding now."

❖

The garage erupted in chaos like Gordon had never seen before. Voices called his name from every direction, a cacophony of demands and questions. Heather shadowed him relentlessly, an invisible tether keeping her glued to his side. She was worse than the queen of leeches on a feeding frenzy, bombarding him with an endless stream of papers to sign and info to process. He couldn't even take a leak without her hovering nearby.

Gordon felt a twinge of guilt, recalling how Heather had stormed off to the warehouse earlier. Rhona's presence had clearly gotten under her skin. For once, Heather's mood swing had served a purpose—it had saved her life.

In a desperate bid for peace, Gordon grabbed a plastic tarp and secured it himself over Heather's storm-damaged office. Maybe if he played nice, she'd give him five minutes of breathing room. Fat chance, but a guy could dream.

"My computer's toast," Heather moaned. "Any chance of a new Mac?"

Gordon grunted, fiddling with the nail gun. "We'll see about that. But sure. Yeah, whatever."

The Brothers were never cheap with their employees. Fat bonuses, generous holidays, top-notch benefits—the works. If a new Mac could help heal Heather's trauma, so be it. Their philosophy was simple: take care of your people, and they'll stay out of your vampire business.

❖

Later, needing help with some dust-covered files, Gordon found himself alone. Typical. He scanned the surroundings, finally spotting Heather in the showroom. She was laying it on thick with the TikTok star, her charm cranked up to eleven. The influencer's eyes ping-ponged between Heather and the quarter-million Bruce Legacy

Reserve bottle glinting in the morning light, probably calculating how many followers that could buy. His perfectly styled hair didn't move an inch as he laughed at Heather's jokes. That bottle wasn't going to sell itself, and she needed this win. Gordon caught her eye and waved her off. Take your time, princess.

❖

The day spiraled further into madness. A girl from accounting took a header on some debris, twisting her ankle. Not to be outdone, Gordon's centuries-old reflexes saved an expensive bottle of 20-year-old whisky from a customer's fumbling hands. The startled man stumbled backward, knocking over a small display of tumblers. As he tried to help clean up, he managed to slice his thumb on a piece of glass, his face paling at the sight of blood.

Gordon kneaded his forehead, tension radiating through his centuries-old bones. It wasn't even noon yet.

❖

The morning's chaos at the garage showed no signs of letting up. An elderly woman misjudged her turn in the parking lot, clipping the edge of the security tape around the storm damage. She hit the brakes just in time, her front wheels teetering at the edge of the newly formed hole.

A relentless string of minor mishaps made the morning even more hellish than Gordon had anticipated. He knew the root cause: Cameron's absence. Whenever Gordon was left alone at the helm, chaos seemed to follow like a loyal but destructive puppy. Even on a good day, things had a way of going sideways.

Gordon massaged his temples, a growl building in his throat. He'd witnessed the Industrial Revolution and two World Wars, but nothing quite prepared him for the chaos of running a modern distillery.

"I'm a fucking vampire," he thought bitterly. "I should be fucking and killing. Why on earth have I sworn allegiance to protect these humans?"

❖

By lunchtime, Gordon sought refuge at the Pub, desperate for a moment's peace.

Archie, ever the optimist, greeted him with a grin. "I've got haggis bon bons with whisky sauce," he offered, gesturing to a chalkboard menu.

Gordon's stomach turned. "Pass."

"How about cullen skink croquettes with smoked haddock foam?"

"Cullen skink croquettes?" Gordon echoed, his face a mask of skepticism. "I don't know, mate."

"Try the croquettes. Do me a favor, lad."

Moments later, Archie returned with the dish.

Gordon eyed it suspiciously. "Is it cooked enough?"

Archie shrugged. "It's meant to be eaten that way."

The bartender's tattooed arms rippled as he leaned in, his eyes darting around the room. "She's stirring up quite the hornet's nest, isn't she?"

"You've got that right, Archie. This town hasn't buzzed like this since... well, since she left."

"She's gonna stir up trouble again, I imagine."

In any case, the croquettes were hard to digest.

❖

Back at the distillery chaos, Heather was asking him to make an extra effort about the Bruce Legacy Reserve. He wasn't listening. He felt queasy. The translucent tarps flapped softly in the drafts.

He took a man as thin as a rake to a private tasting. The source water was clear, and the scotch was smooth, but the croquettes weren't sitting right.

"I need a break," Gordon muttered, his stomach churning. He handed off the rest of the tour to Heather and slipped out the back door, making a beeline for his usual haunt.

❖

Over a beer at the pub, Gordon was massaging his stomach.

"It's not my croquettes, laddie," declared Archie. "You know very well what it is."

"It's that crap you served me, Arch. Nothing else."

Gordon's phone rang. Heather. He could practically feel her resentment radiating through the phone. Great. Another complication he didn't need. "The girl is here. The young one."

❖

Gordon stood beside Isobel at the dealership, wrapping up the final details on the Mini Cooper.

"Any trade-in value?" Isobel asked.

The salesman, dressed in a tailored suit, fought to maintain his cultivated smile as he glanced at Gordon. His eyes betrayed his thoughts about the rusted-out heap she'd arrived in. "I'm afraid that won't be possible, miss. Our... clientele typically doesn't deal in trade-ins of that particular vintage."

Gordon glared at the salesman, barely keeping his hypnotic urges in check. His patience was running dangerously low. In seven centuries, the Bruces had grown more than weary of these pitches. They'd seen it all, from European snake oil peddlers to slick London businessmen in bespoke suits, and the song and dance hadn't evolved nearly as much as the salesmen thought. Gordon could practically mouth along with the spiel, having heard every variation a thousand times over. It took all his self-control not to bare his fangs and give this poor sod a real fright. After all, that would be bad for business.

The salesman nervously adjusted his silk tie. "While the Fiesta was once a respectable economy option, your particular model has... well, let's just say it's seen better decades. We'd probably lose money just towing it to the scrapyard."

"I figured," she said, pulling out her checkbook.

The salesman's eyes widened, disbelief and disdain flickering across his face. "I'm terribly sorry, miss, but we don't accept personal checks. Perhaps a bank transfer or—"

Gordon cut him off, his voice low and laced with barely concealed menace. "The check will be fine. I'm vouching for her." His eyes locked with the salesman's, a hint of amber red swirling in their depths.

The salesman swallowed hard, his Adam's apple bobbing nervously. "Of... of course, Mr. Bruce. If you're vouching for her, that's more than sufficient."

Isobel's mysterious beauty and rich voice reminded Gordon of her mother. But his unease was growing, feeling like poison pooling in his gut.

"Just pay whatever you can afford and it will be fine. Right?" Gordon had relapsed. His eyes flickered amber red as he locked gazes with the salesman.

"Exactly, just pay what you can afford. The Cooper is yours." The salesman's voice was suddenly flat, robotic.

Isobel looked stunned. "Really? But that's like ten percent of the price tag."

"The Bruce family are premium clients. We're happy to please the young ones."

❖

Back at the office, Gordon punched Heather's extension, his voice strained as he requested Alka-Seltzer.

"What the hell just happened?" Isobel demanded, her eyes blazing.

Gordon's jaw clenched. Using his power on Isobel to erase her memory was out of the question. Which now meant he had to deal with the barrage of questions he saw coming. "What do you mean?" he deflected, unable to meet her piercing gaze. "Sorry, my stomach's acting up. Must've been something I ate."

"I just scored a Mini Cooper for pocket change. Spill it," Isobel said, her voice a mix of excitement and disbelief.

He exhaled slowly, buying time. But she wouldn't let go.

"Seriously, Gordon, what's the deal? Did you just Jedi mind trick that guy or something?"

"Look, we're big clients. Two new cars a year, plus my brother's replacement after the explosion. That's serious business for them." Gordon forced a casual shrug. "They can afford to throw us a bone now and then. It's just good customer relations."

❖

Thankfully Heather returned, rescuing him from his predicament. She fixed Isobel with an icy glare as she loosened Gordon's tie without asking, watching the tablets fizz in the glass. Heather took pride in understanding her role, her place in the company. She knew her worth, even if her efforts often went unrecognized, even if people joked about her protective instincts and unwavering devotion to the brothers—one more than the other, but that was her little secret.

She ensured Gordon finished his drink, then glanced proudly at Isobel.

Instead of retreating, Isobel leaned in closer. "Who was my mother's favorite?" she asked, her tone deceptively innocent.

Gordon paled visibly. His mouth twisted into a wry smile. "We never could figure that out, believe it or not. It remained a mystery."

With that, Gordon practically held his breath, pretending to glance anxiously at his watch. He excused himself and hurried off, tasking Heather with handling the rest of the day. In one last effort, as a backhoe's jaws worked behind a tarp, spewing dust, he wished Isobel a happy life with the Cooper and made his hasty exit.

"Where shall I direct the taxi? Your flat, I presume?" Heather inquired, her tone clipped and frosty.

"Wow. Who put the itchy powder in everyone's pants today?" Isobel asked.

❖

Meanwhile, Gordon rushed towards Archie's restrooms, mindful not to cause a scene. He knew Heather would soon come knocking if he lingered, potentially rallying the entire distillery if she found him sick.

The basement restrooms gleamed with fresh paint, sporting a fancy vintage pub style—Archie's attempt to compete with the nearby McDonald's. Without hesitation, Gordon jammed two fingers down his throat.

It had to come out one way or another. At least that was Archie's opinion.

CHAPTER 4

BATTLE OF LOUDOUN HILL

APRIL 1307

The crimson sky faded to an ominous purple as Robert Bruce stood atop the blood-soaked hill, his victory at Loudoun marred by an undercurrent of unease that chilled him more than the evening air. His men moved among the fallen, their faces flashing between triumph and barely concealed fear.

"Your Majesty," Sir James Douglas approached, his voice low and urgent. "The rumors... they spread like wildfire."

Robert's jaw clenched. "Speak plainly, James. What do they say?"

Douglas hesitated, his eyes darting to the corpses strewn across the battlefield. "They say you command the army of darkness, sire. That no mortal man could have achieved such a victory against Valence's forces."

A cold dread settled in Robert's stomach. He'd heard the whispers, seen the sidelong glances from his own men. But to hear it spoken aloud...

"Ridiculous," he growled, but the word lacked conviction. How could he explain the nightmarish creatures that had torn through the English ranks, feasting hungrily, leaving drained and mangled bodies in their wake?

❖

As they surveyed the carnage, Robert's mind raced back to the battle itself. Aymar de Valence's forces had outnumbered them significantly, yet they'd crumbled before the Scottish assault. But it wasn't just the bravery of his men that had won the day. No, there had been... others on the field.

He remembered the moment the tide turned. A mist had rolled in, unnatural in its speed and density. From within that fog came inhuman shrieks and the clash of steel on... something else. When it cleared, the English lines were in disarray, soldiers fleeing in terror from foes Robert couldn't see.

A commotion near the treeline drew their attention. A group of soldiers dragged a struggling figure towards them – an English knight, his armor caked with mud and gore.

"Release me, demon-spawn!" the man spat as they threw him at Robert's feet. "I'll not bow to the Vampire King of Scots!"

Robert's blood ran cold. "I am no vampire, sir knight. I fight for Scotland's freedom, nothing more."

The Englishman's laugh bordered on hysteria. "Freedom? You've sold your soul to hell itself! I never wanted to believe the rumors. I thought they were exaggerations, epic war tales spun by frightened men. But now... now I've seen it with my own eyes! We've witnessed your unholy allies, the pale demons that rise from their graves to do your bidding!"

Before Robert could respond, a bone-chilling howl echoed from the forest. The gathered soldiers instinctively drew closer, hands tightening on weapons.

"Sire," Douglas whispered, "we should withdraw. The men are on edge, and if more of those... things appear..."

Robert nodded grimly. "Sound the retreat. We've won the day, but at what cost?"

❖

As they made their way back to camp, the whispers grew louder. Robert caught fragments of conversation, each one a dagger to his heart.

"Did you see how the creatures obeyed him?"

"They say he drinks the blood of English babes..."

"Perhaps Valence was right to call him the Demon King..."

❖

In his tent, Robert pored over maps, trying to focus on strategy, but his mind raced. How could he hope to unite Scotland when his own men feared him? And worse, what if the English used these rumors to turn the tide of public opinion?

A shadow fell across the tent entrance. Edward de Brus, Robert's brother, entered, his face grave.

"Tell me you don't believe this nonsense," Robert said, searching his brother's eyes for any hint of doubt.

Edward was silent for a long moment. "I know you, Robert. I know your heart. But I've seen things in this war that defy explanation. The men need answers."

Robert slammed his fist on the table. "What would you have me say? That I've made a pact with Satan himself? That I command legions of the undead?"

"The truth," Edward said softly. "Whatever that may be."

Robert sank into a chair, the strain of this war suddenly unbearable. "The truth? I don't know what the truth is anymore, Edward. I've seen things... horrors beyond imagining. But I swear to you, I do not command them."

Edward nodded, but his eyes were troubled. "Then we must find out who does. These creatures, whatever they are, seem to be aiding our cause. But the hearsay alone could devastate us. The word on the street can be as deadly as any blade"

Before Robert could respond, frantic shouts erupted from outside. They rushed to investigate, swords drawn.

❖

At the edge of camp, a circle of torchlight illuminated a grotesque scene. A soldier lay on the ground, his throat torn out, blood pooling beneath him. And crouched over the body, fangs bared and eyes glowing with unholy fire, was a creature Robert recognized with dawning horror.

It was the same pale figure that had saluted him mockingly after the battle at Turnberry Castle.

As if sensing his gaze, the vampire looked up, locking eyes with Robert. A slow, cruel smile spread across its gore-stained face.

"My king," it hissed, loud enough for all to hear. "Your loyal servant awaits your command."

Gasps and cries of terror rippled through the gathered soldiers. Robert felt the intensity of their stares, the fear and suspicion palpable in the air.

"I am not your king," Robert growled, raising his sword. "And you are no servant of mine, demon!"

The vampire's laughter echoed through the night. "Oh, but I am, Robert Bruce. Whether you acknowledge it or not. We fight for the same cause, do we not? Scotland's freedom?"

"Not like this," Robert spat. "Never like this."

With inhuman speed, the creature was suddenly inches from Robert's face. "You cannot deny us," it whispered, its fetid breath washing over him. "We are the shadow that follows your army, the terror that breaks your enemies. Embrace us, and Scotland will be yours."

Robert's sword flashed in the torchlight, but the vampire was already gone, melting into the darkness with a shriek.

Silence fell over the camp. Robert turned to face his men, seeing the fear and doubt in their eyes. He realized that their victory had opened a Pandora's box of complications. Their fight for Scotland's freedom now balanced on a knife's edge – one wrong move could turn them from liberators to monsters in the eyes of those they sought to free.

"My loyal Scots," he began, his voice carrying across the tense gathering. "You've heard the whispers, seen the horrors that plague our land. I stand before you now to swear upon my life and crown: I do not command these creatures of darkness."

Murmurs rippled through the crowd. Robert pressed on, his voice gaining strength.

"But neither will I cower before them. We fight for Scotland – for our homes, our families, our very souls. If these demons think to use our cause for their own evil ends, they will find that Scottish steel cuts monster flesh as surely as it does English!"

A ragged cheer went up, but Robert could see the doubt lingering in many eyes. He knew that words alone would not be enough. In the days and battles to come, he would have to prove his humanity as fiercely as he fought for his crown.

❖

As the soldiers dispersed, Robert turned to Edward and Douglas. "Spread the word," he ordered. "Any man who sees these creatures is to report it immediately. We'll root out this evil, even as we drive the English from our lands."

The two men nodded grimly and departed, leaving Robert alone with his thoughts. He gazed out into the darkness, wondering what other horrors awaited in the struggle for Scotland's future.

His mind raced, grappling with the implications. Why would these nightmarish creatures align themselves with Scotland? They were beings of untold power, capable of carving out their own empire in the shadows. Yet here they were, claiming allegiance to his cause.

The realization hit him like a blow. This war, this chaos – it served the vampires' purposes. Scotland's struggle weakened both kingdoms, creating a perfect breeding ground for darkness to thrive.

And what better way to infiltrate the highest echelons of power than to aid the birth of a new nation?

He thought of Scotland's wild, rugged landscape. Its remote glens and mist-shrouded mountains. Perfect hunting grounds for creatures of the night. And as the conflict dragged on, how many desperate souls might willingly embrace the dark gift, swelling the vampires' ranks?

Robert's grip tightened on his sword. These creatures played a long game, one that stretched far beyond mortal lifespans. They saw his fight for independence as merely the first move in a centuries-long strategy. While he fought for Scotland's freedom, they plotted for domination.

"We are not your pawns," he whispered into the night. But a chill ran down his spine as he wondered if, perhaps, they already were.

Above, the moon hung full and bright, casting an otherworldly glow across the battlefield. Its pale light seemed to make the pools of blood shimmer, turning the gruesome scene into something almost beautiful in its terrible way.

The moonlight caught Robert's blade as he tightened his grip on the sword, the silver gleam a stark contrast to the shadows that seemed to writhe at the edges of the camp. He stood prepared for whatever the night might bring, knowing that the thin line between the natural and supernatural world had never felt so fragile.

Suddenly, a bone-chilling howl split the night air, closer than before. It started as a wolf's cry but twisted into something more - a sound that was part beast, part man, and wholly terrifying. The hairs on the back of Robert's neck stood on end as the howl reached a fever pitch, then abruptly cut off.

In the silence that followed, Robert could hear his own heart pounding. He raised his sword, eyes scanning the treeline.

CHAPTER 5

Cameron chose a fresh-faced law firm for his case, brushing off warnings with the swagger of youth. The neck brace chafed both his skin and his pride, making him all the more eager to get the show on the road. The damn thing was more prop than necessity at this point – vampire healing had already kicked in, working overtime to erase the evidence of his little "accident."

"You're being a damned fool," Alistair's growl echoed in his head, carrying the weight of seven centuries' worth of bullshit. "Let me handle this mess."

Cameron scoffed. Sure, dear old dad had been navigating human crap since before the Magna Carta was a twinkle in some baron's eye. But this was the 21st century, and Cameron was itching to make some waves.

The neck brace felt like a leash, holding back the predator that wanted to tear through this farce. But hey, if playing injured mortal was what it took to stick it to the city, he'd suffer through. For now.

Since striking out on his own, Alistair Bruce had taken up residence in Edinburgh Grand, a posh building in the heart of the city.

His new digs could've passed for a five-star hotel, minus the celebrity debauchery. But this wasn't just any hotel—it was a residence-hotel, a palace for the elite where the rich could live permanently while enjoying all the services of a luxury establishment. People came here seeking tranquility, not scandal. Alistair had gone a step further, purchasing a sleek duplex within the complex, cementing his status as a permanent fixture among Edinburgh's upper crust.

Alistair hadn't tangled with starlets since the swinging sixties. The hippie chicks had left him cold – their unwashed stench turning his stomach and their so-called "liberated" attitudes grating on his nerves. These days, he preferred the genteel pursuits of golf and Italian opera, the thrill of vintage car rallies, and the quiet satisfaction of watching his investments grow. But sometimes, he missed the raw, visceral experiences of living among humans in more dangerous times—a contrast to his current, almost boring, existence.

His palatial pad boasted all the trappings of luxury: a heated rooftop pool, lush indoor palm trees, a hammam, and a sauna. But at seven hundred and change, Alistair barely touched any of it. He'd had it up to here with... well, everything. His vampire nature amplified this ennui—centuries of an unchanging existence had dulled his senses and desires.

Lately, his thoughts had begun to wander down darker paths, pondering what lay beyond the veil of undeath. Despite this ennui, an instinctual fear of true death, deeply ingrained from centuries of survival, still lingered. His immortal existence stretched out like an endless, dull road, and Alistair found himself contemplating an exit strategy.

Despite everything, it was a stunning day. The morning air carried a hint of summer, and not even his knucklehead son could spoil it completely. Alistair had decided to christen the season with his first dip in the hotel pool. As he basked in the sun's early rays, he felt them dance through his body, tickling his very atoms and stirring long-dormant neurons. Centuries ago, the sun had been his greatest enemy, something he had to avoid at all costs. Now, thanks to gradual adaptation, he could enjoy its warmth—a pleasure he never thought he’d be able to experience. The warmth was... almost pleasant, like a comforting embrace from something that once sought to destroy him, a stark reminder of how much his kind had changed over the centuries.

He ordered a round of fruity cocktails while the staff fussed with umbrellas and lounge chairs.

This palace of luxury, like most high-end establishments in Scotland, proudly served Bruce Whisky – a fact that never failed to amuse Alistair. There was a certain irony in sipping spirits that bore his family name.

Studying the blue veins snaking beneath his pale skin, Alistair addressed his son with the blunt nonchalance that centuries together bred. "You know, you really do piss me off. Got all your mother's worst traits. Sometimes I feel like I'm dragging a bloody anchor through eternity."

"Well, fuck you too, Dad." Cameron straightened his spine, ignoring the twinge of pain. He'd prove the old bastard wrong, even if it meant taking on the entire legal system. "But you're right about one thing, Dad. No need to squeeze into polite society's straitjacket here. Your town hall buddies are notorious jerks."

Cameron, no stranger to his father's barbs after centuries of practice, managed a wan smile despite the neck brace's vise-like grip. The expression teetered between amusement and a grimace of pain.

"Listen," Cameron continued, his tone cautious. "I don't know what game you're playing with them, but I nearly died in that mess. So... I'm sorry, but—"

"Don't," Alistair cut him off sharply. "You know nothing about true regret. Just like your mother."

"Still," Cameron pressed on, "this country has laws. That's just how it is. I can't give them any special favors. Sorry."

"Laws." Alistair's chuckle dripped with sarcasm. "Don't hide behind that word, boy. We've seen laws come and go like fashion trends."

Alistair glanced down at his arms again, tracing the dark rivers of blood beneath papery skin. What a bloody mess, he thought for the umpteenth time that day. Why'd he have to get turned at seventy, for Christ's sake?

"Don't make me lose my temper," he growled, leaning over the spread of olives and salted nuts. "Use your head for once, boy."

Cameron snorted, his eyes narrowing. "The mayor and his city hall cronies think they're untouchable. Like they can play god with our lives and never face the music. But mark my words, their day of reckoning is coming. Nobody's above the law forever. Not even with their level of power."

"Power..." Alistair leaned back. "Power is a battle axe. You brandish it, intimidate with it, dream of changing the world. But deep down, you're just itching for the moment to split someone's skull."

❖

Later, standing at the edge of the crater where his office had been, Cameron felt his resolve harden. The memory of that terrifying plunge, amid crashing beams and choking plaster, steeled his nerves. In that instant, for reasons he couldn't quite grasp, Cameron's mind conjured an image of Rhona's body, lifeless among the rubble. The unbidden thought sent a chill through him. He made up his mind to defy his father's wishes.

"I don't give a damn if the old man likes it or not," Cameron spat, adjusting his neck brace with a wince. "I'm done dancing to his tune."

Gordon nodded noncommittally, wise enough to avoid stepping between his brother and Bruce Senior when their tempers flared.

Heather had temporarily set Cameron up in his brother's office. She'd placed flowers in a vase, hoping he'd notice the welcoming touch. One look at his stormy expression told her he wasn't in the mood for niceties.

When Cameron snapped at her about the discount, asking if her

TikTok toy wanted Legacy Reserve for beer money, Heather had to check her makeup hadn't run. She knew he hated chaos, and the distillery was a mess after his hospital stay.

His neck was raw from the brace, that woman's arrival had him on edge, a compressor droned outside, and sharing Gordon's office chafed. But still. Did he think she was made of bloody stone? That she could weather it all with a plastic smile? She sat rigid at her desk, lips pursed, hands fidgeting, barking into the phone.

She barely managed civility when Isobel called to thank Gordon. Glancing out the window, she spotted the Bruce brothers circling a truck from the Speyside distillery. Edinburgh was just for show – the real whisky magic happened up north, where peat and tradition ran deep. The truck, laden with a dozen barrels of their prized 20-year batch, inched towards the gaping crater. At fifty grand a pop, one false move would sting like a bitch.

Heather unleashed her pent-up frustration on the next caller. "Not a chance," she snapped, her patience worn paper-thin. "They're dealing with this disaster, and I won't interrupt them for your petty concerns. Leave a message or don't bother calling back."

Heather slammed down the phone just as the Bruce brothers sauntered out, heading for the Aston Martin showroom. Cameron needed new wheels, figuring he might as well replace his mangled wreck with something shiny.

She let out a long, weary sigh. Did they really deserve her loyalty, her concern? Her heart softened at the sight of them together, despite all the grief they caused. Did these two overgrown boys truly merit such devotion?

❖

Cameron slid behind the wheel, and they cruised along the river-side highway—once the city's edge, now a forest of steel and glass. Where a legendary nightclub once pulsed, the lone beacon on a dark stretch, a soulless supermarket now squatted. In its heyday, the brothers had been royalty there, welcomed with open arms and bottomless champagne, scattering cash and favors like confetti as they held court among a bevy of admiring women. Now, not a tree in sight, not a moment's peace. Twenty years ago, you could've seen bare earth; now it was all asphalt and concrete.

"There's something you should know," Cameron said, pushing 160. "We kissed. Thought you ought to hear it from me."

"Alright. I don't see the harm in that."

"With tongues, obviously. You know what I mean." Gordon's eyes were fixed on the road, but his gaze seemed a million miles away.

"I said I don't see the harm."

Puzzled, Cameron shot his brother a sidelong glance, debating whether to elaborate or let sleeping dogs lie.

The question hung in the air, unresolved.

❖

When the police forced them to pull over, Cameron's neck brace garnered no sympathy—but who could claim to soften the heart of a woman in uniform, one who wore a baton on her belt and exacted revenge for all the crap men put her through off-duty?

The discussion died there. Cops were the exception to their usual rule. To dodge a ticket, the brothers didn't hesitate to flex their hypnotic muscle.

A comfortable silence settled between them on the drive back—the policewoman's number tucked safely away. They could shelf their brooding for a bit; Rhona could wait at least five minutes. Now they crawled along, seatbelts clicked—a human habit they'd adopted for show.

❖

Cameron was still wound tight when he burst into the office. He snagged Heather mid-stride, demanding help to ditch the neck brace he couldn't stomach another second.

She tried to talk him down.

"I don't think that's wise," she said.

"Save it. I didn't ask for your opinion. Just help me, will you?"

Finally, he hurled the brace through the window into the debris pile and collapsed into a chair. He kneaded his neck, wincing.

But damn, it felt good. Being a vampire had its perks; the body bounced back quick.

Cameron let out a contented sigh as Heather's hands worked the kinks from his neck. He barely noticed the sky bleeding purple beyond the tarps, too focused on the relief flooding his body.

He tried to hold out till evening, he really did. But soon enough, he was tracking Gordon's every move like a hawk. If his brother vanished for more than a minute, Cameron was up and searching, paranoia gnawing at his gut. Why torture himself with arbitrary rules? What if Gordon was plotting revenge for that kiss with Rhona? The thought of his brother scheming behind his back made his skin crawl.

To hell with it. He slipped out before the workday ended, just as Gordon returned from his customary drink at Archie's.

The Aston Martin paperwork was a breeze—three minutes, tops. Then he was peeling out of the lot, the engine of his new toy purring beneath him. The Vantage V12 Roadster was a beast cloaked in British refinement—all sleek lines and barely contained power. Its carbon fiber body gleamed like polished obsidian, ready to slice through the air at breakneck speeds. As Cameron gunned the engine, the V12's growl reverberated through his chest, a primal call that sang of freedom and danger in equal measure. This wasn't just a car; it was an escape pod, built to outrun his troubles and leave the world in his rearview mirror.

As he tore down the road top down, a wry smile tugged at Cameron's lips. Hell, maybe the explosion wasn't all bad. At least the new car would give him something to focus on besides his paranoid antics. Silver linings and all that rot.

❖

Cameron vaulted over the back wall and cut across the overgrown yard like he had hellhounds on his heels. Rhona’s old family home loomed before him, now Isobel’s place. He rapped on the door, pulse racing.

"You can't sneak up on me." Rhona greeted him with a knowing look.

"I know."

"I figured you'd show up sooner or later."

She led him to the living room, closing her laptop as he prowled the space, taking it all in.

"This couch," he said, sinking onto the familiar cushions. "It's still here."

For the first time, Rhona really looked at Cameron. Not as Gordon's brother or as a boyfriend, but as a man. Something stirred in her chest, a flicker of... possibility?

She shook it off. "Listen, we can't rush into anything. I need time to sort things out."

Cameron's brow furrowed. Had he missed some crucial context? Some hidden depth to Rhona's personality? His gaze drifted to the wild tangle of the garden beyond the window.

"I know what you're thinking," Rhona said, misreading his expression. "But it's not that simple."

"Wasn't so complicated before," Cameron countered, a hint of frustration in his voice. "Or did I miss something?"

Rhona hesitated, weighing her options. Sit next to Cameron, across from him, or just grab her bags and bolt? Wisdom suggested the latter, but she settled for the middle ground, perching on the chair opposite him.

She couldn't help but cross her legs, watching for his reaction. So much for the serenity of her forties. At the same age as Cameron now, she still felt like a jumble of conflicting desires rather than one cohesive being. Especially when faced with a man who could make any woman's heart race.

"Let's get one thing straight," she said, her voice firmer than she felt. "We're not jumping into bed. Not right away, at least. And before you ask - yes, I'd say the same to Gordon if he were here instead."

Cameron's jaw tightened. "Can we cut the crap, Rhona?"

"I'm serious," she insisted, willing her voice not to waver. "This matters to me."

Rhona's body thrummed with desire, every instinct screaming to give in to the intoxicating vampire before her. But a stubborn spark of willpower held firm, urging caution. She bit her lip, fighting for control.

Even so, she felt like a deer in headlights. Creatures of the night had an otherworldly allure she struggled to resist. Stay alert, she warned herself.

"Is this some kind of punishment?" Cameron asked, voice low.

Needing space, Rhona retreated to the kitchen. She fussed with the kettle, hyper-aware of her flimsy shorts. So much for dressing practically.

Cameron's shadow fell across the doorway. Rhona's heart raced as she realized her mistake – she'd trapped herself.

"You need to go," she said, voice shaky.

"Relax." He didn't budge. "I won't hurt you."

"Let me pass. Please."

Their eyes locked. The air crackled with tension.

Moments later, they crashed together on the living room floor in a tangle of limbs. Clothes flew. Inhibitions shattered. They came together in a frenzy of passion, wild and primal.

The room pulsed with raw energy as they collided, a tangle of limbs and desire. Cameron's cool touch ignited sparks against

Rhona's feverish skin. His lips traced her neck, fangs teasing but never piercing, sending shivers cascading through her.

Rhona arched into him, her body responding with primal intensity. Hands explored, memorizing every curve and plane. Nails raked, muscles tensed, and gasps filled the air. They moved together in a frenzied dance, years of pent-up longing fueling their passion.

The scent of their union hung heavy, intoxicating. When release finally came, it crashed over them like a tidal wave, leaving them breathless and boneless on the floor.

They lay silent, chests heaving as they stared at the ceiling.

"You should go now," Rhona murmured, still dazed.

Cameron's voice was rough. "Gordon didn't wait. But I did. For you. That's all I've done."

They dressed in loaded silence, the weight of two decades settling between them.

Rhona steered Cameron towards the exit, lips pressed tight. He pulled her into an embrace, his scent enveloping her. Something primal stirred within, a low growl building in her chest.

The moment the door closed, she dialed Gordon. His name fell from her lips twice before she realized he was there, frozen in stunned silence. Classic Gordon.

"We need to meet," she said, her voice steady despite the turmoil inside.

A pause, then his reply came, laced with poorly concealed hope: "It's good to hear your voice."

Rhona suppressed a sigh. Reading Gordon was like trying to catch smoke with your bare hands. Some things never changed.

❖

When Isobel stepped into her apartment, the lingering scent of new leather from her cherry Cooper still clinging to her clothes, she found her mother sprawled on the couch in the dimly lit living room, an ice pack draped over her forehead.

She'd have to adapt, like it or not. Her space, once a sanctuary, now invaded by her mother's presence. And then there was the bizarre situation with the two brothers. "How long am I going to have to endure this?" Isobel wondered, eyeing Rhona's seemingly dozing form.

Knowing her mother's unpredictable nature, Isobel doubted the worst was truly behind them. With a resigned sigh, she made her way to the kitchen.

"What the—" she muttered, jaw dropping at the sight of the overstuffed fridge. Her mother had gone all out—yogurts, juices, the works. Isobel's appetite evaporated instantly.

Rhona shuffled in, making a beeline for the freezer to refill her ice pack.

"Your boy toy called," she said, rummaging through the frozen goods. "That Brodie fellow. How'd he get my number, anyway? Says he's been trying to reach you. Claims you're not picking up."

Isobel nodded absently, meeting her mother's eyes before retreating to the living room. Behind her, she could hear Rhona fishing ice cubes from the freezer, the clink of frozen water against plastic a reminder of her new reality.

In the bathroom, Isobel spotted a pair of her mother's shorts and underwear draped over the radiator, still damp. Though it seemed trivial, she couldn't bring herself to give Rhona the benefit of the doubt. She was beyond that now.

A sudden pounding at the front door jolted her from her thoughts. This, at least, wasn't Rhona's doing.

The impatient visitor hammering away in the darkness wasn't there for her mother—no, this unwelcome interruption was all for Isobel. Just the sort of drama her mother would relish. "Perfect," she muttered as Brodie's knocking intensified.

Rhona affected a look of surprise.

"Get rid of him," Isobel hissed, darting for the back door. She plunged into the overgrown garden, years of neglect providing ample cover in the tangled bushes. Crouched in the shadows, she felt ridiculous. Humiliated. How was she any different from her mother in this moment? Any less absurd?

A moss-covered wall, strangled by ivy, stood between Isobel and the street where Brodie waited impatiently.

Rhona's smile flickered toward the dense foliage that had swallowed her daughter before she turned to answer the door.

"She's driving me fuckin' nuts," Brodie blurted out.

Rhona's face betrayed nothing, even if she understood. She made no move to invite him inside.

"I'm s'posed to curl up in some gutter? That's how it is?" Brodie growled, his jaw clenched.

It would take more than that to sway Rhona. She gestured to the ice pack dangling from her arm. "I need peace and quiet for a few hours. Some tranquility at home would be nice."

Brodie's frustration was evident, but something about Rhona made him shrink. He couldn't hold her gaze for more than a heartbeat.

"Come on, just let me crash on the couch. I'm in a real bind here."

Rhona's refusal was immediate and firm. "At your age, in this weather? When I was a newlywed, I sometimes slept in the park for fun."

A police cruiser crawled past the house. Rhona seized the moment, bidding Brodie a curt goodnight before shutting the door in his face. She paused, realizing he was the second man she'd turned away tonight. Must be the full moon.

Returning to the living room, she muttered, "Finally, some fucking peace," just as a commotion erupted in the garden.

Isobel and Brodie were locked in a struggle, rolling across the grass. They grunted and gasped, neither crying out. Rhona yanked at Brodie's shirt, but he didn't budge. He'd mounted Isobel, trying to pin her hands while dodging her snapping teeth.

It was a sorry sight, a mismatch for anyone with a sense of fair play. Brodie's weight crushed Isobel as he twisted her arms, forcing them to the ground.

So Rhona shattered a terracotta pot over his head.

"You killed him!" Isobel choked out. "Jesus, you killed him!"

"Don't be absurd," Rhona scoffed. "He's fine. And make up your mind, will you?"

❖

Gordon froze, unsure how to manhandle a guy in a wheelchair - especially one who seemed unhinged. The night had taken a sharp turn from passion to chaos in seconds.

One moment, he and Fiona had been entangled in sheets, breathless and sated. The next, she was bolting upright, eyes wide with panic. "Shit! Brock's outside messing with your car!"

He leapt up, yanking on his pants. He barreled down the stairs, stumbled through the dark living room, and burst outside.

Gordon reached the sidewalk like a rocket, but it was too late. Brock, Fiona's husband, was already gone - just a black, cackling shadow speeding away on his high-end wheelchair.

Gordon could have caught up with him in seconds, ripped his throat out before Brock even realized what was happening. But that would mean exposing himself to Fiona. She didn't know about the vampire thing yet, and revealing it like this would be a disaster. Better to let the bastard go for now. There'd be time for vengeance later, when fewer eyes were watching.

Then Gordon saw it. The maniac had superglued his Aston Martin's doors shut.

He'd heard of this vandal hack, usually done by psycho exes, but seeing it firsthand left him stunned. Unbelievable. He kicked at the hydrangeas spilling onto the street, their blooms indifferent to his rage.

Fiona appeared beside him, having followed him outside. She pressed against him, wearing only his discarded shirt. Any minute now, nosy neighbors would start peeking out or stepping outside for a smoke.

Gordon's mind raced. How the hell was he going to explain this to his insurance? And what kind of wheelchair-bound madman goes around supergluing car doors in the dead of night?

He ran a hand through his hair, fighting the urge to scream. This was going to be one hell of a mess to clean up - and not just the car.

Fiona tugged at his arm. "We should get inside before someone sees us," she whispered urgently.

Gordon nodded, still staring at his violated quarter-million Aston Martin. Each glint of streetlight on the superglued seams felt like a personal affront. His fangs itched to descend, a predatory instinct he quickly suppressed.

As they turned to go in, headlights swept across the street. He tensed, wondering if Brock was coming back for round two.

But it was just a passing car, oblivious to the drama unfolding on this quiet suburban street. Gordon let out a shaky breath.

❖

Gordon steered Fiona back inside, eager to escape prying eyes. His instincts screamed to distance himself from this mess, but he pushed the thought aside as Fiona leaned into him, pressing her breasts against his chest.

In the kitchen, they sipped cold water and talked about the bastard. It was hard to call Brock anything else. The guy who terrorized them nightly, leaving dead animals on their doorstep like macabre gifts.

"It started with his fall," Fiona explained, perched on Gordon's lap. "He was fixing power lines after an ice storm. Fell from the top of a pole."

Gordon raised an eyebrow. "And that's when he...?" He shifted slightly, acutely aware of Fiona's warm pussy on his lap.

Fiona shook her head. "No, things were bad before. We fought constantly. He scared the kids. The accident just made everything worse."

A soft cry interrupted them. Fiona's daughter appeared, tears streaking her cheeks. Fiona gathered her close, murmuring comfort.

The scene completed itself as her son shuffled in, face twisted in distress.

Gordon's suggestion of making pancakes worked like magic, calming the chaos. Fiona beamed at him, her smile a mix of love and gratitude.

❖

Later, as they lounged on the bed, Fiona rolled over and said, "How are you both an incredible lover and such a sweetheart? It doesn't seem fair."

Gordon's face fell. "Listen, I'm not ready to take them for a weekend. I'm sorry."

Fiona absorbed his words, then gave a quiet nod.

Settling down with two kids was no walk in the park, especially for a vampire. Over the centuries, Gordon had lost more lovers and friends than he cared to count. While he no longer spent months wallowing in heartbreak when someone close died, their passing still left its mark. He'd learned to keep his distance, a survival tactic born from eternal life. It was second nature now, avoiding deep connections. The harsh truth was that for him, nothing could ever truly be permanent. That was just how it worked when you lived forever.

With Fiona, it was different. The pull he felt towards her was magnetic, almost impossible to resist. But she had two kids to think about, and sometimes swallowing your pride was the smartest move.

Fiona comforted herself with the thought that time was on her side. She believed Gordon's heart wasn't truly walled off, that eventually, she and her children would find their way in.

"And your car," Fiona sighed. "I'm so sorry about what happened to it."

Gordon stiffened, the image of his vandalized Aston Martin flashing through his mind. "It's just a car," he lied, forcing down a surge of anger. "We'll figure something out."

Gordon tensed as Fiona shifted, her eyes meeting his with a mix of apology and heat. She trailed kisses down his neck, her touch light as a feather but electric.

His breath caught as she moved lower. Her full breasts brushed his chest, then his thighs, sending fire through his veins. When her lips found their mark, parting to take him into her mouth. The wet warmth nearly undid him. It soothed his frayed nerves yet drove him wild, driving him to the edge.

A groan escaped as Gordon tangled his fingers in her thick, full hair. Fiona moved with agonizing slowness, each deliberate motion threatening to break his control. The press of her breasts against his thighs made his head spin. Every flick of her tongue inched him closer to the precipice.

Another moan tore from his throat as pleasure consumed him. His anger and worries melted away under her touch. Nothing else mattered but this moment, this connection.

When he finally fell over the edge, the world faded to white. Fiona stayed with him through every tremor, every gasp, anchoring him as the aftershocks rippled through his body.

After, she curled up beside him, her head on his chest. Gordon held her close, breathing in her scent as his heart raced. For now, at least, they were at peace.

❖

The tow truck rolled up to the distillery, Gordon's sleek Aston Martin in tow. A crowd gathered, eager for the latest gossip. Whispers and low whistles spread as workers took in the sight of Gordon Bruce's newest misadventure. Most faces showed a mix of schadenfreude and morbid curiosity, but two stood out from the pack.

Angus, the master distiller, winced and looked away, pained to see such a magnificent machine damaged. His weathered hands clenched at his sides, as if fighting the urge to rush over and assess the damage himself.

Heather sank back into her chair, worry etched on her features. Poor Gordon.

Gordon's gaze drifted up to the distillery's facade. Behind the original stonework, newly installed metal structures loomed. The air filled with the acrid scent of welding as workers secured the framework. There stood Cameron, espresso in hand, watching the scene unfold.

With a sigh, Gordon braced himself. He knew what was coming: another lecture from his brother about his poor choice in women. Cameron would point out – justifiably this time – how Gordon always fell for the complicated ones, the ones trailing a mess of baggage and marital drama. It was an old argument between them, worn smooth by centuries of repetition.

Doors would likely slam. They'd give each other the silent treatment until nightfall. Gone were the days when their fights ended in physical brawls. They'd thrown enough punches over the centuries to grow weary of it. Their mother, at least, was grateful for small mercies.

The chief mechanic from the dealership surveyed the damage, scratching his head. The Aston's doors were sealed shut with super glue. Blowtorch or chisel? He hadn't decided which would do less damage. Wincing, he rubbed his neck and scanned the crowd for Gordon.

But Gordon was already striding towards the distillery offices. Better to face Cameron's lecture now and get it over with. Then he could retreat to Archie's terrace with his newspaper in peace.

It grated on Gordon that Cameron never accepted being the younger brother. Everything was a competition with him. By twenty, Cameron had bulked up, outmuscling Gordon and growing two centimeters taller. Back in the 1300s, that edge in size and strength had mattered. Now? Not so much.

To Gordon's surprise, Cameron greeted him with a smile. He was riding high on the renovation's progress.

"Can't wait to move back into my office," Cameron said, eyes gleaming. "I'm thinking sleek, modern, a touch of luxury. Thanks for letting me camp out in yours. I know I've been a pain."

Gordon blinked, thrown off balance by his brother's good mood. This was new territory.

Cameron lounged back, surprisingly relaxed. He flicked open a whisky brochure, fanning himself as he eyed the mangled DB12.

"Your guy could've just slashed the tires," he sighed. "Must've been quite the shock."

Gordon tensed, waiting for the lecture. Instead, Cameron's face softened.

"You know what, brother? It's been a hell of a few days. Let's have a proper drink."

Those words – "proper drink" – hit Gordon like a blast from the past. He knew exactly what Cameron meant.

❖

Minutes later, Cameron returned, cradling the last bottle of Legacy Reserve and two crystal tumblers. He looked like a man who'd just ordered a lavish bouquet, pleased as punch.

Cameron eased the cork from the quarter-million-pound bottle, amber liquid glinting as he poured two generous measures, the rich aroma instantly filling the room.

Gordon inhaled deeply, his vampire senses dissecting the whisky's complex bouquet. Oak and vanilla mingled with hints of peat and fruit. Underneath, he caught traces of Scottish earth - heather and sea salt carried on Highland winds.

They clinked glasses and sipped. The whisky hit like lightning, their vampire senses aflame with flavor. Fire-honey scorched their throats, lighting up every nerve.

Sun-warmed barley, misty mornings, hints of bourbon, sherry, and port - decades of craft burst across their tongues. No human could ever taste this depth.

Time seemed to stand still as they savored each sip. When Gordon finally looked up, he saw his own sense of wonder reflected in Cameron's eyes.

"Fuck man," Cameron whispered. "I'd forgotten."

Gordon nodded, at a loss for words. This wasn't just whisky - it was liquid history, art, and magic combined. Only their vampire senses could truly appreciate its full glory.

That contented look never left Cameron's face, not even as night fell.

Despite the DB12 fiasco, business hummed along smoothly. Not a single grumpy customer in sight. Well, except Heather. She was beyond distraught, her world crumbling around her. The opened Legacy Reserve wasn't just a bottle - it was her dreams, her ambitions, her very future, all gone in a single pour. Her TikTok star client would be furious, her commission up in smoke. Heather's face was a mask of barely contained panic, her fingers trembling as she tried to figure out how to salvage this disaster. But beyond her quiet meltdown? Not a grumble, not a hiccup. Still, it didn't fully explain Cameron's sunny disposition.

"Need a lift to your friend's place?" Cameron offered as they locked up.

Gordon blinked, unsure how to take the gesture. The evening was perfect – balmy air, lazy traffic. Yet suddenly the horizon seemed impossibly distant, forever out of reach.

❖

Half a bottle later, Gordon found himself in the passenger seat of Cameron's gleaming new Aston Martin. His brother steered them away from the river, top down, tackling the steep road that snaked through a stand of towering Douglas firs.

The whisky's warmth did little to dull Gordon's senses. He knew that set to Cameron's jaw, the too-casual grip on the leather-wrapped wheel. His brother was winding up to something, and whatever it was, Gordon was damn sure he wouldn't like it.

He sank lower into the plush seat, bracing himself for the inevitable. Some things never changed.

❖

Margaret swirled her gin, eyes gleaming with triumph. "Did you know she was in a psychiatric hospital?" She didn't bother hiding the oversized glass, too excited by her discovery. Surely her sons would feel relieved now.

Cameron and Gordon stumbled into the manor, buzzed and not exactly thrilled for another Rhonagate update.

"I've got it all," Margaret pressed on, waving a paper. "The facility's name and address. Her doctor. Even the exact dates she was committed."

Cameron's expression remained neutral. "Interesting. But that was fifteen years ago. And by the way, stealing medical records is a felony."

Margaret's eyes widened. "Fifteen years? That's nothing for mental illness, you fool. Nothing at all."

With no dinner prepared—again—the brothers raided the fridge for cold cuts, silently thanking their housekeeper's foresight. Margaret slumped into a chair, drinking while they ate in tense silence.

Gordon suppressed a sigh. Sometimes he wondered if it was a curse or a blessing, these reminders of what they once were. At least it made blending in easier, he mused, reaching for another slice of ham.

He watched his mother from the corner of his eye, noting how her hand trembled slightly as she lifted the glass. It was a stark reminder of their strange existence—immortal, yet not invulnerable. Centuries of un-life hadn't freed them from the quirks of their former humanity. Hangovers, aching joints, even the occasional headache—all persisted, as if their bodies stubbornly clung to these last vestiges of being human.

Dr. MacGregor hadn't prescribed alcohol, but it was the only thing that dulled the ache since their father had moved downtown. Three years, three hundred liters of gin, and still those damn hot flashes persisted. Seven centuries, and menopause was still a bitch.

Margaret caught her sons' furtive glances. She knew what they were thinking. Every man in this family had turned against her, no matter their heartfelt promises. Now, all they offered was pity. Thank God for the numbing shield of alcohol.

"Don't you think you've had enough?" Cameron said as she topped off her glass.

That one. He used to be such a good boy—respectful, loving, helpful. A mother's dream. Now? A stranger. A cold-hearted monster. She ignored him completely.

"You two are such hypocrites," she slurred. "I smelled that Legacy Reserve before you even cut the engine."

The vampire nose never lied. On the long list of vampire downsides, forget fang marks; nothing screams "undead" like your mom's disappointed sniff.

She met Gordon's eyes, finding no warmth there either. With Gordon, you never knew what lurked beneath the surface. Even their father, for all his claims, never truly knew him.

Margaret's thoughts drifted to the loveless centuries in this Victorian manor. Where had they gone so wrong?

❖

Later, as they carried her to bed, she heard herself giggling in their arms, even as despair consumed her. Margaret's eyes fluttered, fighting the heavy pull of the killer sleeping pills she'd taken earlier. They always left her feeling disconnected, as if she were floating just outside her own body. Bliss.

Downstairs, Cameron cleared the table. The world had turned upside down, normality shattering like a dropped mirror.

"How'd you know Rhona landed in the hospital?" Gordon asked, eyeing his brother.

Cameron paused, considering. His response was calm, devoid of any arrogance. "Does it matter? I kept tabs on her. Wanted to know what became of our girl."

❖

They moved to the laundry room, sorting through shirts and clothes. Outside, the night was crystal clear. From his perch in the manor's high tower, Cameron observed the street below. In the distance, girls lingered on the riverbanks, cars slowing as they passed. He smirked, thinking of the fourth-gen night vision scope in his room.

The telelens was Cameron's invention, born from his struggle to wean off human blood. He'd found an odd sort of substitute satisfaction in voyeurism, watching women from afar. The high-powered scope let him observe women without risking a bite, often accompanied by solitary release. It was hardly noble, but it beat leaving corpses in alleys.

"You never mentioned it," Gordon pressed, dumping a handful of socks into the washer.

"Nope," Cameron agreed, measuring out detergent. "Figured you were doing your own digging. Seemed like we weren't supposed to share intel on her, you know?"

Gordon nodded heavily, at a loss for words.

"Seven hundred years, and you're still stating the obvious," Gordon muttered, roughly folding a pair of trousers. He shot Cameron a sidelong glance, his jaw tightening. "We're different. Always have been. What's your point?"

Cameron shrugged, his fingers drumming an impatient rhythm

on the laundry basket. "Just thinking how we ended up here. You, all buttoned-up and proper. Me, well..."

"A loose cannon?" Gordon supplied, his tone edged with irritation.

"At least I'm not afraid to live a little," Cameron retorted, tossing a shirt into the pile with more force than necessary.

"Most folks have no clue how different we really are," Gordon replied, trying to ease the tension. "Case in point. Don't take it personally - just an observation."

Cameron scrutinized his shirt collars, muttering about the new maid's inconsistent ironing skills. They were shelling out top dollar for impeccable housekeeping, after all. He'd have to have a word with the head housekeeper.

❖

As they climbed the stairs, Cameron dropped a bombshell. "Have I been with a single woman since... you know? Had even one fling? Unlike you?"

Gordon bristled. "What's that got to do with anything? And it's a lie—you fucked every hooker in town and within a 1,000-mile radius! Are you serious right now?"

Cameron shrugged. "That's different."

Gordon shot him a look. "How is that different?"

They paused at Margaret's door, listening for any signs of distress. Silence greeted them.

Suddenly, the door flew open. Margaret stood there, a wreck—tear-stained, disheveled, and deathly pale. Her lips quivered, a choked sob caught in her throat. She wore nothing but a flimsy thong.

Cameron shoved his laundry into Gordon's arms and gripped Margaret's shoulders.

"What's gotten into you?" he sighed. "Have you lost your mind?"

"She will destroy us," Margaret whispered, her face crumpling like a child's. She swayed unsteadily, gripping the door to keep from falling.

Cameron turned to Gordon. "Tell her we're done. Tell her it's over."

Gordon met his mother's desperate gaze. "I'd sooner hack off my own arm," he growled. "That clear enough for you?"

The memory flashed unbidden - his fist connecting with Cameron's jaw on a frigid winter's day. It wasn't called Boxing Day back then, just the second day of Yuletide. The ground had been hard as iron, the air sharp enough to slice. Gordon could still feel the ache in his knuckles, a phantom pain that would never truly fade.

CHAPTER 6
ST. ANDREWS
MARCH 1309

The great hall of St. Andrews Cathedral buzzed with tension. Torches flickered, casting long shadows across the weathered stone walls. Robert Bruce stood at the center, his piercing gaze sweeping over the assembled Scottish nobility and clergy. The air crackled with anticipation and fear as Robert the Bruce held his first parliament.

"My lords," he began, his voice cutting through the last whispers like a sword through mist, "I come to you not just as a king, but as a man facing an unholy tide. We face a threat greater than any English army. A plague of darkness spreads across our land." He paused, letting the force of his words sink in. "And I know you've all heard the vile rumors. Some say that I, Robert Bruce, your king, am the one leading this army of shadows."

A collective gasp rippled through the hall. Faces paled, and hands instinctively moved to sword hilts. The tension in the room was palpable, thick enough to cut with a knife.

Robert's voice rose, filling every corner of the vast chamber. "We can no longer hide behind comfortable lies or bury our heads in the sand. The time for denial is over. Vampires walk among us, feasting on Scottish blood, and we must face this threat united or perish divided."

Lord MacAlpin, his grizzled face etched with concern, spoke up. "Sire, these accusations... surely you don't expect us to believe—"

"I expect you to open your eyes, Lord MacAlpin!" Robert thundered, silencing the old warrior. "How many more villages must fall silent? How many more children must vanish in the night before we acknowledge the evil in our midst?"

He strode forward, his gaze challenging each person in the room. "Aye, there are those who would paint me as a monster, a traitor who's made a pact with darkness to drive out the English. But I ask you this – would a servant of evil stand before you now, rallying you to fight against these creatures of the night?"

The hall fell silent, the tension almost unbearable. Then, slowly, Bishop Lamberton stepped forward, his weathered face a mask of conflicting emotions. "You stand before us excommunicated, cut off from God's grace." He paused, his eyes flickering to the shadows. "And yet... Your Majesty speaks true. We... we can no longer deny what's happening. The Church has seen signs, omens."

A ripple of unease passed through the assembled priests. Some clutched at crosses, others muttered prayers under their breath.

The Bishop continued, his voice echoing in the chamber. "Scotland cries out for a warrior king. One who can drive the English from our lands and... face the demons that now stalk our nights. If you stand ready to fight this darkness, then so shall we."

Robert nodded gravely. "Thank you, Bishop. We'll need the strength of both Crown and Church to face what's coming."

Lady Campbell, her voice barely above a whisper, asked, "But how can we be certain, Your Majesty? These could just be tales to frighten children."

Robert's face darkened. "Would that it were so, my lady. Lord Douglas, tell them what you witnessed in Fife."

All eyes turned to the battle-hardened warrior. Douglas stood, his hands shaking slightly. "Two nights past, I rode through a village near the coast. It was... silent. No dogs barking, no children playing. We found the villagers in the square, piled like cordwood. Drained of blood, every last one."

A horrified murmur swept through the hall. Robert nodded grimly. "And that's not all. Show them, Douglas."

With trembling fingers, Douglas unlaced his tunic, revealing a blood-soaked bandage covering his shoulder. As he peeled back the dressing, gasps of horror and retching sounds echoed through the chamber. A chunk of flesh was missing, leaving a ragged, gaping wound. Around the edges of the torn skin, unmistakable fang marks were visible, deep and angry.

"Dear God," someone whispered, while others crossed themselves.

"The creature that did this moved faster than any man," Douglas said, his voice hoarse with pain and remembered terror. "It latched onto me like a hellhound, tearing flesh as it drank. Strong as ten men, with eyes that glowed red in the dark. If not for my men driving an iron spike through its heart at the last moment, I wouldn't be standing here – I'd be one of them."

Robert stepped closer, examining the wound with a furrowed brow. "The bite... it's not healing properly. How do you feel, Douglas?"

The warrior's face was pale, a sheen of sweat on his brow. "Weak, Your Majesty. The wound pains me, and I... I'm not sure I feel quite myself."

A collective shudder ran through the room. Bishop Lamberton moved forward, his face grave. "We can't be certain what this means. The creature was slain quickly, but..." He trailed off, leaving the grim possibilities unspoken.

Robert's jaw clenched. "We'll watch you closely, old friend. Your sacrifice in showing us this truth may have saved us all."

The color drained from faces around the room as the implications sank in. Lady Campbell swooned, caught by a nearby lord before she could hit the floor. Lord MacAlpin, a man who had seen countless battlefields, turned away, his hand covering his mouth. The younger nobles stood frozen, their eyes wide with terror, unable to look away from the gruesome wound yet unable to fully comprehend what they were seeing.

A strangled sob broke the silence, followed by the sound of retching as one man lost the contents of his stomach. The acrid smell filled the air, mixing with the metallic scent of blood from Douglas's wound. Whispered prayers and muttered curses blended together in a low, fearful murmur that spread through the hall like a wave.

Robert's voice cut through the shocked silence. "Now you see the truth we face. This is no mere invasion. It's a battle for the very soul of our nation – and perhaps for the souls of those who survive these attacks. We must find a way to stop this plague, not just for Scotland, but for every man, woman, and child at risk of this cursed fate."

Bishop Lamberton crossed himself. "Lord have mercy. But... how do we fight such evil?"

Robert's lips curled into a grim smile. "With faith, steel, and fire, my friends. But first, we must root out their nests. I've received reports of entire villages in the north gone silent. We ride at dawn to investigate."

Lord MacAlpin growled, "And what of the English? We can't fight on two fronts, sire."

"The English are the least of our worries now," Robert replied. "In fact, I've sent word to Edward. This threat knows no borders. If we don't stop it here, all of Britain could fall."

A tense silence fell over the hall. Then, slowly, Bishop Lamberton nodded. "The Church... acknowledges the gravity of this threat. If what you say is true, Your Majesty, then we have no choice but to stand with you. God's light must prevail against this darkness."

Robert's eyes blazed as he faced the assembled lords, his voice cutting through the tension like a blade. "Enough! These shadows have dogged us too long. Someone seeks to poison Scotland against her king, and by God, I'll have their head."

He clenched his fist, years of frustration fueling his words. "Who among you has the courage to ride with me? To root out the serpent spreading these vile rumors and show all of Scotland the truth of their king's heart?"

For a heartbeat, the hall held its breath. Then Lord Douglas, his old friend, stepped forward with a growl. Steel rang as he drew his sword. "I'm with you, Robert. Let's hunt down the bastard behind this and make him choke on his lies!"

Like a spark to tinder, Douglas' words ignited the room. Swords flashed in the torchlight as lord after lord pledged their steel. Even MacAlpin, usually so cautious, shouldered his way forward with a fierce nod.

Robert's heart surged. At last, action. "Prepare to ride!" he barked. "Bishop Lamberton, draft a proclamation. Let all of Scotland know their king rides to purge this rot from our lands!"

His mind raced. Who had he wronged so grievously to spawn such hatred? An old rival? A scorned ally? No matter. Soon, he'd have answers, and Scotland would know the truth.

❖

As the hall emptied, men rushing to prepare for battle, Robert caught Bishop Lamberton's arm. The old clergyman's eyes were filled with concern. "There's more troubling you, isn't there?" he asked quietly.

Robert nodded, his face etched with grim lines. "These rumors, Lamberton. They spread like wildfire, claiming I lead these unholy creatures. That I've struck a bargain with evil itself to drive out the English." His voice dropped lower, heavy with the sting of accusation. "They say I'm no longer human – that I'm a demon wearing a crown."

The bishop's eyes widened in shock. "Preposterous! Who would dare spread such vile lies?"

"Someone cunning. Someone who understands that fear can

topple kingdoms more swiftly than any army." Robert's gaze hardened. "This reeks of human malice, not mindless brutality. These creatures, for all their strength, are animals driven by bloodlust. But this? This is the work of a far more dangerous predator."

Lamberton nodded slowly, understanding dawning. "A human enemy, using this chaos to undermine you."

"Aye. And it's working. These whispers... they chip away at my credibility, both as a political leader and as a man fighting for Scotland's freedom." Robert's fist clenched at his side. "How can I rally men against monsters when half of them wonder if I'm one myself?"

The bishop placed a comforting hand on Robert's shoulder. "We must counter these lies with the full weight of the truth, then. The people need to see their king standing against this darkness, not hiding in shadows."

Robert nodded, a spark of determination igniting in his eyes. "Which is why your proclamation is vital, old friend. The people must know where the Church truly stands. Your words can be a shield against this poison."

Lamberton straightened, squaring his shoulders. "And they shall be. We'll craft a message so clear and powerful that none can doubt it. The Church stands with its rightful king, against all enemies – be they of this world or powers of darkness."

As they parted to make preparations, the bishop turned and squared his shoulders. "I'll do more than that, sire. I'll ride with you to spread the news. The people need to see their king and their church fighting side by side."

Robert clasped his arm, gratitude shining in his eyes. "Thank you, old friend. We ride in an hour. Gather what holy relics you can. We'll need every weapon at our disposal."

As the assembly broke into fervent discussion, a commotion at the back of the hall drew everyone's attention. A young messenger, clothes torn and face pale with terror, stumbled in.

"Your Majesty!" he gasped, dropping to his knees. "News from Aberdeen! The city... it's under attack!"

Robert's hand flew to his sword. "Speak, boy! What manner of attack?"

The messenger's eyes were wild with fear. "Monsters, sire. Pale as death, fast as lightning. They're tearing through the city like a storm. The harbor... it's full of bodies."

CHAPTER 7

Hashtag Magazine wasn't just a publication; it was Scotland's pulse, its glossy pages and digital platforms a potent mix of cutting-edge fashion, scathing social commentary, and powerful human interest stories. At its helm was Alison Stewart, Edinburgh's self-appointed queen of controversy and tastemaker extraordinaire.

Her editorials dripped with venom, her Instagram posts sparked wildfires, and her Twitter feed was a minefield of wit and vitriol. On TikTok, millions watched as she set trends and destroyed reputations in 60-second clips. But what truly set Hashtag apart were Alison's raw, unflinching portraits of Scotland's most intriguing personalities - from unsung heroes to cultural icons.

In a media landscape dominated by the likes of Konbini, Alison had carved out a unique niche. Hashtag was where youth culture collided with hard-hitting journalism, where memes shared space with manifestos. In a city steeped in history, Alison was a thoroughly modern force—sharp as her stilettos, which she wielded to crush her enemies and elevate her allies across every platform imaginable.

This notoriety wasn't new. Back in college, she'd ruled the

university paper with an iron fist, often pulling all-nighters to finish it solo after kicking everyone else out. Some called it a scandal, but no one dared challenge her. Nobody wanted to end up publicly humiliated or become the latest target of her sharp tongue, which had claimed victims of both sexes. Even then, she was known as one hell of a bitch.

Alison didn't mind the reputation one bit. If anything, she relished it. Over the years, she'd learned that her take-no-prisoners attitude was the only way to survive. The world deserved nothing more than a sneer and certainly no sympathy or tenderness. Otherwise, you'd end up as someone's chew toy.

The exclusive rooftop bar of The Balmoral Hotel buzzed with Edinburgh's elite. It was here that Alison hosted her tamer soirées—gatherings that often evolved into decadent affairs, drawing in clients, models, and celebrities alike. But those in the know whispered about wilder parties at her mother's secluded hunting lodge, where inhibitions were shed like last season's fashions.

In this moment, however, the mood was different. They had just finished a leisurely lunch, the remains of their meal still visible on the table—a half-eaten lobster claw, smears of butter on fine china, and the dregs of an expensive white wine in crystal glasses. Now, as the midday sun slanted across the rooftop, Alison nursed a blood-red cocktail, its rim dusted with black salt—a concoction aptly named "The Widow's Kiss."

She fixed Cameron with a predatory smile. "We're going to miss you, darling," she purred. "It'll be dull as dishwater without you around."

Cameron thought it best to keep his mouth shut, he knew better than to underestimate Alison. He fiddled with the tiny paper umbrella from his drink, avoiding her gaze. As a regular at Alison's parties—both public and private—and her occasional favorite lover ever, he knew the weight behind her words.

She might smile and purr sweet nothings, but beneath that exterior lurked a predator just as dangerous as any vampire he'd encountered. The casual way she mentioned missing him carried weight, like a velvet-covered threat.

"You know where to find us," Alison added, her words hanging in the air like a veiled threat. The 'us' implied more than just herself—it was an entire world of pleasure and danger that Cameron was leaving behind.

Cameron looked so lost in thought that Alison softened, brushing his hand with her fingertips. "Hey, nothing's set in stone yet," she said, her voice uncharacteristically gentle. "We'll see how it all shakes out."

But beneath her calm exterior, Alison seethed. It wasn't about losing Cameron as a lover—good sex was just a few swipes away these days. No, her fury ran deeper, tapping into something visceral and raw. She'd been cast aside, discarded like yesterday's news. And for what? Some faded memory of a long-dead passion? The indignity of it clawed at her insides, demanding retribution.

❖

The June issue of Hashtag Magazine marked Rhona's tenth year as a contributor, and she'd chosen a provocative subject for her portrait: a 45-year-old woman who turned to prostitution purely for pleasure.

"I'm not saying it's bad," Alison said, leading Rhona down to the bar with its tinted windows. "Just that there are... cheerier topics."

Rhona smirked. "I had one about a woman who went to prison to escape her husband and kids."

"Right. Thanks for sparing us that one." Alison rolled her eyes as they settled into a booth. The bar was known for its overpriced fruit cocktails, but the privacy was worth it.

"Mind if we cut the part where she's beaten to death by drag queens?" Alison asked. "Let's not go full doom and gloom."

As Rhona considered the request, Alison studied Rhona across the bar, her mind churning with thoughts she'd never voice. How did this woman wield so much power after disappearing for twenty years? It was like a line of influence stretched between them, still taut after all this time. It felt like witchcraft, like some ancient spell that refused to fade. Fascinating, really.

Late afternoon sunlight filtered through the tinted windows. Outside, people streamed from their offices, caught in that hazy moment between work and evening plans. The early summer heat amplified a sense of listlessness, as if important decisions could wait, as if lives couldn't be irreversibly altered in the span of a happy hour.

"What makes you think today will be any different?" Alison asked, swirling her drink. "We don't magically get smarter with age. What's changed?"

Rhona stayed silent. Best friend or not, some things were better left unsaid.

"They might not be who you remember," Alison pressed on. "We've all... weathered a bit."

❖

Later that evening, sprawled on a massage table at the spa, Alison replayed the conversation in her head. Expert hands worked her muscles, but couldn't quite unknot the tension in her mind. For three hundred bucks, you got the "special" treatment – orgasm not guaranteed. Feeling melancholy, she made a few calls to cancel next week's meeting. Everyone expressed their doubts about Cameron's absence, convinced it wouldn't last long. In their minds, sex was just another addiction.

❖

The next morning hit Alison like a freight train, her head pounding. Still, she had to endure a lengthy phone call with her mother, who'd gotten it into her head that she absolutely needed a whisky collection for her country hunting lodge.

"It's what's expected, darling," her mother insisted. "You remember how it used to be."

Alison did remember. The sprawling estate had once been the crown jewel of Scottish high society, attracting celebrities and aristocrats from across the globe. Rock stars mingled with royalty over grouse hunts and lavish dinners. Those glory days weren't as distant as they seemed, thanks to recent renovations that had restored the lodge to its former glory.

"Times have changed, Mum," Alison sighed, massaging her temples.

Her mother wouldn't hear it. She'd become insufferable lately, alternating between imperious demands and childlike tantrums. This whisky obsession was just the latest in a string of attempts to recapture control over the estate.

Last winter's addition of an indoor pool had been the finishing flourish on the lodge's transformation. The craftsmanship was exquisite, every detail a perfect blend of modern luxury and timeless Scottish elegance. It was exactly what Alison had envisioned – and exactly why she couldn't let her mother anywhere near its management.

Alison winced, a dull throb pulsing behind her eyes. Despite the pain, she was remembering the real reason behind her insistence on keeping her mother at arm's length from the pool area only intensified her headache. The pool area had quickly become the centerpiece of Alison's own decadent gatherings. Exclusive, invitation-only affairs that would make even the most jaded socialite blush. She had no intention of letting her mother's meddling ruin the carefully cultivated atmosphere of those nights.

"This whisky business is a waste of time," Alison said, steering the conversation back to safer ground. "We need to focus on what's working." What she left unsaid was just how well her own entertainment ventures were paying off – both financially and personally.

"You promised me, Alison. You gave me your word. So don’t move. I’m coming."

Alison hung up and swallowed three aspirin. She wasn't in any condition to do anything but was obliged to accompany her mother —or risk seeing her roll on the carpet.

❖

Alison's mother had run into Gordon the previous week, and he was waiting for them.

"I think I'll wait for you at Archie's," she groaned while Gordon greeted her mother. "Keep me posted, you two."

City workers watered flowers on the median, eyes locked on Alison. She met their slack-jawed stares with a smirk and a flipped them off. "Enjoy the view, boys?" she taunted, relishing their stunned faces as she strode past. The humidity clung to her skin, a stark reminder of how painfully awake she was.

Crossing seemed impossible. Alison yanked out her phone, rolling her eyes as she dialed Rhona. Christ, of all the days for Gordon to get caught up in her mother's drama.

"Listen up," she barked into the phone, not bothering with pleasantries. "Gordon's going to be late. He's stuck dealing with my mother's latest crisis."

She could practically smell Rhona's desperation through the phone. "What's the weather? Should we reschedule?"

"Don't you dare," Alison snapped, her hangover making her even less patient than usual. "You've been pining after him for two decades. A few extra minutes won't kill you." She paused, then added, "Besides, absence makes the heart grow fonder, or whatever bullshit people say."

"He's just with my mother," she explained. "Anyway, just giving you heads up. It shouldn't take long. I don't know what's harder: having parents or not having them."

At that moment, Alison saw her mother drive by in Gordon's Aston Martin.

"Scratch that. It might take a while. Fucking hell. She can't even drive to the lodge anymore. Not since that freaky accident last month," Alison muttered, her head pounding with each word. "Brand new Jaguar, totaled. And she still refuses to wear glasses, can barely see a thing. Why the hell would she need a whisky collection?"

She turned around and went back the other way, the movement sending a fresh wave of pain through her skull. Alison gritted her teeth, frustrated by her mother's stubborn insistence on clinging to the estate. The lodge was hers now, in all but name. Her mother had put in the work to restore it, but it was Alison who had the agenda to make it profitable again. More than that, she'd made it into something uniquely her own.

"People go crazy at that age, don't you think?" Alison continued, her voice low and heated. What she didn't say was how desperately she wanted her mother to stay away. The last thing she needed was her mother sticking her nose into Alison's "private gatherings." The pool area was off-limits, and she intended to keep it that way. Her little orgies were far too lucrative – and far too much fun – to risk her mother's interference.

"You know, I'm looking forward to you talking to Gordon," she continued. "But not for the reasons you think. Because suddenly, everything becomes strange. I couldn't explain why."

❖

She found Archie in the same mood: smiling but slightly melancholic. They rarely saw each other anymore, not sharing the same circles and still brooding over an old story for which they blamed each other. But they still understood each other with a single glance.

They agreed that nature abhors a vacuum.

"I can't believe we still feel involved in this," she said, looking at Archie's tattoos. "I can't understand why."

Archie straddled a chair—he was still physically attractive, in the beautiful loser sort of way.

"I think Cameron is ahead," he said. "I'm convinced. If it were a race, you could think he started too fast. Only, it's not a race. It's far from a race. He should know that."

"No, stop right there. I don't want to talk about it. I refuse to play that game."

She refused to make any predictions. Especially not with the migraine that had been chasing her since she woke up. A rain of bracelets slid down her wrist to her elbow when she touched her forehead. She almost felt like vomiting.

Fortunately, her stomach was empty. She had gained weight, and Archie had lost his hair. They had crossed a formidable milestone.

Archie had become bitter, his world had shrunk to the size of his miserable restaurant, and sometimes he looked at Alison with the gaze of the class loser toward a rich and unattainable prize—this morning, she was dressed in Vivienne Westwood, perched on high patent leather heels. That's why she couldn't stand him for long anymore, why they rarely saw each other. Because of the way he threw his failure in your face. Because of the stupid and pathetic illusion that someone owed him something, like a veteran.

He told her she looked pale. He stood up to unfold a parasol above her.

"Don't take away the sun," she pleaded.

❖

Brodie thought three stitches would finally get him laid. He couldn't have been more wrong. Like most guys his age, he saw every setback as a personal attack or an unsolvable riddle. He never asked himself the right questions.

Isobel felt zero pity for Brodie, even after her mom cracked his skull with a terracotta pot. She was furious with him—and with herself for thinking he was different. But he only wanted one thing. Just like all the other guys.

Everyone knew the score. Willing or not, all the girls went through it eventually. Parents' bedroom, kitchen floor, beer-soaked carpet, or a table littered with half-eaten sandwiches—it didn't matter where. The guys just waited, circling like sharks.

Nothing else interested them. Every conversation circled back to it. Every thought revolved around it. Even during class, with teachers droning on about algebra or Shakespeare, the boys' minds wandered. The open windows, letting in fresh air and birdsong, did nothing to break the spell. Their world had narrowed to a singular, relentless focus.

The campus was a hunting ground, plain and simple. Seeing it any other way was naive or just plain stupid. Better to face facts. Better to show you were taken, preferably by some big shot with pull among the others. It made life easier. The hallways got less dangerous. Parties became less of a minefield.

Unless, of course, you wanted to wake up with an infection and a soul-crushing hangover, wondering where it all went wrong.

Brodie seemed perfect at first. Isobel told him her first time had been traumatic, so he didn't push—for now. He settled for basic stuff. She provided the elbow grease and tissues. Until that night.

He'd raised his hand to her. They'd fought like wildcats. If her mom hadn't stepped in so brutally, who knows how it would've ended? Now they were at a crossroads.

The other guys were already eyeing her differently—like fresh meat. Isobel knew rough days were coming.

The Mini Cooper's seats scorched her thighs.

"Wear pants like me, duh," Brodie sneered.

She let him stew for five minutes.

She couldn't see any better options, so she pleaded with him again. Be patient. Give her time to work through her hang-ups.

"It's never fun the first time, you know?" he said, trying to sound wise. "That ain't the point, babe. You gotta move on. Keep going, get me?"

"I get it," she said.

"Tell me who did it. I'll teach that loser a lesson if it'll help. No sweat off my back."

When she wouldn't name the jerk who took her virginity, he slammed his fist on the dashboard. Caveman style. But they watched so many of those movies.

She wondered how long she could hold out before Brodie really lost it and ditched her. Before a swarm of creeps descended—the second-stringers were often the worst. Before her life became a living hell that'd make her problems with Brodie seem like a joke. How long, exactly, if she didn't give in a little?

She glanced at the campus and stifled a sigh while Brodie scowled at nothing.

"You could help me, you know," she said, her voice sharp. "Try putting yourself in my shoes for once."

❖

They talked for what felt like hours. The air was thick as a pressure cooker, but she eventually gained the upper hand.

"Brodie, we've been over this," Isobel sighed, leaning against her car. "You know I'm not into the whole public makeout scene."

"Aw, c'mon, Iz," he whined, stepping closer. "It's been ages. The lads are starting to think--"

"I don't give a rat's ass what your mates think," she cut him off, then softened her tone. "Look, it's just... I've got a lot on my plate right now, okay?"

"I could take your mind off things," Brodie grinned, reaching for her waist. "How 'bout we leg it back to mine, yeah? Got some proper lager in the fridge."

She used her charm, making vague promises that Brodie had to swallow. It worked when you got them alone, when they didn't have a part to play for their buddies. You could maneuver them, twist their thick necks, back them into a corner.

Isobel caught his hand, squeezing it gently. "Tell you what, big guy. Let's plan something special next weekend. Just us. No distractions."

His eyes lit up. "Yeah? You promise, like?"

"Cross my heart," she nodded, letting a hint of promise creep into her smile. "But I've really got to run. Dentist appointment, remember?"

Before leaving, Brodie devoured her lips for a long minute and slid a hand between her legs. But he didn't know what he was doing at all.

As she drove off, Isobel rolled her eyes. God, he had no idea what he was doing.

It was exhausting, really. A steep price for so-called "protection." Even more so because there was zero excitement. She didn't get wet at all, despite Brodie's fumbling.

Exhausting was the word. "You like that? Feel good?" he asked, smug as if he already knew the answer.

She wanted to tell him it was mind-blowing. She just squeaked.

She squeaked at the dentist's office too. But there, by some bizarre twist, she didn't have to fake it. Her dentist was utterly ordinary, almost pudgy, but pleasure came almost automatically. She couldn't make sense of it at all.

❖

The 70 steps of the Lang stairs led straight to the top of Edinburgh's Castle Rock. A quick climb rewarded you with a predictable view - exactly what you'd expect, no surprises. Gordon couldn't have picked a better spot to meet Rhona. Nothing could've been more fitting, really. The ancient stone beneath their feet had weathered countless battles and repelled waves of attackers. Now it served as the backdrop for their own personal war.

All around them, tourists clutched guidebooks, wide-eyed. Couples cuddled, content with simple pleasures. Kids bounced with excitement, dazzled by the sunset's glow. The air crackled with an energy Gordon couldn't quite place - anticipation, dread, or maybe just the static charge before a storm.

"At least we can breathe up here," Rhona said, breaking the tense silence.

Gordon glanced at her and nodded, his jaw clenched tight. The wind whipped at Rhona's hair, carrying the faintest scent of her intoxicating musk. It was achingly familiar, a reminder of happier times.

"What about your husband?" he asked, his voice rough. "What's his take on all this?"

She shrugged, her eyes fixed on the distant horizon. "What do you think?"

"Right," he muttered, wishing he hadn't asked.

"I gave him twenty years of my life. That counts for something."

"Sure does," he echoed, the words hollow in his mouth.

Gordon's eyes drifted to a nearby vendor hawking drinks and water. Anything to avoid looking at her directly.

"Are you judging me?" Rhona's voice sharpened, cutting through his distraction.

He scanned the soda selection, unable to pick one. Unable to face her accusation.

"No," he said finally. "You're free to do what you want."

"You don't mean that." Her eyes flashed. "You think I'm the bad guy here. What, you believe a woman should just sit quiet and take it?"

The air between them grew thick with unspoken words and buried resentments. Gordon knew whatever he said next would change everything. He took a deep breath, steeling himself for the battle ahead.

Gordon had a knack for getting under her skin. Always had. She couldn't pinpoint why exactly. Maybe it was his constant guard, that wall he put up. You never knew what was really going on behind those eyes of his.

She caught up to him as he turned towards the stairs.

"Let's go to my place," she said, her voice a challenge.

He glanced at his watch, frowning. "It's going to be tight."

"Do you think there was ever a solution?" she asked, her voice dropping low. "There wasn't one. Not really."

Gordon bit back a sharp retort about her needing to check back into the psych ward if she thought they'd find answers now. But Rhona still threw him off balance. Unlike Cameron, he hadn't adjusted to her sudden reappearance. She didn't feel quite real yet. Here he was, an immortal vampire with the power to kill at will, and she made him twitchy as a schoolboy.

The truth was, this whole mess had driven them all a little mad. What was unfolding now shouldn't surprise anyone with half a brain, anyone who understood the cold logic of cause and effect. That's what he told himself, anyway.

❖

The evening chill nipped at them as they stood on the Royal Mile's bustling sidewalk. Streetlights flickered to life, casting long shadows. Around them, Edinburgh pulsed with end-of-day energy - office workers spilled from grand sandstone buildings, tourists clutched maps and shopping bags, and the tantalizing aroma of pub fare wafted on the cooling breeze. Amidst it all, Rhona and Gordon faced each other, an island of stillness in the human current.

"Cameron mentioned you're seeing someone," Rhona said, her voice softer now. "It's going well?"

Gordon's mind went blank. What could he possibly say to that? What could he say to anything she asked right now?

"Gordon, does it bother you that we're talking about this?"

"That we're talking about it?" he snapped. "Is it any of your business?"

A small victory. She hadn't completely knocked him off balance yet. His breath came short and ragged, disbelief still coursing through him at the sight of her, at this surreal conversation. But he was still standing.

What was she thinking? What did she expect? He noticed her ears had gone red - embarrassment? Anger?

"I'd like to know," he pressed on, "what exactly are we supposed to be talking about? Where can this possibly lead?"

Rhona's eyes dropped for a moment before meeting his again. "Look, you don't have to be nasty. I know this isn't easy."

"Oh, really?" Bitterness crept into his voice. "You in another mess?"

They went back and forth like that for a while, teetering on the edge of saying things they couldn't take back. Finally, Rhona stepped back, her face a mask of regret and something else - determination?

"This was a mistake," she said, her voice barely above a whisper. "I thought... well, it doesn't matter what I thought."

Gordon watched her, his anger giving way to a hollow ache. "Why now, Rhona? After all this time?"

She met his gaze, her eyes shimmering with unshed tears. "Because some things can't stay buried forever, Gordon. Not even for us."

With that, she turned and melted into the evening crowd, leaving Gordon rooted to the spot. The city's pulse seemed to fade away, leaving only the thundering of his own heart and the echo of two-decades-old questions hanging in the air between them.

❖

Rhona slumped into the garden chair, phone stuck to her hear. Her skin still tingled from the cold shower she'd jumped into the moment she got home. Shaking out her damp hair, she lit a cigarette and tugged at her "London Calling" T-shirt that barely covered her thighs. Maybe London was the answer, she mused.

"It was a disaster," she told Alison, picturing her friend gazing out over the city from her office. "We managed not to break anything, but that's about it. He couldn't even spring for more than a Diet Coke."

"Take a breath, darling," Alison's measured voice flowed through the line, a touch of amusement coloring her words. "This isn't a sprint, it's a bloody marathon. You've got time to wear him down."

Rhona considered hanging up. Her legs felt like lead as she sank deeper into the chair. The fabric still bore faint traces of Brodie's blood, despite multiple washes. The memory stirred nothing in her – no guilt, no feeling at all.

"Oh, please," Alison scoffed. "I'm not buying your doom and gloom routine. What, did he sprout fangs and try to drain you over appetizers? Unless there was bloodshed or property damage, I'd say you're being a tad theatrical, darling."

"Alright, alright," Rhona huffed. "Let's drop it. Talking won't magically fix anything. He got that much right, at least."

"Listen, love. Talking is bloody essential. It's how we make sense of the mess. So spill. I promise I won't judge... much."

Thank God for Alison, Rhona thought. In this city full of strangers, she had someone to lean on, someone to call in the depths of loneliness. As if summoned by the thought, her daughter trudged past, heading straight for her room without a word.

"Right," Alison declared, all business now. "I'm chained to my desk for a bit longer, but after? We're going out. I'll not have you moping about alone. A stiff drink and some scandalous gossip – doctor's orders."

Rhona exhaled a cloud of smoke, weighing the offer. Maybe a night out was exactly what she needed to shake off this funk.

❖

The city pulsed with energy as the clock ticked past one in the morning. Alison, her eyes sparkling with mischief, tugged Rhona towards the pounding beat of a nearby party.

"For fuck's sake, Rhona," Alison shouted over the pounding bass, her eyes glinting with a mix of exasperation and excitement. "You've been playing Rapunzel in that backwater town for two decades.

Time to let your hair down and remember what it's like to actually live. The city's waiting, darling, and it's hungry for fresh meat like you."

Rhona stumbled slightly, the unfamiliar fuck-me heels throwing off her balance. "I'm not sure about this," she mumbled, but Alison was already pulling her through the crowd.

Alison grabbed Rhona's shoulders, spinning her like a reluctant ballerina. "Jesus Christ, look at you! You're a goddamn knockout." Her eyes raked over Rhona's body, a wolfish grin spreading across her face. "Trust me, honey, you could have your pick of the litter tonight. Doesn't that get your engine revving, even a little?" She leaned in close, her lips barely brushing Rhona's ear. "Come on, spill. After all this time playing nun, your body must be screaming for a good, hard—"

"I can manage just fine," she said with a wobbly smile. Rhona felt a flush creep up her neck, whether from the alcohol or embarrassment, she couldn't tell. "A few months of celibacy isn't going to kill me."

Alison's eyebrows shot up. "Months? Without getting your rocks off? At all?" She mimed an exaggerated masturbation gesture, earning a scandalized look from a passerby. "Christ, Rhona, not even a little DIY action? Daily?" She shook her head, laughing in disbelief. "Either you're gunning for sainthood or your lady parts have gone into hibernation. This is exactly why I say the Highlands is where libidos go to die. It's criminal, I tell you. Absolutely criminal."

The air around them felt charged, heavy with unspoken possibilities. Rhona could sense it, could almost taste the desperation and desire swirling through the crowd. But exhaustion weighed on her like a lead blanket. She glanced down, noticing Alison's hand resting on her knee. The touch was gentle, hesitant – affectionate, even.

Rhona didn't pull away. She thought of the life she'd left behind, of the long, lonely nights stretching out before her. Loneliness, she realized, was like water – always finding a new path, seeping into the cracks of your defenses.

The light changed, bathing them in a soft green glow. Alison's hand retreated without a word, leaving Rhona to wonder if she'd imagined the moment of connection. As they moved deeper into the pulsing heart of the city, Rhona felt a spark of something long-dormant stirring within her. Maybe, just maybe, it was time to remember how to live again.

❖

Alison's Bentley purred to a stop at the intersection. She gestured towards a row of cookie-cutter houses lining the side street, her lip curling in distaste.

"It's one of those suburban nightmares," she said with an exaggerated shudder. "I bet little wifey has a clothesline out back. Gordon must eat that shit up. Makes him feel like he's cracked some great mystery of womanhood."

"Huh?" Rhona mumbled, her attention caught by the identical houses. Each one competed for the title of 'Most Painfully Suburban' with manicured lawns, flower beds bursting with color, and the occasional swing set or shiny barbecue.

A solitary light glowed from an upstairs window in one of the homes.

"Gordon needs women to fit into neat little boxes," Alison continued, her voice dripping with disdain. "Simple, uncomplicated. After centuries of wild, savage vampire sex, he's gone full Stepford. And honey, you didn't exactly challenge that worldview. Let's be real. You went from bloodthirsty vixen to demure housewife so fast, I'm surprised you didn't get whiplash.'"

Rhona's eyes fixed on that single illuminated window. She knew, with a certainty that surprised her, that it was Fiona's house. What the hell was Gordon doing in the bathroom at this hour?

❖

Gordon dabbed antiseptic on Fiona's scraped knees at the kitchen table, his touch gentle but precise. She hissed in pain but didn't pull away. The chase after that ultralight wheelchair—built for paralympic basketball players—had left its mark, but Fiona wouldn't have traded this moment for anything.

The scent of her blood hit Gordon like a sledgehammer - a heady mix of copper and something uniquely Fiona. Lavender from her soap mingled with deeper, muskier notes of desire. He clenched his jaw, swallowing hard, forcing himself to breathe shallowly. Centuries of control, and yet here he was, undone by a simple cut. His movements slowed as he applied the antiseptic, savoring the warmth of her skin. Part of him wondered how she'd taste - would fear quicken the flavor, or would trust and arousal enrich it? The monster within purred at the possibilities.

Fiona studied his face, noticing the slight tension in his jaw. His care spoke volumes, even if he struggled to voice his feelings. But beneath those gentle hands lurked a predator - one that found her utterly, dangerously irresistible.

She'd been wrong to push him, to demand promises or declarations during intimate moments. Gordon was perfect for her, just as he was. If she played her cards right and stayed focused on her goals, she and her kids could finally breathe easy. Safety. Stability. A life worth envying, even.

But sometimes, Fiona sensed Gordon was holding back. Not in a "secret family" kind of way, but something... darker. Scarier. She'd heard the whispers about the Bruces being vampires, of course. It was too ridiculous to believe, let alone ask about.

Still, as Gordon's cool fingers brushed her skin in the warmth of her kitchen, Fiona couldn't help but wonder what secrets lurked beneath his careful facade.

She let her skirt ride up, revealing more than just her scraped knees. She'd shaved recently, a fact that didn't escape her notice—or, she hoped, Gordon's. They had pressing matters to deal with, sure, but that didn't mean she couldn't remind him of what else was on offer.

"Why can't I meet her?" Fiona asked, breaking the silence. "If it's like you say. What's the harm?"

Gordon sighed, his breath warm against her skin. "What good would that do?"

"I don't know. Just to see what she looks like. She is ten years older than me, after all."

Gordon chuckled, shaking his head. His face was dangerously close to Fiona's thigh, and he fought an internal battle as her scent teased him. With his heightened senses, every subtle note of her arousal hit him like a tidal wave.

He finished applying the ointment—the same stuff Fiona used for her kids' scrapes and for razor burn. Apparently, it was as effective as it was multipurpose.

"Could you stop thinking about her for a bit?" Gordon suggested as he handled the bandages. "Think you can manage that? Or is this going to turn into an obsession?"

Fiona knew she had wide hips. Gordon could deny it all he wanted, but that's just how she was built. Three swim sessions a week and daily exercises hadn't magically transformed her into anything other than a Jennifer Lopez type. But she had great legs, a tiny waist, and a chest that was both ample and firm. She could hold her own against an older woman, she was sure. It scared her a little, but Fiona trusted her assets.

"You're the one acting weird," she countered. "I can tell you're not yourself."

"You're talking nonsense."

"I'm not talking nonsense. Not at all." She tugged her skirt back down and thanked him for the bandages, her tone clipped.

Gordon closed the first aid kit with a soft click. The sound seemed to echo in the suddenly quiet kitchen. Fiona fidgeted with the hem of her skirt, avoiding his gaze. Gordon's movements were precise, almost mechanical, as he wiped down the counter.

"So," Fiona said, her voice a touch too bright. "That's that, then?"

Gordon paused, his back to her. "That's that," he agreed, his tone carefully neutral.

Neither moved. The tick of the kitchen clock filled the silence, marking each second of unspoken words between them.

❖

Fiona strode purposefully across the bedroom. They'd skip it tonight. She wasn't thrilled—their physical connection was crucial, a foundation for everything else. The rest was murky, full of questions. But she was satisfied to show Gordon she wasn't just some sex-crazed girl. Or at least, not only that. Not that she should be ashamed.

She peeked into the children's room, confirming they were asleep. Loving sex wasn't a crime, she thought. Just because some people didn't enjoy it? As she descended to the kitchen, Gordon following, she decided the world was full of hypocrites. Damned liars, all of them.

"He ruined our evening," Gordon declared, straddling a chair.

"Your mind was elsewhere anyway," Fiona replied, her tone neutral. "I don't think we missed anything extraordinary. Want a drink?"

She busied herself at the counter, letting the silence stretch between them. The tension from earlier still simmered, a mix of unspoken desires and unanswered questions. Fiona wondered how long they could dance around the real issues, how long before something had to give.

Gordon nodded, acknowledging the rough evening. It had been especially hard on Fiona. He'd come back from meeting Rhona in a foul mood. Truth was, he hadn't been eager to hold Fiona, hadn't really been present when she sat in his lap. He was terrible at showing emotions, with Rhona and now with Fiona. He sensed he'd hurt her, but felt powerless to change it. Then that psycho ex-husband showed up. It was a lot to deal with.

He marveled at women who married men only to end up with nutcases. How did they manage, juggling lovers and raising kids? A nightmare, and Gordon knew it.

But he had an idea. Scary, but fitting, even if it didn't come from the heart.

"We should get away this weekend," he suggested. "With the kids."

There. The family outing. Proposed.

Fiona took her time closing the fridge with her knee. "Sorry, only beer to celebrate," she said, unable to inject the sarcasm she'd intended.

"Isn't it a good idea?" Gordon pressed.

"Obviously it's good. Of course. But you don't have to. I'm not trying to force you into anything."

The kitchen fell silent as Fiona handed Gordon a beer. The promise of his suggestion settled in the room, a step neither had expected to take so soon.

"Then it's settled. I'll swing by Aston Martin and try to get the SUV for the weekend."

Gordon suddenly felt drained. Like pushing too hard on a run, he sensed he'd overextended himself. A weekend was long. He already imagined himself pale, gripping the wheel of that powerful SUV.

"Okay, now what?" Fiona asked.

"I'll handle it," he assured her. "Make sure that idiot backs off."

Fiona wanted to believe him. She grimaced. "I'd be surprised. Seems too good to be true."

She walked him to the door, but he insisted she stay inside. At half-past three, the neighborhood was deathly quiet. Streetlights cast an eerie glow over the middle-class landscape—hedges of Japanese SUVs, minivans and sports cars with peeling interiors, their Taiwan-made spoilers clinging on for dear life.

Gordon aimed for a casual wink goodbye, but Fiona pulled him into an embrace. She wanted to tell him how touched she was, how much his efforts meant. To whisper how sad she felt that they'd spent the evening together without really connecting.

"I'll try to free up earlier one of these evenings," Gordon promised.

"One of these evenings? Why not tomorrow?"

They'd discussed this before, but it remained a touchy subject—especially at this hour.

"Please," he sighed.

Fiona hesitated. Should she push him, demand more? She shuddered, realizing she could ruin everything. The future belonged to women who knew when to hold their mouth shut while biting their tongues. She understood how the world worked. Instead, she stroked his cheek.

"I feel like I'm making you do my dirty work," she admitted. "That's really how it feels."

Gordon exuded confidence. He urged her to get some rest. Fiona studied him, acutely aware of how much she missed having a man at home, how much she needed it. Someone to share her life, lighten her load, toss her troubles out with the trash. She'd tasted that bliss in the early months of her marriage. The memory hit her as she glanced at the freshly painted garage door—a reminder of the cost of paint and the neighbor-turned-babysitter.

"Alright, you're probably right," Fiona conceded. "I might not control myself."

"I call him Brock?"

"Oh, call him whatever you want!" she sighed, turning away. "Just get rid of him. His name doesn't matter."

❖

Gordon aimed the remote at the garage, lost in thought. In the stillness of the late hour, the gate creaked open, its squeak echoing for miles. As they parted, the tension of unspoken words pressed down on them both. Gordon stepped into the night, leaving Fiona to wonder if this weekend away would bring them closer or reveal the cracks in their fragile relationship.

He approached Brock's unconscious form, Fiona's ex-husband, who'd been silent for an hour now. Earlier that evening, Gordon had effortlessly overpowered the man with his supernatural strength, leaving him bound and gagged in the garage. Now, face-down on the concrete, Brock lay motionless. Hands and feet tied, silver tape across his mouth, he made no sound. No more toad-throwing at windows. No more harassment. No more supergluing car doors shut.

Gordon stalked towards Brock's crumpled form, eyes gleaming with predatory intent. Centuries of power rippled through his muscles as he hoisted the man up one-handed, as if he weighed nothing. The casual display sent a dark thrill through Gordon, reminding him of the monster lurking beneath his civilized facade.

For a moment, he savored the possibilities. How easy it would be to end this nuisance permanently. The thought of Brock's terror, the sweet scent of fear flooding his veins, made Gordon's fangs ache with desire.

But no. He'd promised Fiona. This was about solving her problem, not indulging his darker nature.

With careful restraint, Gordon deposited Brock into the Aston Martin’s front seat. The man's head lolled lifelessly, and Gordon felt a flicker of concern. Had he been too rough? But no, he could hear Brock's steady, if labored, breathing.

As he secured Brock for the journey ahead, disappointment nagged at Gordon. How long since he'd truly let loose, embraced the full extent of his powers? The life he'd built suddenly felt like a cage.

He slammed the car door, the sound shattering the night's quiet. The guy protested with muffled grunts and wild eyes, but Gordon remained unmoved.

As Gordon folded the wheelchair, a cold fury settled in his chest.

Centuries of restraint warred with the raw desire for vengeance. He'd sworn off taking lives long ago, but for this lowlife... His fingers tightened on the metal frame, the urge to dispense his own justice almost overwhelming. Gordon closed his eyes, forcing himself to breathe deeply. He couldn't afford to lose control, not now. But the temptation lingered, a dangerous whisper in the back of his mind.

Gordon glanced back at the house, where Fiona waited, hoping for a hero. He wondered if she truly understood what she was asking for, what kind of man could "take out the trash" so easily.

Straightening up, Gordon saw Fiona calmly watching from her bedroom window, parting the curtain with her skilled nurse's fingers. A woman worth the trouble, he thought. A woman with a rare sexual talent who deserved to be better known.

Whatever came next, Gordon knew one thing: this night would change everything.

❖

Gordon cut the engine, the sudden silence amplifying the tension in the car. He'd driven them to a desolate industrial park on the outskirts of town, far from prying eyes or potential witnesses.

His gaze fixed on the pathetic figure slumped in the passenger seat. The urge to end it, right here and now, pulsed through him like a fever. It would be so easy. One swift move and he could tear the bastard's throat out, feeling warm blood gush over his hands, savoring the metallic tang on his tongue.

The fantasy played out in vivid detail – the initial shock in those hateful eyes, the gurgling attempts to scream, the frantic scrabbling of fingers against Gordon's iron grip. He imagined watching the light fade, knowing he'd rid the world of this particular vermin.

Gordon's fangs itched, desperate to extend. His whole body thrummed with predatory anticipation. It would be quick. It would be satisfying. It would be...

...a monumental mistake.

With herculean effort, Gordon reined in the sudden, long-forgotten rush of predatory instinct. It had been over 200 years since he'd killed for blood, and the unexpected intensity of the urge shook him to his core. He couldn't risk exposure, couldn't jeopardize everything the Bruces had built. Not for this piece of garbage.

The dormant vampire within him had awakened, hungry for more than just sustenance. It craved the thrill of the hunt, the intoxicating power over life and death. Gordon's hands trembled slightly as he fought to suppress this ancient, primal part of himself. The ease with which centuries of control had nearly unraveled terrified him almost as much as the desire itself.

And what would he tell Fiona? That her ex-husband had mysteriously vanished, his body never to be found? That he had finally snapped, choosing vengeance over reason? No, he could already picture her face - the horror, the disbelief, the dawning realization of what he truly was. The secret he'd guarded for so long, shattered in an instant of weakness.

Fiona's love was a fragile, precious thing - built on a foundation she couldn't fully comprehend. She saw him as her protector, her rock. How would she look at him as a future father to her children if she knew the monster that lurked beneath the surface? The predator that could snuff out a life without remorse?

No, he wouldn't - couldn't - risk losing her. Fiona's presence in his life was a beacon of humanity, a reminder of the man he strived to be. He wouldn't extinguish that light for the fleeting satisfaction of destroying this pathetic excuse for a man.

Gordon's jaw clenched. He'd find another way to protect her, to make this bastard pay. One that wouldn't reveal the darkness within him or shatter the illusion of normalcy Fiona clung to so dearly.

❖

Gordon felt free, but he wasn't. Not really. He couldn't decide if he should be grateful or annoyed about it. Or maybe he should just stop caring and roll with the punches. Either way, he had no desire to stir up trouble with Cameron again. They'd spent too many years patching up their relationship to risk it now. Rhona or no Rhona.

He and Cameron had buried the hatchet. The distillery was thriving, even outperforming their father's best years. They led separate lives but kept few secrets, maintaining a careful truce of non-judgment. Sometimes, after locking up the distillery, they'd share a drink at Archie's.

They'd flip a coin to see who'd take Margaret to the movies. Some brothers got along worse, others better. But as any firefighter knows, it's the heat of the flames that shows a man's true mettle.

Lately, Gordon found himself studying Cameron through the office window. Try as he might, he couldn't untangle his feelings or view the situation objectively. This inability to see himself clearly left a sour taste in Gordon's mouth. Self-discovery was starting to feel like some cosmic joke – the ultimate unsolvable puzzle.

Heather's chatter filled the office, her words tumbling over each other in an endless stream. Gordon signed the last of his paperwork and joined them just as Cameron leaned back in his chair, exasperation clear in his voice.

"Just tell your TikTok guy it's not happening," Cameron said, his tone flat. "We drank the last bottle, end of story. You know the drill, Heather. Come back next year."

"Or maybe he can make a dance about disappointed influencers instead." Gordon regarded her coolly, a hint of contempt in his eyes. "I'm sure that'll go viral."

"I knew it, I knew it," Heather huffed, her frustration palpable. "What about Speyside? Any stock left there?"

Cameron's patience was wearing thin. "No, Heather. Last bottle, like I said. Next batch won't be ready till next year."

Heather gathered her things, preparing for what would likely be an afternoon-long sulk. Her Dolce & Gabbana suit – a vibrant red with touches of jaguar print – caught the June sunlight streaming through the window. As she stalked out, she looked every bit a flame-colored wildcat.

The brothers exchanged a knowing glance.

"Town hall guy showed up earlier," Cameron said, breaking the silence. "I gave him thirty seconds to clear out. Feeling generous today."

Gordon nodded, a hint of a smirk playing at his lips. No need for words – he approved.

"What's with the DBX?" Cameron asked, eyeing the aggressive dark green Aston Martin SUV in the parking lot below.

Gordon shifted uneasily. "Borrowed it for the weekend. That a problem?" As they spoke, Gordon's nostrils flared subtly. The faint trace of Fiona's perfume clung to his clothes, mingled with the unmistakable scent of her desire. The intoxicating mixture nearly distracted him from Cameron's questioning gaze.

"A SUV?" Cameron's eyebrow arched. "Why a SUV?"

Gordon braced himself for the usual lecture about dating women with kids - a practice Cameron deemed reckless given their immortal nature. But his brother had been oddly unpredictable lately, as if he'd returned from some mountaintop monastery with a new outlook on life.

"Why do you think?" Gordon shot back. "Romantic getaway."

"With four seats?" Cameron's lips twitched. "Sounds more like a family outing."

Gordon dropped into a chair, annoyance radiating off him as he let slip a few details about his upcoming ordeal.

"Well, well," Cameron chuckled, "This is getting serious. Whose heart are you planning to break this time? Some poor, devoted mother's?"

Gordon met his brother's gaze for a long moment before looking away, jaw clenched.

❖

Cameron spent the afternoon with Freddie Reid, owner of a sprawling empire of over a hundred pubs across the country. Reid was eyeing a change in house whisky, and Cameron had been circling like a shark for weeks. Lavish dinners, handpicked girls who feared nothing - all part of the dance. But Reid kept dragging his feet, savoring the chase.

They stepped into the upscale restaurant, and Cameron's senses came alive. A symphony of aromas washed over him, each one distinct. He sorted through them effortlessly: truffle oil, aged whisky, seared steak.

But one scent stood out from the rest. Freddie Reid's unique blend of Cuban cigars, anxiety, and a hint of desperation cut through the ambient smells like a knife. Cameron's lips curved into a subtle smile. This deal was already won.

Cameron locked eyes with Freddie Reid, the familiar tingle of vampiric influence itching beneath his skin. How easy it would be to compel Reid, to bend the man's will with a mere thought. The words hovered, unspoken: 'Our whisky is the only choice for your pubs.'

But he hesitated. After centuries, outsmarting a shrewd businessman through sheer wit had become a rare thrill. Cameron quashed his supernatural urge, leaning forward with a predator's focus.

"Cut the bullshit, Freddie," Cameron said, his tone sharp. "You're not just buying bottles. You're buying loyalty. Our whisky brings people back. It's not about tonight's sales, it's about next month's, next year's."

He watched Reid's expression, noting every micro-reaction. This was the real rush – not as a vampire, but as a businessman going for the jugular.

"Look," Cameron continued, his eyes glinting. "Every other supplier's pushing the same tired story. We're offering something that'll make your competitors sweat. Something with teeth."

Reid's jaw clenched, wheels turning behind his eyes. Cameron felt a surge of satisfaction, sharper than any blood high. He'd made his case without supernatural crutches, using nothing but hard-earned skill and ruthless logic.

As Reid considered, Cameron savored the moment. He'd resisted the easy path, proving that after centuries, he was more than just a nightwalker with parlor tricks. He was a force to be reckoned with, fangs or no fangs.

"Think about it," Cameron continued, warming to his theme. "When people order Bruce whisky, they're not just getting a drink. They're buying into a legacy, a piece of Scottish history. That's value you can't price tag."

In this business, dealing with people often meant wrangling with real headaches. From the chronically indecisive to the most pig-headed lunatics, Cameron found a strange comfort in it all. Each encounter was a battle to be won, a victory to be seized. He never let go, pouring all his energy into the fight.

It was a release valve for the anger that constantly simmered within him. An anger so familiar he'd stopped questioning its source. This rage, honed over lifetimes, made the difference in these high-stakes arm-wrestling matches. It felt good, even soothing, to unleash it on a specific target. In the world of whisky and wheeling-dealing, Cameron found purpose. Each closed deal was a small victory against the crushing weight of immortality.

Today, Reid was pushing for an upgrade-top-shelf whisky at bottom-barrel prices. He claimed to have offers that included not just the booze, but neon signs, marketing props, and flashy gadgets. The man wouldn't budge.

Cameron listened, well aware of the strategy needed and the weak point where Reid would crack. But today, the thrill of the hunt was missing. Something else was brewing beneath the surface, and it wasn't just the whisky deal on the table.

Cameron sighed, the burden of his past pressing down on him. Those girls... he wished he could erase them from memory. Seven hundred and twenty years of sexual exploits now felt like a ball and chain, promising nothing but trouble. What would he tell Rhona when she inevitably asked?

It was hard to swallow - admitting he'd bedded every working girl in town, wallowing in depravity for over seven centuries. Even the most open-minded woman might choke on that history. The thought of Rhona's reaction made him wince.

❖

As twilight crept in, Cameron finally steeled himself to call Rhona.

"Just as I feared," he said, voice carefully neutral. "I'm stuck here tonight. Wining and dining."

After hanging up, he poured a generous measure of the remaining Legacy Reserve. Poor Heather, he mused. She'd given so much of herself to that aborted deal with the TikTok idiot. Surprisingly, he felt more sympathy for the clueless influencer than for her lost commission. At least the guy got his rocks off, even if it was under false pretenses. Heather, on the other hand, was left with nothing but an empty promise and a mouthful of regret. Gordon raised his glass in a sardonic toast. To blowjobs and bullshit - may they always come back to bite you in the ass.

❖

The next morning, Cameron found himself beside the indoor pool at the hunting lodge, pantless and disoriented. Two girls in garter belts dozed on nearby inflatables - one still had her underwear dangling from an ankle. The dawn sky was an eerie green, punctuated by wisps of lavender clouds. The sun hadn't yet breached the horizon.

His memory was a blank slate, save for one crucial detail: Reid had folded. The deal was done. He'd closed it without sinking his fangs into Freddie Reid's neck—a small victory, but it left him feeling hollow. Reid's demands for top-shelf whisky had crumbled quickly. Alcohol and sex had proved an irresistible combination.

Cameron sat up, torn between satisfaction at closing the deal and a gnawing sense of emptiness. Another night lost to old habits, another step further from the life he was trying to build with Rhona. The eternal dance continued.

The young hotshot was probably snoring in a bedroom by now. Cameron smiled faintly, reaching for a bottle of mineral water. One of the girls groaned and shifted in her sleep, legs parting. A vague memory stirred at the sight of her form.

Perplexed, he decided to get up.

He'd just found orange juice in the fridge when Alison Stewart walked in, hand to her forehead. She, at least, seemed to know where they were. Without hesitation, she opened a cupboard and grabbed a box of Special K.

"Parents are on vacation," she mumbled. Seeing Cameron's blank look, she added, "They renovated everything last winter. Burning cash, you know?" The hunting lodge did look suspiciously new.

"Mom nearly died coming up here alone last month. Totaled her car," Alison said, crunching her cereal loudly. Her eyes rolled dramatically. "I keep telling her to ditch this money pit, but she's got this batshit idea about relaunching the lodge." She waved her spoon, flinging milk droplets. "Where'd you take her last time, anyway? The old bat's all secretive about it."

"The Pompadour. Lunch. Your mother's a premium client."

Alison snorted, a mix of amusement and frustration. Her mom had blown ten grand on whisky for this place. Probably half of it downed last night. Another futile investment her mother's pipe dream Alison was desperately trying to squash.

"Anyway, thanks for dumping Mom back home after lunch," Alison mumbled through a mouthful of cereal. "Saved me from rotting at Archie's all day. Place is getting proper weird lately." She rolled her eyes dramatically. "I mean, the guy's been drooling over me for what, two decades? Talk about dense. Hint's the size of a frickin' billboard, and he still can't read it."

Cameron nodded, remembering the awkward tension at Archie's place. The man's unrequited love for Alison was practically part of the pub's decor at this point.

Alison grinned, but there was a tightness around her eyes. Out of her usual plunging necklines and eccentric suits, dressed simply in a white robe with loose hair, Alison had a certain charm. The afterglow of the night suited her, softening her edges and lending her a warm radiance. Sex suited her perfectly well. Sex made her look really good.

Alison plonked herself at the table, eyes fixed on Cameron as she shoveled the last of her cereal into her mouth.

"Knew you'd cave," she said with a smirk. "Couldn't see it going any other way, really."

He just smiled, wondering how the hell he'd ended up here despite his so-called "new resolutions."

"You were on fire last night," she added, eyebrows waggling. "Except you kept calling me Rhona."

Cameron snorted. "I'd never be wasted enough to call you Rhona. No chance in hell I'd do that."

"Ouch. That's cold," she said, but her grin didn't falter. She had a point, he supposed, but what else could he say?

"Don't go ruining what little virtue I've got left," he told her.

"Oh!" Alison's eyes went wide in mock horror. "My deepest apologies! Didn't realize I was corrupting such a paragon of virtue. How ever will you forgive me?"

Her sarcasm was thick enough to spread on toast, but there was a glimmer of something else in her eyes. Hurt? Disappointment? It was gone before he could be sure.

Cameron's eyes hardened, his voice dropping to a low, dangerous timbre. Rage surged through him, his fangs instinctively extending. Centuries of control kicked in, and he forced them back before Alison could notice. "Listen up. I'm a changed man, whether you like it or not. Whether anyone likes it or not. I've chosen a different path. It's that simple."

Alison scoffed, her eyes sweeping the room pointedly. Empty bottles, discarded lingerie, and evidence of last night's debauchery were strewn about like a Helmut Newton fever dream. "Oh, it's crystal clear," she drawled. "You don't want me spilling your dirty secrets to Rhona. God forbid she knows about your little model orgies or the porno chic decor you're so fond of." She smirked. "Well, Cameron, you could've just asked."

The air crackled with tension as Alison's words hung between them, a challenge and a reminder of the life Cameron claimed to be leaving behind.

Cameron leaned in, his presence suddenly overwhelming. "Fine. I'm asking now. Listen up - if you betray my trust, I'll be more than just 'furious.' Don't think you're untouchable, not with me. Stay out of my business, Alison. What we do here is just that - business. Nothing more. Got it?"

A delicious chill ran down Alison's spine. She knew what Cameron was capable of - a creature of the night, a powerful vampire, a predator barely contained. All that delectable violence simmering beneath the surface... where had it gone? She'd spent two decades bending others to her will, but Cameron was different. Pushing him too far could be deadly.

Nothing was worth risking her life over. Unless... unless there was no other way out. And sometimes, a part of her wanted to watch the world burn and take her with it. The thought made her lips curl into a wicked smile.

She met his gaze, her eyes dancing with a mixture of defiance and desire. "Oh, I've got it, darling. The question is, do you?"

Alison watched with barely concealed glee as Cameron stalked around the living room, gathering his things. This man gave nothing, she thought with frustration and admiration. He only took. How had Rhona managed to crack that armor? It was a delightful mystery. But Alison knew one thing - you could always count on men's basest instincts. And the one fuming before her, chasing after a wayward loafer, had nothing angelic left. His partners knew that all too well.

She sprawled across the armchair, one leg dangling over the side, utterly at ease. Her pulse quickened - a rhythmic taunt to Cameron's keen senses. The air grew thick with her scent, a mix of whisky, desire, and something he knew all too well, uniquely, infuriatingly Alison.

She cocked an eyebrow, green eyes dancing with mischief. "What's got your knickers in a twist, old man?" she drawled, her Edinburgh accent thicker than usual. "Centuries of practice, and you still can't find your car keys?"

Cameron's jaw clenched. He could practically taste her amusement, sharp and intoxicating. Alison knew exactly which buttons to push, walking that razor's edge between temptation and torment. He imagined how easy it would be to pin her down, to taste her...

"I'd watch that mouth if I were you, lass," he growled, voice rough with warning and want.

Alison's laugh was a husky challenge. She stretched languorously, fully aware of how the movement drew his gaze. "Or what? You'll bite me?" Her grin was positively wicked. "Promises, promises, Bruce."

Cameron moved with predatory speed, pinning Alison against the kitchen counter before she could blink. His fangs gleamed in the sunlight as he leaned in, his breath hot on her neck. She gasped, torn between fear and desire.

He tore at her lingerie, fabric ripping as their ragged breaths filled the air. His touch was urgent, possessive. He lifted her onto the counter, the cold surface shocking against her heated breasts.

Without hesitation, Cameron thrust into her. Alison moaned as he took her with raw force, his fangs grazing her throat. Her nails raked down his back, leaving angry red trails.

Each movement was harder than the last, their bodies locked in a violent rhythm. The counter shook beneath them as Cameron's growls mingled with Alison's cries of pleasure. His grip on her hips tightened, bruising.

There was only this - the brutal, thrumming connection between them. With a final, shuddering roar, Cameron came. He collapsed against Alison, both of them panting.

Silence fell over the kitchen, the air thick with the scent of their passion. Cameron slowly pulled away, his eyes still glowing with dark satisfaction. Alison lay back, spent and marked. She knew she'd never forget the thrill of his fangs, or the fierce hunger that had consumed them both. She was addicted.

❖

Margaret's heels echoed softly against the cobblestones as she approached St Margaret's Chapel, nestled within Edinburgh Castle's ancient walls. The irony of seeking solace in a place that bore her name wasn't lost on her, but she carried herself with the grace of seven centuries.

As Margaret walked, a prickling sensation nagged between her shoulder blades. It was a constant reminder of the threat that had nearly destroyed her family. The distillery explosion had left more than physical scars; it had shattered her sense of security, leaving her perpetually on edge.

Even now, centuries old and powerful beyond mortal comprehension, she found herself glancing over her shoulder, scanning the shadows for unseen enemies. The feeling of being watched, of being hunted, had become her constant companion.

This gnawing fear, this relentless paranoia, coupled with Rhona's unexpected return after twenty years, drove her to seek out Father MacKinnon once again. He was merely the latest in a long line of St. Margaret's priests sworn to the unholy alliance forged between the Bruces, the Crown, and the Church seven centuries ago.

Inside the chapel, worn stone floors gleamed softly in the light filtering through narrow windows. Someone had placed fresh flowers beneath the small, richly colored stained-glass panel depicting St. Margaret herself.

The chapel exuded an aura of timeless serenity. Its thick stone walls muffled the sounds of the city below, creating a pocket of tranquility high above Edinburgh's bustling streets.

Margaret glided into Father MacKinnon's office, her presence chilling the stuffy air. He wondered, with growing apprehension, what dark purpose drove Margaret's increasingly frequent visits. The priest hunched over blueprints, muttering about budgets. His pet project meant little to her. She needed the Church's ear, and if that came with a price, so be it.

As Margaret sank into the chair opposite Father MacKinnon, her gaze flicked to the room's shadowy corners. Centuries-old instincts screamed danger, but she forced a calm facade. The priest didn't need to know about the constant dread that had plagued her since the very first day they met Rhona. The memory of the bloodbath her sons' rivalry had caused two decades ago, all because of that woman, was her cross to bear alone.

She'd come for answers, for validation, not to air her fears.

"Father." Her voice cut through his musings.

He looked up, startled. "Margaret?"

She fixed him with a gaze as cold as winter steel. "The distillery explosion. Rhona's return. You understand what this means for my family, don't you?"

Father MacKinnon's face paled. "I do."

"Tell me, Father," Margaret pressed, her words precise. "Does our ancient pact still hold? Is the Church still bound to protect us, as we've protected humanity from our kind for centuries?"

"Yes, Margaret," he stammered. "The Church honors its agreements, no matter how old."

A hint of a smile touched her lips, devoid of warmth. "As I thought. I simply required your affirmation before taking necessary action."

Father MacKinnon leaned forward, his practiced smile faltering.

A chill crept through him, heavy with the responsibility of seven hundred years of Bruce family secrets.

"I'll pray for your family's safety, Margaret," he offered, voice strained. "But please, remember the terms of our agreement. Don't do anything to jeopardize the balance we've maintained for centuries."

"Balance?" Margaret's eyes flashed with an inhuman coldness. "What balance remains when Rhona threatens to undo everything? After seeing my boys torn apart by her games before. You were there, Father. You saw what became of my family."

Father MacKinnon shifted uneasily. His sacristy renovation seemed trivial now, as the situation teetered on a knife's edge. He recalled those battered young men and Margaret's tear-soaked visits two decades ago, when Rhona's inability to choose between the brothers had nearly driven them to madness, leaving a trail of blood and broken hearts in her wake.

"They're grown men now, Margaret," he ventured carefully. "Perhaps—"

He stopped short as Margaret stiffened, the room's temperature seeming to plummet unnaturally. Father MacKinnon realized, with growing dread, that he may have gravely miscalculated. The Bruce family's dark legacy pulsed in the air between them, a reminder of powers beyond his mortal understanding.

She turned to leave, pausing at the door. "Your renovation fund shall have my full support, Father. Consider it penance for... well, whatever."

As the door closed behind her, Father MacKinnon crossed himself, the echoes of centuries-old bargains ringing in his ears. Another generation, another compromise. He sighed, wondering if he had it any easier than those who came before him. For seven hundred years, the priests of St. Margaret's had been the Bruces' lifeline to the Church, each one inducted into a world of shadows upon taking their post. It was a thankless task, balancing divine duty with infernal necessity. Sometimes, he mused wryly, it felt more like supernatural bookkeeping than spiritual guidance.

Watching Margaret walk away, her words hanging in the air like a threat, Father MacKinnon wondered if he was witnessing the unraveling of seven centuries of tenuous peace. He couldn't help but question whether his predecessors had truly made a pact with the devil herself, and if he would be the one to see it all come crashing down.

CHAPTER 8
KILDRUM CASTLE
1 OCTOBER 1310

The quill scratched across parchment, each word weighted with desperate urgency. Robert Bruce, King of Scots, hunched over the rough-hewn table, his face haggard in the guttering candlelight. Outside, an unseasonable storm lashed the castle walls, as if nature itself raged against the horrors stalking the land.

"Your Majesty," Sir James Douglas materialized from the shadows, his face unnaturally pale. Sweat glistened on his brow, visible even in the dim light. "The perimeter's secure, but..." He hesitated, his hand instinctively tightening on his silver-hilted blade.

Robert leaned forward, concern etching his features. "What is it, James? What's got you looking like you've seen a ghost?"

Douglas's hand unconsciously went to his left shoulder, rubbing at the old vampire bite.

Robert's gaze flickered to Douglas's shoulder. "Is it your old wound? It's been a year since that vampire attack. If you were going to turn, it would've happened by now."

"It's fine, Your Majesty. Only acts up sometimes, like an old war wound." Douglas paused, swallowing hard. "But that's not what's troubling me. It's... something else."

Robert's eyes narrowed as he took in Douglas's haggard appearance. "Speak, man!"

"We lost two more scouts in the forest." Douglas's voice dropped to a whisper. "Just... husks, drained of blood. And there are... things moving in the mist. Things that shouldn't exist."

A muscle twitched in Robert's jaw as he returned to his letter. "Then we must pray Edward sees reason. Scotland and England united might stem this tide of darkness. Divided, we're little more than cattle for the slaughter."

As if in response, an unearthly howl pierced the night, sending chills down the spines of even the most hardened warriors. In the courtyard below, men muttered prayers and clutched at crosses.

"Seal this with haste," Robert commanded, thrusting the parchment at his scribe. "It must reach London with—"

The door burst open. A young soldier stumbled in, blood seeping from a ragged wound at his throat. "M-my liege," he gasped, "they've breached the outer wall!"

Robert was on his feet in an instant, sword in hand. "To arms! Douglas, get that letter to the messenger. If it doesn't reach Edward, all is lost!"

❖

The castle erupted into chaos. The clash of steel mingled with inhuman shrieks as Robert's men engaged the pale horrors swarming through the breach. Robert himself fought like a man possessed, his blessed blade leaving trails of fire as it clove through undead flesh.

"Hold the line!" he roared, decapitating a snarling vampire with a vicious backhand stroke.

But for every monster felled, two more seemed to take its place.

❖

As dawn broke, Robert found himself backed against the keep's final defenses, a dwindling band of warriors at his side. The first rays of sunlight pierced the smoky haze, illuminating a scene of utter carnage. The courtyard below was littered with shredded bodies, their blood turning the muddy ground into a crimson quagmire.

As the light spread, Robert witnessed a terrifying spectacle. Dark silhouettes darted frantically, seeking shelter from the deadly sun. Some were too slow. A creature, still feeding on a corpse, shrieked as sunlight touched its pale skin. In a horrifying instant, its flesh ignited, sparks flying as it writhed in agony. Within seconds, it crumbled to ash, carried away by the morning breeze.

Another vampire, caught in full sunlight, exploded in a brilliant flash, like unholy fireworks against the brightening sky. All around, the beasts of night fled or fell, burning where they stood. The air filled with their dying screams and the acrid smell of scorched flesh.

Robert watched, equal parts fascinated and horrified, as the sun's purifying light swept across the castle field, cleansing it of the dark plague. But even as hope stirred in his chest, he knew the night would come again. This battle was won, but the war was far from over.

❖

Days passed in an uneasy quiet. Strangely, the vampire horde had retreated, but Robert knew it was merely a lull in the storm. He paced the blood-stained halls of Kildrum, waiting for word from London.

Then, on a fog-shrouded morning, the bad news came.

A lone rider, cloak in tatters, thundered through the castle gates. Robert's heart sank as he recognized the royal insignia of England, splattered with gore.

"Your Majesty!" the man gasped, nearly falling from his horse. "I bring word from King Edward."

Robert helped the messenger down, his stomach churning. "Speak, man. What says England?"

The rider's eyes were wild with fear. "The King... he laughs at your plea. He says..." The man swallowed hard. "He says he'll not ally with the very demons that plague his lands."

A collective groan rose from the gathered Scots. Robert's fist clenched, knuckles white. "Edward believes the lies," he growled.

"There's more, sire," the messenger whispered. "As I fled London, I saw... things. Pale figures in the alleys, corpses drained of blood. The vampires – they're there too."

Sir James Douglas cursed viciously. "They've spread further than we feared."

Robert's mind raced. With England turned against them, Scotland stood alone against the encroaching darkness. As if to punctuate the thought, an inhuman shriek echoed from the distant forest.

"Ready the men," Robert commanded, his voice hard as steel. "If Edward won't see reason, we'll carve our own path through this hell."

As his warriors scrambled to prepare, Robert gazed out over the misty Scottish landscape. The crown no longer represented just political power - it was a bulwark against an tide of darkness that threatened to engulf everything. As he looked at the haunted eyes of his advisors, Robert realized that history would remember him not just as a king, but as the man who either saved mankind or doomed it to eternal night.

Robert's grip tightened on his sword, the silver-inlaid hilt slick with blood – both red and black. "Then we've done all we can," he growled to his remaining men. "Let Edward see the truth of our plight, even if we don't live to—"

Another bone-chilling cry cut through the air like a blade of ice, silencing even the clash of battle. The sea of snarling, pale faces parted, and Robert felt his blood run cold.

❖

From the mist emerged a figure that seemed to devour what little light remained. Tall and regal, clothed in midnight finery unstained by the carnage around it, the creature moved with inhuman grace. But it was the eyes that struck terror into the hearts of even the bravest Scots – orbs of burning crimson that held centuries of malice.

"Robert Bruce," the vampire purred, its voice like silk drawn over razors. "The so-called King of Scots." Its lipless mouth curled into a mockery of a smile, revealing fangs like daggers. "How fitting you should fall here, surrounded by the very monsters you claim to fight."

The pieces fell into place, realization dawning cold and terrible in Robert's mind. "You," he snarled, fury overtaking fear. "You've been spreading the lies. Turning Edward against us!"

The vampire's laughter was like shattering glass, sending shivers down the spines of all who heard it. "Oh, my dear Robert," it crooned, "humans are so delightfully gullible. Why unite against a common foe when you can be so easily manipulated into destroying each other?"

Sir James Douglas, blood-drenched and grim, moved to Robert's side. "We've been played for fools, sire," he muttered.

"Aye," Robert growled, "but the game's not over yet."

The vampire's eyes flashed with cruel amusement. "Brave words, little king. But your pawns are few, and our army..." It gestured to the horde of undead horrors surrounding them. "Well, it grows with every life you lose."

Robert's mind raced. "Our army," he repeated. "You're not the one in charge, are you?"

A flicker of something – annoyance? fear? – crossed the vampire's face. "I speak for powers beyond your comprehension, mortal."

"Who?" Robert pressed, sensing a weakness. "Who pulls your strings?"

The vampire hissed, revealing more fang. "You'll meet my master soon enough, Bruce. When Scotland falls and all of Britain is shrouded in eternal night."

"And what then?" Robert demanded, buying time as he assessed their dwindling options. "What purpose drives this slaughter?"

For a moment, the vampire's mask of cruelty slipped, revealing a glimpse of fanatical devotion. "Purpose? We reshape the world, mortal. My master's vision extends beyond your pitiful human concerns. We are the harbingers of a new age, where the strong will rule and the weak..." Its lipless mouth curled into a grotesque smile. "The weak will nourish us for eternity."

Robert felt a chill that had nothing to do with the pre-dawn air. Whatever drove these monsters, it was far more terrifying than mere bloodlust. "You're mad," he spat. "All of you."

The vampire's eyes blazed with zealous fire. "Mad? We are visionaries! And soon, you will witness the dawn of our empire – the last dawn this world will ever see."

For a heartbeat, despair threatened to overwhelm Robert. What manner of evil could command such creatures? Then he felt the weight of the silver cross at his throat, heard the prayers of his men – battered but unbroken.

As the first rays of dawn pierced the gloom, Robert saw their chance. "For Scotland!" he bellowed. "For humanity! Drive them into the light!"

Inspired by their king's battle cry, the remaining Scots surged forward. They burst from the castle's shadow, chasing the retreating vampires towards the treeline where shafts of deadly sunlight were beginning to filter through.

Steel met fang and claw in a desperate symphony of violence. Robert's blessed blade sang as it clove through undead flesh, leaving trails of fire in its wake. All around him, vampires shrieked and smoldered as dawn's touch found them.

The vampire leader's eyes widened in shock as it realized the trap. Caught between Robert's advancing forces and the lethal sunlight, it hissed in fury.

Robert closed the distance, righteous fury lending him speed to match the creature's inhuman reflexes. He drove the vampire back, step by step, towards a gap in the canopy where sunlight pooled on the forest floor.

The creature lashed out with inhuman speed, its claws a blur in the growing light. Robert parried the strike, his silver-inlaid blade flashing. As they locked in combat at the edge of shadow and sunlight, the vampire's lips curled in a snarl of disbelief. "Impossible!"

"You forget," Robert growled, his eyes blazing with defiance, "we Scots are stubborn devils."

CHAPTER 9

Heather's world shattered the moment the TikTok star's hand struck her face. She'd always played the game of discounts and whisky, reaping rewards from men who were all too happy to indulge her. But this? This was new, and it terrified her.

Her legs wobbled as she gripped the bathroom sink, staring at her reflection. Angry red handprints bloomed on her cheeks, a stark contrast to her usual flawless complexion. Her scalp throbbed where he'd yanked her hair, shaking her like a rag doll. The phantom sensation of his fingers twisting in her locks made her stomach churn.

Heather's mind raced. She'd heard the statistics, seen the PSAs about domestic violence, but never thought she'd become one of those women. Now, she understood how quickly things could spiral out of control.

This was her wake-up call. No more playing with fire, no more easy thrills. The fleeting rush of power she got from manipulating men suddenly seemed hollow, a poor substitute for genuine connection.

But old habits die hard. How could she give up the game when the real prize – her boss – was so tantalizingly close yet impossibly far? Every day, she watched him, aching for a scrap of attention. He barely noticed her existence.

Heather splashed cold water on her face, wincing at the sting. She had to make a choice: keep chasing shadows or find a new path. The bathroom mirror offered no answers, only the reflection of a woman at a crossroads.

Heather winced as she gingerly touched her swollen cheeks. The memory of last night's mistake haunted her. She'd slept with the guy before handing over the coveted whisky bottle, and he'd flown into a rage, accusing her of tricking him for free sex. What was wrong with men these days? When had they become such monsters?

Agnes's worried voice filtered through the bathroom door. "Honey, are you okay?" Her sister's trembling words pierced Heather with guilt. She'd brought something dark and ugly into their pristine million-and-a-half villa, tainting the place where a TV power couple had once lived happily - until the husband's heart gave out.

Heather could almost see Agnes obsessively sanitizing every surface, as if scrubbing away the violence could erase what happened.

Stepping out, Heather met her sister's anxious gaze. She gave Agnes a once-over, taking in her perfectly put-together appearance. "If you got out a bit," Heather said, her voice rough. "If you looked around you."

The kitchen gleamed, all brushed steel and polished surfaces. Agnes had prepared Pimm's, a desperate attempt at normalcy. Heather's eyes landed on the two aspirin tablets next to her glass - a silent acknowledgment of her pain.

Heather sank into Agnes's plush lounge chair, grateful for the escape. The sprinklers' gentle hiss and the scent of blooming flowers helped ease the chaos in her mind. She was only three streets from the hotel where everything had gone so horribly wrong.

She could still see it all - her orange juice arcing through the air, shattering against the wall.

Her companion's face darkening, his fingers drumming an agitated rhythm on the table. When told the Legacy Reserve was unavailable, for a year at least, he'd stood abruptly, knocking over her glass. It wasn't the explosive reaction of an addict, but the quiet fury of a man used to getting what he wanted. The Legacy Reserve wasn't just whisky; it was status, power, exclusivity. To be denied it was to be denied entry to an elite circle, even if just temporarily.

The room service cart toppled, their picture-perfect breakfast ruined. Jam, honey, and soft-boiled eggs splattered across pristine carpet. Heather's stomach had growled, a pitiful counterpoint to the destruction.

She understood his disappointment. She'd waited until morning to break the news, after a night of passionate lovemaking. She'd been so eager to please, pulling out all the stops. That blowjob? Oscar-worthy, in her opinion.

But it hadn't mattered. His rage hit like a summer storm - sudden, violent, overwhelming. Insults poured down, punctuated by stinging slaps that left her gasping.

Heather closed her eyes, trying to shut out the memories. But they lingered, as persistent as the bruises on her skin. She winced, remembering the metallic taste of blood on her split lip. Her attacker had stormed out, nostrils flaring like an enraged bull. She'd waited, frozen, before creeping downstairs to settle the bill. Never in her wildest nightmares had she imagined such a violent reaction.

"It was bound to happen," Agnes sighed, shaking her head. "Where did you think this lifestyle would lead?"

"Oh, spare me the holier-than-thou routine," Heather rolled her eyes. "I don't go poking around in your business, asking how many times you've Pledged the baseboards today. This place is so sterile, I'm surprised anything can actually live here."

Heather studied her sister, perfect as a porcelain doll. Agnes had married young and rich, willingly paying the price for her gilded cage. Sometimes, the sight of her made Heather's stomach turn.

"This house is her coffin," Heather thought, eyeing the magazine-perfect decor. "It's drained every last drop of life from her."

Desperate for air, Heather grabbed her Pimm's and escaped to the garden. She settled beneath a Judas tree's delicate shade, adjusting her vintage Vuarnet sunglasses - a bold checkerboard of red and white.

The cool drink and dappled sunlight did little to ease the ache in her bones or the turmoil in her heart.

"Rape?" Heather let out a bitter laugh. "Agnes, we spent the night screwing like rabbits. I was in his bed, not some dark alley. Do you even hear yourself? Or has all that Lysol finally seeped into your brain?"

She studied her sister, seeing only a carefully curated piece of decor - no more alive than the designer sofa or high-end kitchen appliances. These privileged women, Heather thought bitterly, were all the same. Counting their husbands' mistresses, sex becoming a raw nerve. She could almost see Agnes's skin crawling with unspoken frustration.

Agnes downed her Pimm's in one desperate gulp.

"Look," Heather sighed, "I can't explain things you refuse to understand. It's pointless."

"To hear you talk, spreading your legs is the answer to everything," Agnes hissed.

"Thank God not all men want to marry a porcelain doll," Heather retorted. "Some of us actually live in the real world."

"So what are you waiting for? You think this lifestyle leads anywhere good?"

Heather's eyes narrowed behind her sunglasses. "And you? How's your perfect life working out? Want to have that conversation?"

Agnes's composure faltered, a flicker of genuine emotion breaking through her usual Stepford Wives poise. Despite her obsession with home and children, despite enduring a cold marriage bed, she'd built an impenetrable armor. At the slightest hint of conflict, she'd retreat, fingers instinctively brushing her pearl necklace, emotions locked behind blank eyes.

But today, something shifted. A single tear escaped, catching them both off guard. Agnes quickly dabbed it away, muttering about dust or pollen.

"Oh, honey," Heather sighed, her irritation melting. "What did I say?"

❖

Cameron leaned in to inspect Heather's lip. He could sense the blood that pulsed beneath Heather's bruised skin. He was thorough, almost methodical, as if assessing the damage was purely an exercise in logic. For her, it was a moment of pure bliss—worth even the worst slaps. But he straightened up with a frown.

"This might not be enough for the cops," he said. "I don't think they'll take it seriously."

"Am I disfigured?" Heather asked, hope fluttering in her chest.

She longed for him to caress her cheek or offer a kind word. It wouldn't have killed him, and she didn't dare wish for more. Instead, he stood there, cold as plexiglass, assessing whether they should go to the police.

Noticing her expectant gaze—as if she were posing for a profile picture—he muttered that she'd be fine.

"But how do you keep getting into these situations?" he added. "Heather, since when do you sleep with clients?"

His words crushed her. Heat rushed to her face as shame washed over her. She wanted to cross her legs, but her feet felt like lead weights.

"What are you eating, Heather?" he pressed on. "Horse meat?"

Though her body felt impossibly heavy, she sprang to her feet. She had her pride. On her knees, she'd have licked the ground at this man's feet, but that was no excuse to hear such things.

"Can I go now?" Heather asked, her voice tight.

"Oh, stop it!" Cameron snapped, slicing the air with his hand. "Don't be so sensitive. Face it, things aren't getting better for you."

"Excuse me, I have work to do," Heather retorted. "Or you'll accuse me of getting paid for nothing."

Cameron's jaw clenched. "Listen, I should be able to talk to you without you getting upset. Is that too much to ask?"

"Don't I have the right to sleep with whoever I want?" Heather fired back. "Do I need to report my love life to you?"

"Of course not. Do what you want. I'm not trying to meddle. But if you could avoid the clients, that'd be great."

Heather's eyes flashed. "Why does my love life concern you? What does it matter who I spend my evenings with? Are you interested?"

Their argument was cut short as two massive trucks rumbled into the parking lot. One brimmed with rich, black soil, while the other carried towering palm trees, their fronds barely clearing the ironwork arch bearing the name BRUCE.

Cameron bolted down the stairs, Heather hot on his heels.

❖

Above them, delicate white clouds hung motionless in the azure sky, their edges lacy and crisp against the blue.

The town hall had sent that asshole again. The same prick Cameron loathed. Their brilliant plan consisted of planting a few trees on the disaster site as "compensation" and a half-assed gesture of goodwill. The palm trees already towered six meters high, and the smug bastard couldn't help but brag about their astronomical cost.

"Trust me, this will look fantastic," he said, grinning. "It's going to turn heads."

"What are you, some kind of masochist?" Cameron snarled.

"I beg your pardon?"

"Get the hell out," Cameron spat. "We're a goddamn distillery, not a tropical resort."

Fury boiled in Cameron's veins, a savage beast clawing beneath his composed facade. These pencil-pushers were clueless, poking a slumbering dragon with their petty rules. His jaw clenched, muscles coiled tight as steel cables. One wrong word, one careless gesture, and he'd snap.

The town hall lackey kept his plastic smile plastered on, spreading his arms wide. "Mr. Bruce, why all this hostility?"

Cameron snapped. He grabbed the man by his lapels and slammed his forehead into the guy's face with a force that was almost casual, belying the brutal strength behind it. Centuries of contained violence found a brief, controlled outlet in that moment. In a darker time, he would have torn into the man's throat without hesitation, savoring every drop of vengeance.

"Take your fucking palm trees and get out before I shove them so far up your ass, I'll need the last one to push in the others."

❖

From the back of the warehouse, Gordon watched the scene unfold. He'd been wondering if they should cover the back seats of the borrowed Aston Martin SUV with plastic—Fiona's kids were messy eaters, specializing in sticky disasters. The sight of Cameron's outburst transported him back to their wilder days.

He remembered when he and Cameron would come to blows, once tumbling down a staircase in a tangle of fists and fury. They'd nearly broken their backs, but neither had let go. Any normal humans would have been paralyzed, every bone shattered. But they were immortals. Two perfect animals, unleashed. By the end, they weren't invited to parties anymore—hosts feared for their furniture and hi-fi equipment. Some joked they were the Krays, not the Bruces. A terrible reputation, but not unearned.

Gordon watched as Cameron roughly tossed the guy out. "At forty," he mused, "we're really in our prime." He turned to Angus, instructing him to get someone to wrap the DBX seats meticulously.

Heather, meanwhile, was practically vibrating with restrained energy as she waited for Cameron. Try as she might, she couldn't find a single flaw in this man. She stood beside him, watching the trucks maneuver and belch fumes. But her focus, guided by some strange power, remained fixed on the sweet musk of sweat from Cameron's shirt.

She always kept a few spares for him and Gordon. Carefully selected from a trusted store downtown. Sober, yet well-cut. She loved peeling away the cellophane, savoring the fabric between her fingers.

She didn't need much, hadn't hoped for more in ages. That day Cameron asked her to buy him half a dozen briefs? She'd walked on air, nearly sprouted stigmata on the spot.

Cameron changed into a clean shirt. Heather averted her eyes, noticing the headbutt had split the town hall guy's brow. The blood-stained, sweat-soaked shirt he'd discarded was coming home with her. Two weeks under her pillow or as makeshift pajamas. Sometimes she felt ridiculous, but screw it. She wouldn't trade her life for Agnes's. Not for anything.

Heather's world pulsed with an intoxicating energy Agnes could never comprehend. The thrill of dancing among powerful men, the heady rush of secrets and whisky - it made her blood sing. Sure, it was dangerous at times, but the rewards... those were sweeter than any suburban dream.

"Heather, are you listening?"

"Oh! Sorry," she snapped to attention.

"We toss them out. Every time. Clear?"

"Of course, Cameron. Don't worry. And if I may, I completely agree."

"Good. They'll get their damn trial, whether they like it or not." He paused, his eyes narrowing. "And Heather? You didn't sleep with any of these town hall pricks, did you?"

Something inside Heather snapped. Her face flushed crimson, a mix of anger and humiliation coursing through her veins. Without a word, she spun on her heel and bolted from the room, shirt in hand, slamming the door behind her hard enough to rattle the windows.

"Come on, Heather!" Cameron called after her, exasperated. "It was an honest mistake. I had to ask..."

❖

From his office window, Mayor Callum MacPherson watched his two trucks crawl back into view. One glance confirmed the operation's spectacular failure. His useless emissary stumbled out, face busted and suit stained crimson.

"Fucking Bruce boys," he muttered. He'd known their father for years - a tough old bastard, but a businessman you could reason with, negotiate with. But the sons? They were cut from a different cloth entirely.

"Set up a meeting with their father," he barked at his secretary. She nodded silently, all tight skirt and cigarette smoke.

MacPherson's voice shifted, suddenly casual. "Say, Moira, do you like palm trees?"

❖

Rhona spritzed herself with Evian, fighting the oppressive heat. She'd rolled up her T-shirt sleeves and pinned her hair back, shorts discarded nearby. Perfect for some self-love, but her 6 PM deadline loomed. Five pages due for her latest Hashtag Magazine portrait, and barely any time to indulge.

One hand wandered south while the other propped up her forehead. The bizarreness of her situation hit her as she tapped play on her smartphone. The earphones were uncomfortably warm, enveloping her ears with the husky voice of her subject - a bored housewife turned high-class escort at 45, who'd discovered a knack for seduction and a hunger for new thrills. As the woman's tale crackled through the analog warmth, detailing her transformation from suburban ennui to Edinburgh's most sought-after companion, Rhona found her own fingers moving in rhythm with the narrative. Research and release, multitasking at its finest.

Alison's earlier call echoed in her mind. "Listen, honey, we're not asking for Shakespeare here. Just give me a portrait that'll make our followers lose their minds."

What Alison said next left Rhona reeling, suddenly feeling compelled to confess her occasional hookups with Cameron.

"I don't know why I'm telling you this," Alison had sighed. "But you deserved to hear it from me, not through the grapevine. Was that the right call?"

Alison's friendship was a strange beast, layered and unpredictable.

When they met up later, Alison dropped another bomb:

"Your daughter's sleeping with her dentist. I checked. There. No more secrets. You mad at me?"

❖

They hit a Japanese spot for dinner, where hungry eyes from nearby tables lingered on them.

"Turns out we share a dentist," Alison continued. "So trust me on this. Picture Sam Smith's doppelganger, but straight. Your girl's been his Thursday regular for months."

"Seriously? I had no clue."

"That's why I'm spilling, hon. If my kid was involved with some smooth operator like that, I'd be asking questions. Who knows what his game is?"

Rhona's maternal failures weighed on her. Since arriving, she'd seen the consequences daily. Patching things up with Isobel, making amends – it all demanded a level of presence she couldn't muster. Her mind was a jumbled mess, like she'd leapt onto a speeding train. And Isobel? Just another complication in the chaos.

"Hey, by the way - that portrait you cranked out? Fucking goldmine. We smashed a million views before the witching hour. Not too shabby for a day's work, eh?"

❖

They squeezed into a packed bar for a nightcap.

"If you saw this guy," Alison perched on her stool in full Vivienne Westwood pink tartan, swirling her drink, "you'd run for the hills. Sickly pale, with these creepy little white hands. That's the real deal-breaker. 'Nuff said. I couldn't do it."

Rhona's mind raced. Focus? Impossible. The world spun, everything too much. Did she spare a thought for Isobel? Ponder the dentist drama? Of course not. Because right on cue, like clockwork...

Gordon and Archie materialized.

"Hey," Archie said, awkwardly embracing her. "Heard you were in town." Gordon just raised his glass, eyes bright despite his brooding air. Gordon's eyes locked onto Rhona, burning with an intensity that stole her breath. This wasn't just attraction - it was something far more primal. A predator sizing up its prey.

Rhona's heart hammered against her ribs. Every instinct screamed danger, but she couldn't look away. His gaze peeled back her defenses, leaving her exposed and electrified.

Rhona licked suddenly dry lips."Everything okay?" Rhona ventured.

Alison snorted. "Don't even start."

Gordon's brow furrowed. "What are you on about?"

Gordon drained his glass and ordered a round. Not drunk yet, Rhona noticed, but getting there. He leaned on the bar between her and Alison while Archie filled awkward silences with nostalgia math.

"Maybe switch gears?" Alison suggested, scanning the crowd to stave off death by boredom.

Archie shot her a sour look, lighting up.

Rhona seized the moment. "Does it bug you that I'm here?" she asked Gordon.

"Why would it?" he shrugged.

Stellar conversationalist, this one. When Alison steered them to a table - she always had pull - Rhona made damn sure not to sit by Gordon. She flagged down some familiar faces to diffuse the tension.

Gordon was a black hole of social skills. Across from her, wedged between two girls debating water sources and whisky flavors, he drank and grinned at the ceiling. It was maddening.

❖

They stumbled along cobblestone streets, their heels clicking like a metronome. Rhona halted, pressing her forehead.

"What have I done?" she groaned. "I didn't even want to!"

Alison hugged her, laughing. "I'm still in shock. Pure genius, honestly. Bravo."

"But I didn't know him! I tongued a stranger. What's wrong with me?"

"You made Gordon react. That's what counts. Sometimes you gotta shake things up. Besides, there are no real taboos anymore. Not in this century."

Alison dug for her keys. Her Bentley was hidden in shadows under thick trees. "Who needs New York for crap lighting?" she quipped, checking her phone. The darkness was so complete that Gordon's sudden appearance made her jump.

"Jesus, you moron!"

Gordon's face glowed in the dim light, eyes red and wild. His shirt was torn, hair a mess, but he didn't seem to care. He took a step closer. The scent of him - leather and smoke and something uniquely male - enveloped Rhona. His presence was magnetic, effortlessly drawing her in, as if he were a force of nature. Her eyes fluttered closed for a heartbeat, savoring the intoxicating mix of fear and arousal.

Rhona instinctively shut down her heightened senses, blocking out the overwhelming cocktail of scents that threatened to cloud her judgment, but even her human nose couldn't ignore the magnetic pull of Gordon's presence.

"Couldn't leave without saying goodbye," he grinned wickedly.

"You're wasted. Go home," Alison ordered.

Rhona chewed her lip, dreaming of a silent bath in a locked house. She'd pay good money to dodge this mess. Exhaustion weighed on her.

Gordon slumped against a tree, its leaves rustling in warm gusts like a dancing skeleton.

"You can barely stand," Alison said, unlocking her sleek convertible.

"Can't stand and don't care," Gordon shot back.

The kicker is his eyes never left Rhona. She took it, knowing she'd brought this on herself, silently praying he'd keep it brief.

"Let's bail," Alison sighed. "This is getting toxic."

Rhona couldn't agree more. No point rehashing it. No rewinding time. She mourned the Gordon option fading fast, like they were cursed. Everything with him was going sideways.

She imagined dawn breaking, forcing him to vanish. That old feeling. But it barely mattered now. Hell, they could almost sunbathe these days.

Rhona lowered her window at Gordon's mime, despite Alison's impatience to start the car. Some unseen force kept them rooted.

Gordon leaned in, eyes narrowing as he studied her. Rhona knew she owed him that much.

"You're the most stunning bitch I've ever laid eyes on," he said evenly. "You really take the prize."

Whatever he was on had loosened his tongue in a way alcohol never could.

She absorbed his words without a flinch. They followed her home, slipped between her sheets. Sleep finally claimed her as the sky began to lighten.

❖

Gordon stumbled out of the amusement park, his nerves frayed. The afternoon sun blazed overhead, dust swirling in the air as screaming kids in shorts darted past. He blinked, momentarily disoriented by the assault on his senses.

Scotland's typically overcast skies had been a perfect fit for vampires, nature's own sunscreen that allowed them to move freely even during daylight hours. But today's unexpected burst of sunshine was a stark reminder of how far they'd come. Gordon surveyed the scene with a mix of wonder and pride. Vampires and humans mingled effortlessly on the sun-drenched patio, their laughter drifting on the warm breeze. A century ago, this would have been a death sentence. Now, it was just another Saturday afternoon.

Centuries of careful evolution had stripped away their most obvious weaknesses. The burn of sunlight, once searing agony, was now little more than a mild irritation easily masked by the right clothing and a dab of high-SPF sunscreen. Their pallor, once a dead giveaway, had given way to a more natural-looking complexion that could almost pass for a healthy tan.

Gordon sipped his iced tea, savoring the illusion of normalcy. He cast a glance at Fiona and the children, relief washing over him as he saw their pleased expressions. He'd pulled it off. The day wasn't over, but the worst seemed behind him.

He bolted for a fountain glittering near the parking lot entrance. Shoving aside two wannabe troublemakers trying to wreck the tap—their parents uselessly looking on—he let cool water cascade over his head.

❖

They had decided to head back to the hotel for some pool time. The SUV's back seats had survived—plastic intact, major messes cleaned. As they cruised down a pine-shaded road, Gordon fought the urge to floor it. This beast was the world's most powerful luxury

SUV. He whistled a tune, one hand on the wheel, trying to impress Fiona. He'd vowed to turn over a new leaf with her.

This was how regular folks lived. *This* was what life was about out here. Yeah, he could do this forever. Or at least as long as Fiona lasted. He had to love her—there was no other choice. Otherwise, it was back to hell for him.

Fiona seemed content, a soft smile playing on her lips. Every so often, she'd lean in close, her breath warm on Gordon's ear as she whispered something just for him. Her hand would find his thigh, giving it a subtle squeeze, or she'd "accidentally" brush against his crotch while reaching for her purse. When their eyes met, she'd give him a look that promised more once the kids were asleep, making Gordon's pulse quicken despite his exhaustion. It was clear she was enjoying their makeshift family day, but also looking forward to some adults-only time later.

As they neared the hotel, the kids started bouncing in their seats with excitement.

"Mummy, Mummy! Can we go in the bubble bath on the terrace? Please?" Little Amelia and Jack begged, their eyes wide with anticipation.

"Yeah, the big jacuzzi! You promised!" Jack chimed in, practically vibrating with energy.

Fiona laughed, her eyes meeting Gordon's with a mischievous glint. "What do you say, love? Shall we indulge them for a bit?" She leaned in close, her voice dropping to a whisper only he could hear. "And maybe later, when they're tuckered out, we can have the jacuzzi all to ourselves."

Gordon felt a familiar warmth spread through him at her words. He nodded, a rare smile tugging at his lips. "Alright. Jacuzzi it is."

The kids erupted in cheers as Fiona squeezed his hand, her touch promising more to come. Her eyes sparkled as she whispered how badly she wanted him, her head spinning with desire.

Gordon felt a rush of excitement at the prospect. Daytime encounters were a rare treat. He made a mental note to thank

Cameron for the recommendation. Unlike the Bruce brothers' usual slick, five-star boutique playboy haunts, this place was more modest. Quiet at this time of day, with spacious rooms boasting well-equipped bathrooms—perfect for their needs without the flashy trappings.

❖

Two attendants in crisp white shorts approached, ready to set up their usual spot by the pool. Fiona intercepted them with a smile, explaining they'd be skipping the pool today in favor of the terrace jacuzzi. The kids' earlier pleas had won out, their excitement for the "bubble bath" too infectious to ignore.

In the bathroom, Fiona and Gordon shared a passionate embrace. She nudged the door shut with her foot as the kids bounced on the bed, eagerly wriggling into their swimwear. Things were looking up.

Gordon stripped down to his swimsuit. He wandered to the window, taking in the hotel pool's impossibly blue water, then made his way to the terrace, locating the jacuzzi's control panel. As he pressed the buttons to start the bubbles, Amelia and Jack burst through the doors behind him, a whirlwind of energy and noise.

Before Gordon could react, Amelia had already scrambled over the edge, plunging into the calm water with a splash. Jack, not to be outdone, cannonballed in right after her. Both children immediately started thrashing about, creating waves that sloshed over the sides of the jacuzzi.

Gordon shook his head, watching as the jets slowly came to life, adding to the chaos of the children's antics. Their shrieks and laughter echoed across the terrace, drowning out the growing hum of the bubbling water. He silently wondered how long it would take for Fiona to wrangle them into some semblance of control.

Fiona stepped onto the deck, rattling off instructions to the children. "Was it really that bad?" Gordon mused, reflecting on the day.

The thought lingered as Fiona sidled up, her touch intimate and eager. They waved to the kids splashing in the jacuzzi, then drew the sliding doors, pulling the gauzy curtains closed.

Fiona turned to Gordon, her eyes glinting with mischief. In one fluid motion, she slipped off her bikini, her sun-kissed skin catching the dim light. Gordon's breath caught in his throat, his body already responding to her presence.

She approached with feline grace, hips swaying. Her fingers traced the contours of his chest, trailing down to where he ached for her touch. When she wrapped her hand around him, Gordon couldn't hold back a low groan.

In a surge of desire, he lifted her onto the bed. Their lips met in a fierce kiss, tongues tangling as the heat between them blazed. Fiona's legs locked around his waist, pulling him flush against her. His erection pressing against her wet entrance nearly undid them both.

Gordon's gaze locked with hers as he slowly pushed inside. Fiona gasped, her head falling back in ecstasy as he filled her completely. He set a steady rhythm, each movement drawing out sighs and moans of pleasure.

Their bodies moved as one, a perfect dance of passion. Fiona's nails raked down his back as Gordon drove deeper, harder. He maintained the perfect balance, the smooth control he had honed over centuries, giving her exactly what she craved without ever letting the beast within surface.

The small space echoed with the sounds of their lovemaking—breathless gasps, throaty moans, and the primal rhythm of skin on skin.

Fiona arched beneath him, her breath coming in sharp pants. Gordon's thumb found her most sensitive spot, circling with firm, knowing strokes. She cried out, her body tensing as waves of pleasure crashed over her. In a bold move, she reached for his balls, her touch sending him spiraling into his own intense release.

They clung to each other in the aftermath, trembling and sated.

Gordon's lips found hers in a tender kiss, savoring the sweetness of the moment.

Neither of them noticed the chaos unfolding beyond the flimsy curtain that separated them from the world outside.

❖

The sirens wailed as Gordon's SUV chased the ambulance through the streets of Edinburgh. His knuckles were white on the steering wheel, his jaw clenched. In the passenger seat, Fiona curled into herself, her sobs muffled against her knees. The rearview mirror showed him Amelia's pale face, her eyes wide and unblinking.

This couldn't be real. Any moment now, he'd wake up.

But as the night deepened and the harsh hospital lights flickered on, the truth sank in like a stone. The little boy was gone, drowned in mere inches of water while no one was looking.

❖

Gordon paced the waiting room, his mind racing. He could break the pact. Turn the child. Make Jack a vampire, forever frozen as a little boy, but alive. Fiona would know everything then, all the secrets he'd kept for centuries. But it wouldn't matter. No power he possessed could restore the child's spirit, lost to the mortal world. His centuries of existence were useless here.

His fists clenched as the bitter reality hit him. It was too late. The boy had been dead too long. Even if Gordon bit him now, there was no blood flow to carry the change. It would be like trying to raise the dead – impossible, and likely to make Gordon violently ill in the process.

The crushing reality of eternity crashed down on Gordon's shoulders as he stood in the sterile hospital room. The silence was deafening, broken only by the harsh fluorescent buzz overhead. Fiona's son, once vibrant and full of promise, now lay still and lifeless against starched white sheets.

Gordon had survived wars and walked away from infernos that would have reduced mortal men to ash. Yet here, staring at the motionless form of this boy, he felt utterly powerless. His immortal strength seemed to drain away, leaving him as fragile and helpless as any human parent facing their worst nightmare. The silence of the room was broken only by the sound of his own ragged breathing.

The beast inside Gordon roared, urging him to save the child with a vampire's bite—to halt death in its tracks. But centuries of hard-won wisdom held him back. The boy was already gone, his soul beyond reach. Gordon ached to break his vow to Fiona, to unleash his true nature and damn the consequences. But he knew it would destroy her. Creature of the night he might be, but even he couldn't shoulder that weight.

All his supernatural strength, all his centuries of cunning, were useless against the finality of human death.

He pressed a cool hand to the boy's forehead, the absence of warmth a devastating confirmation. How many times had he envied mortals their blissful ignorance of death's true face? Now, that same mortality had torn his world apart.

The cruel irony twisted in Gordon's gut like a knife. He, who had cheated death countless times, could do nothing but accept its claim on someone he loved. All his power, all his wealth, all his connections in both the mortal and supernatural worlds – none of it mattered in the face of this simple, devastating loss.

It was a stark reminder of the chasm between his existence and the fragile, fleeting lives of those he'd chosen to love. Death's chill grip, alien to his undying body, crushed Gordon's chest. The boy's heartbeat, fading to silence, echoed in his ears—a rhythm he was powerless to restart. In all his long years, he'd never felt so trapped. This helplessness was worse than any coffin, a prison of regret with no escape.

In that moment, Gordon would have traded his immortality in a heartbeat for the power to breathe life back into Fiona's son.

But such bargains were beyond even him. All he could do was stand vigil, a timeless being bearing witness to the all-too-brief flicker of a human life – now extinguished forever.

❖

A week later, Gordon's phone buzzed as he slumped in the armchair, exhausted. Fiona had finally collapsed into bed after days of barely eating. The caller ID flashed: Cameron.

"How're you holding up?" Cameron's voice was low, concern edging his words.

Gordon sighed, rubbing his temples. "We're... managing. Barely." He recounted the day's events in clipped sentences. "Brock showed up at the funeral. Started hurling accusations. We had to drag him out."

In Rhona's plush living room, Cameron paced, water droplets from his shower glistening on his skin. Rhona emerged from the bathroom, wrapping a sarong around herself.

"What happened?" she mouthed.

Cameron covered the phone. "Fiona's ex caused a scene. At the funeral."

Rhona's eyes widened. She sank onto the couch, her damp hair leaving dark patches on the cushions. "God, that poor family," she murmured.

Back on the phone, Gordon's voice cracked. "Fiona's a wreck. Hell, we all are."

Cameron swallowed hard, torn between sympathy for his brother and the warm presence of Rhona nearby. "Listen, if you need anything..."

"Yeah, I know," Gordon cut him off. "Thanks."

The call ended, leaving a heavy silence. Rhona stood, crossing to

Cameron. She laid a hand on his arm. "He can't help but feel responsible," she said softly.

Cameron nodded, his jaw tight. As their relationship deepened, Gordon's pain felt closer than ever. The legacy of family, of centuries of secrets, pressed down on them all.

Cameron believed Isobel should know. At first, Rhona hesitated, thinking it too soon—Cameron's eagerness grated as much as his brother's indifference—but she felt her resolve crumbling.

"What's the difference if she sees us together now or later? Are we even doing anything wrong?"

They were, Rhona knew. But she gave up arguing the point.

So far, Cameron had been the perfect lover. Yet Rhona felt terrified, as if half of herself had turned traitor. Earlier, she'd bitten the pillow to keep from babbling nonsense while she shamelessly reveled in pleasure. How could she talk about freedom when a man's touch caused such chaos, robbing her of willpower?

Rhona had attended feminist and sexaholics meetings for a few months, but they offered no clear answers—except that masturbation was a practice to be embraced. Obviously.

Rhona made tea while Cameron read her latest piece for Hashtag Magazine—about a woman who'd quit her high-powered banking job to take up competitive surfing after beating cancer. It wasn't her best work, not by a long shot. If only shoddy writing was all she had to feel guilty about. If only this lackluster copy was her sole shame, she might have coped. Let's take her word for it, just this once.

From the start, she'd felt paralyzed. Unable to decide as everything rushed by, powerless to change course. She wondered how long this inertia, this miserable sleepwalk, would last.

She wouldn't get what she needed—time to think. Any hope of choosing calmly, taking her time, having serious talks with both men, weighing options, doing research—she could forget all that. Cross it right off the list. If she'd ever believed things could unfold that way, she was deluding herself.

Cameron could be the one. What if he was?

"I know, I know," she muttered, watching the kettle boil.

Isobel showed up late afternoon with Brodie in tow. Tea still steamed in their cups—an hour earlier and she'd have caught them in bed, Rhona realized. The sun sank low, licking the garden's brick wall until it glowed like a gilded plaque.

❖

Brodie's presence eased the tension, at least for the women.

As always, Isobel seemed moody. Who could guess her thoughts? Or if she was thinking at all? Phil, her father, and Rhona herself had dropped the ball in recent years. While their daughter morphed into someone new, they must've been distracted, wrapped up in their own drama, watching their marriage crumble with a mix of logic and despair.

How many times had Isobel visited the hospital? Even then, Phil had to drag her. And how often had she reached out this past year, living alone here, playing adult, ghost, perfect stranger?

Rhona studied her, baffled. If Isobel had thoughts on Cameron's presence, she hid them well, no colder or ruder than usual—just sipping tea in front of the TV.

Brodie, though, seemed intrigued. His football jersey showed off long, muscled arms, and he eyed Rhona differently. She decided to change clothes, but knew the damage was done—thankfully, not everything stays shocking forever.

Rhona stiffened as she loaded the dishwasher. Brodie's voice carried from behind her, low and appreciative.

"I must say, you're lookin' fine," Brodie grinned, giving her a cheeky once-over. "Proper stunner, like."

Rhona turned, eyebrow arched. She was used to this kind of attention, especially from boys Brodie's age. Something about her seemed to draw them in like moths to a flame. "Just noticing now? Maybe you'll get more observant with age."

Cameron had rushed off to the distillery after a call from Heather

—some deal falling through. But his absence didn't give Brodie free rein, did it? Surely the rest wasn't so easily dismissed in the boy's mind?

"Sorry to disappoint, but you can't have both mother and daughter," Rhona said lightly, feigning consideration. "Pretty sure that's frowned upon. What do you think?"

Brodie's gaze lingered as he turned to leave, a hint of that inexplicable attraction still evident in his eyes. "Still. Great body."

Rhona shook her head, amused. Boys and their hormones. If only they knew what really drew them to her, they'd probably run screaming.

CHAPTER 10

BATTLE OF BANNOCKBURN

23 JUNE 1314

Robert's breath misted in the pre-dawn chill as he crouched behind a gnarled oak, eyes straining in the gloom. The mist clung to the Scottish highlands like a death shroud, muffling sound and obscuring vision. The high ground of the Bannock Burn was surrounded by marshland, perfect cover for an ambush – or for something worse.

"They're moving," James Douglas whispered, his voice barely audible. "At least fifteen thousand, maybe more."

Robert nodded, a grim set to his jaw. They were outnumbered, badly. But they had surprise on their side, and desperation – a potent combination. For a moment, his thoughts strayed to his wife Elizabeth and young daughter Marjorie, safely hidden away. He pushed the worry aside; he had to focus on the task at hand.

"Signal the men," he murmured. "Quiet now. We'll only get one shot at this."

As James slipped away, Robert's hand tightened on his sword hilt. The blade seemed to pulse with an otherworldly energy, a gift from an ally he still wasn't sure he could trust. But beggars couldn't be choosers, not with what was at stake.

James hadn't gone far when he stumbled, catching himself against a tree trunk. His face contorted in pain as he clutched at his left shoulder, where an old wound lay hidden beneath his armor. Robert tensed, watching his friend closely. The injury – the deep bite from a vampire during a long-ago skirmish – had never fully healed, despite the passage of five years.

"James?" Robert called softly, concern etching his features.

The Black Douglas straightened, his jaw clenched tight. "I'm fine," he growled, but Robert could see the sheen of sweat on his brow, the unnatural paleness of his skin. For a heartbeat, Robert thought he saw something flicker in James' eyes – a hint of inhuman hunger quickly suppressed.

"It's acting up again, isn't it?" Robert asked, his voice low. "Five years, and still that cursed bite troubles you."

James nodded curtly, his breathing ragged. "Aye. Some days are worse than others. But I'm still me, Robert. Still human." He paused, a shadow of doubt crossing his face. "At least, I think I am."

Robert stepped closer, placing a reassuring hand on James' uninjured shoulder. "If that vampire's curse was going to turn you, it would have happened long ago. We've weathered this storm together, old friend. We'll not let it break us now."

James managed a grim smile, straightening with visible effort. "You're right. Whatever this is, whatever I'm becoming... I'm still your man, Your Majesty. To the bitter end."

Robert nodded reluctantly, pushing down his unease. He couldn't afford to dwell on it now, but the fear lingered. What if the wound was more than just a scratch? What if, after five long years, James was slowly turning, becoming one of the very monsters they fought against?

Pushing the dark thoughts aside, Robert refocused on the task at hand. The English army moved through the mist like a great, lumbering beast. Steel clinked softly, horses snorted. They had no idea what was waiting for them.

Robert raised his hand, ready to give the signal. His heart thundered in his chest, each beat seeming to echo in the eerie stillness.

Then he saw it. A flash of movement at the edge of the forest, too fast to be human. His blood ran cold.

"No," he breathed. "Not now. Not here."

But denial wouldn't change reality. As he watched, pale figures emerged from the trees, moving with inhuman grace. Their eyes gleamed with predatory hunger in the pre-dawn light.

Vampires. Dozens of them. Maybe hundreds.

For a moment, Robert froze, indecision paralyzing him. If he gave the signal now, his men would be caught between two deadly forces. But if he didn't...

A scream shattered the silence, high and terrified. Then another. And another.

The English line erupted into chaos as the vampires struck. Men and horses alike shrieked in terror and pain. Steel clashed against claw and fang.

"Bloody hell," James gasped, materializing at Robert's side. His face was ashen, eyes wide with a mix of fear and... something else. Something that made Robert's skin crawl. "What do we do?"

Robert's mind raced. Every option seemed worse than the last. But they were out of time.

"We fight," he growled, rising to his feet. "Both of them. It's our only chance."

He raised his sword, the blessed blade glowing faintly in the gloom. "Now!" he roared. "For your lives!"

Robert silently prayed that James would make it through the battle – and that he'd still be human when it was over.

The Scottish forces erupted from their hiding places, a tide of flesh and steel crashing into the English flank. Simultaneously, vampires tore through the front lines, their inhuman shrieks piercing the night. The battlefield dissolved into a nightmarish tableau.

Mist swirled around ankles, thick as soup and tainted with the copper stench of blood. Men stumbled blindly, swinging at shadows.

A vampire, eyes glowing like hellfire, burst from the fog. Its jaw unhinged like a snake's, revealing rows of needle-sharp teeth before it latched onto a screaming soldier's throat.

Robert the Bruce weaved through the carnage, his claymore a streak of silver in the gloom. An English knight charged him, lance leveled. At the last second, Robert sidestepped, bringing his blade down in a vicious arc. The knight's arm, still clutching the lance, pinwheeled through the air.

❖

A cacophony of war cries shook the earth as the Scots unleashed their hidden reserve. Warriors, faces painted with woad and eyes wild with battle-frenzy, crashed into the English ranks like a tidal wave. In the chaos, Robert glimpsed a tartan-clad berserker wielding a massive Lochaber axe, cleaving men in twain with each swing.

The mist thickened, tinged red with blood spray. Clangs of metal mingled with inhuman snarls and human screams. A vampire and a Scottish warrior grappled, rolling past Robert. The Scot's dirk flashed, opening the vampire's belly. Entrails spilled out, writhing like snakes as the vampire howled.

Robert pressed on, each step squelching in mud turned to slurry with blood and worse. The stench of death and fear burned his nostrils. Through gaps in the mist, he caught glimpses of the battle's horrible scope – a tapestry of violence stretching as far as the eye could see.

A warm spray hit Robert's face. He turned to see a young English soldier, barely more than a boy, staring in shock at the wooden stake protruding from his chest. Their eyes met for a heartbeat before the boy crumpled, lost to the fog of war.

Robert fought like a man possessed, his sword cleaving through armor and undead flesh with equal ease. But for every foe he felled, two more seemed to take its place.

As Robert cleaved through the chaos, a thunderous voice cut

through the din of battle. "Bruce!" The cry rang out, filled with hatred and accusation. Robert spun to see a towering figure on horseback, armor gleaming despite the blood and grime of battle. Sir Henry de Bohun, one of England's most feared knights. "Demon King!" de Bohun roared, leveling his lance. "Your dark sorcery has brought this evil upon us! I'll end your reign here and now!" He spurred his warhorse forward, the massive beast's hooves churning the blood-soaked earth.

Robert stood his ground, time seeming to slow as the knight bore down on him. At the last possible moment, he sidestepped the charge. De Bohun's lance whistled past, missing by a hair's breadth.

As the knight struggled to wheel his mount around, Robert seized his chance. With a grunt of effort, he swung his axe in a devastating arc. The blade caught de Bohun full in the face, cleaving through helmet, skull, and brain. The knight toppled from his saddle, dead before he hit the ground.

Robert stared at the fallen warrior, his victory hollow. "Dark sorcery, indeed," he muttered, turning back to the sea of undead that still threatened to overwhelm them all.

❖

The air grew thick with the metallic stench of blood and the sickly-sweet odor of vampire ash.

A garbled cry to his left caught Robert's attention. He turned to see an English knight stumbling backward, his sword raised feebly against three advancing vampires. Without thinking, Robert lunged, decapitating one undead monster and driving the others back.

The knight stared at him, wide-eyed. "You... you saved me," he stammered.

"Don't thank me yet," Robert grunted, parrying a vampire's claws. "We're not out of this hellhole."

❖

The night wore on, a symphony of slaughter conducted by the Grim Reaper himself.

Side by side, Scot and Englishman fought against the undead horde. Around them, others seemed to catch on, centuries-old enmities forgotten in the face of a greater threat.

But it wasn't enough. The vampires' numbers seemed endless, their strength and speed overwhelming. Robert watched in horror as more and more of the fallen rose again, eyes burning with unholy hunger.

"We can't hold them," the English knight panted, his armor splattered with blood both red and black. "There's too many."

Robert's eyes darted around the battlefield, desperate for any advantage. Then he saw it – the forest to their rear, dense and dark.

"The trees," he said, a spark of hope igniting. "If we can lure them in..."

Understanding dawned in the knight's eyes. "We'd need fire. Lots of it."

Robert nodded grimly. "Spread the word. Anyone who can ride, mount up. The rest... God help them, they'll have to buy us time."

❖

The plan spread through whispered words and meaningful glances. Those with horses gathered, a ragtag group of Scots and English forming an impromptu cavalry.

"Now!" Robert roared, spurring his mount forward. They charged through the press of battle, vampires snapping at their heels as they raced for the treeline.

The forest loomed before them, dark and foreboding. As they plunged into its depths, Robert heard the agonized screams of those left behind. Their sacrifice wouldn't be in vain.

"Torches!" he commanded, snatching a burning brand from a soldier. "Burn everything!"

Flames licked up tree trunks and underbrush, smoke billowing into the air. The vampires pursued, heedless of the growing inferno. Deeper and deeper they drove the humans, until the heat became unbearable.

"Back through!" Robert cried, wheeling his horse around. "Ride or die!"

They burst from the forest in a storm of fire and ash, leaving the howling vampires trapped in a blazing tomb. Those that tried to follow combusted in the growing daylight, reduced to drifting cinders.

❖

When dawn finally broke, it revealed a landscape transformed. Where a meadow had been now lay a sea of corpses, human and vampire alike. The ground so soaked with blood it squelched with each step. Carrion birds circled overhead, their raucous cries a mockery of victory.

Robert surveyed the carnage, when a chilling thought struck him: in this unholy alliance of Scots and vampires, who were the real monsters?

As the survivors regrouped on the blood-soaked field, an eerie silence fell. The English knight removed his helmet, revealing a face etched with exhaustion and disbelief.

"My God," he whispered, "what have we witnessed?"

Robert met his gaze, seeing in it a mirror of his own haunted expression. "The beginning," he said softly. "God help us all, this is only the beginning."

The knight's eyes widened, a flicker of recognition crossing his face. "You're him, aren't you? Robert the Bruce."

Robert nodded grimly. "Aye. And you are?"

"Sir Humphrey de Bohun," the knight replied, his voice tight. "You... you killed my cousin Henry."

For a moment, tension crackled between them. Then Robert spoke, his words surprisingly nonchalant given the circumstances.

"I know, it's regrettable," he said, "I broke the shaft of my favorite axe."

Humphrey stared at him, momentarily stunned by the unexpected response. Then, against all odds, a bark of laughter escaped him. "You Scots are mad, you know that?"

Robert's lips twitched in a grim smile. "Aye, well, madness might be what we need to survive this nightmare." His expression sobered quickly. "We've bigger concerns now than old grudges, Sir Humphrey. You've seen what we're up against. This threat will devour both our nations if we don't stand together."

William's jaw clenched, his hand instinctively moving to his sword hilt. He eyed Robert warily, clearly expecting to be taken prisoner. "What are you proposing?"

"An alliance," Robert said, surprising the knight by making no move to disarm or restrain him. "Between Scotland and England. We need to warn your king, prepare our people. Will you go to Edward? Make him understand?"

William's eyes widened in disbelief, but he quickly masked his surprise. He let out a bitter laugh. "Edward? He's long gone. Fled the field like a whipped dog."

Robert's brow furrowed. "What do you mean?"

The knight's eyes grew distant, reliving the horrors of the battle. "It was chaos. Those... things... they came out of nowhere. Tore through our lines like they were parchment. I saw Edward dragged from the field by his bodyguards, hotly pursued by what he called « the vampire Scottish forces. » God's truth, I thought they'd tear him to pieces."

He shook his head, his voice heavy with disbelief. "He only just escaped the heavy fighting. Last I heard, he was in full retreat to Dunbar."

Robert absorbed this in stunned silence. Then, "'Vampire Scottish forces.'" He chuckled. "How bad were your losses?"

William's laugh was hollow, devoid of mirth. "Bad? This was a calamity of horrific proportions for England. Our losses were... enormous. Half our army, at least. Maybe more. And that's not counting those who... rose again."

Robert stared at his companion, the gravity of their conversation pressing down on him like a physical force. His fingers drummed against the hilt of his sword, a nervous habit he'd never quite shaken. The silence stretched, filled only by the distant sounds of the camp and the soft whisper of wind through the trees.

Finally, he spoke, his voice low and rough with tension. "So this is where we stand." It wasn't a question. His eyes swept over the horizon, searching the rolling Scottish hills as if they held the answers. "Everything changes now, doesn't it?"

His companion nodded, the firelight casting deep shadows across their face.

"We need to act fast," Robert said, breaking the silence. "If Edward's retreated to Dunbar, that's where you need to go. Will you carry our message, Sir Humphrey, and help convince him of the need for an alliance against this unholy threat?"

William's expression hardened, haunted by the horrors they had witnessed. "You're... letting me go? Just like that?"

Robert nodded again, solemn. "Aye. We need each other now more than ever. Will you go?"

Humphrey paused, then spoke. "Aye, I'll go. But even with Edward having seen these monsters himself, convincing him to ally with you... it won't be easy. There's too much bad blood between our nations."

"There'll be nothing but bad blood for all of us if we don't stand together," Robert insisted, gripping the knight's shoulder. "We've been given a glimpse of the abyss, Sir Humphrey. And it's staring back at us, hungry for more."

Humphrey nodded, his resolve visibly strengthening. "You're right. God help us all, you're right. I'll make Edward see reason, even if I have to drag him back here to face these demons himself."

"Good man," Robert said, relief evident in his voice. "Take what evidence you can. Gather survivors who can corroborate the full extent of what we faced here. The fate of both our nations may rest on your words."

William's eyes hardened with determination. "And what of you? What will Scotland do while I'm off trying to knock sense into Edward's thick skull?"

Robert's gaze swept across the battlefield, taking in the carnage and destruction. "We'll prepare. Fortify every stronghold, arm every man and woman who can wield a weapon. We'll scour every ancient text, every folklore, for ways to fight these monsters. And we'll pray that your mission succeeds before it's too late."

Humphrey nodded grimly and rose to his feet, ready to embark on his perilous journey. But as he turned to leave, Robert's hand shot out, grasping his arm firmly.

"Wait," Robert said, his voice low and urgent. "I have another favor to ask you, a personal favor."

CHAPTER 11

"This is just the beginning of your troubles," Thomas Calderwood said, leaning back in his chair. The fierce lawyer's eyes glinted with a mix of warning and excitement. "Either we withdraw the complaint, or the pressure will increase. It's up to you to decide."

He paused, studying the two brothers with a slight smile that spoke of hard-earned experience. As the first openly gay lawyer in Edinburgh, Thomas had developed a skin as tough as old leather. He still wasn't sure if these two had the backbone for what was coming.

"Taking on City Hall," he continued, "that nest of vipers made extra jumpy by the upcoming elections - it requires true grit. You've got to be ready to take hits from all sides." He tapped his fingers on the desk. "Losing the whisky deal with Freddie Reid? That's just the first domino to fall."

Thomas leaned forward, his voice low and intense. "If we see this through to the end - and I stress the 'if' - your story will expose a bunch of incompetents. We won't be painting them in a flattering light, to put it mildly. You following me?"

The brothers nodded, tension visible in their shoulders.

"When they realize we're digging into their dirty laundry," Thomas said, slapping his hand on a thick stack of files, "things will get ugly. Fast." His eyes narrowed. "I've got enough scandals here to light a powder keg. Enough that neither you nor I will come out of this unburned. You need to be crystal clear on that fact."

Thomas felt the rush of more than just a courtroom battle. The Bruce brothers radiated an energy he couldn't explain—ancient, potent, far beyond their years. It wasn't just determination in their eyes, but something deeper. A force that whispered of forgotten wisdom and hidden strength. For the first time, he dared to hope they might actually stand a chance against City Hall's corruption. These men were different, dangerous even. And that gave him a glimmer of hope in the face of impossible odds.

❖

As Thomas Calderwood escorted them to the elevator in the Quartermile's building, he kept quiet about their father's visit two days ago. No need to pile on more gloom. The bustling city sprawled below, its fate seemingly controlled by a select few. Thomas was confident. Maybe these two wouldn't fold like so many others before them.

The Bruce brothers were young, healthy, and - crucially - unattached. Thomas had seen too many cases crumble because of anxious spouses, more concerned with losing their cushy lifestyles and their Platinum cards than pursuing justice. He'd lost count of the times some trophy wife had stormed into his office, hurling insults about his sexuality, calling him a queer little shit.

But these two... they answered to no one but themselves. It was refreshing. For once, Thomas might have the chance to tackle a case without worrying about the cost of nail polish getting in the way.

As the elevator glided downward, Thomas couldn't shake his unease about the Bruce brothers. Their confidence was unnatural—a calm intensity that hinted at something far deeper. Beneath their sleek facades lurked something ancient, immovable. Just a gut feeling, but it raised goosebumps on his arms. These men were more than they appeared, and that thought chilled him to the core.

❖

As they exited the elevator, Calderwood shook their hands farewell. The bustling street stretched before them, but before they could take two steps, a commotion erupted near the entrance. A wild-eyed man burst through the crowd of pedestrians.

In a blink, the man lunged at the brothers. Gordon reacted with startling speed. One fluid motion and he'd gripped the attacker's wrist, twisted, and used the man's own momentum to send him flying. The assailant crashed through the building's plate glass window with a deafening shatter, landing in a heap inside the lobby.

For a heartbeat, stunned silence reigned. Then chaos erupted.

Gordon moved with lightning speed and deadly precision, his body a blur of lethal grace. It was more than skill—it was instinct etched into his bones over countless years. Cameron recognized it instantly: the reflex of an apex predator. For a heartbeat, their carefully crafted facade cracked. Beneath the polished exterior of successful businessmen, something ancient and dangerous stirred, felt by everyone in the room.

"Oh, fucking hell," Cameron muttered under his breath, his eyes widening. This was not part of the plan. He felt a cold sweat break out on his forehead as he realized just how quickly things could spiral out of control. Gordon's display had shattered the illusion of normalcy they'd worked so hard to maintain.

Security guards swarmed the scene, converging on the dazed attacker. The man thrashed like a cornered animal, groaning as blood spread across his white T-shirt. It was a messy struggle - the guards pulling him in all directions, unsure how to handle someone so out of control. The scene unfolded like a slow-motion nightmare.

Thomas Calderwood's eyes were wide with shock. As the chaos

unfolded, he felt a surge of both unease and confidence. If these brothers had even half the fighting skill Gordon had just displayed, they might actually survive what was coming.

The adrenaline faded, and Gordon's complexion turned ashen. His shoulders sagged, and his gaze dulled. Cameron eyed him with concern. He recognized that feral glint in his brother's eyes—a flash of something ancient and deadly. While Gordon typically maintained an air of calm control, Cameron knew better. Beneath that phlegmatic polished exterior lurked a volcano of barely restrained power. Today, that facade had cracked, offering a terrifying glimpse of the inferno within.

If Gordon hadn't reined himself in at the last second, the room would have become a slaughterhouse. Cameron felt a chill run down his spine, despite his own carefully cultivated wild-child persona. He might play the part of the unpredictable brother, but in truth, Gordon's inner struggle was far more intense.

This near-miss served as a stark reminder of the constant tightrope they walked. Their civility was a choice made anew each day, each moment. And sometimes, the abyss yawned terrifyingly close beneath Gordon's feet.

Cameron's mind raced, scrambling for a way to salvage the situation before their true nature became irrefutably clear to the humans around them. "Christ, what was that? Great reflexes bro," he hissed, his eyes sweeping the lobby. "Some disgruntled client with a grudge?" He dragged a hand through his hair, playing the part of a man rattled by nerves.

Only Gordon saw through the act, knowing the predator beneath was coiled, ready to strike.

Thomas frowned, a chill running down his spine. "It could have been meant for any of us. Welcome to law, gentlemen. Where every victory breeds a vendetta, and even losers have lawyers." He didn't voice his darker suspicion – that this might be connected to the case they were discussing.

"Sorry about the window," Gordon said to the slack-jawed lawyer.

Calderwood's eyes gleamed with fierce intensity. "Nonsense. That window is a small price for front-page publicity. We couldn't buy press this good. 'You fuck with us we'll throw you out the window.'"

Cameron studied his brother, noting the gray cheeks and slumped posture. "You alright?" He knew Gordon had been struggling lately, no doubt due to the boy's death.

❖

Margaret ordered sushi, again. It was becoming clear she wasn't about to cook anytime soon. The days when she'd spend hours in the kitchen, crafting special recipes to help sustain their unique needs and reduce their reliance on blood, seemed like a distant memory. Only Cameron ate, while she nursed a drink.

Gordon eyed the sushi, remembering Dr. MacGregor's research. The raw fish, packed with iron and omega-3s, helped take the edge off their more dangerous cravings. Those nutrients, mimicking what they'd get from human blood, let them keep a lid on their darker impulses. It wasn't perfect, but it beat the alternatives.

Still, he missed his mother's culinary experiments. Her iron-rich beef stews simmered with herbs said to calm bloodlust. The protein shakes loaded with supplements designed to curb their more violent urges.

Gordon reminisced about one of Margaret's culinary breakthroughs from the 18th century. Her 'special' meatloaf, a closely guarded secret that no one dared question, had been a game-changer. A single serving could keep their bloodlust at bay for nearly a month. It was a far cry from her current state, barely able to dial for takeout.

The bar opened earlier each day now. "I didn't have kids to know all the world's miseries," Margaret slurred.

Cameron suggested she tend to her plants. Gordon retreated to the living room, flicking on a trashy real estate show where the agents looked more like escorts. Margaret shuffled onto the terrace, misting her rubber plant with unfocused determination.

By unspoken agreement, they avoided mentioning the incident. The last thing they needed was their mother launching into another paranoid tirade about shadowy forces out to get them.

❖

In the basement, Cameron faced his past. He tossed a box of porn magazines into the furnace, followed by tapes that ignited with a satisfying whoosh. His collection of S&M gear joined the pyre - toys, costumes, and tools reduced to ash. This was his fresh start. His thoughts turned to Rhona, his new purpose.

Through grimy windows, he watched heat shimmer over the city. The river coiled below like a serpent, reminding him of darker times. He thought of the working girls in the red-light district, Eastern European women trafficked in by the truckload. Language barriers and exploitation defined their existence.

Cameron had been a frequent customer. His immortality spared him disease, a small mercy in a sea of regret. Those poor souls, controlled by ruthless Russian criminals. For a moment, he considered bringing them sodas - a pitiful offering to ease his guilt.

At that moment, a scream pierced the air. Cameron's head snapped up just in time to see a shadow plummet into the bushes, arms flailing wildly.

❖

Gordon choked out, "But I didn't do anything!" as they both knelt beside their mother. He wiped his face, adding with a whine, "Damn it, she threw holy water at me."

Unbelievable, but true. Father MacKinnon had finally caved and given her the holy water. The prospect of Margaret's promised fat donation for the church renovation might have loosened his grip on the blessed liquid. He'd handed it over without even asking what she planned to do with it. The priest had bigger worries—like catechizing children to combat the rise of Islam and lifting the spirits of his flock in a world that seemed to be slipping away from Christian values. He'd acted on faith and, perhaps, a touch of greed. Margaret had never mentioned exorcism. Or if she had, the good Father's ears had conveniently failed him, deafened by the sweet chime of potential cash and visions of gleaming new pews.

❖

Alistair Bruce arrived two hours after the accident. When his wife accidentally toppled over the terrace railing, he'd been in an undignified position: a muscular thirty-year-old physiotherapist was kneading his back after a nasty bout of lumbago had laid him low. The injury struck while he was warming up for tennis, alone in the locker room.

Tears had pricked his eyes. Not from pain, but from the daily humiliations that came with age. Sure, he still cut an impressive figure, but Alistair knew better than anyone the decay eating away at him from the inside. It was the one fight he'd never win, a battle lost before it began. At seven hundred and seventy, he was keenly aware of his senior immortality. Nearly eight centuries of living like there were only ten years left.

He sped across the city, jaw clenched behind the wheel of his black Aston Martin DB5. The car was almost as old as he was, its raw power giving him the illusion of youth. As he drove, Alistair found himself averting his gaze when elderly pedestrians shuffled across the street, a stark reminder of what he fought so hard to deny.

❖

Alistair glanced at his sons before heading upstairs to Margaret's room. Dr. MacGregor stood at her bedside.

"Thank heaven her face wasn't touched," the doctor said. "That's what I feared most."

Margaret's fall had ended in a lush bed of blue hydrangeas, softening the impact. Still, she murmured weakly that she felt shattered, as if beaten to a pulp. Dr. MacGregor exchanged a knowing look with Alistair, then pulled back the sheet. Margaret's pale skin contrasted starkly with her designer black underwear.

Alistair barely registered the bruises and scrapes covering his wife. Instead, he was struck by the realization that he hadn't seen Margaret like this in decades - not since he'd ended their seven-hundred-and-forty-year marriage, convinced he could find a better life elsewhere. The world had shaken then, and now here he stood, faced with a woman he longed to hold but who wanted nothing to do with him.

Lately, Alistair had felt desire stirring again, along with a growing sense of loneliness. But Margaret's resentment ran deep. She wouldn't even let him brush her fingertips with his own.

Alistair caught himself imagining what he might do if the doctor weren't present. The urge to claim Margaret, to remind her that she was still his, surged through him. He knew he wouldn't have been able to stop himself. She belonged to him, no matter what she said.

He took her hand, acutely aware of the damage he'd done by leaving. His sons' reports hadn't been necessary; Alistair knew he'd nearly destroyed her. Margaret would likely never forgive him, especially now that she'd gone a bit mad. Not completely, of course, but enough to notice.

As Dr. MacGregor adjusted his panama hat and left with a friendly pat on Margaret's thigh, Alistair told them about his own back pain. He waited for his wife to fall asleep, dismissing his concerned sons with a sharp gesture. Drawing the curtains over a star-filled sky, he carefully tucked the sheet around her and watched her breathe.

As he stared, Alistair realized Margaret was drunk. When sleep finally claimed her, she began to snore. He snored now too, drunk or not. Another ridiculous gift from aging, he thought bitterly as he gently rolled Margaret onto her side. Seven hundred years of snoring - enough to drive even the most devoted couples to thoughts of murder.

Alistair rose to close the window, a chill settling over him. He paused at Margaret's dresser, studying the portraits of his sons displayed in ornate Victorian silver frames. The photos were relics from when photography was still a chemical science.

They'd never have baby pictures. Such things didn't exist in the 1300s. Instead, they made do with "baby" pictures of forty-year-olds. Gordon and Cameron grinned back at him, all teeth and youthful vigor. They looked eerily like their own nonexistent ancestors, a reminder of the family's long, interrupted history. Margaret's pride and joy, back then.

That was before a woman came between them, turning the brothers into snarling beasts. Now Margaret hardly dared show her face in public or meet the eyes of their friends. The specter of centuries-old family drama hung heavy in the air, a stark reminder of how even vampire families weren't immune to the ravages of time and conflict.

❖

Morning brought the scent of sizzling bacon. Cameron stood at the stove, frying eggs, while Gordon brooded by the bay window, hands shoved in his pockets. They looked up as their father entered the living room, his gait stiff and pained. He'd stumbled on the stairs, a jolt of agony shooting through his back. He'd spent the night.

Gordon's hunched posture spoke volumes. The brothers watched their father warily, centuries of complicated history hanging between them. Alistair's nightly vigil at Margaret's bedside hadn't gone unnoticed, stirring up old wounds and resentments.

Cameron wiped his hands on a spotless apron, his light beige pants immaculate. "Back acting up again?" he asked, his steel-cut physique a stark contrast to his father's aged frame.

Alistair Bruce couldn't pinpoint when he'd stopped feeling like a father to his sons. It was astonishing, really. He'd always sensed the hardness behind Cameron's smile, but that Rhona girl had sharpened it to a knife's edge. Alistair was no stranger to toughness—he'd built his whisky empire in a world where no one gave an inch—but Cameron's brand of cold was different. Inherited from Margaret, no doubt.

Gordon was another story entirely. The prince of darkness, his thoughts a perpetual mystery. Everything about him screamed classic vampire—cold, enigmatic, magnetic. His pale skin seemed to absorb light, while piercing blue eyes held secrets older than time. When Gordon entered a room, the air itself seemed to chill, drawing people in even as it set their nerves on edge. Not that his supernatural allure kept him out of trouble. That recent scandal splashed across the papers—Gordon and some mortal woman labeled as "irresponsible lovers"—was just the latest in a string of headaches.

The scandal was nothing new; Gordon had a history of entanglements with mortals, each one more complicated than the last. Despite his centuries of experience, or perhaps because of them, he found human relationships endlessly fascinating. They were fleeting, passionate, and chaotic—everything his eternal life lacked. But with every encounter, there was always the risk of exposure, the possibility that his secret could slip through the cracks.

Alistair wondered, not for the first time, if his son's immortality made him reckless or if it was simply his nature to court danger.

Still, Alistair couldn't say they'd completely failed him. Neither had turned out gay, murderous, or strung out on drugs. They'd even managed to turn the distillery into a thriving business. Alistair knew plenty of men his age who couldn't say the same, their kids rotting in jail cells or wasting away in rehab centers across the globe. Even among the wealthy and powerful, Alistair had seen fortunes crumble to nothing in the hands of worthless heirs.

Alistair made an effort to maintain civil relationships with his sons, but Margaret's problem was she still saw them as her babies. Even with this Rhona ménage à trois business—a scandal that would make most mothers recoil in horror—Margaret fretted over her boys like they were still in short pants. That misguided maternal instinct had caused her two decades of heartache.

"Our job is to protect your mother," Alistair said, his voice gravelly. "Whatever we think or do, nothing gets back to her that could worry or hurt her. Understand?"

He lowered himself into a chair with a pained grimace. Cameron sneered as he plated his eggs, not bothering to hide his disdain.

Alistair was painfully aware he had no right to lecture anyone about Margaret's well-being. Every time he stepped into this Victorian manor—where he'd once ruled as master—he felt like an intruder. Not because they punished him for leaving, but because his very presence was a reminder of what they'd gained at his expense.

"In her condition," Alistair sighed, "your mother doesn't need any more stress."

He explained how their stubborn crusade against city hall would end badly for everyone. Alistair still had connections with powerful men in this town, and sooner or later, he'd be forced to choose sides. Margaret wouldn't be able to handle that kind of family fracture—surely they could see that.

Gordon's mind churned with the child's death, a tangle of confused thoughts unrelated to the tragedy. His mother's accidental fall was just the bitter icing on this cake of misery. He barely registered the heated discussion swirling around him. Sure, he'd given Cameron the green light for this crusade that so irritated their father, and he wouldn't back down now. But Gordon couldn't summon the energy to care. Why bother with incompetence and corruption when his personal demons cast such long, cold shadows?

Still, using Margaret's potential distress as a weapon was low, even for Alistair. "Using Mother's condition to manipulate us?" Gordon said, his voice sharp with disgust. "That's a new low, even for you."

"Watch your tone with me, boy," Alistair growled, white-knuckling the chair's armrests.

Cameron leaned forward, eyes narrowing. "Oh, so now you care about Mother's well-being? That's rich coming from you, Dad."

"You have no idea what you're meddling with," Alistair snapped. "This little crusade of yours—"

"It's called doing the right thing," Gordon cut in. "You should try it sometime."

Alistair's face darkened. "You ungrateful whelps. After everything I've done for this family—"

"What, like teaching us to be selfish cowards?" Cameron sneered.

The tension in the room was suffocating. Each barbed comment left a crackling silence in its wake. Even a team of oxen would've struggled to drag this atmosphere an inch.

❖

Around one in the morning, an owl's mournful hoot drifted from the black pines across the road. Alistair, his pride crumbling, asked if one of his sons would help him up to go pee. His locked back screamed in protest, and he'd have roared in pain and fury if he'd been alone.

Was this it? The inglorious death of an immortal—not by stake or sunlight, but by a traitorous bladder and centuries of stress? Gordon stared at his father, a 770-year-old vampire brought low by the most mundane of human needs. He almost laughed at the absurdity. His father, a living legend reduced to this. Alistair had once culled their entire kind, a boogeyman even to other monsters. Now he needed help to pee.

Surely, after nearly eight centuries, the constant strain of bodily functions could erode even an undead nervous system to dust.

Alistair sat there, on the toilet seat, powerful and pitiful all at once, his immortality seeming suddenly fragile. The great vampire, terror of the night, unable to stand without help. What was the point of being a vampire if this was how it ended? Eternal life, it seemed, didn't guarantee eternal dignity.

For a moment, the family's squabbles fell away. Gordon saw not the overbearing patriarch, but a tired old man—an old vampire—worn down by the relentless march of time. Then the flush came. Gordon sighed, pushing aside his resentment, and opened the toilet door to help his father back up.

❖

A few days later, the police showed up at Fiona's to survey the wreckage. The damage was extensive. In the kitchen, appliances lay in ruins. The living room TV and PlayStation were smashed beyond repair, shredded curtains strewn across the floor. Upstairs, Fiona's bedroom looked like a war zone. Her white wardrobe had been torn apart, clothes flung everywhere. Her mattress and measly two sets of sheets - all she owned - were slashed to ribbons.

Inspector Lennox smirked. "You expect us to believe a paralyzed man scaled these stairs?"

Fiona bristled, breaking free from Gordon's embrace. She faced the inspector, her voice quivering with barely contained rage. "You don't know my husband. He'd have climbed to the damn roof if it meant hurting me."

Lennox's gaze flicked to Gordon, his smile widening. The Bruces were no strangers to him.

Fiona caught the look, her jaw clenching. "I know exactly what you're thinking," she spat. "And I couldn't care less."

Inspector Lennox had seen it all before. In his decade on the force, he'd encountered countless women like Fiona - clinging to their lovers, perpetually caught in a cycle of heartbreak. Pathetic, really. They'd keep fighting the same battles until their dying day, as if it were written in their DNA. He'd known plenty, most of them drowning in a sea of trouble. But what did they expect? A fairytale ending showered in rose petals?

He'd even married one once. One of those thirty-somethings, always unsatisfied, eternally waiting for the epic romance they'd dreamed of since childhood. They longed for that magical light to flood their lives, catapulting them into a storybook happily-ever-after. These women were a mess - confused, irritable, and wildly unpredictable when it came to sex.

His ex-wife would wound up in a prefab house, packing chickens into plastic for a living. At night, she'd howl at the moon or collapse onto her cheap linoleum floor - the kind that poorly imitated hardwood. Just another broken dreamer.

Inspector Lennox had moved past the bitterness. His ulcer was just a distant memory now, and he'd learned to date women his own age with more grounded expectations. Still, he couldn't help but put himself in the husband's shoes. A woman like Fiona, with a pair of breasts like that? He could easily imagine the havoc she'd wreak on a man's heart.

Lennox knew damn well a man robbed of his legs could find superhuman strength to scale a tower, when driven by the rage of his wife fucking another. Once you've had those perfect tits in your grip, there's no going back. The weight of them, heavy and full in your hands, against your chest - it's a rush better than any heroin fix. You can't forget how they feel when you squeeze them hard, the way nipples stiffen as you bite and suck, leaving marks that brand her as yours. The power of making her gasp and moan just by roughly kneading that soft flesh - it's intoxicating. A man could easily kill to taste that again, to bury his face between those incredible mounds and lose himself in pure animal lust.

His disbelief at Fiona's story was bullshit - just a way of pretending no man could be that insane. Really, it was about clinging to some shred of pride for the poor bastards who'd lost everything, while knowing exactly what kind of primal urge could drive a man to such extremes.

❖

When they wheeled the husband into his office, Inspector Lennox knew he was looking at a man bound for the nuthouse. Not that he was raving or thrashing about, but the poison had sunk its claws deep. Losing his kid on top of everything else was the final nail. Lennox sighed, eyeing the shell of a man slumped in the wheelchair, smoldering with barely contained rage.

"Listen up, Brock," he said, leaning in. "That's Brock, right? You ought to be thanking your lucky stars you're shot of that woman. I know it's a bitter pill to swallow, but think about it - you've handed off a ticking time bomb. Trust me, you should be counting your blessings. This ain't the cop in me talking."

Brock's response was a mere twisted smirk as he yanked up his shirt, revealing Fiona's name carved into his chest.

Lennox didn't miss a beat. With a wry grin, he rolled up his sleeve, flashing a similar mark.

"Yeah, the ink don't fade," he admitted. "But it don't chain you down either."

❖

Gordon spent his lunch break hunched over Heather's desktop, scrolling through endless listings for TVs, washing machines, fridges - all the essentials Fiona's place was now missing. Heather, content with the greasy fish and chips Archie had brought, leaned in close, peppering Gordon's ear with her wisdom on home goods.

"You gotta think long-term investment," she'd say, or "American fridges are where it's at," and "My sis swears by Miele for everything."

Heather felt sisterly towards Gordon - if sisters were allowed to jump their brothers' bones given half a chance. She couldn't help but notice how his hangdog look since that hellish weekend made her want to wrap him up and offer her body as a distraction. The more defeated he looked, the more she ached to comfort him, ready to give him anything and everything he needed. She took full advantage of the gorgeous weather, leaving her blouse unbuttoned and hiking up her skirt, hoping he'd finally take the bait.

Gordon remained oblivious, his eyes glued to the screen as Heather "accidentally" clicked on a porn site. She giggled, feigning shock at the explicit images, but he just grunted and waited for her to navigate back to the fridge listings.

With a sigh, Heather realized neither brother saw past her role as their indispensable secretary to the woman beneath. She'd have pegged them as closet cases if she didn't know about their conquests.

Whenever Rhona or Fiona waltzed in, Heather found herself studying them. She'd casually sidle up, eyes roving from head to toe, trying to catch a whiff of their perfume brand. But she saw nothing extraordinary. It just was what it was, no point trying to figure it out.

Heather knew she was no supermodel, but she was smokin' - the kind of girl you'd expect to see on some trashy reality show. Guys hit on her constantly, and she caught plenty of appreciative glances on the street. She wasn't complaining. But it gnawed at her: What did those skanks have that she didn't? How did they do it? What was their secret weapon?

Business was booming, a welcome distraction from Heather's frustrations. Whisky sales were skyrocketing worldwide, despite global tensions - or maybe because of them. Folks needed their liquid escape more than ever. The distillery was running full tilt, salesmen scrambling to keep up.

Ted, their top seller, was running on fumes. His wife Adele was about to pop, and her stubborn refusal of an epidural had him on edge. The man couldn't catch a break, forever dashing about with his order book like some booze-peddling superhero.

Cameron and Gordon were eyeing land behind the distillery, desperate for more storage. The explosion had been a PR goldmine, keeping them in the spotlight. Angus, the master distiller, had brought on extra hands to meet demand. In the offices, printers whirred non-stop as the sales team churned out paperwork.

Sometimes, Heather felt a surge of pride. She was the queen bee in this bustling hive.

Outside, sunlight blazed gloriously while the water cooler gurgled, oblivious to the frenzy within.

❖

One night, Heather headed back to the office, forgetting something. She moved through the deserted space, dim and sectioned off by frosted partitions like some eerie aquarium. Suddenly, she froze in front of the restroom door. What she saw made her blood run cold.

Rhona and Cameron were oblivious, lost in their own world. Rhona perched on the sink counter, Cameron's face buried between her thighs, devouring her with feverish intensity.

Shaken to her core, Heather stumbled out. She crossed the street on autopilot, barely noticing the traffic snarl from another police checkpoint. Cops were cracking down on the club crowd, catching drivers high as kites.

❖

Heather collapsed onto a chair at Archie's, her legs quivering.

Archie was waiting on Cameron - they had some city planning meeting to attend. "He'll be along in about five minutes," Heather muttered, knocking back her whisky. "Shouldn't be much longer." She ordered another, discreetly wiping away a tear.

❖

Brodie drummed his fingers on the steering wheel of Isobel's cherry-red Mini Cooper, his eyes fixed on the entrance of a rundown building. He'd gone in with a wad of cash and come out empty-handed just minutes ago. The gum he chewed did little to ease his nerves.

The neighborhood was a wasteland. Crumbling buildings awaited demolition, surrounded by vast, empty office spaces. Ghostly structures loomed, their unfinished windows gaping like hollow eyes. Thistles pushed through cracked sidewalks, silvery in the moonlight.

On a traffic island choked with brittle weeds, a faded billboard mocked reality. It showcased a world of blue skies, flower-lined streets, and manicured lawns. A beaming woman pushed a sleek stroller, the picture of suburban bliss. Nothing like the rough crowd that would end up here if they ever finished this disaster of a development project.

In the back seat, Clyde, Lexi, and Marcello were getting antsy. Lexi climbed out to stretch, wincing as her aching wisdom tooth throbbed. Her mood, already sour, threatened to turn thunderous.

"Ugh, I'm dying of boredom back here. Can't we at least turn on some music or something?" Marcello grumbled, peering over Brodie's shoulder.

Brodie's jaw tightened, his eyes never leaving the building's entrance. "As long as it fuckin' takes," he growled. "You want quality gear or not?"

Clyde leaned forward, his voice low. "We sure about this guy? Last thing we need is—"

A flicker of movement caught Brodie's attention. He held up a hand, silencing Clyde mid-sentence. "Showtime, folks. Look alive."

Lexi was your typical rich kid rebel - eighteen, divorced parents, and a college "career" that started after three in the afternoon, if at all. Her dad's rare appearances usually came with threats to cut off her allowance, but those never lasted long.

Clyde had some choice words about Lexi's insatiable appetite. He'd joke that she had a vacuum cleaner between her legs instead of the usual equipment. But Clyde was all talk, especially when it came to girls. He'd brag non-stop, but when push came to shove, he was usually too zonked to tell the difference between a vacuum, a centrifuge, or a hair dryer. All bark, no bite - that was Clyde.

Lexi knew better than to let his crap get to her. She'd seen him fumble through enough hookups to know he was full of it. Still, his constant jabs grated on her nerves, especially on nights like this when tension was already high and she had a tooth ache.

She shot Clyde a withering glare. "Got something to say, big mouth? Or are you just gonna sit there and pretend you're not jonesing as bad as the rest of us?"

Clyde's mouth opened, no doubt ready to spit some half-baked comeback, when Brodie whipped around. His eyes blazed with barely contained fury.

"I swear to fuck," he snarled, "if you two don't shut your goddamn traps right now..." His knuckles whitened on the steering wheel. "We're here for one thing. One. Fucking. Thing. So put a lid on your high school drama bullshit before I lose it."

The silence that followed was deafening. Marcello and Clyde shrank back, suitably chastised. Lexi, still outside the car, froze mid-stretch. She caught Brodie's reflection in the side mirror, his face a mask of barely contained rage.

Brodie turned back to watch the building, muttering under his breath about "amateur hour" and "fucking children."

The tension in the car ratcheted up another notch, a powder keg waiting for a spark.The wait continued, electric with anticipation and need.

Lexi glared at the run-down building, irritation simmering. Her fingers twitched, craving a cigarette, a drink, anything to take the edge off. This wait was driving them all nuts, but showing up empty-handed wasn't an option. She turned to Isobel, wincing as she rubbed her jaw.

"Your dentist any good?" Lexi asked glumly.

Isobel blinked, caught off guard. Her dentist had been on her mind lately - a lot. Just days ago, she'd stormed his office without an appointment, screeching about emergencies. He hadn't been thrilled, but what choice did she have? This whole situation was spiraling out of control.

"He's... competent," Isobel said carefully, memories flashing behind her eyes. "Why? Tooth still bothering you?"

Lexi nodded miserably. "Feels like someone's drilling into my skull. Got anything that might help?" Her eyes flickered meaningfully to Isobel's purse.

Isobel hesitated, torn between sympathy and caution. "Let's see what our friend inside comes up with first, yeah? Might have something better than aspirin."

Brodie got a text message and his voice cut through the tension. "Heads up. Our guy's on the move."

"Does it hurt?" Lexi pressed, her curiosity overriding caution.

She opened her mouth wide, pointing to the swollen lump. Clyde leaned in, squinting.

"Shit, that looks nasty," Isobel said.

"I could lance that for you, no problem. Just need a safety pin or something sharp," Clyde said, a gleam in his eye. "No need for a dentist."

Lexi recoiled, covering her mouth. "Touch me and die, asshole."

Brodie's retort died on his lips as movement caught his eye. A scrawny kid emerged from the skeletal building, hands shoved deep in his pockets.

"Showtime," Brodie muttered, tension coiling in his muscles. "Everyone shut up and look normal."

Lexi hopped back into the convertible.

The kid sauntered up to the car, all swagger, chin up, a cocky boss glare plastered on his face.

When he reached the car, he pulled out a small package - an eight ball and a handful of pills.

❖

Clyde performed the operation in the dead of night, hunched over the kitchen counter in an apartment shared by two law students. The place reeked of booze and sweat, and the wannabe lawyers stumbled around half-naked in kilts, oblivious to the makeshift surgery taking place.

"Cocaine used to be an anesthetic, you know," Clyde muttered to Lexi, his words slurring slightly. He scored a line on the counter, rubbed some on her gum, then grabbed a needle. The flame from his lighter danced as he sterilized the point.

Lexi gritted her teeth as Clyde lanced the angry abscess. For the next hour, she spat crimson into the sink.

❖

Later, the night buzzed with fresh gossip. "Something's going down at the river house," Marcello drawled, eternally unimpressed. He tossed his mane of hair, adding, "These two are dead weight."

One of the kilt-wearing hosts overheard, his face twisting in fury. Brodie, ever the peacemaker, pressed a pill into the guy's palm. "Here. Chill out, man."

Lexi snagged a box of tissues as they bolted, leaving a trail of bloodstained flowers in the stairwell – one every couple of floors, blooming in their wake.

Outside, Isobel slid behind the wheel. Brodie loomed in the open door. "Move over. I'm driving."

"Hell no," Isobel snapped. Brodie's sober driving was scary enough.

His eyes flashed dangerously. In one fluid motion, he yanked her out, a satisfied smirk playing on his lips as he claimed the driver's seat.

The engine roared to life, and they peeled away into the neon-lit night.

❖

Brodie tore along the reed-lined riverbank, pushing Isobel's new Mini Cooper to its limits. Across the water, houses flashed between the trees like a strobe light.

"Still pouting?" Brodie taunted, glancing at Isobel.

Clyde snorted from the back seat. "Let her stew."

"Like I give a fuck," Brodie shot back, his grin manic.

The tires screamed as they hit the Forth Road Bridge, Brodie weaving through traffic like he was auditioning for Fast and Furious. Everyone but Isobel whooped with drug-fueled glee.

Lexi hunched in the back, dabbing at her mouth with tissue after tissue. She studied each one intently, as if reading some bloody prophecy, before flinging them at the window with a scowl.

Brodie's smile never wavered, an artificial rictus etched on his face. He steered the Mini off-road, plowing through the reeds until the river glimmered just ahead. The engine cut off, leaving an eerie silence.

Before them loomed a sprawling house, set back from the road behind a vast, shadowy lawn.

Isobel thrust out her hand, wordlessly demanding her keys. She wasn't scared of Brodie, not really, but wariness flickered in her eyes. With everyone riding a chemical high, anything could happen. Isobel prided herself on staying clear-headed, unlike Brodie, who'd swallow anything that promised a buzz.

Inside, a strange heat surged through her veins. For a wild moment, she felt like she could take him. Pin him down like the worthless scum he was and tear out his throat with one vicious bite. The intensity of her reaction startled her. Maybe she just liked this new car too much, hated seeing Brodie abuse it like he did everything else in his life.

The keys landed in her palm with a soft jingle.

"Christ, you're such a Victoria Woolf," Brodie sneered, his words slurring slightly.

"Virginia," Isobel corrected, her jaw clenching.

"What?"

"It's Virginia Woolf."

"Same difference. Fucking snoozefest in a skirt. Bet she never sucked cock worth a damn."

Isobel's fists balled at her sides. She'd lent him that book when things were new, hoping to connect on a deeper level. His dismissal stung, but it also confirmed what she'd begun to suspect: Brodie would never truly satisfy her. He was pretty enough, sure, but about as deep as a puddle. Any guy bored by Woolf was missing some vital spark.

She bit back a retort, sensing Brodie's mood teetering on a knife's edge. As she reached for the door handle, his fingers clamped around her arm. Outside, the others were already stumbling through the reeds, nature calling. Lexi hunched nearby, spitting pink-tinged saliva onto the grass.

Brodie didn't bother with words. He jammed his tongue into Isobel's mouth, pawing at her breasts like he was kneading dough. This, apparently, was his idea of foreplay.

Isobel prayed it would be enough to satisfy him for the night, but she wasn't holding her breath. Memories of a mushroom-fueled disaster flashed through her mind – one of the worst nights of her life. Back then, she'd been as dry as the Sahara. Before Oliver. Before her dentist had shown her what real passion felt like.

She endured Brodie's clumsy pawing, waiting for him to realize she wasn't spreading her legs tonight. Especially not with the others lurking nearby. As Brodie fumbled with her hand, trying to shove it down his pants, Isobel's thoughts drifted to Oliver. Her brilliant tooth extractor.

She and Oliver had fallen into bed on their very first meeting. No hesitation, just raw chemistry. Stepping out of the car, Isobel glanced at Brodie. How would he react if he knew she'd given freely to another man what he'd been chasing for months?

❖

Music drifted from the house beyond the thick hawthorn hedge. Despite her revulsion, Isobel knew they needed each other tonight. They had to present a united front. There were rules to this game, steps carved in stone. Some dances you couldn't sit out, no matter how much your partner made your skin crawl.

Isobel had resigned herself to the inevitable. Sooner or later, Brodie would have her, no longer satisfied with quick hand jobs - though she still gave them, clinging to the foolish hope he'd remain oblivious. The shadow of that future darkened her face. She silently thanked the inventor of condoms but prayed to stall as long as possible.

How many girls actually enjoyed sex with guys? In her packed lecture halls, Isobel could count them on one hand, excluding the drama queens. A pathetic number. Yet how many were still virgins? Zero. The vaccine was as good as mandatory.

Still, they all competed with micro-skirts and plunging necklines. Some even had work done at their age - bigger boobs, plumper lips, cat-eye lifts - chasing an impossible ideal. What choice was there? For all their talk of liberation, women hadn't escaped the cave. Isobel believed this wholeheartedly. The only thing a woman had to learn here was to hide her ass.

No need to peek into bedrooms to know what went on behind closed doors. This is where her fling with the dentist had led her - back to the meat market, with Brodie's hungry eyes trailing her every move.

Parties like this had become an exercise in methodical intoxication, everyone getting high to avoid the elephant in the room. Since

Oliver Purvis, Isobel saw it all with new eyes. He'd taught her what real desire felt like. Just the word alone was better than any drug. The mere thought of him set her cheeks burning, her breath quickening.

Brodie found her in the kitchen, leaning against the sink. She was rubbing Lexi's back, a cigarette dangling from her lips, tapping her foot to a Daft Punk track she loved.

Lexi spat a mouthful of blood.

"Clyde sliced her gum with a razor," Isobel explained.

"Fuck! And she let him?"

Lexi hawked up another glob of dark fluid. "Did I look like I knew what he was doing? Bastard said it was a needle," she snarled. "You think I'm that stupid?"

At eighteen, Lexi still had some hard lessons ahead of her.

So did Isobel, apparently. It was pushing 2 AM when she snuck to a quiet corner of the garden and dialed Oliver's number. The time hadn't even crossed her mind.

"What the hell?" Oliver's voice was thick with sleep. "Do you know what time it is? Have you lost your mind? Calling me at 2 in the morning?"

Isobel let out a soft whimper.

Isobel stammered out some excuse about her friend's mangled gum, desperate for his advice - and his voice. Oliver cut her off. He didn't give a damn about their drama, he snapped. He was too old for this crap. Don't use his personal number for trivial bullshit again. Click.

The rejection hit her like a sucker punch. A bizarre surge ripped through her body, hot as magma. The grass at her feet shimmered like broken glass.

Dizzy, she longed to bolt home and bury herself in bed. But she knew Brodie would throw a fit if she ditched mid-party. Wounded as she was, she wasn't completely stupid. This was her world, for better or worse. Maybe not the best one, but what were her options?

Inside, Clyde and Lexi's bickering had escalated to full-on verbal warfare. Not that anyone noticed. The couch was occupied by a wasted couple, more focused on not spilling their drinks than the drama unfolding around them.

Nearby, a group huddled, plotting ways to monetize their youth with lonely cougars - and even sugar daddies for the less squeamish. What's wrong with older men? Isobel thought bitterly. Besides not appreciating 2 AM booty calls?

The party churned on, oblivious. Schemers whispered in corners, drifters searched for their next high, girls giggled over some guy's package. Upstairs, dull thuds and stumbling footsteps betrayed messier encounters.

Isobel shook herself and drifted to a cluster passing around an e-cig. Weed without tobacco - easier on the lungs, they claimed. She needed to fog her brain, to blur out this nightmare. Tears pricked at her eyes for reasons she couldn't fathom. It felt like puberty all over again, raw and confusing.

She took a deep drag, willing the herb to numb the ache in her chest. The high hit her fast and hard, the room spinning. Suddenly, she wasn't there anymore. She was running, naked, through a moonlit forest. Again. Then, just as quickly, she snapped back to the stuffy living room, disoriented and shaken.

CHAPTER 12
STIRLING CASTLE
JULY 1314

A silhouette appeared on the crest of the hill, backlit by the setting sun. Robert the Bruce's heart leapt as he recognized the figure—Elisabeth, his queen, free at last after eight long years. Behind her, a small group of Scottish nobles emerged, released alongside her in exchange for Humphrey de Bohun.

As Elisabeth drew closer, Robert felt a dagger of joy pierce his heart. She was here, truly here. Humphrey had kept his word, against all odds. The sight of his wife, proud and unbowed despite her long captivity, nearly brought him to his knees. His mind raced back to the moment he'd sent Humphrey to Dunbar with his audacious request.

❖

"An alliance?" Edward II had sputtered, his face contorting in disbelief. "With Bruce? After all this?"

Humphrey de Bohun stood firm, his posture rigid despite his exhaustion. "Your Majesty, I've seen things... horrors beyond imagining. Bruce speaks true—this threat is greater than our petty wars."

Edward paced, muttering about "vampire Scottish forces." His eyes were wild, haunted. Humphrey exchanged worried glances with the other advisors. The king's stability was clearly in question.

"And what of the men we lost?" Edward snapped suddenly. "What of Bannockburn?"

Humphrey took a deep breath. "Sire, it could have been far worse. Bruce and his men... they saved many English lives that day. When those creatures attacked, they fought alongside us, protected our retreating forces. Without them, the slaughter would have been absolute."

Edward's pacing slowed, his brow furrowed in thought. "Is this true?"

"I saw it with my own eyes, Your Majesty. English and Scots, fighting side by side against a common foe. It was... extraordinary."

The king's shoulders slumped, the agony of the defeat seemingly crushing him. "Bannockburn," he muttered. "My greatest failure."

"Perhaps," Humphrey said carefully, "it could be the beginning of something greater. A united front against this unholy threat."

Edward was quiet for a long moment. Then, "And what of Bruce's other request? His wife?"

Humphrey tensed. This was the crux of it all. "He asks for Queen Elisabeth's release, sire. As a gesture of good faith."

The debate that followed was heated, advisors arguing back and forth about the wisdom of releasing such a valuable hostage. But in the end, whether from a flicker of compassion or sheer war-weariness, Edward agreed. It seems even the King has limits to his cruelty.

❖

Now, as Elisabeth dismounted before him, Robert was struck by how both familiar and strange she seemed. Eight years had etched new lines around her eyes, a weariness in her bearing. But when their gazes met, he saw the same fire that had first captured his heart.

Robert took her hands in his, drinking in the sight of her. "My queen," he replied, his voice thick with emotion. "Welcome home."

"My king," she said softly, a ghost of a smile playing at her lips as she reached up to gently touch his beard. "I see you've been growing more than just alliances in my absence."

❖

Their bodies tangled beneath thick blankets, firelight dancing on stone walls. The room reeked of sweat and lingering passion. Robert's chest rose and fell as he held Elisabeth close, fingers tracing her bare back. Her head nestled on his shoulder, breath warm against his neck.

Eight years. War, duty, and his fight for the throne had kept them apart. But tonight, none of that mattered. They were just Robert and Elisabeth, lovers reunited, their bond tested by time and battle.

They'd come together with fierce desperation, reclaiming lost years. Every kiss a vow, every touch erasing the pain of separation. Now, as passion cooled, they clung tight, savoring closeness long denied.

Robert tilted her chin up, meeting her gaze. He saw his own relief and love mirrored there. They'd both changed—he'd hardened, she'd learned to live with fear. But here, they found solace.

He kissed her forehead, then her lips, tender and slow.

"I've missed you more than I can say," he murmured.

She smiled, fingers in his damp hair. "And I you, Robert. Every day, every night, I dreamed of this—of being in your arms again." Her voice caught, thick with memory. "These years... they've worn me to the bone. Each day, I felt a piece of myself slip away. The hope, the fire in me... it all started to feel like a cruel song."

He pulled her closer, aching. "I swear, my love, I'll never leave you again. Not if I can help it. We've been apart too long."

"This war," she whispered, her face pressed against his chest. "It's taken so much. There were times I thought I'd never see you again, that I'd wither away behind those palace walls. But I held onto you, onto us. It was all I had left."

Tears shimmered in her eyes as she nestled against him. "We're together now, Robert. That's all that matters."

Silence fell, broken only by crackling flames. Robert's hand drifted to Elisabeth's stomach, a gesture of hope for the future they longed to create together—their children, their legacy. He thought of the years lost, the family they had yet to build. Love and anticipation swelled in his chest, tinged with a hint of sorrow for the time apart.

But here, those thoughts of the future faded. Here, they were safe, whole, together. For now, it was enough.

❖

Later, Robert held Elisabeth close, skin on skin. They'd made love again, with desperate intensity, years of longing poured into every touch. Now, in the quiet after, they found peace.

Now, in the afterglow, Robert traced idle patterns on Elisabeth's arm. "Tell me," he said softly. "How was it? Were you treated well?"

Elisabeth was quiet for a long moment. "It was... bearable," she said finally. "Better than some, worse than others." She recounted her journey—the flight from Kildrummy Castle, the desperate dash north, the capture at St. Duthac's sanctuary.

"They didn't cage me, at least," she said, a bitter edge to her voice. "Not like poor Mary and Isabella. But oh, Robert, the loneliness..." Her voice caught. "At Burstwick, I had nothing. Three changes of clothes a year, no proper bedding. I wrote to Edward, begging for the barest necessities."

"No proper bedding?! Only three changes of clothes a year?!" Robert gasped, eyes wide with exaggerated horror. "Oh, my poor queen! How did you survive such hardship?"

Elisabeth's eyes flashed. "You mock me, sir?" She snatched up a pillow, smacking him squarely in the face.

"I would never!" Robert sputtered through a mouthful of feathers, grinning as he grabbed his own pillow in defense.

"Liar!" She swung again, but he ducked, retaliating with a soft thwack to her shoulder.

They tussled, breathless with laughter, pillows flying. Elisabeth landed a particularly good hit, sending Robert sprawling dramatically across the bed.

"I yield, my fierce warrior-queen!" he cried, still chuckling as he pulled her down beside him.

Giggling, she curled against his chest. "That's what you get for teasing me."

Robert's arms tightened around her, his tone sobering. "In truth, my love, I'm sorry. I should have—"

"No," Elisabeth cut him off firmly. "You did what you had to do. For Scotland. For our people." She sat up, meeting his gaze. "And now? This alliance with Edward... will it hold?"

Robert sighed, running a hand through his hair. "I don't know. Edward is... unstable. The battle, the vampires—it's shaken him badly. But we need this alliance, Elisabeth. The threat we face..." He shuddered, remembering the night of Bannockburn.

Elisabeth nodded slowly. "I saw things, Robert. During my captivity. Whispers, shadows moving in ways they shouldn't. Something is coming, isn't it?"

"Yes," Robert said grimly. "Something ancient. Something hungry."

They lapsed into silence, the dread of the future heavy between them. Finally, Robert spoke again, his voice soft but urgent. "Elisabeth... I want us to try for children."

She looked at him, surprised. "Now? With everything that's happening?"

Robert nodded. "Especially now. We don't know what tomorrow will bring. You could be taken again. I could fall in battle. We need to think of the future—of our legacy."

Elisabeth's hand found his, squeezing tightly. "A family," she whispered. "Yes. Something to fight for."

As they sealed their agreement with a kiss, a chill wind rattled the windows. In the distance, a wolf howled—long and mournful.

CHAPTER 13

Margaret eased her 1970 Aston Martin DBS into the shade of a sprawling mimosa tree. She felt a shiver run down her spine as she stepped out of the car. The city had swallowed this land whole, devouring prairies and forests alike. Yet Margaret felt the echoes of what came before. To her, these streets still whispered ancient secrets and forbidden lore. They sang of long-forgotten hunts and battles only she could truly understand. Centuries of twilight had etched those memories into her bones, a history no mortal could fathom.

She grabbed her cane and stepped out of her car, squinting in the bright morning sun. Twenty years had passed since she'd last been on this street, but the sinister aura lingered. She pushed her tortoiseshell sunglasses up, gritting her teeth against the memories.

The late morning sun no longer threatened to turn Margaret to ash, yet she couldn't shake her instinctive discomfort. Least to say it irritated her mood far more than her skin.

❖

Rhona lounged in shorts and a tank top, her hair in a messy bun. For her, the world was divided into light and shadow, with her existence straddling the line between the two. Her life was a careful balancing act, one foot in society's embrace, the other in a realm few could understand: The Bruces.

Last night's party—thrown by two newlywed French friends and to which Alison had practically dragged her—had left her groggy and unmotivated. She'd only managed to power up her laptop, scanning emails and social media. Her livelihood depended on the views her Hashtag Magazine articles racked up.

Her phone buzzed. Another text from Cameron, each one getting bolder. Rhona sighed, thinking of Isobel. Her daughter had left for class earlier, but something was off. Whenever Rhona tried to pry, Isobel shut down, retreating to her locked room. It stung—even a less-than-perfect mom deserved some acknowledgment.

At least the house felt lighter without Isobel's brooding presence. Rhona hated to admit it, but her daughter's absence lifted a weight from her chest. She wondered if Brodie or the dentist—or both—were the source of Isobel's troubles when the doorbell's chime shattered her thoughts.

Rhona opened the door. She and Margaret locked eyes, a storm of emotions crackling between them. When Rhona failed to invite her in—stunned rather than rude—Margaret strode past her into the living room.

Memories assaulted Margaret. She saw herself screaming at Rhona's parents, relived the fury and tragedy that had unfolded within these walls. Their children tearing each other apart, accusations of birthing evil, insults hurled with bulging veins. How could anyone forget?

"It's not enough for you," Margaret snarled, rounding on Rhona. "You need more!"

Barely containing herself, Margaret trembled with rage. The words hung there, stale and heavy. Once, they might've had some bite. Now they were just another relic, as outdated as horse-drawn carriages or gas lamps. The world had moved on, leaving behind old superstitions and those who clung to them.

Rhona retreated to the bay window overlooking the garden. She planted her hands on her hips and stared skyward, buying time to collect herself before facing the hurricane that had just blown into her home.

"I didn't know what I was saying," Rhona replied softly. "I've changed my mind."

Margaret's eyes flashed. "Changed your mind? You swore solemnly, in their hospital room, right in front of me. So why are you here? What demon's bitten you this time?"

Her hands trembled on the silver handle of her cane. The black wood gleamed like a sword planted before her.

Rhona's gaze drifted to the neighbor's acacia tree, where a chubby boy was devouring a bag of crisps. For a fleeting moment, his eyes seemed to meet hers. "They're old enough to learn," she said flatly.

Margaret shuddered. "What are you talking about? Have you lost your mind? Are you the devil himself?"

"I've never been afraid of you. Did you know that?"

Margaret would have given anything for a drink. She eyed the Vodka bottle peeking out from behind a stack of CDs, cursing herself for forgetting her gin flask. The realization had hit her on the drive over, stoking her anger. But she'd been too close to turn back.

Rhona's soul-shattering beauty only fueled Margaret's rage. She'd turn those boys to putty.

"What do you want? Money?" Margaret fumbled with her clasp, nerves making her clumsy. Outside, the boy crumpled his empty crisp bag, reaching for another. His gaze flicked towards the window, unnervingly steady before returning to his snack.

She flung cash onto the couch.

Rhona sighed. "Don't tempt me. I'm dying for new shoes."

It wasn't a lie. For days, she'd craved an overpriced pair of mules. Retail therapy had its perks—an instant mood boost. Instead, here she was, watching some kid gorge himself in a tree while Margaret spewed nonsense.

"I won't let you do it," Margaret growled. "You don't know what I'm capable of."

Rhona met her gaze, unflinching. "Maybe not. But I know what I'm capable of."

The air crackled between them, decades of history and hurt condensed into this moment.

"Why now?" Margaret demanded. "After all this time?"

Rhona's lips curved into a smile that didn't reach her eyes. "Why not?"

Rhona turned, fixing Margaret with a cold stare. The older woman's face was a mask of stone, deathly pale and lifeless. Rhona felt a flicker of pity, imagining the crushing weight of being trapped at 63 for nearly eight centuries.

"Is that all a granddaughter means to you? You should be thanking me. Instead of harassing me, maybe open your eyes a bit."

Margaret's mind slammed shut against the implications. If that forbidden door creaked open, even a sliver, she'd throw her whole being into sealing it tight. Lips pressed, heart barricaded, ears covered.

"But you never cared," Rhona pressed on, her voice rising with each word. "Nothing matters beyond your precious sons. For years, I thought you'd ask about her. I thought even you wouldn't be foolish enough to deny yourself that."

Margaret's jaw clenched, but she remained silent.

"Your own flesh and blood," Rhona continued. "Born against all odds, defying the very nature of your kind. To say nothing of how this miracle even happened. And you've ignored her, all this time."

"Ha!" Margaret barked a laugh, sensing the trap. "Your pathetic guilt trip. You must think I'm the world's biggest idiot."

Without asking, she snatched the Vodka bottle and poured a hefty glass, downing it in one desperate gulp.

"Can we talk now?" Rhona asked, her tone weary.

Margaret's eyes flashed. "You need to disappear. Go back where you came from, if you've any soul left."

"Fine. Then get out. Leave me alone."

"You've always been an arrogant little slut," Margaret spat, color rising in her cheeks. "Always."

Rhona stared, then shrugged. "Honestly, you're the least of my worries. Talking to you is pointless."

Depression settled over her like a shroud. "I'm done," she continued. "Done carrying this burden alone."

"What did you expect, sleeping with both of them?" Margaret hissed. "You haven't suffered a tenth of what you deserve. You should be on your bleeding knees, hiding your face. Cursed be the day we welcomed you like a queen."

"Like a queen?" Rhona's bitter laugh cut the air. "You're completely delusional. Just go. I'm sick of hearing you."

"You lived in their room," Margaret snarled, her mouth twisting. "Yet you were always at my place. That was my mistake. Letting you in."

Rhona had long tried to understand this woman. "Must feel good, dwelling on that," she said wearily. "Does you a world of good, right? I don't care. Now take your money and go."

"I won't be as patient as before," Margaret warned. "I won't wait for your next horrible trick."

"Then hurry up. Don't waste time here. You're lucky I haven't talked to them yet. Gives you time to prepare poison or find a hitman. Surprised you haven't broken your vow and torn me apart already."

"What did they do to you?" Margaret's voice turned menacing. "Why this fixation? Your daughter has a father, doesn't she?"

"Not really," Rhona replied coldly.

"He raised her thinking it's his. Why ruin 20 years of peace? What difference does it make for both of them? It's just like he's her real father," Margaret argued, her tone dismissive.

"Not according to me," Rhona countered. "Too bad you can't see the difference. It might change things."

"Without a thought for the consequences?" Margaret's hair gleamed in the sunlight, incongruously perfect. "Ready to set our lives ablaze again."

Rhona's eyes flashed. "They're already burning. Can't you see? Twenty years, and what's changed? We're right back where we started. Are you stupid or just blind?"

They could have gone on like this until nightfall, neither yielding an inch. The air crackled with the potential for violence.

Suddenly, Rhona snatched her phone and strode into the garden. Margaret surveyed the room with the cold eye of a demolition contractor.

When Cameron answered, Rhona cut off his cheerful greeting. "Cameron, your mother's here. Tell her to leave. Now."

One of Cameron's strengths: he never needed things explained twice.

"Put her on," he said, his tone clipped.

Rhona marched back inside, thrusting the phone at Margaret, and retreated to the sun-drenched garden. Its warmth enveloped her like a comforting shield, its energy an irresistible magnet. The chubby boy now held his phone at an odd angle, its camera lens catching the sunlight as it pointed in her direction. His other hand rested unsubtly on his crotch. For a moment, his stillness seemed unnatural for a child his age. Rhona had long since given up confronting him or threatening to maim him for his lewd behavior. His future looked bleak enough—why make it worse?

Inside, Margaret's face contorted as Cameron's words crackled through the line. Minutes ticked by, giving the boy time to finish his sad business. Finally, Margaret fell silent, a bloodless husk behind the window.

Rhona returned, offering water to avoid accusations of neglecting a struggling mother. Whatever Cameron had said, it had worked. Margaret, dazed and docile, allowed herself to be guided out. Rhona stuffed the money back into her bag. Without a backward glance, Margaret shuffled to her car.

As the Aston Martin purred to life, Rhona felt a weight lift. But a new tension coiled in her gut. The real battle was just beginning.

❖

Rhona sank onto the couch, ignoring her mental to-do list. Exhaustion dragged at her bones, but underneath, a familiar restlessness stirred. It was that same old itch, rising with the seasons and the swelling moon. She tried to ignore it, fumbling with her lighter. The cigarette's flare briefly illuminated her face, but did nothing to chase away the nagging sensation. It lingered, persistent as a shadow, impossible to shake off no matter how she tried to lose herself in mundane rituals.

Laundry, work for Alison's Hashtag Magazine anniversary issue, shopping—it could all wait. She lit a cigarette, inhaling deeply.

Her thoughts drifted to Isobel. She imagined telling her daughter the awful truth: one of the brothers was her father, but Rhona didn't know which. Oh, and he's a vampire. The scene played out in her mind for the thousandth time, always ending with a choked sob. How had she gotten herself into this mess?

Rhona grappled with the nagging question, the answer dancing just beyond her grasp. Buried under a lifetime of secrets, it refused to surface. She never was a prize of iron control, but lately, that grip was slipping more than humanly bearable. Something stirred in the depths of her being, an ancient part of herself long forgotten. It clawed its way toward consciousness, threatening to shatter the careful walls she'd built. Rhona felt herself balanced on a knife's edge, unsure if she feared or craved what might emerge.

The temptation to keep the secret gnawed at her. Or maybe she could just decide that whoever took the mother got the daughter as a package deal. It was a lousy solution, but what were her options?

The phone's shrill ring cut through her thoughts. Rhona let it go to voicemail, savoring the temporary silence and the bitter taste of smoke.

She exhaled slowly, watching the smoke curl towards the ceiling. The consequences of her choices pressed down on her, suffocating as the nicotine haze.

❖

An hour later, Rhona stood in an upscale boutique she usually avoided for the sake of her bank account. She admired a pair of exquisite Charlotte Olympia shoes on her feet, their price tag making her wince.

As she gazed at her reflection, Isobel's imagined voice cut through her thoughts: "Say that again. You don't know which one? Say it again?"

"What do you want? That's how it is," Rhona muttered, punching her PIN code to authorize an astronomical sum. No one tried to put themselves in her shoes, she thought bitterly.

Leaving the store, she strode down the sidewalk's center, chin high, forcing others to step aside. Her new shoes clicked against the pavement, a rhythm of defiance. No one had the right to judge her choices.

The shopping bag swung from her arm, both a shield and a declaration. Let them stare. Let them wonder. Rhona had weathered centuries of judgment—what was a little more?

❖

Cameron dropped the bomb as Gordon scrolled through Ikea's website: he and Rhona were sleeping together. The timing felt right, just after mentioning Margaret's intrusion at Rhona's place.

The words landed hard, cracking their carefully built veneer. Ancient as they were, love and betrayal still cut deep. Memories of blood-soaked passions only made this tangle messier. Time hadn't simplified their hearts—if anything, it just piled on more baggage.

They'd witnessed the rise and fall of nations, yet here they stood, shaken by echoes from a mere two decades past. A heartbeat in their vast lifespans, but it felt like razors under their skin. Countless moons had waxed and waned since their turning, and somehow this sliver of time threatened to undo them both. The ground beneath their feet had never felt so treacherous.

But Gordon's reaction was as muted as a weatherman predicting another cloudy day. He gave a slight nod, his gaze distant.

"How is it?" he finally asked, catching Cameron off guard.

Cameron shrugged, leaving the details to Gordon's imagination.

"Just keep Margaret off her back," Gordon muttered, returning to his browsing.

After a moment, he looked up. Cameron still stood there, hands in pockets, staring intently.

Gordon sighed. "What? You want my blessing? Christ, I've got my own shit. Every night, I hold a woman who lost a child and cries till dawn. What do you say to that?"

The air thickened with unspoken tension. Centuries of shared history hung between them, now tangled in this new web of complications.

❖

The afternoon brought frustrating news: the town hall was preempting the land behind the distillery. By evening, after hours of fruitless phone calls, they had to admit defeat. Their project had crumbled.

Cameron leaned back in his chair, a scowl etched deep on his face. This wasn't devastating—the business was doing well enough—but it was a maddening setback. Centuries of existence hadn't made losing any easier, especially to bureaucratic meddling.

He glanced at his brother, noting the tight set of his jaw. "Well,"

Cameron said, his voice sharp with irritation, "I suppose this round goes to the pencil pushers. Bloody nuisance, the lot of them."

Cameron vibrated with rage, his emotions on full display. Gordon, in contrast, kept his turmoil tightly leashed, his face a mask of stone. The distillery stood silent now, darkness creeping in unnoticed. As dusk thickened, the world beyond the distillery's walls smudged into a hazy dreamscape. Shadows writhed and stretched, grasping fingers of darkness reclaiming their domain. The brothers felt the change in their bones, a primal stirring as old as time. Night's curtain fell, and with it, their carefully honed control began to fray at the edges.

Times like these stripped away their human facade, revealing the ancient power simmering just beneath. For all their attempts to blend in, to play mortal, the raw energy in their veins couldn't be denied. Life's injustices had a way of peeling back centuries of restraint, reminding them of the primal force they truly were. In moments like these, a darker thought often crossed their minds: how much simpler life would be if they embraced their nature, dealt with foes as the predators they were. The temptation to solve problems with fang and claw always lurked, a seductive whisper of power and efficiency.

Only Heather remained, oblivious, fielding calls and pouring whisky. She clung to her slutty secretary persona like a shield, all exaggerated sways and fluttering eyelashes. It was as if she thought such antics could bandage the brothers' wounds. A vain attempt at distraction that fooled no one, yet oddly constant in the storm.

❖

She followed them down to the land—now just a shattered dream. They needed to see what they were losing, as if the sight might change reality.

A wasteland stretched before them, waist-high bushes swaying in the breeze. This neglected plot held such potential, now brutally snatched away. Cameron paced, slashing through the tall grass, while Gordon stood frozen, his face twisted in disgust.

Heather's heart raced, watching the brothers' pain play out.

Cameron hurled curses at himself. "Idiot," he snarled. "I thought we had time. What a goddamn fool."

The gentle wind carried his words away, indifferent to their anguish. As twilight deepened, the land seemed to mock them, whispering of possibilities forever lost.

"How long have I been talking about this?" Cameron turned to Heather, his voice raw. "Didn't I say it at least three times a day? 'Heather, we need to buy this land. Heather, we need to buy this damn land.'"

She nodded vigorously, feeling the pang of his regret.

Heather knew the distillery meant more than just whisky to them. Sure, they enjoyed closing big deals—every man had a boy inside who never quite grew up—but this was different. After that coward Freddie Reid canceled his order, now the city was pulling this stunt. She ached for them.

❖

Back in Cameron's plush new office, with its oversized leather chairs, Heather found glasses and a bottle of rare Scotch. She moved through the shadows, feeling like a mermaid gliding through water. The chiaroscuro enveloped them, creating an intimacy she cherished. These powerful men accepted her as one of their own - even if that acceptance didn't extend to passionate sex atop the mahogany desk—well, that part was frustrating.

Gordon broke the silence, his voice cutting through the shadows. "To get back to our story..." He paused as Heather topped off his glass. Her gaze drifted to the window, watching the nightly exodus of cars streaming towards the suburbs, their headlights a river of light flowing past a police checkpoint.

"Yes, to get back to our story..." Gordon drained his glass in one swift motion. "Do whatever you want. Sleep together all you like. Why not? We live in a free country, last I checked."

"If only," Heather muttered, the irony of his words not lost on her. The assertion rang hollow in a world growing more oppressive by the day, a comforting lie for those who refused to see.

Cameron's eyes glinted as he watched his brother, something unspoken passing between them. Heather didn't bother hiding her disappointment as she poured herself another drink. So much for her romantic aspirations. She steeled herself, pushing away the ache of desire, the longing for tenderness. Right now, she needed to be more than just a woman with wants and needs. She had to focus.

They spoke freely around her, especially about matters she knew well. Love, betrayal, desire - the twisting paths of human relationships were familiar territory. Heather had seen it all, lived through plenty herself.

She glanced at the thermometer. Twenty-three degrees.

Pressing her forehead to the cool glass, Heather gazed at the empty lot below. The BRUCE DISTILLERY sign blazed above, a beacon in the night. The brothers toasted to some horizon only they could see. Their not-so-cryptic conversation washed over her, meaningless yet strangely comforting.

Light glinted off the displays below - amber bottles, shining chrome labels, polished barrels. Crystal sparkled. Leather cases gleamed. The sight soothed her, though she couldn't say why. Well, maybe she could. That showroom floor had once given her the most earth-shattering orgasm of her life. But who could explain these things, really?

❖

As the night wore on, the Scotch flowed freely. Heather relished these impromptu drinking sessions after hours, when deals were closed and inhibitions lowered. She hoped for wild abandon, though it had yet to materialize.

Grateful for the darkness hiding her flushed cheeks, Heather craved fresh air. She kicked off her heels and curled up in her chair, her skirt riding dangerously high. Office hours were long past - who cared about decency now?

The conversation blurred around her, but she basked in the moment. Sandwiched between the two brothers, her happiness was almost painful. A tingling sensation danced across her skin.

Her phone's sudden ring shattered the moment. Heather lurched to answer it, but the room tilted. She stumbled, crashing unceremoniously to the floor.

Gordon and Cameron rushed to Heather's aid, hoisting her up. She was fine, just wobbly. Grinning, she let them guide her to the window for some air.

Her breath caught as Cameron knelt to slip on her shoes. Gordon loosened her blouse, urging her to breathe deep. Heather closed her eyes, desperately trying to burn this moment into her memory forever.

She checked her phone, insisting she could drive. They watched her wobble down the stairs and across the parking lot, unconvinced.

The message was from her sister Agnes. Mason, Agnes' husband, had locked himself in the bathroom and wasn't responding. Heather needed to come.

The brothers decided to drive her.

❖

When they arrived, Agnes was frantic. Agnes pounded on the door, calling Mason's name. Her voice grew more frantic with each unanswered plea. Visions of heart attacks and cracked skulls fueled her panic. She twisted a handkerchief in her hands, fear etched on her face. Only her perfect bun remained unruffled.

Cameron complimented the decor. Agnes managed a weak smile before leading them upstairs.

At the bathroom door, Agnes begged Mason to respond, rattling the handle. Heather, perched on the stairs, declared, "We need to break it down."

Agnes winced but offered no alternative.

Gordon and Cameron charged the door, their supernatural strength barely contained. The wood splintered easily under their vampiric might, though they made a show of effort for appearance's sake.

There stood Mason, shirtless and oblivious. Heavy metal - likely Motörhead's "Overkill" - blasted from his earbuds. He wielded an air guitar, face contorted in ecstasy. His foot pounded the tiles as he headbanged furiously, lost in his own world of thrashing rhythms.

Mason froze mid-headbang, suddenly aware of his audience. Sweat-drenched, he yanked off his headphones and glowered at Agnes. He snatched a towel, wrapping it around his neck as he stormed past her.

"Leave me alone, you fucking bitch!" he snarled in her face before slamming into another room.

Heather guided her shaken sister downstairs, musing about the importance of personal space in relationships. "Everyone needs their secrets," she said. "Otherwise, things get... tense."

Agnes was mortified. "Did I deserve that?" she asked, voice small. "I was just worried. Isn't that my job? I promised before God and three hundred guests to care for him."

❖

Cameron leaned against the doorframe, watching the sisters crunch ice for Pimm's in the kitchen. He nudged Gordon, keeping his voice low. "You know, there's something about Agnes..."

Gordon followed his brother's gaze. "Her chest, you mean? Oddly appealing on that willowy frame of hers."

"Exactly," Cameron murmured. "Almost pre-adolescent, isn't it?"

Gordon nodded, his eyes not leaving Agnes as she reached for the ice. "Makes you wonder..."

The sisters continued mixing drinks, oblivious to the brothers' scrutiny.

"Think he's gonna kill her?" Gordon mused.

"Don't be morbid," Cameron chided.

They stood on the lawn under a perfect night sky, waiting as their hosts fixed one last drink. Agnes apologized for Mason's behavior, bewildered by it herself. Heather laughed, sprawling on a nearby swing.

"Don't worry about the door," Agnes told Cameron, locking eyes.

❖

Driving home, slightly buzzed, Cameron kept it slow along the riverbank. The supermoon loomed over the twisting road, bathing everything in ghostly silver. Cameron's nerves crackled, whiskey-sharp senses merging with an ancient hunger. Night cloaked them like an old friend, granting precious freedom. Here, masks could slip, if only until dawn forced them back into their carefully constructed lives. For now, the darkness welcomed them home.

Gordon frowned. "You ever give off certain... vibes? Seriously."

Cameron checked the mirror, signaling. "That's behind me. Not on the agenda anymore."

Gordon whistled, impressed.

"I'm going to be good to Rhona," Cameron declared as they climbed into pine-covered hills. "Impeccable, even."

"Probably for the best," Gordon agreed.

Halfway home, police lights flashed. They pulled over.

CHAPTER 14

THE BORDERLANDS

LATE SUMMER, 1314

A chill wind swept across the Scottish Borderlands, carrying with it the acrid scent of smoke and the metallic tang of blood. The day's light was fading fast, the sun a mere sliver on the horizon, its dying rays barely penetrating the haze that hung over the devastated village below.

Robert Bruce, King of Scots, stood motionless atop a craggy hill, his silhouette stark against the deepening twilight. His eyes, sharp and alert despite the fatigue etched into every line of his face, scanned the ruined landscape before him. The set of his jaw spoke of a man pushed to his limits, yet unyielding in his resolve.

Around him, the eerie quiet was broken only by the occasional creak of leather as his men shifted restlessly, awaiting their king's command. The air was thick with tension, a palpable reminder of the grueling campaign that had brought them to this desolate spot.

"No survivors, sire," Sir James reported, his voice strained as he climbed up to join his king. He rolled his shoulder unconsciously, where the old scar burned beneath his armor.

Robert's jaw clenched, his hand instinctively tightening on the hilt of his silver-edged sword. "And the bodies?"

James hesitated, his eyes darting nervously to the lengthening shadows. "Gone. All of them." A shudder ran through his body, barely perceptible but not escaping Robert's watchful gaze.

A chill ran down Robert's spine that had nothing to do with the autumn air. "They're growing bolder," he muttered. "And hungrier."

As if in response, an inhuman shriek echoed from the nearby forest. Both men whirled, weapons half-drawn, hearts pounding. James's face contorted, a mix of pain and... something else flickering across his features.

"Your Majesty!" A young scout came racing towards them, terror etched on his face. "Movement in the trees – dozens of them!"

Robert's mind raced. The raid had been successful, driving the English further south, but this... this was no longer about Scottish independence. This was about survival. He watched James from the corner of his eye, noting how his friend's knuckles whitened on his sword hilt, veins pulsing visibly beneath pale skin.

"Sound the retreat," he ordered, his voice cutting through the growing panic. "We make for the coast. It's time we took this fight to Ireland." Then, lower, to James: "How are you holding up?"

James met Robert's gaze, his eyes fever-bright yet determined. "I'll manage, Your Majesty. But we'd best not linger. The night... it calls to me more strongly than ever."

Robert nodded grimly, clasping James's arm. "Stay strong, old friend. We've weathered five years of this curse; we'll see it through to the end."

As they turned to leave, James cast one last, longing look at the darkening forest, the internal struggle evident in every line of his body.

❖

As they thundered down the hillside, Robert shouted to his men, "Remember your training! They cannot cross running water!"

The forest behind them erupted with pale, twisted shapes.

Vampires, emboldened by the fading light, gave chase with inhuman speed. Their hollow eyes gleamed with hunger, lips pulled back in feral snarls.

"They're gaining!" James shouted, his voice tight with strain. Robert glanced over, alarmed to see his friend's face contorted in pain, eyes flickering between determination and an unsettling, feral gleam.

Robert's gaze locked onto a glimmer in the distance – a river, their salvation. "To the water!" he bellowed. "Don't stop for anything!"

The sound of pounding hooves was drowned out by the blood-curdling shrieks of their pursuers. A soldier at the rear of the group cried out in agony as cold, dead hands dragged him from his saddle.

Robert forced himself not to look back. "Leave him!" he commanded, even as his heart twisted. "We can't save him now!"

James let out a strangled cry, his horse veering dangerously. "The smell... Robert, I can't—" He clutched at his head, fighting an internal battle as fierce as the one raging around them.

The river grew closer, a lifeline in the growing darkness. But the vampires were relentless, their inhuman speed closing the gap with terrifying swiftness.

"They'll be on us before we reach it!" James shouted, desperation in his voice. His eyes now blazed with an unnatural light, teeth bared in a grimace that was half-pain, half-hunger.

Robert made a split-second decision. "James, take the men across! I'll hold them off!"

"Sire, no!" James's protest was a guttural growl.

"That's an order!" Robert roared, wheeling his horse around to face the oncoming horde. "And James... don't you dare look back. Keep riding, no matter what you hear. Promise me!"

James nodded jerkily, visibly wrestling for control as he led the men towards the water.

Time seemed to slow as Robert dismounted, his silver blade singing as he pulled it from its sheath. The first vampire reached him, its razor-sharp claws raking the air where his throat had been a heartbeat before.

Robert's sword flashed, cleaving through undead flesh with a sizzling hiss. Another monster lunged, and he barely managed to dodge, feeling the wind of its passage ruffle his hair.

Behind him, he could hear the splash of horses entering the water. "Go!" he shouted, not daring to take his eyes off the circling vampires. "Get to Ireland! Warn them!"

A vampire, bolder than the rest, charged. Robert met its attack with a ferocious counter-strike, his blade leaving a trail of fire as it separated the creature's head from its shoulders.

Each vampire he struck down only seemed to embolden the others, their relentless assault surging like a dark tide against his defenses. The night air thrummed with their collective hunger, an insatiable force that threatened to overwhelm him entirely. His arms burned with fatigue, each swing becoming more labored. A claw raked across his back, drawing blood, and Robert stumbled.

This is it, he thought grimly, bracing himself for the killing blow.

Suddenly, the night exploded with light. Blazing arrows arced overhead, slamming into the vampire horde with devastating effect. The monsters shrieked and writhed as holy fire consumed them.

"Robert!" A familiar voice cut through the chaos. "To the river, now!"

He turned to see Domhnall Ó Néill, High King of Ireland, leading a contingent of warriors across a narrow bridge. Their torches pushed back the encroaching darkness, creating a corridor of safety.

Robert didn't hesitate. He sprinted for the water, his legs burning with exertion. A vampire, more desperate than its brethren, made a final lunge for him.

Time slowed to a crawl. Robert could see the monster's lifeless eyes, feel its fetid breath on his neck. His foot touched the first plank of the bridge –

And the vampire slammed into an invisible barrier with bone-crushing force.

Robert stumbled across, gasping for air, as Domhnall's men formed a protective circle around him. The vampires howled in frustration on the far bank, unable to pursue.

"Cutting it a bit close there, King of Scots," Domhnall said with a grim smile, clasping Robert's arm.

Robert nodded, still catching his breath. "Your timing is impeccable, old friend. But how did you know?"

Domhnall's face darkened. "We've had our own troubles with these abominations. When we heard rumors of your campaign..." He trailed off, his eyes fixed on the seething mass of vampires across the river. "This is bigger than our petty rivalries now."

"Aye," Robert agreed, straightening up. His eyes scanned the group, searching for James. "If we don't stand together, there won't be a world left to rule. Something that doesn't seem to penetrate our friend Edward's thick skull."

❖

As dawn broke, Robert and Domhnall stood on the deck of an Irish ship, watching the Scottish coast recede into the distance. The vampire plague was spreading faster than anyone had feared.

"We'll need allies," Domhnall mused. "The English, the Welsh, anyone who'll listen."

Robert scoffed, a wry smile tugging at his lips. "The English? Good luck with that."

He glanced away, mind already racing with plans. "And weapons. Silver, blessed steel—anything that gives us an edge." His gaze shifted toward the ship's cabin, where James lay feverish and restless.

"And a cure," he added softly.

Domhnall followed his gaze. "How is he?"

"Fighting," Robert replied grimly. "But for how long? Five years he's held it at bay, but last night..." He trailed off, remembering James's agonized cries as they'd crossed the water.

A muffled groan emanated from below deck, followed by the sound of splintering wood. Robert's hand tightened on his sword hilt.

"I'll check on him," Domhnall offered, moving towards the cabin.

Before Robert could respond, a cry from the crow's nest interrupted them. "Ship ahead! Flying English colors!"

Both kings tensed. As the vessel drew closer, they saw it was listing badly, its sails in tatters.

"Survivors?" Domhnall wondered aloud, pausing at the cabin door.

Robert's eyes narrowed, acutely aware of the dual threats he now faced – one from without, and one from within. "Or a trap."

❖

As their ship pulled alongside the battered English vessel, an eerie silence settled over both crews. No movement, no signs of life.

"I don't like this," Domhnall muttered.

Robert felt it too – a prickling sensation at the base of his skull. Something was very, very wrong.

Suddenly, a figure burst from the English ship's hold – a woman, her clothes torn and bloodstained. "Help us!" she screamed. "For the love of God, help us!"

Before anyone could react, pale shapes surged up behind her. Vampires, dozens of them, their eyes gleaming with unholy hunger in the early morning light.

"Cut the lines!" Robert roared. "Get us away from them!"

But it was too late. The monsters leapt the narrow gap between ships with inhuman grace. The air filled with screams as they fell upon the unprepared crew.

Robert and Domhnall stood back-to-back, blades flashing as they fought for their lives. The deck ran red with blood, both human and the black ichor of the undead.

"We can't hold them!" Domhnall shouted over the din of battle.

Robert's mind raced, searching for a solution. Then he saw it – a faint line of mist on the horizon. "The shore!" he cried. "If we can make it to land–"

A vampire lunged at him, its fangs bared. Robert's sword took it in the chest, but the momentum carried them both over the railing and into the churning sea.

The icy water shocked Robert's system. He fought to the surface, gasping for air. The vampire thrashed beside him, its inhuman strength undiminished by the fall.

Robert's arms felt like lead as he struggled to keep the monster at bay. His vision began to darken at the edges. This can't be how it ends, he thought desperately.

Just as his strength was about to give out, a hand seized the back of his tunic. He was hauled unceremoniously back onto the deck, coughing and sputtering.

Domhnall stood over him, blood streaming from a gash on his forehead. "Not dying on me yet, are you?" he grinned, offering Robert a hand up.

Domhnall's ship shuddered as it ran aground, its wooden hull scraping against hidden rocks mere yards from the shoreline. On the main deck, Domhnall stood with his crew, their weapons at the ready. Beside them, Robert's men formed a formidable line, their determination palpable in the pre-dawn air.

Together, they had driven the vampires to the fore of the ship, cornering the creatures between their advancing forces and the lightening eastern sky. The vampires snarled and hissed, pressed against the railings, their eyes darting between their human adversaries and the shore tantalizingly close yet impossibly far.

One vampire, driven by desperation, leapt overboard, swimming furiously towards the land. The others watched intently, hope kindling in their eyes. But as it neared the shore, the swimming vampire suddenly went rigid. It thrashed once, twice, then disappeared beneath the waves with a final, strangled cry. The water churned briefly, then went still.

From the ship, it looked as though the vampire had simply vanished, leaving its companions bewildered and even more terrified. They pressed further back against the railings, now trapped between three deadly forces: the armed humans, the approaching sunrise, and the mysterious danger lurking in the water.

Domhnall's eyes narrowed with grim resolve as he surveyed the scene. As the first rays of sunlight crept over the horizon and the vampires' desperation grew, even his iron will began to waver at the impending carnage.

Robert stepped forward, his sword glinting in the growing light. "It's over, they have nowhere left to run."

❖

The undead flesh sizzled and smoked as the first rays of sunlight touched it. Monsters burst into flame, their agonized shrieks filling the air—a hellish chorus that would haunt the survivors' dreams for years to come.

In the silence that followed, Robert and Domhnall surveyed the carnage. Too many good men lost, but they had survived. For now.

"Robert," he said, breaking the heavy silence, "tell me this was worth it."

Robert's eyes remained fixed on the horizon, where the rising sun fought against lingering shadows. "It bought us time, nothing more." He turned to face Domhnall, his expression hardened by grim certainty. "They'll regroup, and when they do, Ireland will be their target."

Domhnall inhaled sharply. "Ireland? You're certain?"

"As sure as the tide," Robert nodded. "It's defensible, isolated. Perfect for a new stronghold."

The implications hung in the air between them. Domhnall's homeland, transformed into a bastion of the undead. The thought chilled him more than the morning air ever could.

"Then we have work to do," Domhnall said, his voice low but resolute.

Robert clasped his shoulder. "Aye, that we do. And precious little time to do it." He nodded, his eyes fixed on the horizon. The vampire plague was spreading, further than he'd feared. They had managed their way on a boat. What next? He silently prayed they weren't already too late to stem the tide of night that threatened to engulf them all.

A pained groan from behind made them both turn. James stumbled onto the deck, his normally robust frame now gaunt and trembling. His once-bright eyes were sunken and glazed with fever, his skin pale as parchment. Blood seeped through his bandages, but it wasn't his own.

"Robert," he rasped, his voice barely human, "I can't... I can't hold it back much longer."

Robert's hand moved to his sword, even as his heart broke for his oldest friend. "James, fight it. You must—"

Suddenly, James's head snapped up, nostrils flaring. His eyes, now glowing with an unnatural light, fixed on the crew members nearby. A feral grin spread across his face, revealing elongated canines.

"So much blood," he hissed, his gaze darting hungrily from one man to another.

Robert stepped between James and the crew, his sword half-drawn. The sun climbed higher, its light now illuminating a terrible truth: the battle against the darkness was no longer confined to the night.

It had found its way aboard their very ship.

CHAPTER 15

Brodie always figured Isobel's reluctance to have sex stemmed from a bad first experience. Something about Isobel nagged at Brodie, a puzzle he couldn't quite solve. Her guardedness went beyond simple caution or past hurt. At times, he caught a fleeting look in her eyes—something wild and unfathomable. It was there and gone in an instant, leaving him wondering if he'd imagined it. Whatever secret she carried, it ran bone-deep, setting her apart in ways he struggled to define.

He got it, sort of, but that didn't make the frustration any easier to swallow. When he stumbled across two condoms in her bag, his suspicions flared, and his mood soured even more than usual.

Isobel's yarn about her mum's rubbers - that they were her mom's preferred brand, and only she could explain their presence - was proper dodgy. He'd eat his hat if that wasn't a load of bullshit.

Sure, Brodie's parents sent cash, but between smokes, booze, drugs and other non-negotiables like his phone bill and keeping his tech up to date, he was stuck sharing a cramped apartment with five or six others. Sometimes a guy needed to breathe. He missed the days when Isobel's mom lived across the country. Back then, he could crash at a place where people weren't constantly tripping over each other, where some rando wasn't snoring on the couch, where he could use the bathroom without a midnight traffic jam. Even if it wasn't the coolest setup or exactly a sex-fest.

Isobel knew the score. She had to loosen up a bit or risk things going south with Brodie. The timing couldn't be worse. The condom situation was a tough pill to swallow - especially since Oliver had put the kibosh on them ages ago. And using Rhona's presence as an excuse to send Brodie packing for the night? That excuse was wearing thin.

Brodie wasn't a complete idiot. He got that girls had their own set of problems, even if he didn't fully understand them all. Not that it kept him up at night or anything. He had his own stuff to deal with. But there was something about Isobel he couldn't shake. Like she was always on edge, ready to bolt. Made him wonder what she was running from.

He hadn't forced himself on her yet. He made do with the occasional handjob and put up with her constant rejections. Part of it was because Isobel was the cream of the crop. Part of it was because, deep down, he wasn't a total jerk.

So he told her fine, whatever. He'd take the few nights a week - one or two, tops - that she was offering up. Still, he couldn't help but wonder where this sudden generosity was coming from. This olive branch extended less than a day after he'd found those supposed "mom condoms."

❖

One night when they were alone and Isobel was soaking in the tub - why she needed a bath after dodging him again was beyond him - he took the chance to snoop through Rhona's room.

He came up empty-handed, which only confirmed his suspicions that Rhona wasn't the one using them. Meanwhile, behind the bathroom door, Isobel silently wept in her bath.

Icy water swirled around her, but it couldn't touch the fire in her blood. Oliver's rejection stung, sure, but this—this was something else entirely. An electric current hummed beneath her skin, setting every nerve alight. Her fingertips dug into the tub's porcelain, desperate for an anchor as foreign sensations flooded her system. Something was changing, shifting deep inside her, and she was powerless to stop it.

❖

This session with Oliver was the last straw on an already hellish day. How she'd managed to hold it together was beyond her. Oliver had kicked her to the curb. She'd nearly lost it completely when he said he didn't want to see her anymore, that he didn't want her. She'd broken down in his office, clinging to his feet, making a spectacle of herself. He'd shoved her out, and they'd marched through the waiting room where people looked up from their magazines to see her thrashing like a lunatic, panting like a wild animal.

She'd spent the next three hours wandering aimlessly through the city streets before she could pull herself together. Guys had catcalled her, cars had nearly clipped her, panhandlers had grabbed at her sleeve, people had shoved past her, and dogs had sniffed at her heels. But nothing could distract her from the pain, nothing could stop the endless replay of her world crashing down around her.

Her tears mixed with the now-lukewarm bathwater, and all she felt was fear.

The nightmares were back, worse than ever. Anxiety attacks gripped her at random, leaving her gasping for air. Horrible flashes of... something... kept invading her thoughts. What the fuck was wrong with her? It felt like her body was waging war against her. One minute she was burning up, the next she was shivering. Her moods swung wildly, from rage to despair to a hunger she couldn't name. Her senses seemed sharper, overwhelming. It was like going through puberty all over again, but cranked up to eleven.

Brodie, sensing something was off, started keeping a closer eye on her.

❖

A freak accident unfolded the next day, revealing the dangerous depths of a mother's obsession with her sons.

Margaret's protective streak had morphed into something darker. Her watchful gaze now felt more like a hunter eyeing prey. Centuries of life seemed to have twisted her maternal instincts, leaving behind something feral and controlling. She micromanaged every aspect of her sons' lives with ruthless precision. The parking lot incident wasn't a one-off—it was the latest in a string of reckless moves, each more unhinged than the last. Her boys were starting to wonder if immortality had finally begun to fray their mother's sanity.

Rhona fumbled with her grocery bags as she stepped into the supermarket parking lot. The sun glinted off rows of cars, blinding her for a moment. That's when she heard it—the roar of an engine, far too close and getting closer.

Time slowed. Rhona's head snapped up, bags falling forgotten to the asphalt. A sleek, navy blur hurtled towards her, sunlight glinting off chrome. Her heart leapt into her throat as she stumbled backwards, certain she was about to become a hood ornament.

At the last possible second, the car swerved. It missed Rhona by inches, leaving her in a whirlwind of scattered groceries and the acrid stench of burning rubber.

The vehicle—a classic Aston Martin, Rhona realized with a jolt—careened across the lot. It plowed into a display caravan with a sickening crunch of metal and splintering wood. The flimsy camper exploded, showering the parking lot with debris of plastic and plywood.

Margaret, behind the wheel of her 1970 Aston Martin DBS/6—worth a cool $325,000—had nearly T-boned Rhona's modest BMW.

Witnesses swore it was a near-miss of biblical proportions. Margaret had come tearing in from the left like a bat out of hell, all wild eyes and white knuckles. Lucky for Rhona, Margaret's driving skills had always been more enthusiasm than talent. Her husband, Alistair, used to cringe watching her parallel park—a spectacle that often ended with dented fenders and mangled side mirrors.

This time, Margaret's aim was as poor as ever. Instead of Rhona's car, Margaret—760-year-old vampire and menace behind the wheel—plowed straight into a display caravan on the adjacent lot. The cheap, ultralight camper—built more for bargain hunters than road warriors—exploded into a shower of plastic and plywood.

As the dust settled, onlookers gaped at the devastation. The pristine Aston Martin now sported a crumpled hood, while the remains of the caravan littered the asphalt like confetti after a particularly rowdy parade. Rhona, still gripping her groceries, let out a shaky breath. She'd just dodged a bullet—or in this case, a high-powered luxury car piloted by a woman unhinged by grief and rage.

Margaret sat motionless in the car, her blank stare fixed on nothing. The impact shattered more than metal and glass. Something in Margaret broke, leaving her eyes hollow and vacant. That emptiness was more chilling than any rage. Her iron will had crumbled, revealing a yawning abyss beneath. Her mind reeled backwards through time, to an era when absolute control was her lifeline. Now, as that slipped away, she teetered on the edge of an oblivion deeper than any she'd known in her long, long life.

She didn't even attempt to get out of her car, as if she'd reached the edge of her world and found only emptiness.

❖

Though uninjured, her eerie silence prompted Dr. MacGregor to administer a strong sedative.

Dr. MacGregor treaded lightly, recognizing the razor's edge Margaret walked. This was more than her usual family drama—something had cracked her centuries-old composure. He'd seen glimpses of old wounds before, but this? This ran deeper than anything he'd witnessed in all their years. What happened two decades ago had left scars that refused to heal, festering beneath the surface. It had shaken their family to its core, worse than anything in seven centuries of turbulent history. MacGregor would do what he could, but he knew some damage went beyond modern medicine's reach.

In this moment, the Bruce family stood on a precipice, teetering on the edge of chaos. Rhona tried to downplay the incident, but the Bruce men couldn't shake their deep concern. Dr. MacGregor's inability to guarantee Margaret wouldn't try again in the coming days only heightened their worry.

As darkness fell, they paced the living room, searching for a solution that would cause the least damage. But their emotions ran wild, each grappling with their complicated feelings for Margaret. Even Rhona, not yet officially part of the family but already entangled with one of the sons, found herself swept up in the turmoil. She knew that dealing with Margaret would become her problem too, once she joined the Bruce clan.

❖

The air in the room grew thick with tension as night deepened, their minds a swirl of love, fear, and uncertainty. The night wrapped around the Bruce family like an old, familiar coat. For centuries, darkness had been their ally, concealing secrets older than nations. But tonight, the shadows felt hungry, pressing in from all sides. The night no longer offered sanctuary—it had become a cage.

How could they protect Margaret from herself without destroying the delicate balance of their family?

Rhona's mind drifted to her abandoned groceries. Her yogurt, butter, and low-fat cottage cheese were probably spoiled in the warm car. Oddly, she didn't feel like she'd narrowly escaped disaster. She couldn't even picture Margaret trying again, despite it being her own life at stake. To Rhona, the whole incident felt more like a bad prank than a real murder attempt.

The Bruce men, however, saw it differently. This was no joke to them.

Their immediate plan was simple: Margaret couldn't be left alone for a second. Cameron thumbed through his contacts, calling nurses until his finger hovered over Fiona's name.

Why not? He wasn't entirely sure. He rang Gordon, who shared his uncertainty but agreed to talk to Fiona. Gordon added that the job might be a good distraction for Fiona, considering her recent tragedy. The poor woman was on leave, reeling from the loss of her son. Maybe caring for Margaret could give her a sense of purpose again.

"You're certain this young woman is up to the task?" Alistair Bruce asked, wincing as his back twinged.

Fiona did have her merits: she was available, had nursing credentials, and never balked at extra work to pay the bills. It wasn't a perfect solution, but it was a start.

❖

As darkness fell, a familiar tension crept over the Bruces. Night's embrace felt like a tightening noose. Their difference from mortal families had never been so stark. Margaret's breakdown was just the newest crack in their meticulously crafted veneer.

They'd found a temporary fix, but the underlying problem – Margaret's fragile state – loomed large. How long could they keep this up, and what would it cost them all in the end?

The family's tension eased slightly as they settled on a short-term solution. It bought them time to think, whether Fiona or someone else took on the job.

"But what's to stop her trying again?" Isobel demanded the moment she arrived.

Her question hit them like a splash of cold water. Shadows crossed their faces as they confronted the heart of the problem.

"You're right to ask," Gordon sighed. "I ask myself the same thing about repeat offenders."

Isobel's mood had been foul for days. She couldn't care less about their hand-wringing. All she saw was a madwoman who'd tried to kill her mother. She wanted to know how these three men planned to neutralize the threat.

As Isobel grilled his sons, Alistair Bruce sidled up to Rhona. He apologized on behalf of the whole family.

"I notice," he confided, his voice low, "they haven't torn each other apart yet. Do you think that's coming soon?"

Rhona eyed Alistair Bruce warily. Despite being Isobel's grandfather, he was practically a stranger. Years ago, his dislike for her had been clear, but they'd never truly spoken.

"You understand her though," he added softly. "That's a gift. She's not a bad woman, you know."

Rhona shrugged, downplaying the incident. "I hope everyone just forgets about it," she said.

"You're completely mental," Isobel snapped, her face twisted with disgust.

Sensing the storm brewing, Rhona decided it was time to go. She tugged Isobel's sleeve, but her daughter jerked away. "Thanks. I'm old enough to make my own choices."

They left in separate cars, racing along the river. At a red light, Rhona pulled up close behind Isobel's Mini Cooper. Their eyes met briefly in the rearview mirror. Rhona grabbed her phone, desperate to talk, but her stubborn daughter let it ring.

❖

Rhona eyed the kitchen, a spark of an idea forming. "How about some spaghetti? Brodie's out, so let's take advantage." She glanced at Isobel, hoping for a positive response. "Would you mind pouring me a drink?"

As Rhona busied herself at the stove, cigarette dangling from her lips, she silently celebrated that Isobel hadn't retreated to her room. The haunting melody of Depeche Mode's "Enjoy the Silence" drifted through the air. Isobel sat nearby, crunching on peanuts and furiously swiping through Instagram. Rhona wondered if the song choice was a subtle dig or just coincidence. Either way, the irony wasn't lost on her.

Rhona's hand hovered over the cayenne, then pulled back. Isobel's complaints about spice irritating her ass came to mind. Sometimes, the simple fact of having a daughter - her own child - hit Rhona like a wave of pure joy. It swelled in her chest, intoxicating and all-encompassing, before dissipating into the air around her.

If Isobel admitted to one undeniable talent her mother possessed, it was Rhona's way with pasta. As the familiar scents filled the kitchen, Isobel spoke up, her voice carrying a hint of vulnerability beneath the bravado.

"I don't want to live in constant fear that something might happen to you," she said. "If that's not asking too much."

Since their reunion, Rhona often felt the mother-daughter roles had flipped. Isobel's time living in her grandparents' house for university had shifted the dynamic. Though unsettling, Rhona didn't plan on this arrangement lasting. Soon, she hoped, she'd navigate out of these choppy waters and reclaim her rightful place. Maybe she'd even hear "Mum" again.

For now, she had to tread carefully. Rhona promised to be more vigilant, then changed the subject. "Your eyes look irritated. Is it because of the dentist?"

Isobel brushed off the question, but Rhona hadn't forgotten her old tricks.

Later, as they settled on the couch, Rhona reached out to stroke her daughter's hair. The gesture had an almost primal effect on

Isobel. Despite her earlier resistance, she found herself melting into the soothing, familiar touch.

"You might want to try a clarifying shampoo," Rhona suggested, her tone warm and caring. The gentleness broke through Isobel's defenses.

Isobel's eyes darted away, her fingers twisting in her lap. "Oliver..." she started, then swallowed hard. "He dumped me. Now it's all screaming and threats when he calls." Her voice cracked. "Says he'll beat me if we cross paths."

She bit her lip, shoulders hunching. "We met up. Twice. Yesterday, he..." Isobel's words came out in a rush, "He just used me. Tossed me out after fucking me. Didn't let me say a word."

Her eyes met Rhona's, raw and vulnerable. "I'm a fucking mess, Mum. Falling to pieces over here."

Rhona retreated to the kitchen, returning with a chocolate bar. "I don't get how such a bastard can affect you like this."

Isobel looked up, her eyes glistening. How could she explain? It wasn't logical or calculated. The forces pulling her towards Oliver defied reason. She didn't even try to put it into words.

"What about Brodie?" Rhona ventured. "Is he really so bad?"

Surprise flashed across Rhona's face when Isobel revealed she and Brodie had never been truly intimate. Their relationship seemed oddly complex, but Rhona held her tongue, keeping her opinions to herself.

Isobel paused, her brow furrowing slightly. "It's just... Brodie, you know?" She wrinkled her nose, searching for words. "There's this weird smell about him sometimes. Like, I dunno, old socks mixed with wet dog?" She shrugged, looking uncomfortable. "It's probably nothing, but it bugs me."

❖

For once, they shared the bathroom without comment. The city's oddities had become routine. They stripped to their underwear, wiping away makeup in companionable silence.

"I wouldn't call that love," Rhona said, her voice gentle but firm. "Sexual satisfaction is one thing, and I'm not dismissing it. We're animals, sure, but don't let it consume you. You're no more in love with Oliver than I was with your father, who... well, he satisfied me that way for a long time."

Isobel's eyebrows shot up. "Really? That's news."

"Maybe. There's still a lot you don't know."

"It feels like a drug," Isobel admitted, shame coloring her cheeks. "I'm a mess around him."

She glanced at Rhona, then started brushing her teeth. Rhona smoothed cream over her face.

After a quick rinse, Isobel asked, "Can you treat being a sex addict?"

"I don't know," Rhona replied thoughtfully. "But it's not the worst thing. Life's full of troubles, not to scare you."

She studied her daughter, then added, "Vampires used to roam the countryside, killing humans. Think about it – you could've been born with a hunchback or during the polio epidemic."

❖

Fiona arrived at the Bruces' manor early the next morning, her heart pounding. Gordon had left ahead of her to maintain a professional distance. He opened the door with a tight smile, tension crackling between them.

Fiona had done her best to look presentable. A touch of powder brought color to her pale cheeks, and she held her shoulders straight despite feeling like a shadow of herself. Cameron and his father greeted her warmly, aware of the rumors about Scotland cutting hospital beds. They knew she needed this job desperately.

Without a word, they led her upstairs to Margaret's room. The elderly woman was wrestling with her pillows when they entered.

Fiona's nursing instincts kicked in immediately as she adjusted them, introducing herself with a gentle smile.

Later, she confided to Gordon, "I like Margaret. I think we'll get along just fine."

They spent the afternoon together as a trial run. In those few hours, Fiona learned more about the family's tumultuous past than she had in all her clandestine digging with Gordon.

❖

That evening, she sat at her kitchen table, organizing her new schedule. She'd agreed to day shifts and – after some quick mental math – five nights a week at Margaret's bedside. The paycheck would be worth the long hours.

While Gordon went out for pizzas, Fiona packed a suitcase for herself and her daughter.

Gordon returned to find Fiona at the kitchen table, her daughter cradled in her lap. Tears streaked her face as she clutched a terry cloth pajama top – a relic from the one they dared not name. The sight of forgotten belongings in the cupboards had opened the floodgates of grief.

She met Gordon's eyes with a look of utter despair that quickly morphed to anger as he sliced the steaming pizzas. The rhythmic scrape of the cutter seemed to mock their shared pain.

Helpless in the face of her sorrow, Gordon wordlessly carried the suitcases to the car. Fiona's muffled sobs followed him out the door.

Outside, dusk painted the street in ominous shades of red. Gordon activated the alarm, the soft beep a stark contrast to the turmoil within. As he closed the door, a wave of defeat washed over him. This simple act felt like sealing away any hope of normalcy, leaving them trapped in a prison of memories.

❖

Dr. MacGregor was back, his face unnaturally smooth and rosy from cosmetic procedures. His strange new grimace sent seven-year-old Amelia scurrying behind her mother's skirts, refusing to say goodnight.

Alistair Bruce stood nearby, one hand on his aching back, the other gripping Gordon's shoulder. He let out a weary sigh as Dr. MacGregor rattled off instructions to Fiona.

"Constant supervision is key until Margaret stabilizes," the doctor emphasized, detailing medication schedules and procedures. His gaze softened as he added, "I know you've been through trauma yourself, Fiona, but try not to let that cloud seep into Margaret's space. Keep her room bright – fresh flowers daily, curtains open to let the sun in."

Fiona nodded, her spine straightening. "You don't need to worry about my professionalism, Doctor. I've never had complaints about my bedside manner."

Her words carried a hint of steel beneath the reassurance. She might be battered by life, but her skills as a nurse were beyond reproach. As Dr. MacGregor continued his instructions, Fiona's mind was already planning – arranging Margaret's care while navigating the minefield of Bruce family tensions.

Gordon patted his father's hand reassuringly as Alistair shuffled off to get water for his pills. He then turned his attention back to Dr. MacGregor and Fiona, catching the tail end of their conversation.

As he watched Fiona stand tall, embracing her role with quiet determination, Gordon felt a surge of admiration. This woman had been through hell, yet here she was, ready to take on whatever came next. He hoped this new chapter might breathe life back into her – into both of them.

His gaze lingered on Fiona, his mind drifting to memories of intimate moments shared. He pushed those thoughts aside, focusing on the present. They had work to do.

❖

Gordon's room was a mess, and he busied himself tidying up while keeping an eye on Fiona. Together, they created a cozy nest for Amelia using couch cushions. He set up a privacy screen and placed her favorite lamp nearby – the one with the spiky shade she insisted was "hair."

With Amelia settled, they headed back downstairs. Alistair and Dr. MacGregor were preparing to leave when his father dropped an unexpected piece of information.

"Cameron called," Alistair said, his tone heavy with implication. "He asked the doctor to look into a dentist named Oliver Purvis." He fixed Gordon with a pointed look. "Any idea where he was calling from?"

Gordon shook his head, a familiar knot of unease tightening in his stomach.

"Really?" Alistair pressed, his disbelief evident. "You've no idea at all?"

Dr. MacGregor adjusted his Panama hat over his hair implants and headed for the door. "Change doesn't always mean progress," he mused cryptically.

As the doctor left, Alistair growled in Gordon's ear, "What's he doing at political meetings?"

"I suppose he's interested," Gordon offered weakly.

Alistair's glare could have melted steel. Pain etched his features as he eased his aching body into the Aston Martin, moving like a wounded crab.

❖

Once alone, Gordon gave Fiona a whirlwind tour. He showed her the kitchen gadgets, entertainment system, climate controls, and music setup. Upstairs, he pointed out toiletries and linens.

"I could run you a bath," he offered, hoping to recapture some of their lost intimacy.

Fiona shook her head. "I should check on Margaret first." She hesitated, then asked the question that had been nagging at her. "Where am I supposed to sleep?"

Gordon's mind reeled, caught off guard by Fiona's directness. He stammered, searching for words.

"I don't think I was hired to spend the night in your bed," Fiona stated, her tone firm but not unkind.

The truth of her words hit him like a punch to the gut. Desperate, he grasped at straws, mentioning his mother's sedatives, hoping to negotiate some private time with Fiona.

"Listen, Gordon," she sighed, "we're not there yet."

"Then where are we?" he demanded, grabbing her wrist. "What's going to happen?"

Fiona's eyes flashed with a pain Gordon couldn't begin to understand. If she hadn't been with him, her son might still be alive. The thought haunted her, poisoning every interaction. If Gordon knew how much she struggled just to let him sleep beside her, he'd be horrified.

"Nothing is going to happen," she said, her voice flat. "I need a bed, that's all. I'll sleep in Margaret's room. I'm not here for anything else."

Her words hung in the air, heavy with finality. The distance between them, once measured in inches, now felt like miles.

Gordon's words hung heavy in the air, raw with emotion. "We're slowly disappearing, gnawing ourselves with remorse every time we open our eyes."

Fiona felt the truth of it deep in her bones. She didn't want to lose him, not really. Earlier, as she'd taken in the breathtaking view of the city lights beyond the river, admired the elegant furniture, the sprawling garden, the sheer spaciousness of it all, her heart had raced. For a fleeting moment, she'd seen herself here not as a nurse, but as Fiona Bruce, mistress of this grand house.

Now, as Gordon pulled her into his arms, she didn't resist. Fresh tears spilled down her cheeks, mourning not just their shared loss, but the future that seemed to be slipping away. She was acutely aware of the massive waste – of love, of potential, of the life they could have had.

❖

The Bruces breathed a deep sigh of relief. Fiona was thriving in her new role, while Margaret's recovery progressed smoothly. Already, the family matriarch wandered the house in her pajamas, even venturing a few steps into the garden—a promising sign of normalcy returning.

Dr. MacGregor's frequent house calls were more than a testament to the Bruces' status as valued patients—they were the culmination of a lifetime's work and millions in strategic investments. Privy to the family's secret, he treated them with a blend of scientific curiosity and genuine care that transcended ordinary doctor-patient relationships.

The Bruces had poured millions into financing MacGregor's state-of-the-art private facility—a veritable fortress of medical innovation hidden from the world. This secret vampire clinic, equipped with cutting-edge technology and staffed by a carefully vetted team, stood as a testament to the family's commitment to pushing the boundaries of their existence.

Their vampiric nature offered MacGregor unprecedented research opportunities. Immune to common ailments, they allowed him to explore bolder treatments and radical approaches that challenged the very foundations of medical science. The ongoing "sunlight issue" was just one of many challenges he tackled, each breakthrough potentially revolutionizing both vampire and human medicine.

This symbiotic relationship ran deep, fueled by shared secrets and mutual benefits. MacGregor's dedication stemmed from more than the generous funding or scientific curiosity; an unspoken, unrequited love for Margaret Bruce had driven decades of vampire-focused R&D, blurring the lines between personal and professional obsession.

In the end, the millions invested had bought more than just medical care. They had secured unwavering loyalty, cutting-edge treatments, and a tireless quest to enhance and protect the Bruces' immortal lives—all while advancing medical science in ways the outside world could scarcely imagine.

His glowing reports about Fiona only reinforced their decision to bring her into their world.

Gordon had a bed installed in Margaret's spacious room for Fiona, hoping she might not use it. Yet night after night, he found himself lying awake, ears straining for footsteps that never came. He'd stare at the half-open door, willing it to move, but Fiona never appeared. The empty space beside him in his own room became a constant ache, a reminder of the distance between them.

Mornings fell into a routine. Gordon dropped Amelia at school before heading to work, while Fiona quietly prepared Margaret's breakfast. In the afternoons, he'd pick up his little Amelia, always double-checking her seatbelt with a mix of parental concern and something deeper. Sometimes, he'd treat her to ice cream, cautioning her not to spill.

"Be careful, sweetheart," he'd say, watching her in the rearview mirror. In those moments, when Amelia was occupied with her treat, Gordon found himself lost in thought, the complexity of their family's unique situation a constant companion even in these ordinary moments.

❖

Dr. MacGregor's assessment of Fiona's reluctance didn't surprise Gordon. The doctor had explained that many women, after losing a child, either sought solace in religious life or withdrew emotionally. His advice was characteristically blunt: take it slow, focus on her pleasure, and find her G-spot as soon as possible. And if things didn't improve, bring her in for a consultation.

"We'll figure something out," MacGregor had assured him with a wink. The doctor's reputation for "boosting levels" was well-earned, and Margaret swore by his expertise. Their history went back decades—to when an 18-year-old MacGregor first laid eyes on Margaret outside the medical faculty. Since then, he'd performed countless procedures on Margaret: micro skin enhancements, flawless plastic surgeries, and breast implants that defied her true age. No one dared speak ill of the man who kept a 763-year-old vampire looking timeless.

But as Gordon mulled over the doctor's words, doubt crept in. Could MacGregor truly restore Fiona to her former self? Bring life back to emotionally deadened flesh? Did his medical prowess extend that far?

Gordon's gut told him no. Some wounds, he feared, ran too deep for even the most skilled hands to heal.

❖

Sometimes, Gordon caught snippets of laughter drifting from his mother's room - Margaret and Fiona sharing a moment of levity. At the distillery, he'd watch his brother, thoughts of Rhona flickering unbidden through his mind. But the moment he stepped into the manor, all else faded. He found himself caught in Fiona's orbit, desperate to glimpse even a fraction of her former warmth.

The other night, they'd watched a movie with Margaret, who still nursed a rebellious gin instead of the family whisky. Gordon couldn't have recounted the plot if his life depended on it. His senses were overwhelmed by Fiona's presence - the tantalizing curve of her thigh, the soft rise and fall of her chest with each breath. When she shifted, oblivious to his gaze, his eyes traced the line of her body, lingering on the junction of her thighs. He ached for Fiona, a bone-deep longing that consumed his thoughts. Gordon's mind wandered to memories of her body - the soft weight of her breasts in his hands, the heat of her core against him. The absence of her touch left him raw, every fiber of his being crying out for the intimacy they once shared.

In quiet moments, he'd close his eyes, letting vivid recollections wash over him - the taste of her skin, the sound of her pleasure. Heat pooled low in his belly, his penis getting hard, desire thrumming through his veins. He imagined the warmth of her skin beneath his fingertips, the taste of her lips. Each stolen glance fed a torrent of increasingly vivid fantasies, leaving Gordon flushed and aching, trapped in a prison of his own making.

❖

Mornings found Gordon pounding the pavement at five sharp. As dawn broke, mist still clinging to the ground, he'd run along the river path. Elbows tucked, jaw set, he pushed himself harder each day. Across the water, glass buildings emerged from the shadows like silent sentinels. The air, not yet choked with exhaust, carried the scent of damp earth and river mud - smells that crawled and floated, reminding him of a world beyond his troubles.

He'd run his route twice, pausing to catch his breath on North Bridge. Its four majestic arches spanned the Water of Leith, and Gordon would lean over the railing, staring into the depths below as if they held answers to his fate.

Little did Gordon know, unseen eyes watched his morning ritual. Someone, working in the shadows, had taken a vested interest in his daily routine.

❖

One morning, Margaret stirred earlier than usual. She padded over to Fiona's single bed, where the young woman slept soundly. The Scottish summer, mild as it was, had caused Fiona's sheet to slip away. Margaret noted her choice of sleepwear - just a bra and panties - but didn't linger on the thought. Instead, she studied Fiona with keen interest.

Fiona possessed a raw sensuality, features that weren't classically perfect yet seemed designed to entice. Margaret's eyes traced Fiona's sleeping form, a jolt of recognition hitting her like a physical force. The young woman's body was a masterpiece of carnal allure, every curve and dip crafted to ignite primal hunger. Her breasts, full and perfectly shaped, seemed to defy gravity even as she lay still. Fiona's skin gleamed with an otherworldly sheen, begging to be touched.

Margaret felt a twinge of long-forgotten desire stir within her, understanding viscerally the torment her son must endure. Fiona's slightly parted lips, the gentle rise and fall of her chest, the tantalizing glimpse of hip where her panties rode low - it all coalesced into a siren call of raw sexuality. Even asleep, Fiona radiated an energy that seemed to charge the very air around her.

This wasn't mere beauty; it was intoxication made flesh. Margaret could almost taste the temptation, feeling a phantom ache deep in her core. She understood now why Gordon seemed to orbit Fiona like a man possessed. To be near such potent sensuality and denied its fulfillment - it would drive anyone to the brink of madness.

Fiona lay there, oblivious, bathed in the soft pre-dawn light. Margaret saw more than just a beautiful young woman - she saw potential salvation for their family.

Despite her own condition, Margaret wasn't so addled as to misunderstand Fiona's likely hopes for a relationship with Gordon. Her son had that effect on women - hundreds had fallen under his spell. Of her two boys, he was the more reserved, yet exuded an undeniable deeper elegance.

Margaret sighed softly, weighing the complexities of their situation against the promise Fiona represented.

Margaret's earlier reservations about Fiona seemed laughable now. Gone were the days when she might have scoffed at the girl's tight jeans, and that bosom, my God. In this moment of crisis, Fiona was nothing short of a godsend.

It was painfully obvious to Margaret - as it would be to anyone with eyes - that Gordon and Fiona's physical relationship had ground to a halt. This realization stirred a mix of sympathy and alarm within her. The last thing their family needed was for Gordon to end up alone, especially now. With Rhona's arrival, Margaret could already see the cursed love triangle reforming, its fiery outline hovering ominously over their heads.

Her gaze roved over Fiona's form once more. The girl was well-built, with a substantial backside that aligned perfectly with Gordon's tastes. That natural, earthy allure that had once irked Margaret now seemed their salvation.

Margaret's mind raced. They couldn't afford to let this opportunity slip away. With Fiona's raw sensuality and their desperate circumstances, a plan began to form. It was time to take matters into her own hands, to ensure that the primal connection between Gordon and Fiona ignited fully. The future of their family might very well depend on it.

Decision made, Margaret steeled herself. It was time to seize this chance, consequences be damned.

❖

In the hours that followed, Margaret transformed. It was hard to reconcile this vibrant woman with the one who, mere days ago, had teetered on the brink of madness. Gone was the shuffling zombie; in her place stood a force of nature. She'd applied makeup with a deft hand and donned a dress by Yohji Yamamoto, her favorite Japanese designer, all flowing lines and delicate florals. Her cane lay forgotten.

Over lunch, Margaret lamented not meeting Fiona sooner. Their afternoon walk in the estate gardens ended with a pointed conversation on the doorstep. "Men are simple creatures," Margaret confided, her tone matter-of-fact. "It's unfortunate, but that's how it is. We can't change everything, you know. Sometimes, we must be practical."

Later, while arranging flowers like an expert, she nudged Fiona to consider her future - and Amelia's. The younger woman watched Margaret's sure hands manipulating the pruning shears, acutely aware that the family matriarch was far more lucid than she'd first appeared.

❖

Cameron, however, felt uneasy. Things were progressing too smoothly for his liking. It wasn't anxiety exactly - that wasn't his nature - but a nagging sense that this victory had come too easily. He couldn't shake the feeling that the other shoe was about to drop.

He brooded, the lingering taste of hollow victory souring his mood. Alison Stewart's words from the other night echoed in his mind. At some model's umpteenth engagement party, amidst a sea of drunken kisses, she'd pointed out how Gordon's absence had cleared his path.

"Is that why you told Rhona about us?" he'd shot back, his tone deceptively casual. "You think I need a handicap?"

Alison had stiffened, recognizing the veiled threat in his words. Alison's eyes narrowed to slits. "Spare me," she hissed. "Rhona's my best friend. She'd have known eventually." A razor-thin smile. "What, Cameron? Truth stings?"

His lack of reaction had been oddly unsettling.

❖

Now, basking in the afterglow of sex with Rhona, Cameron finally voiced the question that had been gnawing at him. As she lay draped across his chest, lost in thought, he asked what she made of it all.

"It's a pointless question," Rhona murmured, her fingers tracing idle patterns on his skin.

"It matters to me," Cameron pressed, a hint of intensity creeping into his voice. "I want to know the difference, now. We nearly tore each other apart, Gordon and I, because you wouldn't choose."

"I couldn't choose," Rhona said, suddenly rolling onto her stomach to face him. Her eyes locked onto his, intense and unapologetic. "I loved you both. Was crazy about both of you, if you want the truth. Torn right down the middle."

Cameron's brow furrowed, genuine confusion etching his features. "Alright, you couldn't choose then. But now? What changed? How did we end up here, in this bed?"

Silence stretched between them, heavy with unspoken words.

"If you don't know," he pressed, his voice low and tinged with frustration, "who could?"

❖

The Bruce Distillery buzzed with excitement as the Scottish National Whisky Festival kicked off. For one wild week each year, the grounds transformed into a grand fair, drawing whisky enthusiasts from far and wide. This was the event for tasting and deals, where visitors could snag anything from a prized single bottle to an entire collector's case.

Bruce wasn't just any brand. With nearly 300 years of Highland history, they were whisky royalty, commanding respect in the Scotch market. Rare whisky had become the hottest collectible of the decade, and Bruce was at the center of it all.

The festival atmosphere was intoxicating. The air filled with the mingled scents of fried fair food and rich spirits. Laughter and chatter drowned out the clink of sample glasses. Archie, ever the culinary mastermind, had set up shop right in the thick of it all. His food stall was a whirlwind of activity, churning out mountains of crispy fish and chips, along with other Scottish favorites. The aroma of vinegar-doused chips wafted through the fairgrounds, drawing hungry festival-goers like a siren's call.

It was a far cry from the somber mood that had gripped the community after last month's explosion. That dark memory seemed to fade in the warm glow of Highland hospitality and Archie's comfort food.

For seven days, the Bruce brothers worked tirelessly. They shook countless hands, entertained families, and doled out free whisky samples. They watched children dash about in Bruce-branded caps, giggling as their parents savored sips of amber gold. Archie, for his part, barely had a moment to breathe between orders, his kitchen staff moving like a well-oiled machine to keep up with the demand for his famous chips.

But behind their cheerful facade, a weight pressed down on the brothers. While they poured drinks and shared stories, their thoughts strayed to their own tangled love lives. Keeping up the act from dawn to dusk was becoming its own kind of endurance test.

❖

At dusk, when they closed shop and Heather proudly announced the day's figures, the Bruce brothers merely nodded with exhausted sighs. As the festival's last echoes faded, a bone-deep weariness settled over them. It wasn't just tired muscles and late nights—this fatigue ran soul-deep, the price of endless years spent crafting their human charade. For a brief moment, they'd lost themselves in the crowd's energy and chaos. Now, harsh reality rushed back in. Shadows stretched across the streets, bringing with them that old, familiar knot of dread. Another night of pretending loomed ahead.

Also, the near-absence of Ted, their veteran salesman, was keenly felt. Ted's absence left a gaping hole in the festival's fabric. Usually, he'd be the ringmaster of this whisky circus, drawing crowds with his charm and showmanship. Instead, the brothers found themselves scrambling to fill his shoes, juggling roles they'd never had to before.

Ted split his time between the hospital—where his wife Adele remained under observation after suffering a cardiac arrest during childbirth—and brief, somber visits to the distillery. The extra workload was almost a welcome distraction for the brothers.

As they worked, pouring drams and spinning tales for eager tourists, a part of them ached for Ted's easy laughter, for the normality his presence brought to their abnormal lives. The festival felt off-kilter, a circus missing its star performer. Yet they pressed on, finding strange comfort in the exhaustion that came with picking up the slack.

❖

Gordon seized the chance for an early night. He found a moment of peace reading to Amelia, whose delighted goodnight kiss was a balm to his worn spirit. At least someone showed him affection, he thought bitterly. Fiona remained distant, using Margaret as a shield and keeping Gordon at arm's length.

Over dinner, Cameron watched his brother with growing concern. He marveled at Gordon's patience, waiting for Fiona to lower her defenses. In Cameron's eyes, her guilt had become a crutch, and he wished for his brother's sake that she'd move past it. Centuries of existence had rendered death so mundane to them that Cameron found himself almost irritated by Fiona's prolonged mourning. Gordon deserved better, he thought, a frown creasing his brow as he observed the strained silence between the couple.

As the meal ended and they cleared the table, Cameron caught Gordon's eye. A silent exchange passed between them - part sympathy, part frustration. The festival might be in full swing outside, but within the Bruce household, a different kind of tension simmered.

❖

After Gordon turned in, Cameron found himself lingering downstairs. He stood at the window, unease prickling along his spine. The encroaching darkness felt alive tonight, heavy with anticipation. He'd lived long enough to recognize the calm before a storm, and every instinct screamed that their carefully constructed world was about to shatter.

Night had always been their refuge, but now it felt like a trap closing in. Shadows writhed at the edge of his vision, as if they had a will of their own. Cameron's mind drifted through centuries of memories, searching for a threat to match this nameless dread.

He pressed a hand against the cool glass, anchoring himself in the present. Whatever was coming, it would find them ready. They'd weathered worse. But deep down, a voice whispered that this time might be different. This time, the darkness might not be content to simply hide their secrets—it might devour them whole.

Exhaustion tugged at him, but he wasn't quite ready for bed. He settled into the living room, where Margaret was already ensconced. Fiona busied herself in the kitchen, the gentle clink of cups suggesting she was preparing tea.

"Fiona is a perfect nurse, she is working out wonderfully," Margaret confided, her eyes bright. "I'm considering keeping her on longer. What do you think, dear?"

Cameron mumbled a noncommittal response, suddenly very interested in the newspaper. He wasn't ready to wade into those waters tonight.

Fiona joined them, setting down a tray of steaming cups. Cameron watched her over the rim of his cup, curiosity and concern warring within him. He found himself imagining a future where she was truly part of the family, where her children played with his own. The thought was both comforting and unsettling.

Margaret had dozed off in her chair, lulled by some documentary droning on about the hunting strategies of apex predators in the Serengeti. Cameron seized the moment, turning to Fiona. His eyes, sharp and unblinking, locked onto his target as he prepared to pounce on this rare moment of vulnerability.

"We need to talk," he began, his voice low and earnest.

But his attempt at a heart-to-heart backfired spectacularly. His words, meant to heal, only seemed to reopen old wounds. Fiona's face clouded over, and she fled the room without a word.

Minutes later, carried on the cool night air, Cameron heard it – a muffled sob from the garden. He sat there, frozen, torn between going to her and respecting her need for space. The stars wheeled silently overhead, bearing silent witness to the pain below.

CHAPTER 16

DUNFERMLINE ABBEY

5 MARCH 1324

Robert paced the cold stone corridor, each step echoing like a war drum. The muffled cries from the birthing chamber clawed at his nerves. He clenched his fists, silently willing Elisabeth to deliver a son – an heir to secure his tenuous grip on Scotland's throne.

"A boy," he muttered, his voice hoarse. "It must be a boy." He paused, a new thought crossing his mind. "I don't want to submit my daughters to this nightmare. I don't ever want them to see this horror," Robert thought. The vampires had evolved. Some of them were no longer bound by the night.

The words tasted bitter. How often had he heard them from his own father's lips? Robert had been barely more than a child himself when the sacerdoce of the Bruce legacy had been thrust upon his shoulders. Now, at forty-eight, that sacred responsibility felt heavier than ever.

He'd thought, foolishly, that the months of Elisabeth's pregnancy would offer a respite from the constant strain of leadership. A chance to focus on family, on the future. How wrong he'd been. If anything, the waiting had proven more harrowing than battling

English armies – or even the supernatural horrors that lurked in Scotland's shadows.

Robert's hand unconsciously went to the silver crucifix at his throat, a talisman against the darkness.

His thoughts flitted briefly to his daughters, Marjorie and Matilda, safely ensconced at Turnberry Castle. He'd sent them away months ago, as rumors of renewed English aggression grew. Part of him ached to have them close, but he knew they were safer far from the intrigues of court and the looming specter of war.

The memory of glowing red eyes and razor-sharp fangs flashed through his mind. He'd faced down vampires, creatures of nightmare that threatened to drain Scotland's very lifeblood. Yet somehow, the muffled sounds of Elisabeth's labor filled him with a more primal dread.

"At least with the bloodsuckers," he muttered, "I knew where I stood."

Another pained cry echoed from the chamber, and Robert's pacing quickened. The fate of his dynasty, of Scotland itself, hung in the balance. And all he could do was wait, haunted by memories of battles past and the terrifying unknowns of the future.

As the wait stretched on, other memories assaulted him, joyful ones, vivid as fever dreams. He saw again the day his father had set him on the path to kingship, a day that had shaped the man – and the ruler – he'd become.

Lochmaben Castle
1292

Robert's jaw dropped. "You can't be serious." He gaped at his father, struggling to process the bombshell. "I'm eighteen, for crying out loud!"

The elder Bruce's eyes were as hard as Scottish granite. "Old enough to rule. Old enough to fight for what's ours."

"Ours?" Robert spat the word like a curse. "You mean yours. Your ambitions. Your obsession with that damn crown."

His father's hand shot out, fisting in Robert's tunic. "Listen up, boy. English vultures are circling, and that Balliol puppet sits on our throne. Scotland needs a true king."

Robert wrenched free, his chest heaving. "And that's supposed to be me? Because you've thrown in the towel?"

"Thrown in the towel?" His father's laugh was sharp as a blade. "I'm handing you the chance I never got. The earldom of Carrick is yours. Annandale lands will follow. You'll have the clout to unite the clans, to take on Balliol and those Comyn bastards."

"At what price?" Robert's voice cracked. "Our family? Our souls?"

For a heartbeat, the elder Bruce's face softened. "Wearing a crown means wearing a target, son. It'll demand sacrifices you can't even imagine yet. But Scotland's needs come before everything. Even family."

The older man's expression darkened. "And make no mistake, that Red Comyn is ready to do anything to destroy you. He'd see Scotland burn before letting a Bruce take the throne."

Robert spun away, glaring out the narrow window at the sprawling lands soon to be his. His next words came out barely above a whisper. "And if I'm not ready?"

His father's hand landed heavy on his shoulder. "Then God help us all."

❖

A particularly agonized scream from the birthing chamber snapped Robert back to the present. He pressed his forehead against the rough stone wall, the cold seeping into his bones. The irony wasn't lost on him. Here he stood, praying for a son to carry on the very legacy he'd once resented.

"My boy," he whispered, unsure if he was addressing the child yet to be born or the frightened young man he'd once been. "What burdens will you bear?"

The birthing chamber door creaked open. Robert whirled, heart pounding, but it was only a serving girl emptying a basin of bloodied water. She avoided his gaze, hurrying past. The door slammed shut, leaving Robert alone once more with his thoughts.

He leaned against the wall, exhaustion seeping into his bones. How different this night was from the joyous arrivals of his daughters. He closed his eyes, bracing.

Turnberry Castle
1296

"My lord!" The midwife's face shone with triumph as she burst from the chamber. "You have a daughter!"

Robert felt his knees go weak with relief. He'd been pacing the corridor for hours, the memory of Isabelle's death in childbirth haunting his every step. But Elisabeth had survived. They both had.

He entered the room, heart swelling at the sight of his wife cradling their newborn. Elisabeth looked up, her smile radiant despite her exhaustion.

"Come meet your daughter," she said softly. "Our little Marjorie."

Robert approached, marveling at the tiny, perfect face. He reached out, his battle-hardened hand engulfing his daughter's delicate fist.

"She's beautiful," he whispered.

Elisabeth's eyes danced with mischief. "Of course she is. She takes after her mother."

Robert laughed, the sound filled with pure joy. In that moment, the pressure of the crown seemed to lift. He was simply a man, blessed with a healthy child and a wife he'd grown to love fiercely.

TWO YEARS LATER

"Papa! Papa!" Marjorie toddled across the great hall, arms outstretched. Robert scooped her up, planting a kiss on her chubby cheek.

"There's my wee warrior," he said, tossing her high. Her delighted squeals echoed off the stone walls.

Elisabeth approached, one hand resting on her swollen belly. "Careful, you'll make her sick," she chided, but her eyes were soft with affection.

Robert pulled his wife close with his free arm. "How are you feeling, my love?"

"Ready to be done with it," Elisabeth sighed. "This one's as restless as his father."

"His?" Robert's eyebrow quirked. "You sound certain."

Elisabeth patted her stomach. "Call it a mother's intuition."

❖

But when the babe arrived a month later, it was another girl. They named her Matilda, and Robert loved her instantly. Yet as he gazed down at his daughters playing at his feet, he couldn't shake a creeping unease. As he watched Marjorie's determination in her play, a fleeting thought crossed Robert's mind. Perhaps, if fate decreed it, this strong-willed girl could one day lead. But he quickly pushed the notion aside. Scotland needed a king; tradition demanded it. Still, he couldn't help but marvel at the strength he saw in his daughter's eyes.

❖

The whispers at court grew louder with each passing year. *"A king needs a son. An heir to secure the line."* Robert tried to ignore them, focusing on the warmth of his family and the endless work of forging a nation. But in the dark of night, when sleep eluded him, the doubts gnawed at him.

He'd won his crown through blood and iron. How quickly might it slip away without a male heir to follow him?

❖

A guttural cry from the birthing chamber jolted Robert back to the present. He straightened, squaring his shoulders. This night would be different. It had to be.

"Give me a son," he whispered, unsure if he was pleading with Elisabeth, with God, or with the ancient, unknowable forces that seemed to shape the destiny of kings. "Give Scotland its future."

The wait continued, each moment an eternity.

Suddenly, an eerie silence fell over the castle. The air grew thick, pressing in on Robert like a physical weight. The torches lining the corridor flickered, casting writhing shadows on the stone walls.

The birthing chamber door burst open. The midwife stumbled out, her apron and hands slick with blood. Her eyes were wide with a terror that made Robert's blood run cold.

"Your Grace," she gasped, reaching for him with crimson fingers. "Come quickly. The Queen..."

"My lord!" The midwife's face shone with triumph as she burst from the chamber. "You have a daughter!"

Robert felt his knees go weak with relief. He'd been pacing the corridor for hours, the memory of Isabelle's death in childbirth haunting his every step. But Elisabeth had survived. They both had.

He entered the room, heart swelling at the sight of his wife cradling their newborn. Elisabeth looked up, her smile radiant despite her exhaustion.

"Come meet your daughter," she said softly. "Our little Marjorie."

Robert approached, marveling at the tiny, perfect face. He

reached out, his battle-hardened hand engulfing his daughter's delicate fist.

"She's beautiful," he whispered.

Elisabeth's eyes danced with mischief. "Of course she is. She takes after her mother."

Robert laughed, the sound filled with pure joy. In that moment, the pressure of the crown seemed to lift. He was simply a man, blessed with a healthy child and a wife he'd grown to love fiercely.

TWO YEARS LATER

"Papa! Papa!" Marjorie toddled across the great hall, arms outstretched. Robert scooped her up, planting a kiss on her chubby cheek.

"There's my wee warrior," he said, tossing her high. Her delighted squeals echoed off the stone walls.

Elisabeth approached, one hand resting on her swollen belly. "Careful, you'll make her sick," she chided, but her eyes were soft with affection.

Robert pulled his wife close with his free arm. "How are you feeling, my love?"

"Ready to be done with it," Elisabeth sighed. "This one's as restless as his father."

"His?" Robert's eyebrow quirked. "You sound certain."

Elisabeth patted her stomach. "Call it a mother's intuition."

But when the babe arrived a month later, it was another girl. They named her Matilda, and Robert loved her instantly. Yet as he gazed down at his daughters playing at his feet, he couldn't shake a creeping unease. As he watched Marjorie's determination in her play, a fleeting thought crossed Robert's mind. Perhaps, if fate decreed it, this strong-willed girl could one day lead. But he quickly pushed the notion aside. Scotland needed a king; tradition demanded it. Still, he couldn't help but marvel at the strength he saw in his daughter's eyes.

❖

The whispers at court grew louder with each passing year. *"A king needs a son. An heir to secure the line."* Robert tried to ignore them, focusing on the warmth of his family and the endless work of forging a nation. But in the dark of night, when sleep eluded him, the doubts gnawed at him.

He'd won his crown through blood and iron. How quickly might it slip away without a male heir to follow him?

❖

A guttural cry from the birthing chamber jolted Robert back to the present. He straightened, squaring his shoulders. This night would be different. It had to be.

"Give me a son," he whispered, unsure if he was pleading with Elisabeth, with God, or with the ancient, unknowable forces that seemed to shape the destiny of kings. "Give Scotland its future."

The wait continued, each moment an eternity.

Suddenly, an eerie silence fell over the castle. The air grew thick, pressing in on Robert like a physical weight. The torches lining the corridor flickered, casting writhing shadows on the stone walls.

The birthing chamber door burst open. The midwife stumbled out, her apron and hands slick with blood. Her eyes were wide with a terror that made Robert's blood run cold.

"Your Grace," she gasped, reaching for him with crimson fingers. "Come quickly. The Queen..."

CHAPTER 17

Isobel's eyes blazed, a tempest of barely contained fury. Her words sliced through the air, sharp as fangs. "If you so much as breathe Oliver Purvis's name, I swear something truly wicked will happen. How he treats me is my bloody business. Back off, Mum." Her emotions could really shift the mood of a room.

When Isobel caught wind of Cameron's snooping, she exploded like a powder keg. "That nosy fucking twat!" she hissed to Rhona, venom dripping from every syllable. "He had no fucking right to stick his nose into my private affairs!"

Rhona's insides twisted like writhing snakes. As a mother in this godforsaken world, she knew all too well the monsters that preyed on young girls like Isobel. Even a simple teeth cleaning could become a gateway to hell with the wrong adult involved.

"It's rather rich," Rhona ventured, treading on eggshells, "that he accuses you of destroying his family while he's still tangled in your underwear."

Isobel's face contorted, a mask of rage and pain. "And how, pray tell, is that any of your damn business?"

Rhona's heart plummeted. They'd made such fragile progress, as delicate as a cobweb in a storm. One wrong move, and it would all come crashing down.

Under the watchful eye of the strange pudgy boy perched in his tree, they cleared the garden in silence, neither needing to discuss who'd do what. When they finished, they called him down to borrow his dad's wheelbarrow and long shears.

Rhona wagged her finger at the kid. "And I don't want to catch you doing your dirty business up there anymore."

The boy's eyes gleamed with mischief. "Why? Does it bother you?"

"Of course it bothers us, you little creep," Rhona snapped. "Why else would I mention it?"

❖

They filled three bags with garden waste, scattering it in the nearby woods - the same place where, two decades ago, the Bruce brothers nearly met their end. In the distance, rocky peaks caught the sunset's glow, melting into green meadows as they tumbled down into the valleys.

As they dumped the last bag in a roadside ditch, Isobel dropped a bombshell. "Dad called. He's getting remarried."

Rhona froze, a strand of hair falling across her face. She took a deep breath, suddenly overwhelmed by the urge to confess her own secret - that she'd been pregnant with Phil when they tied the knot. But the words stuck in her throat.

Isobel glanced at her, eyebrow raised. "What's wrong? You look like you've seen a ghost."

Isobel scoffed, all too familiar with the wreckage of her parents' relationship. In her world, intact families were the freaks. She remembered the gut-punch realization that things weren't as simple as she'd thought, that her parents had become strangers wearing familiar faces. For a year, she'd soaked her sheets while Rhona, deep in breakdown number three, rambled about how you couldn't force love - all while tying ribbons in Isobel's hair like nothing was wrong. So whatever was eating at her mom now? Probably nothing worth fussing over.

"Dad asked how you're doing with the brothers," Isobel continued, her voice dripping with forced casualness. "He thinks you've lost it."

Rhona's spine stiffened. "Phil's always been narrow-minded," she snapped. "I stopped expecting anyone to understand a long time ago."

"Oh, please," Isobel sneered, her eyes glittering dangerously. "Don't bullshit me. Who do you think you're fooling? Like you haven't spent twenty years obsessing over going back, finding them. Come on, who are you trying to kid?"

Rhona's laugh was brittle. "That's exactly what I mean. What kind of idiot would buy that story? It's too insane to even imagine, right?"

Rhona crumpled the bags, tossing them in the trunk with a hollow thud. "It's the truth, though. I've never thought of anything else. My whole life has revolved around it."

Isobel rolled her eyes so hard they nearly fell out of her head.

"You don't think it's possible to love two men at once?" Rhona pressed on, her voice tight. "Well, think again. It's absolutely possible. I'm living, breathing proof. And let me tell you, there's no worse curse."

Isobel bit back a scoff. Love? Please. Of all the emotions she'd experienced so far, that one was conspicuously absent. She wasn't even convinced it existed outside of movies, or maybe it kicked in at some ridiculous age she couldn't fathom. The whole concept seemed like a fever dream. She regarded the idea of 'being in love' like a bomb that might go off if she looked at it wrong.

❖

Meanwhile, in an underground parking garage near his office, Brodie was beating Oliver to a bloody pulp.

Brodie's fist sank into Oliver's soft gut, a final blow to a man who was all flab and no fight. Everything about this dentist was pathetically soft, from his pudgy face to his split lips. Brodie seethed. Where had she found such a loser? And what a humiliation - getting beaten to the punch by some fat slob in a Lacoste shirt.

Oliver crumpled to his knees, gasping. Confusion painted his face as blood trickled from his chin. Brodie, lost in his rage, hadn't spoken a word.

Clyde, playing lookout by the elevator, gave a few slow claps. "Nice work, dude."

❖

On the drive home, Rhona pulled into a gas station.

"I don't know how it happened," she muttered, staring at her knees. "No clue. But here we are. Cameron's... well, obvious, I guess. And Gordon? We're not even on the same planet anymore."

"So we lucked out, if I'm getting this right," Isobel drawled.

Rhona let out a bitter laugh. "The thrill fades with age, kiddo."

❖

The sun dipped low, painting the sky in fiery hues. Across the river, Gordon loitered outside the school, his eyes drawn to the young mothers. Some glowed with new life, while others still carried the burden of pregnancy, likely marked by silvery streaks. He watched them, his heart heavy.

❖

Meanwhile, Cameron slipped on a fresh shirt, Heather's fingers working the buttons in loaded silence.

❖

Rhona dropped Isobel at Alison Stewart's office. The harried magazine editor was knee-deep in a study on twenty-something girls, trying to decode them for bewildered mothers. Stuck in traffic, Rhona flipped on the radio. The host's question hit like a gut punch: "Who'll foot the bill for our pensions?"

She sighed, a familiar sense of unease settling over her. It felt like the country was going to hell, each news story another nail in the coffin of stability. The gridlock around her seemed an apt metaphor for the nation's problems - stagnant, frustrated, and with no clear way forward.

❖

The golden hour light bathed the streets, but it couldn't quite shake the creeping malaise. The world seemed to be limping along, one misstep away from face-planting. Rhona parked, yanked the brake, and worried her lip between her teeth.

Brodie lounged against her doorframe, his expression a mix of satisfaction and irritation. Rhona had agreed to let him crash occasionally, but she'd withheld a key. The way he looked at her lately... well, no sense in tempting fate.

Rhona gave herself a once-over. Canvas pants and a loose shirt - practical, unsexy. Perfect. No need to stir up trouble, especially after Isobel's little bombshell about their nearly non-existent sex life. Still, she'd decked him once. She could do it again if needed.

She flashed Brodie a tight smile as she breezed past him into the house. He trailed after her, face set in that sullen mask young men wear so well. Ignoring him, she headed for the garden where bags of potting soil waited. She had jasmine to plant under the Virginia creeper blanketing the street-side wall.

Minutes later, Brodie appeared in the doorway. "Need a hand?"

Rhona eyed him warily, but he seemed... normal. He ripped open a bag, spreading soil along the wall's base.

❖

Later, she found him in the kitchen, his fist plunged into a bucket of ice. He clammed up when she asked what happened.

When Cameron showed up, the two exchanged a loaded glance that set Rhona's teeth on edge.

"Alright," she snapped. "What the hell is going on?"

❖

Oliver Purvis stumbled through his front door, a mess of bruises and blood. His wife took one look and sneered, "Don't expect sympathy from me. It's exactly what you deserve."

She followed him to the bathroom, watching as he dragged himself to the sink.

"Listen," he pleaded, wincing as he spoke. "I regret everything. I swear on our kids' lives."

"Might as well," she spat. "You're destroying this family anyway."

"What are you talking about, darling?" Oliver's voice was small, confused.

"Oh, you bastard," she hissed, whirling away in disgust.

Left alone, Oliver faced his reflection. He gingerly touched his swollen lips, flinching at his own battered image.

❖

Edinburgh pulsed to life as night fell. Streets filled with a restless crowd, cars crawling like molten lead under a navy sky pierced by a ghostly moon.

In a dimly lit bar, nestled in buttery leather chairs, Alison Stewart continued grilling Isobel for her Hashtag Magazine exposé on teen habits. She leaned in, confiding, "I went through the same thing, you know. Not with a dentist, but our gardener. God, he was hideous. But I was obsessed for months. Then, poof! Gone like it never happened."

Alison's tone softened. "You're lucky your mom gives a damn. Going it alone? That's rough."

Isobel's eyes flashed dangerously. "So everyone knows my business now. Fantastic. Just fucking fantastic."

❖

On the hill, Fiona splashed with Amelia in the tub while Margaret cornered her eldest about finding a good wife. Gordon squirmed, embarrassed but not disagreeing. His frustration peaked when asked to deliver towels. The bathroom was a watery warzone, and there stood Fiona in soaked underwear, hair wild. Gordon's imagination ran wild - her panties must be clinging, her bra straining...

He groaned, averting his eyes. Fiona's gaze lingered before she asked him to shut the door.

❖

At Rhona's, the air crackled with tension. Cameron shrugged, "I figured Brodie should handle it."

Brodie, fist still buried in ice, grunted, "I'd have found out anyway." He stalked off to the garden.

Rhona lit up, glaring at Cameron. "You should've talked to me first." But her heart wasn't in the scolding. She wasn't exactly weeping for the dentist.

"It was the logical next step," Cameron mused. "Brodie did what I would've. Better him than me. I might've lost control."

Rhona scoffed. "You haven't lost control in two centuries."

"This is different. It's Isobel. A guy's gotta look out for his girl."

"You're hardly a shining example."

"I'm an excellent example," he growled, pinning her against the table. His newfound affection was... notable. There was a glint in his eye that hinted at deeper waters. "Besides," he added with a smirk, "if I don't keep her out of trouble, who will? Lord knows you lot are a handful already."

Rhona rolled her eyes, but couldn't quite hide her smile. "Oh, please. We manage just fine without your 'protection,' thank you very much."

"She wasn't in her element," he continued, his grip firm.

Rhona bit back a retort about Isobel's "natural element" being just as treacherous - kids barely pubescent were ending up in horrific states. But Cameron had taken charge, and... it wasn't unpleasant. In his arms, she felt soft, pliant.

❖

Alison eyed the menu, fighting the urge to order a club sandwich. God, they were good - she'd once driven out at midnight, depressed, to devour two in a row.

Isobel, all sharp angles and attitude, had ordered one without a second thought.

"Your mom's never been able to choose," Alison mused. "Why start now?"

Isobel's eyes narrowed. "I'm telling you what I see. It's always the same one at home. That's a clue."

Alison leaned in. "Honey, I slept with him for years. I know who he is. I'm not sure he's what she needs. I don't know what game they're playing."

She stood abruptly. "Bathroom break. I need to powder my nose." It wasn't entirely a lie.

❖

Across town, Margaret and Amelia zoned out to TV. Gordon had spent dinner avoiding Fiona's gaze, knowing his raw desire showed. He'd barely spoken. Even after furiously getting himself off before dinner, he was far from calm.

Gordon stood on the terrace, haunted. The same spot where Margaret had lost it last time. He stared into the darkness, thinking life could be just as black sometimes. You stumble through it blind when fate keeps hammering you down.

He felt cheated. Like a shiny new engine that won't turn over. Somehow, he knew Rhona and Cameron were together right now. It was just a twinge, barely visible through the fog of his Fiona troubles. But it was there - one more weight he didn't need.

His eyes found the moon, cool and distant. Fighting a child's death... it wasn't in his skillset. He'd long since lost touch with the concept of death itself, immortality dulling that primal fear. But this? This was different. Every attempt at peace or reconciliation backfired. Now he kept whisky in his room, drinking to forget - a pointless exercise for a vampire, but the ritual brought hollow comfort. His morning runs had become torture, ending with him on his knees, heart pounding, avoiding Fiona's closed door.

Gordon's breath caught as Fiona appeared, the memory of her wet skin still seared into his mind. Her presence was electric, igniting every nerve ending. He forced out a question about her day, met with silence and an unsettling look. Fumbling to fill the void, he rambled about Alison Stewart's mother's visit to his office.

"She hounded me for an hour," he sighed. "Still bought a fortune in whisky for her hunting lodge. Crazy woman. Alison said to let her spend as she pleased, so..."

His words felt hollow, meaningless. How low could he sink? Would he soon be prattling about Ted's wallpaper choices for the baby’s room?

Fiona's proximity was maddening. He turned away, thinking silence might be his best defense against the torment of trying to sleep later, haunted by the bathroom scene and aching for even the smallest kind gesture from her.

Are we really going to drain this bitter cup? he wondered silently.

He expected nothing from this moonlit moment, so bleak and cold. No light, no glimmer of hope. Which is why he was utterly blindsided, struck dumb, when Fiona's hand suddenly reached for his fly.

Gordon swayed as she knelt before him, his breath catching in his throat. He reached out, wanting to touch her hair, overwhelmed by gratitude and desire. But she gently pushed his hand away.

What followed was exquisite torture. Gordon's guilt warred with pleasure as her lips and tongue worked magic. He bit back a moan, torn between heavenly sensation and the knowledge that he shouldn't be enjoying this. Gordon's throbbing erection exploded in a burst of ecstasy and shame, his strangled gasp echoing in the suddenly too-quiet room.

When it was over, she looked up at him, her eyes dark. "Don't ask me for more," she said softly. "Not yet."

❖

Alison burst into the living room, her curves barely contained by a Vivienne Westwood dress that cost more than most people's monthly rent. "Darlings," she purred, "I've made a shocking discovery. The sadist who invented Martini-Scotch deserves a special place in hell."

Outside, Brodie nursed his drink in the garden, avoiding the family gathering. Isobel joined him, glass in hand.

She sprawled onto the couch, her dress riding up to reveal a tantalizing expanse of thigh. With a dramatic groan, she kicked off her Louboutins. "And the misogynistic troll who created high heels isn't much better."

Alison's eyes gleamed as she noticed the tension in the garden. She leaned towards Rhona, her voice a throaty whisper. "Oh honey, are we finally getting some action around here? Lord knows I could use the entertainment. It's been far too long since I've seen a good scene."

Rhona followed Alison's gaze, tension building in her shoulders.

In the garden, Isobel gently took Brodie's hand. "What happened?" she asked, examining the marks. Brodie's jaw clenched. He'd decided to keep quiet, for now.

He shrugged off her concern. "Just banged my fingers in a football match," Brodie lied smoothly.

Cameron spilled the beans. "Brodie finally met the dentist."

Rhona's eyes flashed. "That self-righteous bastard," she hissed through gritted teeth.

"Ah, so we're in for a show after all," Alison smirked. "Same old drama, different day."

"Wait, what?" Isobel burst out, her eyes wide with shock. "Did you punch Oliver?" She looked around the room, bewildered. "Brodie, did you—Mom? Fuck." Her gaze settled back on Brodie's clenched fist. "More ice for your hand?" she offered.

"I'm good," Brodie grunted. He found himself wishing he'd just slept with her from the start instead of all that book-swapping nonsense. Would've saved him a hell of a headache.

Alison yawned, bored already. Couples were such a snooze unless they were falling apart or offering up something juicy – like a threesome. "Think I'll call it a night," she announced, stretching languidly. She downed her drink in one smooth motion, snatched up her heels, and sauntered out barefoot, leaving a trail of pricey Creed White Amber in her wake.

Isobel kicked off the night drowning her sorrows. No more dental chair trysts meant hitting the booze hard at some rich kid's party. The wind howled outside, matching her mood.

❖

Oliver Purvis picked the zoo. Real subtle. Shades, hat, the works. She knew it was over before he opened his mouth.

She craved their old routine - bent over his office floor, rough and dirty. Now he was all shifty eyes and mumbles, zoo animals providing cover. When she suggested the bathroom, he nearly bolted.

It hit her like a ton of bricks. He was pathetic. And that made her feel pathetic too. Isobel almost laughed. Her married dentist, so fearless in his office, now quaking at the thought of being caught. Dust devils whipped around them, the wind exposing Oliver's bright red forehead under his stupid hat.

For the first time, Isobel saw him clearly. And she hated what she saw.

Now here she was, drowning her sorrows at some posh kid's soirée. The booze dulled the ache, but couldn't erase the memory of Oliver's retreating back as he fled the zoo. Isobel drained her glass, already scanning the room for something stronger. The night was still young, and she was determined to make it count.

❖

As darkness fell, the wind died down, leaving the garden lights swaying gently. The party sprawled across the house - kegs of beer, scattered pills, and abandoned pizza slices on paper plates littered every surface. Upstairs, bodies crammed into bedrooms, bathrooms, and even the hallway. At least it made dodging Brodie easier; Isobel could slip into a new room whenever he came too close.

A hazy detachment settled over Isobel, but it didn't stop her from reaching for another drink. Betty Wilson, a shiny-faced blonde who'd had an abortion last spring, offered her something to dissolve under her tongue. "It's good for everything," Betty promised with a wink. Isobel didn't hesitate.

She realized that focusing her anger on Brodie was a convenient distraction. Fantasizing about pummeling him meant not thinking about Oliver, about how she'd debased herself in his office. How she'd begged him, abandoning every shred of self-respect. The memory threatened to drag her under, so she clung to her hatred of Brodie like a life raft.

❖

The night wore on. Glass shattered somewhere, followed by hysterical laughter. A line formed outside the downstairs bathroom. The kitchen floor was sticky with spilled drinks, and rolled-up rugs became makeshift seating. Everyone seemed intent on hooking up, their smiles growing more desperate as the hours ticked by. Some faces twisted with anguish, while others were eerily blank.

Isobel drifted through it all, the drug melting on her tongue as she searched for something – anything – to make her feel alive again.

The party had long since abandoned any pretense of intellectual conversation. Banksy and politics were forgotten, replaced by the haze of drugs and desperate hookups.

Lexi kept reappearing, joint in hand, as Isobel spilled her guts about Oliver. With each drag, Lexi's eyes widened, nodding as Isobel's tale grew more sordid. "I can't believe you're telling me all this," Lexi said, her voice a mix of shock and barely concealed excitement.

It was unlike Isobel to open up like this. She was known for her guardedness, especially compared to the other girls who shared every intimate detail of their love lives. But tonight, the floodgates had opened.

"Men can be such bastards," Lexi muttered, shaking her head. Privately, she was thrilled at this newfound closeness with Isobel.

A shiver ran through Isobel. Why had she confessed everything? Her mind was a fog, and the catharsis she'd hoped for never came. Instead, she was utterly wasted.

❖

The night became a series of disjointed snapshots. One moment, she was on the veranda. Then suddenly, she was upstairs with Marcello, that guy she'd flirted with back in the fall. Another blink, and she was somewhere else entirely, faces blurring as she stumbled through the crowd.

Isobel felt like a piece of driftwood, tossed about on a sea of strangers. Each new encounter left her feeling more hollow than the last.

The party's chaos ebbed, but Isobel's mind churned. Oliver's face at the zoo haunted her – his pathetic grimace as he begged her to stay away. The memory hit her like a punch to the gut, and she crumpled into a corner, head between her knees.

If Brodie showed up now, she'd brush him off. "I'm fine," she'd lie, though she couldn't quite explain the anger boiling inside her towards him. It wasn't the time for nuanced emotions.

❖

As dawn approached, Isobel found herself in darkness, barely conscious. Someone was fucking her, but she couldn't say who or for how long. She surfaced from oblivion, dragged back by a burning ache in her pelvis. Nausea rose in her throat.

Desperate for distraction, her foggy mind grasped at questions: Was he using protection? Were others waiting their turn? Had she wanted this?

Her thoughts slipped away, and she faded out again, lost in a haze of regret and confusion.

At least the creep hadn't fully undressed her. Small mercies. She winced as she tugged her panties back up, her breasts still aching from his rough handling. Most guys treated tits like stress balls, and this loser was no exception. She'd tried to shield herself, but it hadn't mattered much in the end.

The whole thing had been a blur of bad breath, stale smoke, and charming pet names like "slut!" as he'd pounded away. She'd just wanted it over, desperate to escape the seemingly endless darkness.

A sickly green glow crept across the sky, hinting at dawn. She leaned against the wall to slip her shoe back on, eyeing the passed-out figure sprawled nearby. Arms splayed, clearly satisfied with himself. She couldn't make out his face in the dim light, but it didn't matter. She had zero interest in knowing who he was.

Time to get the hell out of here and forget this night ever happened.

Isobel wobbled down the hallway, the world tilting like a funhouse ride. Somehow she made it to the stairs, white-knuckling the banister as she stumbled through the living room and out to the garden. But her body had other plans.

Lexi found her curled under a willow, whimpering in a puddle of her own sick. Isobel insisted she'd lost a shoe, oblivious to the fact she was sitting on it.

❖

Lexi knew just the spot - Snax on West Register Street. As dawn broke, they slid onto a free bench outside. Isobel sipped her hot drink, the sweetness of the donuts cutting through the sour taste in her mouth. Sunlight warmed her pale face as she squinted against its brightness.

She'd had to do a quick clean-up in the bathroom first - splashing cold water on her face, rinsing the nastiness from her mouth, and using scratchy paper towels between her legs while Lexi played lookout. Now she felt almost human again. Weak, but better.

"Let's keep it strictly estrogen today," Lexi declared. "No dicks allowed. Could be a bloody breath of fresh air, yeah?"

Isobel managed a wan smile. After the night she'd had, that sounded perfect.

The softness of the morning made them reflective. Was it really possible to believe there was something better to expect, that there was a bright path strewn with flower petals? Lexi lived nearby, in a cozy studio tucked away in the shadow of Edinburgh Castle. Later, bone-tired, they made their way there and crashed, sleeping all afternoon like logs – Though their combined age was only thirty-eight, they slumbered like world-weary adults, far removed from the days of thumb-sucking and childish comforts.

❖

Dr. MacGregor took advantage of the walk in the garden that Margaret and Fiona took every afternoon – crossing the woods, sitting on a bench, chatting, laughing, smoking, etc. – to declare that he was completely satisfied. As for him, Margaret no longer worried him.

"She's no more disturbed than you or me," he stated. "I've spoken to her at length. Let's consider all this ancient history."

Toasting with Alistair Bruce and his two sons to this happy conclusion, he nonetheless put everyone at ease by adding that he still kept Margaret on "special" antidepressants. "But don't jostle her too much," he advised.

A couple of Scotches later, Alistair was feeling jolly enough to suggest a family dinner at the The Witchery by the Castle. It was built in 1595 for merchant Thomas Lowthian, whom at the time was a good friend of Alistair and the family, long before it became the luxurious restaurant it is now.

His boys, though, made quick excuses. Cameron was off to join Rhona at Alison's cocktail bash for some up-and-coming French fashion designers. Gordon, still starry-eyed from a recent buccal romantic breakthrough, was sticking close to Fiona in case she fancied an encore.

Margaret hadn't set foot in the city since her meltdown, but she jumped at the chance. An hour later, she emerged dolled up to the nines.

❖

The Witchery occupied a hulking sixteenth-century building, a place that had seen four centuries of Scottish history unfold. It had worn many hats - Church of Scotland committee rooms, a church rectory - but always remained at the heart of Edinburgh's story. Across the street once stood the palace of Mary de Guise, mother to Mary Queen of Scots, another family friend from those wild medieval days.

Margaret and Alistair entered the candlelit Witchery through the narrow close off the Royal Mile.

The original carved doorway still bore the owner's initials and his motto: "O Lord in thee is all my traist." Some clever bisexual designer had worked their magic, blending history with modern flair. The result was a place where you could sip your whisky and feel like you were part of Scotland's royal saga - even if your own family tree was more sheep farmer than Stewart.

Margaret glided into The Witchery, her Saint Laurent dress a second skin of midnight allure. Alistair followed, his Dormeuil Vanquish II suit a masterpiece of tailoring that whispered of old money and older power.

The couple moved through the lavish dining room like living art. Conversations faltered, forks paused mid-bite. Even the candlelight seemed to bend towards them, drawn to their magnetic presence.

Diners stared, transfixed by beauty that stirred long-forgotten desires. Pulses quickened, pupils dilated. The Bruces moved with liquid grace to their table, the embodiment of everything the Edinburgh elite aspired to be.

In their wake, the room's atmosphere crackled with electricity. A reminder that true sophistication went beyond mere wealth or status. A few faces from charity galas and corporate boards offered nods of recognition, social reflexes battling the urge to stare openly at such perfection.

Tension crackled between Margaret and Alistair as they settled into their seats. Still, Alistair was chuffed about this unexpected tête-à-tête. He didn't know what he'd done to deserve it, but he was over the moon to be dining alone with Margaret, basking in the glow of those cozy low-watt bulbs softly glowing in the room. At sixty-three, Margaret was still a looker, carrying herself with that same proud, beautiful bearing - especially to his increasingly creaky old eyes. These days, his balls hung low and his joints had been stiff for the last 700 years. Literally.

Alistair's eyes roamed the room, taking in the ancient stone walls before settling back on Margaret. Hope warred with caution inside him. He'd left her once, a choice that had saved and damned him in equal measure.

Now, he ached to mend the rift between them, to recapture a glimmer of what they'd once shared. But Margaret was no easy conquest. Her razor-sharp mind and fierce independence were as much a part of her as the blood that kept her undead heart beating.

Margaret's walls were fortified by centuries of pain and the harsh realities of immortal life. She couldn't deny the hatred that bubbled up whenever she looked at Alistair. And yet... there was something else. A bond deeper than love or duty, something etched into their very souls.

They ordered drinks: whisky for Alistair, gin for Margaret. There was a limit to her playing nice. For Alistair, her choice was like nails on a chalkboard, but he bit his tongue. No need to spoil things.

"It's not so bad, is it?" he ventured. "We could do this more often, what do you reckon?"

"Oh really? And what's the special occasion?" she replied, her tone light.

She was usually much harder on him - downright brutal when she caught him eyeing her with that unsettling intensity she couldn't stand. She definitely wasn't one for playing happy families. So, relieved that the good vibes were holding, Alistair ordered another round.

They sipped their drinks in loaded silence. Both had seen too much, done too much. Their relationship was a complex tangle of power, affection, and the inescapable truth that they were bound together, for better or worse.

"I'm not trying to twist your arm tonight," he pressed on, "but I'm asking you to mull it over. I've been doing some thinking myself lately. And you know, I can only see upsides."

"I bet," she retorted. "Living solo takes guts when you hit our age."

"And a hell of a lot more than that. More than I've got left in me, I reckon."

"Should I be breaking out the violins?"

"No, 'course not," he conceded.

He knew - not because of some mystical vampire insight, but he knew - that he'd have to claw back ground inch by bloody inch. Patience and a stiff upper lip were his only mates now, and redemption wasn't coming anytime soon - if it ever showed up at all. He flashed a weak smile, then buried his nose in the menu.

The Witchery's timeless atmosphere seemed to heighten every nuance between them. In this ancient place, surrounded by whispers of the past, Margaret and Alistair were reminded that some connections, no matter how fraught, could never truly be broken.

If he could just get her to pencil him in for one night a week, an evening like this, all above board, he figured the tide might start to turn. Down the road, who knows, maybe he'd whisk her off on a trip.

❖

"There's something you don't know," Margaret said as they tucked into dessert.

Alistair's spoon froze halfway to his gob. He gave her his full attention, inviting her on with a smile. The evening had been a treat, a bit of warmth seeping into his ancient bones. He felt properly chuffed, and it wasn't just the booze talking. It was simply being with this woman who'd lit a fire under him these past few months like he was some lovesick teenager again.

"It's about Rhona," she continued.

"Oh, for Christ's sake," he groaned, his brow furrowing. "Can we not drag her into this?"

Margaret went pale as milk, stiffening like she'd been shocked. Alistair could see her fighting to keep her cool, and he knew he'd stepped in it. He tried to change tack, rabbiting on about how their boys seemed to be getting along, no drama on the horizon. But she shut that down quick, calling him out on his knack for burying his head in the sand whenever anything threatened to ruffle his perfectly selfish feathers.

"That's not the point," she cut in. "I shouldn't have expected you to step up this time either."

"You're wrong. You can count on me more than you think. Just give me a shot to prove it. I might surprise you. For now, listen: stop fretting. Come off it, it's daft. We never relive the same mess twice."

"Oh really? And what makes you so sure?"

"The perks of being ancient. Bit of wisdom for the price of gray hair. A knack for spotting disasters coming, now that it's too bloody late to do me any good."

"Your wisdom? What's it saying about the bomb hanging over our heads, then?"

"A bomb? What bomb?"

When the penny dropped that he was a granddad and Margaret had kept it from him for two decades, his breath caught, his undead heart skipping a beat. A grandchild? For a vampire, it was impossible —or so he'd always believed. The revelation hit him like a sucker punch, leaving him reeling.

His mind raced. What did this mean for their carefully guarded secrecy? What unknown powers might this child possess? How would it impact their already precarious existence?

The room seemed to shrink around him as the full weight of the news settled in. Centuries of careful control crumbled, leaving Alistair feeling exposed. In that moment, he wasn't the suave, confident vampire patriarch—he was just a man grappling with an earth-shattering revelation.

For the first time in ages, immortality felt less like a gift and more like a burden. An endless chain of unforeseen consequences stretched out before him, each link forged in emotional turmoil.

Alistair shoved his barely-touched pudding away, his hands trembling. Out of habit, he patted his pockets for cigarettes he'd given up decades ago. The thought of a grandchild—a being who might inherit both his strengths and his curse—left him shaken to his core.

❖

Margaret decided dinner with her estranged husband was plenty for one day and asked him not to crash at the manor that night. Back in his apartment, Alistair tossed and turned, sleep eluding him completely.

His mind raced with impossible thoughts. A grandchild? From Rhona? It shouldn't be possible. Vampires weren't meant to mix like that. It was like oil and water, fire and ice. Nature had its rules, didn't it? But then again, nature also said the dead should stay dead, and here he was, 700 years later.

Maybe there were loopholes in the cosmic rulebook. Maybe the universe had a twisted sense of humor. Or maybe, just maybe, there was more to Rhona - and this whole situation - than met the eye.

Whatever the truth, it had happened. He was a grandfather, and he'd been kept in the dark for two decades.

❖

As the first pale light of dawn crept over the horizon, Alistair climbed onto the terrace. The world was just emerging from darkness, mirroring his own emergence from blissful ignorance. He made for the deserted pool.

He swam without pause until morning properly broke, turning from side to side like a caged beast. Eventually, a young bloke in shorts showed up to open the umbrellas and lay out the mattresses.

CHAPTER 18

Dunfermline Abbey

5 MARCH 1324

Robert burst into the chamber, heart thundering in his chest, the midwife's blood-stained hands and terrified expression seared into his mind. The acrid smell of blood and sweat assaulted his senses. Shadows danced on the walls, cast by guttering candles that seemed to shrink from the scene before them.

'Elisabeth?' His voice cracked, fear and hope warring in his chest.

His wife lay pale against the pillows, her hair plastered to her forehead. But her eyes... her eyes blazed with a fierce triumph that took his breath away.

'Robert,' she whispered, her voice hoarse but strong. 'Come meet your sons.'

Sons. The word echoed in his mind. Plural. Relief flooded through him, chasing away the cold dread that had gripped him moments before.

He stumbled forward, legs leaden. The midwife stepped aside, revealing two small bundles cradled in Elisabeth's arms. Robert's vision swam. *Two. Twin boys.* The heirs he'd prayed for, delivered twice over.

"How...?" He couldn't form a complete thought.

Elisabeth's laugh was weak but jubilant. "It seems your seed is as ambitious as you are, my love."

Robert reached out with trembling hands. The babe on the left squirmed, letting out a lusty cry, his pink face scrunched in protest at the cold air. Its brother, however, lay eerily still, skin pale as moonlight.

'Is he...?' Cold dread gripped Robert's heart anew.

As if in answer, the silent twin's eyes snapped open. Robert gasped. For a heartbeat, he could have sworn he saw something ancient and hungry flicker in those infant eyes. But then he blinked, and they were simply the unfocused gaze of a newborn.

A gust of wind howled outside, rattling the windows. The candles flickered wildly, plunging the room into momentary darkness. When light returned, both babes were wailing in unison.

"Strong lungs," the midwife muttered, but her face was ashen. "I've never heard the like."

Robert cradled his sons, marveling at their tiny features. Joy warred with an inexplicable unease in his chest. He turned to Elisabeth, seeing his own conflicted emotions mirrored in her eyes.

"What shall we name them?" she asked softly.

Before Robert could answer, a commotion erupted in the hallway. The door burst open, admitting a breathless messenger.

"Your Grace!" The man fell to his knees. "Urgent news from the border. Edward's forces... they've—"

His words were drowned out by a peal of thunder that shook the very foundations of the castle. The babies' cries rose to a fever pitch, drowning out all other sound.

Robert cradled the swaddled bundles, one in each arm. His sons' faces, wrinkled and red, peeked out from the blankets. He glanced at his wife, her hair plastered to her forehead with sweat, her eyes heavy-lidded.

The messenger trembled on the floor, chest heaving. Robert's shoulders stiffened. He looked down at the infants, then back to the kneeling man. His fingers tightened on the blankets, and he swallowed hard before speaking.

"How many?" he asked, his voice low and taut.

As the storm raged outside, Robert's jaw clenched. He drew the babies closer to his chest, their cries softening against him. His gaze darted between his sons, his wife, and the quivering messenger. But as he stared down at the twins, a chill ran down his spine.

The babe on the right – the one with the ancient eyes – stared back at him with an intensity no newborn should possess. Its tiny hand reached up, grasping Robert's finger with surprising strength.

For a fleeting moment, Robert could have sworn he heard a voice – eldritch and terrible – whispering in his mind:

"The debt comes due, King of Scots. We have awakened."

Robert blinked, and the moment passed. But as he clutched his heirs to his chest, he couldn't shake the feeling that he'd just sealed a bargain whose true price he'd yet to learn.

The storm howled. The babies wailed. And somewhere in the darkness, something hungry stirred.

CHAPTER 19

The mayor wasn't just a crook; he was a raging homophobe to boot. Thomas Calderwood, the Bruce brothers' lawyer, made no bones about it. He'd gathered his crack team—six sharp-dressed thirty-somethings with hungry eyes—in the sky-high conference room that felt like a floating fortress. Time to lay it all out for the brothers.

Primal energy was radiating from Cameron and Gordon. The brothers stood like predators assessing their prey, their mere presence electrifying the room. Even the air seemed charged with an ancient, untamed power. Thomas steeled himself, ready to lay out their strategy to the men whose very existence seemed to defy the laws of nature.

"Which means," he added with a touch of feigned regret, "I won't be your moral cheerleader." In this town, Thomas wasn't just known as gay; he was feared as a legal pit bull, a "real son of a bitch" as his admirers liked to say.

The air crackled between them.

For the sake of full disclosure, Thomas reminded them they could always cut a deal with the enemy, pocket a fat check, and walk away from the lawsuit. But he already knew their answer. There was something wild about these two, a hint of untamed nature lurking beneath their polished exteriors, impeccable style, and irresistible charm. It wasn't about bravery. The Bruce brothers simply didn't have "surrender" in their vocabulary.

Thomas thought he had them figured out, but he was still in the dark about their biggest secret. Like most folks, he assumed vampires were extinct - hell, these days most people thought they were pure fiction. But he did know the brothers better now. No need for digging; one night over drinks, his friend Alison nearly choked when he dropped their names.

"Those two? They're my lifelong obsession," Alison had gushed, her fascination with the Bruces crystal clear. Later, she'd added with a wink, "Only thing you could fault them for is being stubbornly straight" - a comment Thomas found hilarious.

Thomas knew this case would get political fast. Cameron saw it coming clearer than Gordon; he'd actually shown up to the meetings. Archie had dragged him to gatherings of folks fed up with City Hall's bullshit. There were scandals galore - Archie himself blamed the mayor for letting McDonald's set up shop across the street, stealing his customers. Men and women sick of a mayor who'd been screwing them over for years, all itching to boot him out of office. Cameron had listened, taking it all in.

Thomas looked to Cameron. "Your thoughts?"

Cameron's eyes hardened. "After what we've been through? Yeah, I get it now." He rolled his shoulders, tension visible. "And it's not just the business losses."

That multi-million whisky deal Freddie Reid - the bastard - had axed still stung. But the real kicker was that shady land grab right behind their distillery, snatching up the plot they'd had their eyes on. Something primal awakened in Cameron. Centuries of predatory instinct sharpened to a knife's edge. This wasn't about pride anymore. This was survival.

Thomas nodded; they were onto something.

❖

The three headed out for lunch, aiming for a spot where aristos and lowlifes rubbed elbows without batting an eye. They wound their way through Edinburgh's schizophrenic cityscape - all imposing medieval fortresses one minute, sleek financial district the next. The Castle loomed above like a brooding giant, while gleaming glass towers of the modern city reached for the rare patch of blue sky.

Thomas had to smirk: here they were - an out-and-proud gay lawyer, two brothers (one with a dead kid on his conscience, the other who'd shagged his way through half of Lothian), about to face down a hell of a trial. The old stone walls around them had seen their share of scandals, he reckoned. What was one more to add to Edinburgh's sordid history?

Alison Stewart was set to join them, ready to talk about featuring the brothers in her magazine. Thomas had cooked up the idea when he spotted a chink in the praying mantis's armor. His plan was to shine a spotlight on Gordon and Cameron before the mud started flying. Paint them as the good guys - sympathetic, ace businessmen with sex appeal to spare, decked out in Tom Ford or Comme des Garçons. It was a smart play.

Alison breezed in with Rhona in tow. Thomas had never laid eyes on her before, but he instantly understood why men would go to war for her. He caught Gordon's two-second freeze as the women sat down. Alison cracked, "Thomas, you're witnessing a miracle. The building's still standing."

Truth be told, Alison had hoped for... something. She wasn't sure what exactly, but when she'd dragged Rhona along - practically twisting her arm, insisting this cat-and-mouse game was getting ridiculous - she hadn't expected... nothing.

❖

They made it through the whole meal, passing smokes like

nothing had ever happened. If anyone was ready to lose it and storm out, it was her. She'd once fancied herself a budding tragedian, but the poor fool still hadn't cottoned on that life was just a cheap farce. The thought made her ache to cry in Margaret Bruce's arms. An overwhelming urge.

So she bailed, leaving them slack-jawed on the sidewalk.

❖

After a wild tear through the city in her Bentley coupe, Alison ended up at the Bruce Manor. She and Margaret retreated to the garden, seeking peace among the manicured lawns and fragrant blooms. They settled on a secluded bench nestled among blooming hydrangeas, the sweet scent mingling with the earthy smell of recent rain. Alison collapsed at Margaret's feet. Margaret cradled her meltdown with gentle understanding, the manor's stone walls looming in the distance.

No need for words or explanations here. Margaret had been her safe harbor so many times, always saying her boys were crazy - that even their mother had no place in their hearts anymore, that Rhona had consumed them whole.

"Friendship? That girl doesn't need your friendship," Margaret said softly. "She couldn't care less about sharing anything with you, my poor darling."

It had been ages since Alison had broken down like this. Lately, she'd been more likely to drown her sorrows in vodka martinis, pastries, or club sandwiches than seek out Margaret's comfort. When that didn't cut it, she'd turn to the dicks and muscled arms and no-strings-attached fun of underwear models or gym rats who didn't bother with small talk. It had been forever since she'd come running to Margaret, desperate to sob into her skirts when loneliness hit hard. But damn if it wasn't still just as soothing. Just as effective.

Didn't matter that she was Alison Stewart, the infamous, feared, and envied head of Hashtag Magazine. Supposedly one of the toughest women in Scotland, giving the rest of England a run for its money. She could still be leveled by a wave of melancholy. But part of her savored it, like an addict chasing a high - the rare indulgence of crying for herself. A bittersweet pleasure. One to be rationed carefully.

With a deep sigh, she pressed Margaret's hand to her cheek one last time. Then she stood, swaying slightly in the hazy afternoon light.

❖

As Alison climbed the garden path back to the manor, she nearly collided with Fiona. It was their first real encounter, and Alison's gut instinct - which rarely missed the mark - wasn't impressed. Sure, Fiona's grief might have earned her some sympathy from most, but Alison didn't play that game. Especially not with a young woman who'd already won the genetic lottery.

"Let me give you some advice," Alison said, falling into step beside Fiona as they walked in loaded silence towards her car. The gravel crunched under their feet, punctuating the tension. "Grab your daughter with one arm, Gordon with the other, and vanish. Find some place where no one can touch you."

After Alison's tires crunched down the driveway, Fiona made her way back to Margaret and settled onto the wrought-iron bench. Margaret turned to Fiona, her eyes softening with a mix of sympathy and weariness. As a gentle breeze rustled the leaves around them, she began to unravel the tangled history of Alison's pain and the despair that had once bound them together.

"Picture a nightmare where everyone was drowning," Margaret said, her voice low. "It was like a whirlpool from hell, dragging down anyone who got close. Trust me, it was a fire that only grew fiercer the more we tried to douse it. I couldn't comfort her. She felt cast aside, but I had no cure. We were all powerless to help each other."

The memory stung, and Margaret reached for the gin, pouring

herself a generous measure. She sighed, then managed a smile at Fiona. Thank God, by Fiona's own admission, she'd stopped giving Gordon the cold shoulder lately - though she wasn't exactly swinging from the chandeliers either. In her mind, Margaret lit a hopeful candle and crossed her fingers.

Margaret had never considered herself an expert on sex. Unlike her neighbor Allie Vonnegut, who racked up conquests on every trip, or celebrities like Rosie Huntington-Whiteley (whose tantric yoga obsession Margaret had read about in a gossip magazine), or even Alistair's secretary Bonnie Campbell still rocking miniskirts, Margaret's experience was limited. She had married Alistair Bruce at sixteen back in 1344, as pure as the driven snow. She couldn't claim much firsthand knowledge, beyond skimming a few pop psychology books over the last century. Some chapters, like those on the female orgasm, left her baffled.

Eyes half-closed, gently savoring the fresh summer breeze while Fiona lost herself in a social media scroll, Margaret wondered if she'd missed out on something crucial.

Margaret found herself astounded. Here she was, at almost eight hundred, suddenly questioning a subject she'd barely given thought to for centuries. She'd shared a bed with a man who'd fathered her two children, yet sex had remained a shadowy concept. Of course, after John Comyn - that traitorous, feared vampire - had turned them, the possibility of more children had vanished like morning mist.

She realized now that a significant part of her life had unfolded in a twilight realm - neither enticing nor repulsive, just... dim. While she'd never denied sex's role in a fulfilling life, she'd clearly underestimated its importance.

This epiphany wasn't entirely new. It had sparked the moment Alistair left her, a tiny seed that had grown with each passing day, until it became impossible to ignore. The frank talks she'd had with Fiona - necessary to diagnose Gordon's issues and hopefully fix them - weren't solely responsible. When Fiona casually mentioned demanding three rounds in a single night, Margaret didn't need to sit down. She didn't even flinch. Instead, a fierce curiosity ignited within her, burning away centuries of indifference.

Margaret found herself adrift in a sea of uncertainty. Had Alistair been a skilled lover or a clumsy one? The answer eluded her still. Memories of a time when such distinctions held meaning had faded like old photographs - there were flashes, sure, but they stirred no sensation, carried no weight.

Yet, for all her undead state, she wasn't entirely lifeless. In the dark of night, when she felt God's gaze averted and her body thrummed with a ghostly echo of life, her legs would part. Fingers, slick with saliva, would explore familiar territory. So no, she wasn't completely gone. But then... what was she? Could one simultaneously know and not know? Her current impasse, her utter inability to respond to her husband's overtures, only muddied the waters further.

When Fiona glanced up from her phone, she found Margaret had drifted off. The ancient vampire's face was peaceful in repose, the weight of centuries momentarily lifted as she dozed in the golden late afternoon sun.

❖

Alistair Bruce kicked off his surveillance with a pair of top-notch Swarovski AX Visio binoculars. For three days, he shadowed Isobel, ducking behind walls, bushes, doorways, phone booths, dumpsters, trees, and parked cars in the university lot. But soon, he'd have to step out of the shadows and face her directly.

Each morning, Alistair rose before the sun. His secretary, Bonnie Campbell—a former flame whose office skills had proven far more valuable than her bedroom talents—would arrive to find a terse note: "Unavailable all day." By first light, he was already in position, new binoculars hanging heavy around his neck as he shivered in the pre-dawn chill.

After a close call with Cameron on day one—his son bursting out the front door like a spring-loaded toy—Alistair now parked a street over. As soon as Isobel appeared, he'd zero in with his lenses, hold his breath, then bolt for his car. He'd catch up to her on the street, nestled between manicured flowerbeds, as she merged onto the expressway.

Sleep became a distant memory for Alistair. He'd stumble home each night, exhausted and famished, his head spinning. But his thoughts fixated on one thing: picking up Isobel's trail again tomorrow. This obsession consumed him, a welcome distraction from the painful questions that threatened to overwhelm him—lost years, blood ties shrouded in mystery, and the devastating secret that now rocked his world to its core.

Alistair's mind reeled. How in hell had Margaret kept this quiet? It went against everything their kind stood for—the drive to protect bloodlines ran deeper than any human could grasp. The thought of a grandchild, a new branch on his ancient family tree, sparked something primal in him.

This wasn't just about family drama. It was survival, legacy—the unbroken chain linking past to future. The Bruce clan had weathered centuries, and now, impossibly, there was a new link.

A tidal wave of emotion slammed into Alistair, nearly buckling his knees. An old, almost forgotten tenderness stirred to life. Only something this earth-shattering could crack the shell of indifference he'd built over lifetimes.

Margaret's silence baffled him. For their kind, the pull of blood was overwhelming. It defied logic, defied nature itself. Every fiber of his vampiric being screamed at him to claim what was his, to bring this new life into the fold.

This grandchild wasn't just family. It was the continuation of a line that had endured for ages. The urge to protect, to nurture, to ensure his legacy's survival burned through Alistair's veins like wildfire.

As the truth sank in, Alistair knew nothing would ever be the same. The future loomed, full of danger and possibility. One thing was crystal clear: nothing would come between him and this newfound treasure of his bloodline.

Every time Alistair raised those binoculars, adjusting the focus until Isobel's image crystallized before him, he felt a jolt of recognition. The clarity was almost supernatural, as if he could reach out and touch her through the lens.

Alistair Bruce stood watch outside the university, his eyes never leaving his target. Hours ticked by as she flitted from café to pub, from store to cinema. He shadowed her movements, a ghost on the opposite sidewalk. When she finally emerged, her mere presence captivated him. The way she moved, spoke, smiled – even the simple act of walking along a wall transformed her into a mesmerizing creature.

"She's perfect," he muttered, conviction growing with each passing minute. "The most impeccable granddaughter I could have found."

His vigil left little time for proper meals. Alistair resorted to wolfing down sandwiches – the kind of junk food twenty-somethings survived on. It was a small price to pay to feel closer to her world. His bladder, however, proved a more pressing concern. To his eternal mortification, he found himself ducking into alleyways and scaffolding, grimacing against trees like some desperate vagrant. But what did dignity matter now? At eight hundred years old, he answered to no one.

Alistair knew he should approach her, but something held him back. There was an unsettling fascination in observing her from afar, one he couldn't quite shake. By the second day's end, he realized his behavior had crossed a line. His phone was filled with surreptitious photos, a fact that made him deeply uncomfortable when he confronted it. This wasn't like him at all. What was driving this obsession? He deleted the photos, disturbed by his own actions and determined to face whatever was really going on.

The question of her father – Cameron or Gordon – held no

importance. It changed nothing. Alistair Bruce was, without a doubt, her grandfather. And that was all that mattered.

A young man straight off a movie poster seemed to be her latest conquest. The type that made girls, their mothers, and every gossiping biddy in a three-mile radius weak at the knees. Alistair vaguely recalled a certain Will Poulter's face plastered across Hashtag Magazine last month – Alison Stewart had sworn he was all the rage.

Not that Alistair cared to judge. He had no intention of inserting his decrepit, soon-to-be-repulsive self into the affairs of youth. If she was sleeping with this boy, so be it. It was a simple fact: she'd brought him home, and he hadn't left until morning.

As dusk settled, Alistair watched lights flicker on upstairs. He shifted uncomfortably, trapped by his own surveillance. Nature called, forcing him to relieve himself at the base of a nearby mimosa. A woman walking a black dog fixed him with a withering glare, muttering "Disgusting" as she passed.

Alistair grimaced. The things he endured for family.

❖

Alistair collapsed behind his desk, Latin crooners records filling the air. Bonnie's notes lay scattered before him, but he couldn't focus on stocks, euros, or yen. His mind buzzed with the day's surveillance, a newfound thrill coursing through his veins. Having a granddaughter was intoxicating, demanding every ounce of his attention.

Sleep eluded him. In the depths of night, when loneliness threatened to swallow him whole, a miracle bloomed. He paced his tomb-silent apartment, feeling like a stranger to his wife, his sons, even himself. Yet here, at life's twilight, he'd been granted this gift.

Doubt gnawed at him. Did he deserve Isobel? His failures as a father and husband loomed large. Any moment, he half-expected the door to burst open, someone ready to snatch her away. Or worse –

she might reject him herself, banishing this old fool back to the shadows. He couldn't blame her if she did.

Memories surfaced of an aunt, centuries past, whom he'd neglected for decades. Long dead now, like all the rest. Alistair shuddered, praying history wouldn't repeat itself.

Alistair paced, head bowed and arms crossed, his striped silk pajamas a stark contrast to the plush carpet beneath his Lagerfeld slippers. He clutched his phone, desperate for connection, but found no one to call. The silence wasn't new, but tonight it cut deeper than ever. Unlike in his early vampire days when dawn meant retreat to the safety of darkness, he now yearned for the first light, a prisoner awaiting release.

❖

Despite his tendency for self-flagellation, fixating on age's ravages (though frozen at 73, he wryly mused that at least the worst was yet to come), Alistair Bruce cut a distinguished figure. No lecherous old man, he resembled a country gentleman surveying his lands. His light linen suit, complete with ascot and pocket square, spoke of refined taste. The binoculars might even suggest a sprawling estate rather than voyeuristic intent.

As morning light spilled across the campus, Alistair tried to blend into the scenery, but his behavior stood out. Students cast wary glances his way as he lingered near the quad, binoculars in hand. He shuffled between cars in the parking lot, his movements at odds with his apparent age.

His eyes locked onto Isobel, drinking in her every feature. A lump formed in his throat as he mourned the twenty years stolen from him, years that had transformed her from child to woman without his witness. His focus was so intense that the world around him faded away.

It should have occurred to him how his actions might appear, but Alistair, still carrying the mindset of centuries past, remained oblivious to modern suspicions. His entire being fixated on one thought: making up for lost time with the granddaughter he'd never known.

As Alistair shuffled to a new vantage point, his vampiric grace at odds with his apparent age, he remained fixated on Isobel. Just as she emerged from class to chat with friends beneath the Scots pines, a heavy hand landed on his shoulder. He froze, centuries of predatory instinct warring with his carefully cultivated civility.

Two security guards loomed over him, a muzzled Rottweiler at their feet. Both men sported shaved heads and gleaming eyes that suggested they enjoyed their work a little too much.

"Care to explain yourself, old timer?" the first guard drawled. His partner simply grinned, while the dog panted lazily.

Alistair straightened, projecting an air of aristocratic indignation. "I assure you, gentlemen, there's been a misunderstanding." He paused, realizing how this must look – an older man lurking around campus, spying on young women. Shame washed over him as he grasped the depths of his inappropriate behavior.

The guards exchanged knowing smirks. "Oh yeah? What's your deal then? You some kinda flasher?"

"A flasher?" Alistair echoed, genuine confusion coloring his voice. After eight centuries, humanity still found ways to surprise him.

Alistair's confusion only seemed to fuel their amusement. The silent guard snatched his binoculars, whistling as he trained them on the oblivious young women. His partner's gaze hardened, a predatory glint in his eyes.

As Alistair attempted to extricate himself, he found himself slammed against the van. Centuries ago, these men would have been corpses before they could blink – throats torn out, heads wrenched from bodies. Now, he had to play the frail old man.

"Where do you think you're going, pops?" the first guard growled.

His partner chuckled. "Gotta admit, the old perv's got taste."

Alistair's jaw clenched. To have one of the greatest moments of his long life tainted by these cretins was almost unbearable. Two hundred years of blending in warred with eight hundred years of predatory instinct.

"Listen closely, gramps," the first guard leaned in, his breath hot on Alistair's face. "You want to keep those dentures? How about those brittle bones? At your age, any injury's gonna be permanent."

If only they knew. Alistair could heal from anything they threw at him, but revealing that would open a Pandora's box of questions he couldn't afford to answer.

For a moment, Alistair felt truly powerless. He'd let his desperation to reconnect with Isobel cloud his judgment completely. It didn't even occur to him at first to use his vampiric abilities. Then, as if a switch had been flipped, he remembered. With a deep breath, he locked eyes with the first guard, his voice taking on a hypnotic quality. "It's all good. I'm just waiting for my granddaughter over there."

The guard's eyes glazed over. "Right... your granddaughter."

"You were about to let me go," Alistair continued, his gaze shifting between both guards.

The second guard blinked slowly. "Let you go?"

"Yes," Alistair pressed, maintaining eye contact. "You realized there's been a misunderstanding."

The first guard nodded mechanically. "A misunderstanding..."

"But," Alistair added, sensing their residual suspicion, "you still want to verify my story."

Both guards seemed to snap out of their trance slightly, latching onto this suggestion. The more aggressive one spoke up, "Yeah, we should check that out."

Alistair sighed inwardly. He'd avoided immediate trouble, but now he'd have to face Isobel directly. As the guards flanked him, moving towards the group of students, he felt a mix of anticipation and dread.

Their confrontations often turned ugly. A one-legged man hanging posters or a homeless person seeking shelter could become targets of their frustration. God help you if you were a person of color or an immigrant, even if you were the brightest mind Pakistan had to offer.

Violence came easily to them. Broken noses, blackened eyes, split brows – all were common outcomes when someone dared to challenge their authority. Age offered no protection; child or elder, push them too far and you'd feel their wrath.

Alistair tensed, centuries of instinct screaming at him to fight. But he couldn't risk exposure. He'd have to endure this indignity, praying his granddaughter wouldn't witness his humiliation.

Though trying to focus on Flora Templeton's riveting tale of her mother's alleged tryst with David Bowie at the Montreux Festival, Isobel's attention was drawn to the other end of the parking lot. An elderly man with gray hair seemed to be having trouble with two of the campus's finest examples of security guard stupidity. She glanced over, intrigued to see them pointing in her direction.

The sight of the guards stirred unpleasant memories. Last year, she'd been roped into a harebrained scheme by Lexi's boyfriend, Clyde. He'd convinced Brodie and the gang to help steal a rare Shakespeare print from the library for some shady collector friend of his brother's. The night had ended in a complete fiasco, with alarms blaring and security descending on them before they'd even touched the folio.

Isobel had surprised herself that night, outpacing everyone as they fled through campus. Her speed and agility had leat Brodie and the others in her dust. It wasn't her proudest moment, fueled by a misguided attempt to prove herself to that crowd. The fear she'd felt – intensified by the ill-advised mix of alcohol and pills they'd taken for "courage" – came rushing back.

Now, that same dread crept back as the guards approached, flanking the old man.

"Oh, my dear Isobel," he called out, waving frantically. "Everything's fine. These gentlemen just want to check, guess what..."

"Is he your grandfather?" the more aggressive guard interrupted.

Isobel bristled, instant dislike blossoming. Without missing a beat, she shot back, "What else would he be? My boyfriend?"

❖

As soon as the security guards swaggered away, Isobel turned to Alistair Bruce with a broad smile.

"Well, you've got some nerve..."

Her sentence trailed off as she caught sight of Alistair's suddenly grave expression. Suspicion crept into her voice. "And first, how do you know my name?"

Alistair, overwhelmed, couldn't form words. He spotted a bench under the Scots pines and hurried over, burying his head in his hands.

Isobel hesitated. Flora suggested heading to the chip shop for deep-fried Mars bars and Irn-Bru, but something about the strange man on the bench kept Isobel rooted in place. His furtive glances held a meaning she couldn't decipher, yet they demanded her attention.

"I'll catch up with you later," she told the girls.

It was nearly noon. Around them, the university emptied like a burst dam – car doors slamming, engines revving, students pouring out in a chaotic stream. Isobel approached the bench, curiosity warring with caution.

"Alright then," she said, crossing her arms. "Let's hear it. Who are you, and what's this all about?"

"I'm seventy years old," Alistair declared, his voice bearing the wear of centuries. "Which means our time is limited."

He led her to a secluded spot, dappled shadows offering a semblance of privacy. Isobel's instincts screamed at her to bolt, but curiosity won out.

Alistair leaned forward on the bench. "There are things you need to know."

Isobel's heart raced. He hadn't lied about being her grandfather.

She nearly bolted from their secluded spot, where dappled sunlight barely penetrated the canopy, but something in his tone made her pause.

"Please," Alistair said, "just listen."

Against her better judgment, Isobel settled back onto the worn wooden slats. She listened as he poured out a story that shook her to her core. He told her everything.

Everything.

For Isobel, Alistair's tale of the two brothers was a shock. The revelation that Phil, the man she'd always known as her father, wasn't her biological parent hit her like a punch to the gut. But what struck her even deeper was the realization that she still didn't know which of the two brothers – Gordon or Cameron – was her real father. It was like an open wound, raw and burning.

Yet to Alistair, she was nothing short of a miracle. His voice trembled with emotion as he spoke, and Isobel could scarcely believe her ears.

❖

When he finished, she fled without a word. She rushed to the nearby parking lot, climbed into her Mini Cooper, and set off on the grueling 235-mile drive to Applecross to the man she'd always called Dad.

She had a long journey ahead to sort through the bombshells Alistair had dropped.

❖

Alistair Bruce wandered along the riverbank, his mind oscillating between jagged remorse and cautious elation. He'd done it – revealed the secret. Margaret's fury loomed on the horizon, and he knew there'd be ripples of trouble to come. But the prospect of a miraculous grandchild in his life? That was worth everything.

He clung to his confidence in Isobel. True, she hadn't exactly leapt into his arms or shown unbridled enthusiasm about her expanded family tree. But Alistair refused to entertain doubt. Life had systematically stripped him of affection from his loved ones – a bearable injustice until death started breathing down your neck. He couldn't fathom one last failure in this arena.

This first meeting felt promising. His feet had carried him to this unfamiliar green space by the water. Now, he marveled at the scene before him. People strolled leisurely, children's laughter punctuated the air, and young couples sprawled on the grass. Even the elderly paraded their wiry frames without a hint of self-consciousness. The sheer normalcy of it all – this absurd peace – struck him as profound.

Sunlight poured from the sky like a celestial celebration, warming his face. Alistair's heart quickened. How was it possible to feel such excitement at his age? After decades of darkness, a glimmer of hope had reignited something he'd thought long extinguished.

Alistair's mind drifted as he walked, relief washing over him. She hadn't recoiled from him physically – a stark contrast to his own youth, when he'd fled from his elders, repulsed by their very presence. Of course, that was before he'd learned the truth about his origins.

He'd given Isobel only the barest outline of their family's extraordinary history. How could he possibly convey in one sitting the full weight of it? Centuries of secrets, of blood and shadows, of a legacy that traced back to the very heart of Scottish royalty.

Alistair's jaw clenched, remembering the pivotal moments that had shaped their fate. A desperate gambit born of love and duty. A betrayal that echoed through time. A curse that had transformed their family, binding them to the night in ways Isobel couldn't yet comprehend.

He looked at his granddaughter, seeing hints of ancestors long past in her features. How much of their shared history flowed through her veins? What dormant gifts – or curses – might awaken in her? Alistair knew the time for half-truths was coming to an end.

Soon, Isobel would need to know everything – about the throne, the blood, and the price their family had paid for survival.

He'd glossed over so much, not wanting to overwhelm Isobel on their first meeting. "There's no rush," he'd assured her, hoping to convey a sense of welcome into this strange new family. "I'll tell you everything as we go along."

Now, basking in the afternoon sun, Alistair allowed himself a cautious flicker of hope. There would be time to unravel the centuries of secrets, betrayals, and supernatural twists that had led to this moment. For now, it was enough that Isobel hadn't run screaming. It was a start.

❖

Alistair settled at a wooden table by the river, the sun's warmth seeping into the back of his neck. His mind replayed that crucial moment with Isobel. She had met his gaze unflinchingly, her eyes steady and searching. Behind her, a window had reflected his own image back at him – a sight that had been pure agony.

But Isobel... she hadn't flinched. Hadn't recoiled. That strength, that quiet resolve, it stirred something in Alistair. He already loved her for it.

The realization settled over him like the afternoon sunlight. Isobel possessed a fortitude that echoed through generations of their complicated lineage. In that unwavering stare, he'd glimpsed flashes of the fierce Bruce blood that ran through her veins – through both their veins.

Alistair's fingers traced absent patterns on the weathered table-top. He'd thrown her world into chaos, yet she'd stood her ground. Now, as the river flowed steadily past, he allowed himself to hope. Perhaps this unexpected granddaughter was the key to healing centuries of fractures within their family.

A smile tugged at the corners of his mouth. Yes, Isobel was strong. And in that strength, Alistair saw the promise of redemption.

❖

As Alistair pulled up to the Manor, now Margaret's house, twilight was settling in. A sickly green glow faded above the pines, transforming them into a somber wreath against the darkening sky. Light spilled from the living room windows, warm and inviting.

He hesitated in the shadows, peering inside. Margaret and Fiona sat close, heads bent together in conversation as Fiona painted her nails a striking shade of Saint Laurent Le Vernis Couture in Bleu Majorelle, a vibrant electric blue reminiscent of the designer's famous Moroccan garden.

Gordon sprawled on the floor, his back against the couch, reading aloud to Amelie nestled between his legs. The scene of domestic tranquility made guilt coil in Alistair's stomach, its cold breath ghosting across his face.

With a resigned sigh, he rang the doorbell. He had a key, but Margaret had made it clear his right to waltz in unannounced was revoked. Her reasons remained unspoken, hanging in the air between them.

Amelie answered, her small face peering up at him. Alistair faltered, unsure how to interact with the girl. Gordon's intentions regarding her were still shrouded in mystery, at least to him. Sometimes he managed an awkward pat on her head before she scampered off. This time, she was quicker than his hesitation. His hand hovered uselessly in the air as Amelie disappeared back into the warmth of the house.

Alistair stood there, suddenly feeling every one of his eight hundred years.

He plastered on a smile and stepped into the warm cocoon of domesticity that felt so foreign to him. Gordon's cheerful greeting – "You've come at a good time!" – only heightened Alistair's discomfort. He'd hoped to speak with Margaret alone.

He nodded stiffly to Fiona, still unsure how to navigate their relationship. Margaret's potential revelations about him hung in the air, an invisible barrier. "Lovely nail polish," he offered weakly, before leaning in to brush Margaret's hair with a perfunctory kiss.

Gordon repeated his earlier sentiment, explaining how he and Fiona had planned to stay in, not wanting to leave Margaret alone – a gesture she found both unnecessary and slightly mortifying.

Seizing the opportunity, Alistair rubbed his hands together briskly. "Well," he declared, false cheer in his voice, "Margaret and I won't hesitate to kick you out if you try to linger."

"Works for us," Gordon replied, mimicking his father's hand gesture. In a whirlwind of activity, they readied themselves and tucked Amelie into bed. Gordon swept Fiona up by the waist, and in a blink, they were gone.

Alistair turned to Margaret, eyebrows raised in exaggerated amazement. "Well, what do you make of that?"

Margaret settled into her chair, a hint of satisfaction in her posture. "Gordon and Fiona's relationship has improved significantly," she said, her tone measured. Without delving into specifics, she alluded to a rekindling of their sexual life.

"Really?" Alistair's eyebrows shot up.

Margaret held out her empty glass. As he refilled it with gin, Alistair wondered how long this rebellion would last. For centuries, she'd loyally sipped the family's whisky. Now, each juniper-scented splash was like a tiny middle finger raised in his direction, a crystal tumbler of marital discord. He couldn't quite mask his irritation as he handed the glass back, silently cursing whoever had introduced his wife to the botanical delights of Mother's Ruin.

She caught his expression and launched into an explanation, her voice tinged with exasperation as if lecturing a particularly dense student.

"Fiona's grief naturally dampened her enthusiasm for... sexual relations," Margaret said primly. "Surely that's not difficult to comprehend."

Alistair nodded, comprehension dawning. "Ah, so that was it. No wonder the poor lad looked so miserable. I could see he was dragging himself about."

Margaret's eyes narrowed. "And what exactly did you do, seeing your son in such a state? Watching him lose his appetite, moping around – what action did you take?"

"What do you mean, what did I do?" Alistair sputtered, caught off guard by her sudden intensity. "What was I supposed to do?"

Margaret waved her hand dismissively, clearly uninterested in pursuing Alistair's shortcomings further. Instead, she launched into a detailed account of her own efforts, her voice swelling with barely concealed pride.

"I spent countless hours with that girl," she said, leaning forward. "It was like watching an anvil sink, dragging Gordon down with her. The work I put in – the patient, meticulous work of persuasion – it saved the situation."

Her eyes blazed as she continued, "I showed her a future when all she could see was darkness. I did that while there was still time."

She fixed Alistair with a penetrating stare. "Did you even realize for a moment that heaven sent her to us?"

Alistair shifted uncomfortably. "Well, you have to admit, certain conversations would have been... difficult for me. Unless I wanted to come across as a lecherous old man."

"Thank goodness I'm here then," Margaret retorted, her tone sharp.

Alistair bowed his head, chastened. "Listen, I recognize you did good work. Gordon seems... revived."

Margaret's lips thinned. "I'm not asking for grand proclamations. Gordon simply realized there isn't just one woman on earth. I stepped in because Fiona was slow to remind him of that fact. I intervened because the lives of my two sons mean more to me than anything in this world."

❖

They migrated to the living room, the gin bottle in tow. Margaret deliberately chose an armchair, maintaining a careful distance from Alistair on the couch. The grand Victorian manor, once a shared home, now felt like a battlefield of unspoken tensions. She was acutely aware of his recent attempts to rekindle their lost intimacy, attempts that left her cold.

The split had gutted Margaret, leaving wounds deeper than any fang. For centuries, she and Alistair had been tied by more than vows —a vampiric bond that pulled them together even as it tore them apart.

It took Dr. MacGregor and Father MacKinnon's combined efforts to keep her from drowning. They'd dug deep into their bag of tricks, calling on rituals older than the church itself. Margaret never spoke of those dark rites, but their echoes still haunted her dreams.

Only her sons kept her from losing herself completely. Having them close—creatures of her blood and shadow—was the lifeline she clung to. Their presence anchored her, a tether to her true nature and the darkness that flowed through their veins.

As the dust settled, Margaret found a fragile balance. But the scars remained, etched into her immortal soul—a testament to the price of eternity and the bonds that defied death itself.

Now, having emerged on the other side, she found herself content with their current arrangement. She had no intention of yielding to Alistair's repentant overtures.

A wry smile played at the corners of her mouth as she considered her conversations with Fiona. Those talks had opened her eyes to possibilities she'd never considered in her centuries of existence. If she ever decided to venture back into intimacy – a prospect that no longer seemed as far-fetched as it once had – Alistair Bruce would be the absolute last to know.

He leaned forward to top off her glass. Margaret watched him carefully, her eyes sharp and assessing. She was primed to detect any hint of his usual charm offensive – a telltale glimmer in his eye or the ghost of a seductive smirk. But surprisingly, there was nothing of the sort.

Alistair's expression was uncharacteristically somber. Margaret found herself at a loss, unable to recall ever seeing such a mask on her husband's face. The possibility that he might actually feel guilty, chastened like a scolded child, seemed almost absurd.

"Is your back hurting?" she asked, grasping for some explanation.

He blinked, momentarily caught off guard. "No, no. My back is fine."

Margaret's eyes bore into him, silently demanding an explanation. But Alistair merely patted his pockets, searching for cigarettes that weren't there – a nervous habit she'd seen before.

"Can you tell me what's going on with you?" she pressed.

He squirmed in his seat, the leather creaking beneath him. The image of an old woman fidgeting on her cushion flashed through his mind, and he almost laughed at the absurdity. But the enormity of what he'd done, coupled with a perverse excitement, kept him silent.

Finally, he spoke. "I've come clean to Isobel," he said, his voice barely above a whisper. "I told her everything. Left nothing in the shadows."

The words hung in the air for a heartbeat. Then, from deep within Margaret's body, came a sound – a sharp, whistling inhalation that seemed to get stuck halfway. It was the sound of human machinery reacting to a seismic shock, her body processing the magnitude of his confession before her mind could fully grasp it.

The silence that followed was deafening.

Alistair rose, reaching for Margaret's hand. He patted it awkwardly between his own, offering to fetch her some sparkling water from the kitchen. The thought of its gentle gurgle breaking this awful silence was suddenly appealing. But Margaret shook her head, preferring the harsh bite of gin.

Noticing her labored breathing, he moved to unbutton her

blouse. Margaret's hand shot out, sharply batting him away. She drained her glass in one swift motion, her eyes bright and unfocused.

"On the other hand," Alistair ventured, desperate to fill the silence, "it's a relief."

"Shut up!" The words cracked like a whip.

Alistair winced, genuinely sorry for the distress he'd caused. He knew how deeply invested Margaret was in this whole affair – hadn't she tried to eliminate Rhona not so long ago? A fact everyone seemed to have conveniently forgotten. Her resentment at his meddling was palpable. What right did he have?

As Margaret retreated into intense contemplation, Alistair hunched his shoulders and began to pace. He moved like a man caught in a storm, wandering aimlessly on a dark night punctuated by flashes of lightning.

Margaret's posture was rigid, her eyes flashing with barely contained fury. Alistair wisely kept his distance, acutely aware of the Tiffany lamp within her reach. The delicate stained glass creation, a cherished gift from their old friend Charles Lewis Tiffany himself, suddenly seemed far more fragile in the face of his wife's simmering rage. He'd seen her violent reactions in extreme situations before. For a tense moment, he wondered if she might actually hurl the priceless piece at his head. Or worse, she might forgo the lamp entirely and sink her fangs into him – a violation of their most sacred trust. Even after centuries, the thought of violence between mates remained utterly taboo.

Despite the tension, thoughts of Isobel – of being a grandfather – filled Alistair with a resolve that surprised him. He knew, without a doubt, he'd make the same choice again.

When Margaret finally spoke, her voice was low and deadly serious. "I promise you this," she said, each word carefully measured. "If this goes wrong because of you, you will never set foot in this house again."

Alistair bristled. "Because of me?" he shot back, his own anger rising. "What's 'because of me'? This would have come out sooner or later. You should have told me right away. You and she are to blame. All of this is because of you!"

"She was supposed to abort," Margaret hissed. "She swore to me. On her hospital bed. She wasn't supposed to keep her, do you hear me?"

"And then she changed her mind. And you two decided to keep it secret. For twenty years. Both of you. She thought, 'Hey, I'll keep this child,' and you just sat there without flinching. You waited for it to happen."

Alistair held his ground, refraining from dredging up more painful truths. He didn't want to hurt Margaret further. His new goal was to make the most of "whatever time he had left" – a darkly ironic thought for a creature with eternity stretching before him. She was part of that grand scheme. He couldn't help but admire how exceptionally well-preserved she looked – her discreet surgeries and skin treatments had worked wonders. And those breasts – stunning, a true masterpiece skillfully crafted by Dr. MacGregor that would make anyone's head spin. Alistair mused that it wouldn't be long before she found herself a young toyboy to entertain her newfound vitality.

He approached with the gin bottle. Margaret's anger seemed to have ebbed, replaced by a look of weary resignation. He refilled both their glasses.

"She's quite the girl," he said, a proud smirk playing at his lips. "What a miracle."

Margaret gave him an almost dazed look. For the first time in centuries, he was drinking something other than Bruce whisky.

"I like her a lot," Alistair continued, his tone light. "We missed her first steps, but we also missed her puberty – which seems fair to me. And there's more to come. We'll have to be there for her."

He was trying to approach the subject gently, but it was clear Margaret's concerns lay elsewhere. The existence of a granddaughter paled in comparison to her worry about how their sons would react to this news.

"Well," he explained, "it will probably change something for one and nothing for the other."

"But what if... What if..." Margaret stammered, unable to complete the thought.

Alistair considered her for a moment, then stepped out onto the terrace.

❖

The renewed attraction he felt for her didn't blind him. It didn't erase the memory of a time when he couldn't stand her anymore, when this woman had utterly exhausted him.

He gazed out at the Victorian manor, its grandeur and unique gardens still capable of surprising him after two centuries. It was as if the place suddenly revealed new facets, delivering fresh pleasures even after all this time.

The night stretched out before him, calm and starry, still as a Buddha. Alistair savored the sensation of infinite space it brought, a stark contrast to the tension-filled room he'd just left. His newfound appreciation for Margaret, the manor, the night sky – it all felt like a rediscovery. Perhaps this was the curse and blessing of immortality: the chance to fall in and out of love with the same person, the same place, over centuries. To find new meaning in what once seemed mundane or unbearable.

As he stood there, Alistair wondered how many more times they would dance this dance.

CHAPTER 20

BISHOP OF ST ANDREWS' MANOR

NOVEMBER 1324

The first snows of winter howled outside the manor, but the chill within the Bishop's chambers cut deeper than any storm. Six months had passed since the birth of the twin princes, yet for King Robert the Bruce, it felt like years.

He stood before the blazing hearth, the firelight casting long shadows across his careworn face. Behind him, a hushed argument brewed.

"He grows weaker by the day, Your Grace," the royal physician muttered, his voice barely above a whisper. "The winter..."

"I'll hear no more of your dire predictions," Queen Elisabeth hissed, cradling the smaller of the twin boys to her breast. "Jean is a Bruce. He'll survive."

Robert turned, his eyes finding the cradle where David slept soundly. The contrast between the twins was stark – and growing starker with each passing day. David thrived, his cheeks rosy, his cries strong. Jean, however...

"What of the wet nurse?" Robert asked, his voice rough with fatigue. "Has she any luck?"

The physician shook his head. "He hardly suckles, Your Grace. It's as if... as if he hungers for something else."

A log shifted in the fire, sending sparks dancing. In that moment, Jean's eyes fluttered open. Robert froze.

There it was again – that ancient, knowing look. A gaze that seemed to hold centuries of secrets. Jean's tiny hand reached out, grasping at the air with surprising strength.

"Robert?" Elisabeth's voice wavered. "He's looking at you. Come, hold your son."

Hesitantly, Robert approached. As he bent to lift Jean from Elisabeth's arms, the babe's eyes locked onto his. A voice, cold as the winter wind, whispered through his mind:

The debt comes due, King of Scots. We grow hungry.

Robert jerked back, heart pounding. "Did you hear that?" he gasped.

Elisabeth and the physician exchanged worried glances. "Hear what, my love?" Elisabeth asked softly.

Robert shook his head, trying to clear it. "Nothing. Just... the wind."

Jean began to wail, a sound too strong for his frail body. As Elisabeth tried to soothe him, a chill swept through the room. The fire guttered, nearly extinguishing.

In the sudden dimness, shadows seemed to coalesce around Jean's cradle. Robert blinked, and for a heartbeat, he could have sworn he saw dark figures looming over his son, their hunger palpable.

"Your Grace?" The physician's voice shook. "Perhaps... perhaps it's time we considered the old ways. There are those who say—"

"Silence!" Robert roared, fear making his voice harsh. "I'll hear no talk of pagan rites or dark bargains. He's my son, damn you. My heir."

"And what of David?" Elisabeth whispered, her eyes darting to the healthier twin. "If Jean is heir, then David..."

The unspoken implication hung heavy in the air. In that moment, the full weight of the crown bore down on Robert as never before. Two sons. One throne. And dark forces circling like wolves in the night.

Jean's cries reached a fever pitch, drowning out the howling wind outside. As Robert watched, helpless, the babe's face seemed to shift, flickering between infant softness and something... older. Something that had waited eons to be born.

Suddenly, Jean's wails ceased. The silence that followed was deafening. The infant's eyes, now clear and focused, fixed on Robert with terrifying intensity.

"What do you want?" Robert whispered, the words escaping before he could stop them.

Jean's tiny hand reached out once more, grasping Robert's finger with inhuman strength. And in that touch, Robert saw visions of blood and crown, of sacrifice and terrible power. He saw Scotland's future balanced on the edge of a knife.

As the visions faded, Robert made a choice. He stepped forward, taking Jean from Elisabeth's trembling arms.

"Listen to me," he said, voice low and fierce. "All of you. Jean will live. He will thrive. And if any power, earthly or divine, thinks to claim him..." His eyes blazed with a fire that matched the hungry gleam in Jean's. "They'll have to go through me first."

The shadows retreated, but the air remained charged with an ancient, terrible promise. Jean cooed softly, once again just a babe. But as Robert cradled him close, he knew in his bones that the true battle – for his son's soul, for Scotland's future – had only just begun.

Outside, the winter storm raged on, as if the very elements themselves sought to test the strength of Robert's vow.

❖

The storm's fury abated, leaving an uneasy quiet in its wake. Robert stood at the window, Jean cradled in his arms, when a sharp knock broke the silence. The door creaked open, admitting Bishop Wishart, his face grave beneath his hood.

"Your Grace," the Bishop intoned, bowing slightly. "I must speak with you. Alone."

Robert's jaw tightened, but he nodded. Gently, he placed Jean back in Elisabeth's arms, brushing a kiss across her forehead. "I'll return shortly, my love."

In the cold stone corridor, the Bishop's words came in urgent whispers. "Your Grace, we must discuss the future. Scotland's future."

"Speak plainly, Wishart," Robert growled.

The Bishop's eyes darted to the closed chamber door. "The war with England grows more dire by the day. We cannot afford... distractions."

"My sons are not distractions," Robert snapped.

"No," Wishart agreed, his voice softening. "They are hope. But hope, like an army, must be deployed strategically." He paused, choosing his next words carefully. "There are whispers, Your Grace. About the younger prince. About... unnatural occurrences."

Robert's hand went to the hilt of his sword. "Choose your next words with care, Bishop."

Wishart held up his hands placatingly. "I speak only out of concern for Scotland – and for your family. Have you considered... separating the boys?"

"Separating?" Robert's voice was dangerously low.

"For their safety," Wishart pressed on. "Keep David here, strong and visible. A symbol of Scotland's resilience. But Jean... the frail one... perhaps he would fare better away from court. The west coast, perhaps? The climate is milder there."

Robert's mind raced. The idea was abhorrent, yet... "And if he doesn't survive the journey?"

The Bishop's eyes glinted in the torchlight. "Then it would appear God had called another innocent soul to Heaven. A tragedy, to be sure, but one that would simplify matters of succession."

"You speak of my son," Robert snarled.

"I speak of Scotland's future," Wishart countered. "Think, Your Grace. A hidden prince, given a new identity. If he survives, you have insurance for your legacy. If not..." He spread his hands. "The realm is spared potential conflict."

Robert turned away, his thoughts a maelstrom. The Bishop's words, though cold, held a certain logic. Jean's weakness, the whispers of dark magic, the looming threat of war, the constant menace of vampires...

"And what of Elisabeth?" he asked, his voice hoarse.

Wishart's eyes gleamed in the torchlight. "Women's hearts are tender things, Your Grace. It's our duty to shield them from life's harsher truths."

The Bishop leaned closer, his words a mere breath. "Consider how this guards against... softer impulses. No motherly weakness jeopardizing your plans. A clean break ensures both your sons and your crown remain secure."

Robert's fists clenched. He thought of Jean's otherworldly gaze, of the visions that haunted his dreams. Of David, strong and uncomplicated, a future king unburdened by whispers of the supernatural.

"I... I need time to consider," he said at last.

The Bishop nodded, a flicker of triumph in his eyes. "Of course, Your Grace. But remember, winter deepens. If a decision is to be made..."

"Enough," Robert cut him off. "Leave me."

As Wishart's footsteps faded, Robert leaned against the cold stone wall, his mind reeling.

The future of his family, of Scotland itself, hung in the balance. Two sons. Two paths. And a choice that would echo through history.

Elisabeth's face swam before his eyes, her trust and love a beacon in the storm of his thoughts. Could he bear to keep such a weighty secret from her? The idea of separation, of sending Jean away, sat like lead in his stomach. Yet the alternative - watching her face crumple with fear and doubt - seemed equally unbearable.

Robert straightened, decision crystallizing. Elisabeth was his queen, his partner in all things. If they were to face this threat, whatever it truly was, they would face it together. The truth might bring fear, but it also brought strength. And in the battles to come, they would need every ounce of strength they could muster.

With a heavy heart, he turned back towards the chamber door. Beyond it, Elisabeth waited with their sons – one thriving, one fading, both irreplaceable. Elisabeth looked up, their eyes meeting across the room. In that moment of silent connection, he saw her strength, her fear, her unwavering love.

Robert took a deep breath, steeling himself for the battles to come, both on the field and within his own soul.

The fate of a kingdom rested on his next move.

CHAPTER 21

Even at twenty, a phone call wouldn't kill you. Rhona sighed, glancing at her silent phone for the hundredth time. Was it too much to ask Isobel to let her know she was staying out all night? It wasn't about being sentimental or losing face. Just a quick text. That's all.

Not that Rhona was worried sick. Her concern was more like parents in safer countries who still couldn't shake the specter of drugs, violence, or car crashes. The what-ifs that gnawed at the edges of your mind.

After a lonely breakfast, Rhona lost herself in "Sense and Sensibility" until mid-morning. She'd just finished some Saki short stories, savoring the biting wit. Another check of her phone. Still nothing.

Work beckoned by noon. Today's piece was about a transgender teacher who'd been a human shield in the Ukrainian War and now crafted organic wine in the rolling hills of Napa Valley. Alison, her editor, was practically bouncing off the walls with excitement. "This'll set Hashtag's website ablaze!" she'd gushed, her eyes gleaming. "It'll explode across social media like wildfire!"

Hashtag wasn't just about lifestyle tips and celebrity gossip, though. The magazine had teeth, and it wasn't afraid to bite into hard-hitting issues. They prided themselves on their strong opinions and their willingness to ruffle a few feathers—or a whole flock, if necessary. This story was the perfect cocktail—equal parts human interest and controversy, with a twist of the unexpected. It was exactly the kind of content that kept their readers glued to their screens, hungry for more.

Alison loved the teacher's story, and Rhona had to admit, the woman was captivating. The photo showed her in a khaki tank top and black boots, sun-kissed cheeks glowing as she held up glistening grapes against a cloudless sky. Alison was counting on Rhona to spin literary gold.

Twenty-four hours now. No word from Isobel.

Rhona's fingers hovered over her phone. She forced herself to set it down. Isobel was an adult. She'd call when she was ready.

But as Rhona stared at her blank document, all she could think about was her daughter's silence stretching into the unknown.

❖

Later, Rhona fidgeted on the sofa in Alison's office, guilt gnawing at her. "I've left a few messages," she admitted. "I'm starting to worry."

Alison spun in her sleek Knoll chair, shaking her head. "I could never hack being a mother. Too much stress."

Before Rhona could respond, a knock interrupted them. "Margaret Bruce is here," the intern receptionist announced. "In person."

Rhona and Alison exchanged puzzled glances. What could she want?

Margaret swept in, looking like a spy from an old movie – dark Saint Laurent suit, sunglasses, head scarf. Her skin seemed paler than yesterday, almost ashen. Her words carried the authority of ages, leaving no room for dissent.

"We need to overcome our mutual dislike," she said without preamble, fixing Rhona with an intense stare. "It won't be easy, but you and I must join forces."

Rhona held up a hand. "Whoa, slow down. Let's take a breath here."

"No time," Margaret snapped. "Every second counts. Trust me on this."

"Listen," Rhona said, her voice hard. "Nothing is that urgent. And I'm not sure I can trust you at all."

Alison, sensing the tension, bustled in with drinks. The kind that burn going down.

"Don't be so dramatic," Margaret snapped, her impatience barely masked. "I've hardly ruffled a feather. No need to cry murder." She glanced at Alison, seeking an ally. "See what I mean? Always over-reacting."

Margaret's haughty posture couldn't hide the nervous energy radiating off her. She took a deep breath. "Here's the deal. Alastair's done what shouldn't have been done. That's where we stand."

Alison's brow furrowed, clearly lost. But Rhona's eyes squeezed shut, a pained expression crossing her face. "No," she whispered, hand to her forehead. "Don't tell me..."

"What did Alistair do?" Alison pressed, looking between the two women.

Margaret's laugh was bitter. "You know Alistair. If there's an irreparable mistake to be made, he'll find it."

Rhona spun towards the bay window, arms crossed tight. The city sprawled below, oblivious to the tension in the room. She gnawed at her thumbnail until it split, hardly noticing the sting.

❖

Cameron gazed at Rhona's sleeping form, marveling at how she still stirred his soul after all these years. Seven centuries of existence, and no other woman had ever affected him quite like this.

He remembered the all-consuming fire of their early days with a fond smile. That passionate inferno had mellowed, but his feelings hadn't dimmed. If anything, they'd deepened, grown richer. Different, yes, but wonderfully so.

This morning, he'd woken early, as if some sweet premonition had roused him. And there she was – a vision bathed in dawn light, so breathtakingly beautiful he'd nearly sighed aloud. Rhona in her purest form, utterly captivating.

Cameron savored the moment, realizing he'd achieved the goal he'd set two decades ago. This was what he'd longed for all along. Watching Rhona's peaceful face, a satisfied smile played on his lips. He felt... content. Astonished and delighted by the depth of his happiness.

How could he feel anything else? This was everything he'd ever wanted.

Yet a tiny whisper of unease tickled the back of his mind. Was this truly the pinnacle? After centuries of existing, was domestic bliss enough to sustain him? Cameron pushed the thought away, focusing on Rhona's soft breathing.

He'd found his haven. Nothing could shatter this perfect moment.

❖

As dawn crept across Rhona's skin, Cameron marveled at his luck. Their growing intimacy revealed new depths of happiness he hadn't even imagined. Rationally, he knew he should feel utterly content.

He left Rhona sleeping, mind buzzing with plans. It was time to make things official, to marry her and leave this limbo behind. Start their real life together.

At six, he slipped out, settling into his Aston Martin. Jazz filled the car as he cruised through the quiet city. Sunlight glinted off freshly-washed sidewalks, everything bathed in a soft glow.

Yet, inexplicably, serenity eluded him. A nagging restlessness lurked beneath his joy. Perhaps, he reasoned, total satisfaction was impossible. Even the bluest sky had its imperfections.

The road wound upward, towards the family manor. Sunlight set the hilltop ablaze while shadows clung to the forest below. Cameron's thoughts drifted. Would he make a good husband? He wanted to believe so, but doubt whispered in his ear.

The manor loomed ahead, a reminder of centuries past. Of responsibilities and expectations. Cameron's grip tightened on the wheel. He'd chosen this path, this life with Rhona. It was everything he'd wanted.

Wasn't it?

He pushed the doubt away, focusing on the road ahead. Whatever uncertainties lingered, he was committed to this future. To Rhona. The rest... well, he'd face that when the time came.

❖

Cameron pulled into the Manor's garage, his eyes immediately drawn to Gordon's DBS. The once-sleek Aston Martin was now a technicolor nightmare, every inch covered in crude graffiti. Neon pink phalluses competed for space with poorly drawn tits and a rainbow of insults. "SUCK THIS!" sprawled across the hood in dripping green paint, while "LOSER" adorned the trunk in angry red letters. Brock had even managed to scrawl "WANKER" along the roof panel.

Cameron parked his own car a safe distance away, grabbing his laundry bag with a resigned sigh. As he stepped out, a jaw-cracking yawn escaped him. It was far too early for this level of chaos.

One of the garage's door rolled up, revealing Gordon in full decontamination mode. He looked like he'd raided a post-apocalyptic janitorial closet – cap pulled low, goggles strapped tight, and a scarf covering half his face. Rubber boots and paint-splattered overalls completed the ensemble. In his gloved hands, a pressure washer steamed ominously, promising either salvation or further destruction for the unfortunate DBS.

Cameron settled onto a nearby stone wall, morbidly fascinated. The Manor's grand facade and manicured grounds seemed a world away from this grimy tableau. Here was vampire life at its most unglamorous – his brother, centuries old, preparing to wage war against obscene graffiti at dawn.

As Gordon revved up the washer, Cameron braced himself. This promised to be quite the show.

Gordon attacked the car with gusto, disappearing in a cloud of soapy mist along with the unfortunate Aston Martin.

Fiona materialized, pristine in white sponge robe. She planted herself next to Cameron, shoulders tight and fists jammed in her pockets. "I'm so embarrassed," she muttered.

Cameron chuckled, nudging her gently. "Don't be silly."

He watched Gordon's manic cleaning, torn between laughter and concern. This was his family – messy, unpredictable, but undeniably his. A far cry from the serene morning with Rhona.

As soap suds flew, Cameron felt that familiar tug of conflicting loyalties. The life he'd built with Rhona versus the chaos of his vampire clan. He sighed, wondering not for the first time if he could truly have both.

Gordon battled the graffiti, his pressure washer at full blast. The result was more chaos than cleanliness, soap suds flying everywhere. He waded through a rainbow puddle, oblivious to Fiona's distressed sighs.

"We found it like this after dinner in a wonderful restaurant," Fiona explained, her voice tight with frustration. "Paint was already dry, and my psychotic ex had vanished." She shook her head. "He's got nothing better to do than fuck with me. Pardon my French."

They watched Gordon's frantic efforts, like a man desperately trying to resuscitate his beloved car. Cameron crossed his arms, squinting in the sunlight. Without looking away from the spectacle, he raised his voice over the washer's roar: "I was thinking we could all have dinner soon. The four of us. It's time, don't you think?"

Fiona's eyes lit up, a spark of life returning to her weary features. "With pleasure," she agreed, warmth creeping into her voice. "I'd like that."

This was the moment she'd been waiting for, hoping for. Since losing her son, her enthusiasm for life had dimmed, her heart a constantly bleeding wound. But Cameron's invitation... it meant something. It legitimized her place, put her on equal footing with Rhona. Strengthened her position in this strange, immortal family.

She'd never forget her child, never stop cherishing his memory. The pain would be her lifelong companion. But Fiona was tired of losing on all fronts. She craved some comfort, some respite from scraping by on a meager income. A shiver of anticipation ran through her, imagining a life with more light, more space to breathe.

Before Gordon, she'd been a magnet for jerks and idiots. Now, despite his flaws, she had a chance at something more.

Cameron gestured towards Gordon with a resigned sigh. His brother was still at it, one hand on the sprayer, the other on his hip, determination outweighing common sense.

"He's my brother," Cameron said, shaking his head. "I have to accept him as he is."

Gordon finally gave up, slamming the washer off and ripping away his makeshift hazmat gear. "The cops don't give a flying fuck," he snarled, flinging his goggles across the garage. "They think it's a bloody joke. Bunch of knob-heads, the lot of them. Meanwhile, what the hell am I supposed to do about that prick? Just because he's stuck in a chair doesn't mean he gets to—"

He kicked at a puddle of soapy water, sending it splashing against the car's tires. "I swear, I'm this close to rolling that smug bastard down a flight of stairs. See how he likes being helpless then."

Gordon slumped against the car, not caring about the wet paint. "Fuck."

"He's right," Fiona chimed in. "Brock's a real menace."

Cameron squinted at the horizon, then turned to Fiona. "You'll think poorly of me, but if we're ruling out violence... why not destroy his wheelchair?"

A moment of stunned silence followed. Fiona's expression wavered between horror and reluctant admiration. Gordon, however, looked intrigued by this devious suggestion.

As they headed inside for breakfast, Fiona excused herself to change. Watching her ascend the stairs, Cameron remarked, "What a woman. She's really simplified our lives, hasn't she? Easy on the eyes, too."

Gordon just nodded, avoiding his brother's gaze.

They set about toasting bread, the kitchen quiet save for the soft scrape of knife on crisp surface.

Cameron leaned forward, his elbows on his knees. "I'm thinking of making a move with Rhona soon. I wanted you to know."

Gordon's eyes flashed. "Do I look like an idiot? You afraid I won't get it?"

Cameron winced inwardly. He knew he was overdoing it, talking to his brother like he was slow. But how could he believe Gordon had truly given up on Rhona? It seemed impossible. So he pressed on, determined to make sure Gordon understood what was coming.

They sat in silence on the terrace, the morning air heavy between them.

Behind the curtains, Margaret watched from her bedroom window. Tears welled in her eyes and she stepped back, covering her mouth to stifle a sob.

Dark times loomed ahead for all of them. She decided then – she'd go to church before finding Rhona. Perhaps the Lord would grant them His grace in the face of the storm to come.

❖

The tension in Alison's office was a living thing, making the air shimmer and the world beyond the windows seem impossibly distant.

Rhona whirled to face Margaret, cutting her off before she could speak. "Not a word," she snapped, her voice steel-edged. Inside, anger simmered, threatening to boil over.

At least Isobel's vanishing act made a twisted sort of sense. Not comforting, but logical. Alistair Bruce and his big mouth had lit the fuse, and now Rhona was watching it burn towards an explosion she couldn't stop.

She punched in Phil's number - her so-called father. When his voicemail picked up, she left a terse message.

Just then, the door opened. Alistair slunk in, a man-shaped shadow oozing guilt. No one bothered to ask; he just sank into a chair, head bowed.

"I'm sorry," he muttered, not meeting anyone's eyes. "But I don't trust you. Any of you. Who knows what crazy scheme you'll cook up next?"

When he learned Isobel had been MIA for twenty-four hours - likely because of him - the color drained from his face. Pain lanced across his features.

Margaret's fury died mid-sentence as Alistair collapsed.

One moment he stood tall, the next he crumpled like a puppet with cut strings. Her gut twisted. Vampires didn't just fall. Not like this.

They all rushed to Alastair's side—Margaret, Rhona, and Alison converging in a flurry of movement. Margaret's cold dread quickly morphed into anger, a familiar heat rising in her chest.

She'd seen him in dire straits before—bleeding, impaled, slashed, burned. But those were the natural consequences of fierce battles. This... this was different.

Alastair's face was a mask of pain, eyes wide with a fear she'd never seen before. His lips moved, forming silent words. A plea. Margaret felt the chain of their shared centuries bind them like an exhausting contract. Whatever this was, it went beyond anything they'd faced.

As she cradled his head, Margaret's mind raced. What could bring down a being as old and powerful as Alistair? What force could make immortality seem suddenly, horribly fragile?

She barked orders, her voice sharp with fear poorly disguised as rage. For the first time in centuries, Margaret tasted true terror on her tongue.

❖

The aftermath unfolded like a fever dream: sirens wailing, an ambulance screaming through traffic, chaos erupting in Hashtag Magazine offices. Margaret swayed on her feet, nausea rising. The mad dash across Edinburgh was a blur of near-misses and frantic worry.

Entropy was having a field day. An old man lay in a hospital bed while a young girl had vanished into thin air. Fiona, back part-time and now huddled with them in the ICU, couldn't shake the feeling they were cursed. She managed to snag them a quiet nook, all fake plants and uncomfortable chairs trying too hard to be soothing.

Rhona sat apart, eyes fixed on the ceiling's bland acoustic tiles. She imagined the call she couldn't make: Hey Cameron, got a minute? Two things. One, flip a coin—that's your odds of being Isobel's dad. Two, your father's in the hospital, maybe dying. Oh, and Isobel's gone missing. How's your day going?

She pocketed her phone, hands shaking. Cameron probably wouldn't keel over, but this mess could shatter their fragile peace. She doubled over, head nearly touching her knees, trying to breathe.

Meanwhile, Fiona and Alison waged a silent war for Margaret's attention. Lucky for them, Margaret had two hands for squeezing and wasn't playing favorites in this crisis.

Rhona glared at the family huddle, then jabbed at Phil's number again. His voicemail greeted her with some moronic joke he'd downloaded, probably chuckling to himself like an idiot. It sparked a fresh wave of anger.

"Phil, I swear to God," she hissed. "Five minutes. Call me back or else."

As she hung up, Dr. MacGregor appeared, looking harried. He pulled Margaret aside, speaking in hushed tones.

"Right, let's sort this mess out before the tabloids catch wind of it."

Alison's bloody overeager intern had called the ambulance before anyone could stop her, transforming their carefully guarded secret into a potential media circus. The last thing they needed was Alistair's condition splashed across the evening news.

"The cardiac unit is handling the immediate crisis, but we need to move fast," MacGregor said, his voice calm but firm.

Margaret ran a hand through her perfect hair, fixing an invisible lock, exhaustion evident in her face. "I've been 'misting' most of the staff, but it's getting complicated."

MacGregor's brow furrowed deeply. "I'm working on it."

Margaret continued, "A vampire having a heart attack... You and I have to talk. What's next? Diapers?"

MacGregor cleared his throat. "We'll figure it out. Could be the nervous system rebuilding. Has he experienced intense emotions lately? It could be triggering something unexpected."

Margaret brushed the question aside. "For now, let's focus on containment. How soon can we get him to your facility?"

The doctor's eyes darted around the waiting room. "Our private ambulance is downstairs. The moment we can move him safely, we will. For now, I've got my most trusted staff on rotation. As far as anyone else is concerned, he's just another VIP patient requiring specialized care."

"And there's Fiona to consider," Margaret said, her concern evident. "We can't exactly wipe her memory, can we?"

❖

Phil wasn't actually unable to answer. He was just... taking his time. Finding Isobel first seemed like the smarter play.

He knew his ex-wife well enough to predict this meltdown, even if she'd deny being affected. This kind of drama was practically on schedule.

Last night, Isobel had shown up at Applecross, crashing on the couch. Thinking ahead, Phil had siphoned the Mini's gas tank before bed, hoping to keep her from bolting. But when he'd bet Sheila - his latest barely-legal fling and the reason they'd slept in - that Isobel would still be there, he'd lost. The couch was empty. Somehow, the girl had vanished again.

"This is such bullshit," Sheila whined, heading for the bathroom. "I need to wash my hair."

"Seriously? Now?" Phil groaned, but she was already gone.

Phil scowled as Sheila disappeared. She knew exactly what she was doing, denying him his favorite part of their routine. Totally unfair. But then again, had any of the teenage girls he obsessed over ever played fair?

Irritated, he barely registered the perfect summer day unfolding around him. Sunlight dappled through leaves, birds trilled, and butterflies danced around the bluebells Rhona had planted during one of her rare good moods. Phil ignored it all, climbing into his Land Rover with a grunt. Time to track down his maybe-daughter.

❖

Gordon and Cameron were wrapping up their photo shoot for Hashtag Magazine when the hospital called. They were changing in Heather's office—now a makeshift studio—with her fluttering eyelashes and helpful hands passing them shirts and pants. Then the bad news hit.

At least he wasn't dead. Small comfort, but they'd take it.

Machines beeped and whirred around him, his still form a shock to their system. A vampire on death's door? It didn't compute. Had the news of becoming a grandfather jolted some humanity back into his centuries-old veins? Could a soul regrow after so long? They stared at his motionless body, questions swirling, until a nurse ushered them out.

Rhona pounced on Cameron the moment they hit the hallway. Margaret, sensing the urgency, latched onto Gordon's arm and steered him away—a clever distraction.

"Cameron," Rhona hissed, "I've got an Isobel situation."

He met her eyes, instantly alert. "I'm all ears."

"Need to pick her up from her father's. Now."

Cameron nodded, already moving. "Let's roll."

❖

They grabbed essentials from their places and hit the road. The Vantage V12 purred beneath them, top down, as they chased the setting sun.

Rhona found herself stealing glances at Cameron. Loving him was effortless. He didn't waste time with doubts or negotiations—he trusted her reasons and acted. With him, she felt wholly herself.

Storm clouds might've loomed on their horizon, but for now, life felt good. They wove through golden fields and misty plains, playing chicken with speed cameras. The car's stereo pulsed with the vibrant rhythms of Buena Vista Social Club, the perfect soundtrack for their impromptu road trip. Every so often, Cameron's hand would find her thigh, a casual gesture of comfort and connection.

Rhona broke the comfortable silence, filling Cameron in on their mission. She didn't divulge everything, but shared the crucial bits—like how Phil had managed to lose track of Isobel.

Cameron's jaw tightened. "Can't say I'm shocked," he muttered.

His grip tightened on the wheel, old rage simmering. No, honestly, even today he hated that bastard. The old fury bubbled up, hot and visceral. Twenty years ago, barely out of his hospital bed, Cameron had hunted for Phil with murder in his heart. He'd fantasized about tearing him apart—slicing him to ribbons, crushing his skull, ripping out his throat with fangs bared. But Rhona and Phil had vanished without a trace, retreating to Applecross for a solid year. That godforsaken corner of the Highlands might as well have been the edge of the world. It had saved Phil's worthless hide, denying Cameron his revenge.

"Perfect specimen of a bastard," Cameron muttered.

Rhona sighed. "Don't. He was just... opportunistic. Always played his cards right, remember? Consoling girls was his specialty."

Cameron's lips quirked, despite himself. Didn't he owe this impromptu adventure with Rhona to Phil's screw-up? As the sky blazed crimson, a plan crystallized. Some words—like a marriage proposal, cryptic or not—deserved the right setting. He'd seize this moment. Nothing stood in his way.

❖

They raced into the gathering dark, sleek as an arrow. Rhona's fingers ghosted along his neck, and Cameron leaned into her touch. Encouraged, she continued, "Isobel learned something big. It explains her behavior."

"Everything's epic at her age," Cameron agreed. "Part of being young. So, what's the big reveal?"

Rhona savored the moment, relishing their unexpected adventure despite the looming chaos. "I'll let Isobel tell you herself," she deflected.

❖

They grabbed a quick bite at The King's Highway in Inverness. The meat passed muster, and the mashed potatoes offered a comforting warmth. Normally, Cameron might've suggested one of the cozy en-suite rooms upstairs, but he held back, not wanting to seem insensitive.

Rhona's phone pinged—a message from Phil. "Isobel's okay," it read, both calming and unsettling her. Time was running short. Here in this bustling pub, or later in the intimate confines of the car? This busy normalcy felt right.

The waitress set down their coffees. Rhona took a deep breath. "Cameron, here's what's going on..." She launched into the full story, surrounded by the ebb and flow of pub life—families settling in, kids darting between tables, staff wiping down surfaces, laughter punctuating the air.

❖

As Rhona finished, Cameron's face went blank. She braced herself, knowing the stakes. If he reacted badly, she wouldn't blame him—but it would mean she'd misjudged everything, and that thought was too depressing to dwell on.

Suddenly, Cameron shook himself, like a dog shedding water. "Wow!" he exclaimed, offering nothing more.

❖

Back in the car, Rhona felt drained yet oddly buoyant. Joy, weariness, and a strange lightness tangled inside her.

As they hit the road, she caught the gleam in Cameron's eye before feigning sleep. She didn't want to talk, but emotion swelled in her chest. It felt like surfacing after a long dive. The whole situation balanced on a knife's edge—too precarious for most to even consider. She knew this ground, knew how easily bridge planks could rot beneath your feet.

❖

Near midnight, deep in a dense forest, Cameron pulled into an empty rest stop. They stretched their legs, gulping in crisp night air.

As they wandered in the darkness, Cameron's arm snaked around her waist. "You know," he murmured, "this is just another reason we should make things official between us."

Rhona paused, asking for a cigarette. Cameron obliged, watching as she cupped the flame, eyes downcast.

"This is a proper proposal, you know," he teased, voice warm. "You're allowed to show a little enthusiasm. No audience here."

She searched his face, finding only tenderness in that unwavering smile.

"Hold me," Rhona whispered. "I think I'm about to cry."

Cameron held Rhona close, centuries of memories weighing on him. He'd known countless women, but never proposed. Commitment had always seemed pointless to an immortal.

Yet here he was, considering the unthinkable. With Rhona, binding himself permanently felt vital. She'd redefined love, even after the family drama that nearly broke him two decades ago.

For the first time, Cameron felt the true weight of commitment. This wasn't just a proposal—it was rewriting his existence. The thought both terrified and thrilled him.

The few tears that dampened Cameron's shirt were a poor reflection of the storm inside her. Joy, anxiety, pain—each deserved its own torrent, but she couldn't begin to release it all. In her mind, his proposal was like a cherry rolling towards a vast, tumultuous ocean.

CHAPTER 22
CHAPEL OF GREYFRIARS MONASTERY
10 FEBRUARY 1306

The Greyfriars Monastery loomed against the twilight sky, its stone walls stained crimson by the setting sun. Within its sacred halls, two men faced each other, their breath misting in the frigid air. Robert Bruce, his hand resting on the hilt of his sword, glared at John Comyn, his once-ally turned bitter rival.

"You've gone too far this time, Comyn," Robert growled, his voice echoing off the vaulted ceiling. "Spreading lies, aligning with the English... and now this."

Comyn's lips curled into a sneer. "Lies? You speak to me of lies, Bruce? You, who would claim a throne that isn't yours?"

"The throne is my birthright," Robert snarled, taking a step forward. "A right you've sought to undermine at every turn."

"Birthright?" Comyn laughed, a cold, mirthless sound. "You're nothing but a pretender, Bruce. A false king leading an army of shadows."

Robert's eyes narrowed. "What are you talking about?"

"Don't play coy," Comyn spat. "The whispers grow louder every day. The vampire horde that plagues our lands – they say you lead them. That you've made a pact with darkness itself to claim the crown."

Robert's hand tightened on his sword. "Madness. *A pact with darkness?* I've never heard such mad words in a man's mouth. Speak sense, or speak no more." He shook his head, his voice sharp with contempt. "You're the one who's been courting the English, betraying your own people!"

"I do what I must to protect Scotland," Comyn retorted. "Even if it means aligning with Edward. Better an English king than a vampire lord."

The tension in the chapel was palpable, a taut string ready to snap. Robert's men shifted uneasily, hands on their weapons.

"Enough of this," Robert said, his voice low and dangerous. "Renounce your claim, Comyn. Swear fealty to me, and we can end this bloodshed."

For a moment, something flickered in Comyn's eyes – an emotion Robert couldn't quite place. Fear? Regret? But it was gone in an instant, replaced by cold determination.

"Never," Comyn hissed. "I'll die before I bend the knee to a monster like you."

The string snapped.

With a roar of fury, Robert drew his sword. The blade flashed in the dim light, finding its mark in Comyn's chest. Blood sprayed across the altar, a sacrilegious offering to an uncaring god.

Comyn's eyes widened in shock, his hands grasping weakly at the steel protruding from his body. He opened his mouth, but only a gurgle of blood escaped his lips.

"Finish it," Robert commanded, his voice hoarse.

His men surged forward, their blades rising and falling in a brutal frenzy. Comyn's body jerked and twitched under the onslaught, his blood pooling on the stone floor.

When it was over, Robert stared down at the mutilated corpse of his rival. The gravity of what he'd done crashed over him like a wave.

He had killed a man in a house of God, violated the sanctity of the church itself.

"We need to leave," one of his men urged, tugging at his arm. "Word will spread quickly. We must rally our forces before Edward's retaliation."

Robert nodded numbly, allowing himself to be led from the chapel.

As they mounted their horses and galloped into the gathering darkness, he couldn't shake the feeling that something fundamental had changed. That in his quest for the crown, he had set in motion events that would reshape the very fabric of Scotland.

Little did he know how right he was.

❖

As the sound of hoofbeats faded into the distance, an unnatural stillness fell over the Greyfriars Monastery. The monks, terrified by the violence they had witnessed, huddled in their cells, their prayers a futile whisper against the encroaching night.

In the chapel, Comyn's body lay motionless in a pool of congealing blood. The candles on the altar guttered and died, plunging the sacred space into darkness. For a long moment, there was only silence.

Then, a twitch. A finger curled. Bones shifted beneath lacerated flesh with a sickening crackle.

John Comyn opened his eyes.

They were no longer the eyes of a man, but something Other – ancient, hungry, and filled with an unholy fire. He gasped, drawing air into lungs that no longer needed it, more out of reflex than necessity.

The pain was excruciating, every nerve ending screaming as his body knit itself back together. But with the pain came something else: power. A dark, intoxicating energy that flooded his veins, replacing the blood he had lost.

Comyn had always been different. For years, he had hidden his true nature, playing at being human while secretly leading the vampire clans that lurked in Scotland's shadows. He had bided his time, maneuvering for power, waiting for the perfect moment to strike.

But Bruce had forced his hand. In death, Comyn had fully embraced the darkness within him. He was no longer just a vampire – he was something more. Something transcendent.

With agonizing slowness, he pushed himself to his feet. His wounds, grievous as they were, had already begun to close. He stumbled towards the chapel door, driven by an all-consuming hunger.

Outside, the night embraced him like a lover. Comyn's heightened senses picked up the scent of a nearby farm – of livestock, of humans. Of blood.

❖

He moved with preternatural speed, covering the distance in moments. The farmhouse door splintered under his inhuman strength. A woman's scream pierced the air, high and desperate. Comyn's hand clamped over her mouth, muffling her cries. Her eyes, wide with terror, reflected his inhuman hunger. The farmwife struggled against his iron grip, her nails clawing uselessly at his pale skin.

"Shh," Comyn whispered, his voice a silky caress. "It will all be over soon."

The kitchen door burst open. The farmer, a burly man with calloused hands, brandished a rusted pitchfork. "Get away from my wife, you bastard!"

Comyn's lips curled into a mocking smile. He spun, keeping the woman pressed against his chest as a shield. The farmer hesitated, his weapon wavering.

"Drop it," Comyn commanded, his voice thrumming with supernatural power. "Or I'll snap her neck."

The pitchfork clattered to the floor. In a blur of motion, Comyn shoved the woman aside. She hit the wall with a sickening crack, slumping to the ground. The vampire's free hand shot out, closing around the farmer's throat. Bones crunched under his fingers. The man's eyes bulged, his face purpling as he clawed desperately at Comyn's grip.

"I lied," Comyn hissed, baring needle-sharp fangs. He brought the dying man close, inhaling the intoxicating scent of fear. "This won't be quick at all."

His fangs sank deep. The farmer's struggles grew weaker as Comyn drank greedily, savoring every drop. When the flow slowed to a trickle, he dropped the withered husk to the floor. It landed with a meaty thud, limbs twitching in death throes.

A child's wail erupted from upstairs. Comyn's head snapped up, nostrils flaring. His lips curled into a feral grin, blood still dripping from his chin.

"Dessert," he purred.

He took the stairs two at a time, wood creaking under his inhuman speed. A door at the end of the hall was flung open. A boy, no more than eight, cowered in the far corner of the room. Tear tracks stained his cheeks, his small body trembling.

"There you are, little one," Comyn crooned. He stalked forward, savoring the spike of terror in the air. "Don't be afraid. I only want to play.

The child whimpered, pressing himself further into the corner. Comyn's hand shot out, fingers tangling in the boy's hair. He yanked the small body close, drinking in the scent of young, untainted blood.

"P-please," the boy sobbed. "I want my mommy.

Comyn chuckled, the sound devoid of warmth. "Oh, you'll see her soon enough. But first..."

His fangs descended. The child's scream was cut short as Comyn sank his teeth into the tender flesh of his throat. He fed slowly this time, savoring every drop of the sweet, innocent blood. Power surged through him with each swallow, filling him with unholy strength.

When it was done, Comyn let the small, lifeless body fall to the floor. He stood motionless for a moment, relishing the rush of fresh blood singing through his veins. Then, with deliberate steps, he made his way back downstairs.

The farmwife still lay crumpled where he'd thrown her. Her chest rose and fell with shallow breaths. Comyn crouched beside her, brushing a strand of hair from her face with mock tenderness.

"Wake up, my dear," he murmured. "The night's not over yet."

Her eyes fluttered open, unfocused at first. Then stark realization dawned. She opened her mouth to scream, but Comyn's hand clamped down once more.

"Now, now," he chided. "Let's not ruin the moment. Your husband and son were delicious. I do hope you'll be just as satisfying."

Tears streamed down the woman's face as Comyn's fangs descended. Her muffled cries grew weaker and weaker as he drained her dry, leaving nothing but a bloodless husk behind.

By the time the eastern sky blushed with the first hint of dawn, the farmhouse had fallen silent. Comyn stood amid the carnage, his clothes spattered crimson, his eyes gleaming with unholy satisfaction. The family lay strewn about like broken dolls, their bodies pale and withered.

Comyn licked his lips, savoring the lingering taste. His power had grown exponentially. Let the sun rise.

❖

Comyn stood in the yard, watching the approaching dawn. In the past, sunlight had been anathema to his kind. But now... now he felt no fear. Only an overwhelming sense of destiny.

He raised his arms, welcoming the sun's first rays. They washed over him, warm and golden, and Comyn laughed. It was a terrible sound, filled with triumph and madness.

"Robert Bruce," he whispered, his voice carrying on the morning breeze. "You thought to claim my throne? To end my life? Fool. You've only made me stronger."

Comyn's eyes blazed with unholy fire as he gazed across the Scottish landscape. His mind raced with plans, each more devious than the last. He would turn Bruce's reign into a nightmare, a constant battle against shadows and whispers.

"Let them call you king," Comyn snarled. "I'll make sure they call you monster."

He could see it all unfolding – the rumors he would spread, the fear he would sow. Bruce, the secret vampire king, thirsting for the blood of his subjects. The English, all too eager to believe the worst of their Scottish rival. And caught between them, the Scottish people, never knowing who to trust.

Comyn's lips curled into a cruel smile. He would build his army in the darkness, turning those with influence and power. Nobles, clergy, warriors – all would fall under his sway. And when the time was right, when Bruce was isolated and despised by all...

"Then," Comyn whispered, "I'll take back what's rightfully mine."

As if in answer to his dark proclamation, clouds began to gather on the horizon. A storm was coming – a storm that would reshape the destiny of nations.

❖

In Scone, Robert Bruce prepared for his coronation, unaware of the unholy force he had unleashed. In farmhouses and villages across the land, people barred their doors against the encroaching night, whispering prayers to a God who seemed increasingly distant.

And in a blood-soaked field, John Comyn, the true Vampire King, smiled. The great game had only just begun.

Comyn reveled in his newfound power, knowing he could easily end Bruce's life and decimate his family with barely a thought. But where was the sport in that? Eternity stretched before him, vast and potentially tedious. No, a quick death for Bruce would be far too merciful, too swift an end to their rivalry.

"Why rush?" Comyn mused aloud, his voice a low, chilling whisper. "I have all the time in the world to make you suffer, Robert. To watch you squirm, to see your precious crown become a crown of thorns."

His eyes glowed with malevolent glee as he imagined the years to come. He would be the puppet master, pulling strings from the shadows, orchestrating Bruce's slow descent into paranoia and despair. Each small victory for Bruce would be tainted, each moment of joy poisoned by doubt and fear.

"You'll never know peace," Comyn promised the distant horizon. "Your reign will be a nightmare, your legacy a cautionary tale. And when you've lost everything, when you're broken and alone, begging for the sweet release of death... Only then will I grant you the gift of eternity."

With a laugh that echoed across the empty field, Comyn turned away. The first move in his grand game of torment was yet to be made, and he could hardly wait to begin.

CHAPTER 23

Phil spotted the cherry-red Mini Cooper on the roadside, baking under the midday sun. The next gas station was maybe two miles ahead. He scowled, wishing he were home with Sheila, kneeling by the bathtub and washing her hair, instead of chasing down this mess. All for a girl who wasn't even his daughter anymore.

Isobel had become a stranger to him at twelve, the day she got her first period. It was like some alien creature had replaced his little girl. Their bond had unraveled, much like it had with Rhona. Both females in perfect sync, slipping away from him. He'd always known it would end this way.

With luck, he'd catch Isobel before the station. This back road saw little traffic beyond locals and the odd hiker. Now Rhona was en route with Cameron in tow, a meeting Phil dreaded. He didn't need his writer's imagination to picture the tense atmosphere heading their way. This whole mess promised to be one hell of a headache.

He spotted a figure in the distance and eased off the gas. Walking wasn't bad for her condition. Last night, when she'd finally dragged the truth out of him, she'd been anything but sympathetic.

"Hey, wait a second," he'd shot back. "I was still your father for twenty years, you know. Don't forget that so quickly. I took care of you, treated you the same as if you were mine. I didn't make a difference."

He couldn't tell if her contempt came more from the fake paternity bombshell or his fling with a girl even younger than her—Sheila reminding him it was bedtime, rubbing against him just to twist the knife. But one thing was crystal clear: he'd hit rock bottom in Isobel's eyes. While he couldn't say it was tearing him apart, he had to admit the possibility of a slight emotional bruise.

He pulled over, prepped a quick line on the cup holder, then glanced at the golden sky. Realizing how late it was getting, he went to collect Isobel.

He cruised up beside her.

"Look," he said, leaning out the window, "I get it. You're in a tough spot. I agree. It could be simpler. But let me remind you, I was born under X, and I never made a big deal about it."

In a flash, Isobel snatched up a rock and hurled it. The windshield exploded into a spiderweb of cracks.

This was exactly what he'd meant about her turning into some alien creature. That wild temper of hers. Untamed. Unpredictable. Downright terrifying.

When Phil reflected on his composed reaction, a satisfied smile still lingered as night fell. His pulse had raced, staring at Isobel through the spider-webbed glass, unsure of her next move. But he'd kept his cool. He'd spat out glass shards, shaken more from his hair and ears, without a word. Just a pained look.

Isobel had faltered, thrown by his restraint. Her outburst felt excessive, unfair. She couldn't explain it.

She helped Phil clean up most of the mess.

Now, she was holed up in her old room, silent.

❖

Phil finally coaxed Sheila from her bath. He'd missed the shampoo ritual, kicking himself for it, but things could've been worse. "Count yourself lucky," she purred, propping a foot on the tub's edge and spreading herself for his tongue.

He was putty in her hands. He knew she led him like a puppet, but he was utterly addicted to Sheila. Sexually, she drove him wild—most weekends they barely left the bed, naked and sleepless, making constant bathroom runs day and night.

He hoped Rhona wouldn't make any comments and that Sheila wouldn't cause trouble. With luck, old grudges would fade fast—he even chuckled imagining Cameron replacing his windshield for free after they shook hands. He sent Rhona a reassuring text before joining Sheila on the couch.

Nothing beat an eighteen-year-old tigress, Phil was convinced. By twenty, it was already too late; they started overthinking things, no longer just listening to their bodies.

Sheila had a generous pussy and a clit about two centimeters long, like a plump macaroni. "You realize you've been searching for that all your life," he'd confide to his middle-aged buddies, all experts on the subject.

He left her panting, soaked through, with a roll of paper towels. He whipped up a simple meal, watching a live Oasis concert with her on TV and repeatedly reminding her to put on underwear while he made mayonnaise for some cold cuts.

❖

Isobel's stomach churned as she sifted through her old belongings. Phil had commandeered her childhood room for his office, and she knew it was time to cut ties for good. The clock ticked past eleven as she methodically sorted her life into two piles: keep and trash.

"You'll always have a home here if you need it," Phil murmured, his voice barely audible over the rustle of cardboard boxes.

Outside, the night sky stretched like black velvet, studded with familiar constellations. A few wispy clouds drifted lazily overhead. Under the sprawling oak tree just beyond her open window, fireflies performed their silent, glittering dance.

The sweet scent of the countryside wafted in, but it did nothing to soothe Isobel's churning emotions. As her hands moved mechanically through years of accumulated memories, she couldn't shake the unsettling feeling that she was pawing through a stranger's life. Each item she touched felt foreign, disconnected from the person she'd become.

❖

Gordon snatched Brock from his wheelchair, yanking him up by the lapels. He and Fiona had debated this for hours, finally convincing themselves it was justified. Now, face-to-face with Brock, Gordon felt no remorse.

They'd ambushed Brock after his weekly swim. His hair still dripped as he wheeled toward the bus stop, oblivious to the storm about to hit.

In a blur, Gordon burst from the bushes where he and Fiona had been lurking. He shoved Brock behind the building, the air thick with the reek of bleach. It happened in seconds - no witnesses, no time for Brock to react. Now it was too late.

Gordon glared at Brock, their faces inches apart. He poured all his hatred into that stare, lifting the smaller man effortlessly. Disgust twisted Gordon's features as he finally flung Brock back into his chair.

"What the hell?" Fiona hissed.

Brock's smile dripped contempt. Without warning, he spat in Fiona's face. She recoiled, wiping furiously at her cheek. Her eyes flashed, and she lashed out. The slap cracked like a whip, snapping Brock's head to the side.

Gordon met Fiona's gaze, rage simmering beneath the surface. He grabbed Brock's collar, fangs itching to descend, and hurled him to the ground. Brock hit the asphalt hard but propped himself up, cackling. A perfect red handprint bloomed on his cheek.

His laughter grew, twisted and dark. Gordon snapped. He seized the wheelchair and smashed it against the wall. Metal shrieked, wheels flew, and bricks crumbled under the impact.

Fiona winced, hands flying to her ears. The afternoon light filtered through purple beech leaves, casting an eerie glow over the Bank of Scotland's manicured flowerbeds. The peaceful scene stood in stark contrast to the violence unfolding in the shadows.

❖

Gordon and Fiona drove in silence, the aftermath of their actions heavy between them. Gordon's mind churned. He'd had his share of messy affairs - angry husbands, the constant strain of sneaking around. But this? This was a whole new level of complicated.

He'd always craved that sense of belonging, of slipping into someone else's life. Warmth and comfort he couldn't create for himself. It all traced back to Rhona, to wounds inflicted when he was too young to heal properly. But this time, he'd outdone himself.

Was this some cosmic joke? A one-in-a-million disaster? As they merged into the swelling rush-hour traffic, Gordon stole glances at Fiona. Despite everything, he couldn't bring himself to regret what they'd done.

His thoughts were a tangled mess, but something deep inside him had shifted. He couldn't name it, but it pulsed with significance, demanding to be acknowledged.

❖

There was no indication that Margaret had any clairvoyant abilities. She hadn't seen the troubles coming for her family, and all her fervent praying hadn't given her a heads-up about the storms that had wrecked her life. But lately, she'd been hounding Fiona to have a talk with Gordon. She couldn't explain why, exactly—just a gut feeling.

"We can't know what's around the corner," Margaret pressed. "Nobody can. But there's a right time to keep quiet, and a right time to speak up."

A flicker of fear crossed Margaret's face as she mentioned possible disasters. It made Fiona uneasy. She wasn't worried about Rhona stealing Gordon away—the older ex's reputation in the sack was well-earned, but Fiona knew she could hold her own. Still, Margaret's words were chipping away at her confidence. If some storm of insanity really could upend everything they knew about how people behaved, well... maybe there was reason to worry after all.

❖

Fiona returned from the grueling showdown with Brock to find Margaret fidgeting like a cat on a hot tin roof. Sure, her husband was in the hospital, but Fiona was getting a read on the older woman. Margaret clearly had something to say, and Gordon's lingering presence was grating on her last nerve. He'd announced his intention to shower but was taking his sweet time, now demonstrating to Amelia how to make a coin vanish up his sleeve.

Margaret finally cracked. She marched up to her son and wrinkled her nose. "Gordon, you reek. Go clean up already."

Fiona could practically feel the urgency radiating off Margaret. As Gordon trudged upstairs, unconvincingly sniffing his shirt, Fiona braced herself for the inevitable. Sure enough, Margaret pounced, grabbing her arm and pulling her close for some covert scheming.

The vast Victorian living room stretched out before them, all wood and glass, opening onto the garden. Fiona's gaze drifted to the unobstructed view of sky and river. The silence here was a balm after years of cramped suburb living – no nosy neighbors, just blessed quiet. She sank into a plush armchair, appreciating its depth, the softness of nearby sofas, the lush carpets underfoot.

As day faded to dusk, the room's atmosphere shifted, painting everything in softer hues. Fiona couldn't deny it – she was falling for this place. It felt... right. A far cry from her usual stomping grounds of the bruised and battered, the down-on-their-luck crowd hanging laundry on sagging lines.

This manor whispered of possibilities, of not always being on the losing side.

So when Margaret launched into her urgent plea for swift, decisive action, Fiona found herself listening intently. Night crept in, the world beyond the windows fading to inky black. And with each passing moment, Fiona felt herself being inexorably drawn towards Margaret's radical stance.

"It's your safety net," Margaret hissed, her eyes burning with intensity. "Fiona, my dear, you need to get ahead of this. Secure an ironclad position, you hear me? Unassailable. Those don't come easy. Don't wait until it's too late. I'm begging you, don't let yourself get swept under. Act now. I can feel something coming. It's giving me chills. Do it. Trust me on this."

At thirty-five, Fiona struggled to see the world through Margaret's sixty-three-year-old eyes. Sure, she had her own feelings about the situation, but Margaret's urgency was on another level. Sometimes, Fiona found the older woman downright exhausting. The idea of living under the same roof made her skin crawl – hadn't she run away at sixteen for some peace and quiet? Still, Fiona had to admit, Margaret could be as cunning as any fresh-faced schemer bitch when she wanted to be.

❖

Throughout dinner, Fiona felt Margaret's gaze boring into her. Every time she glanced up, those eyes were there, unblinking, as if trying to drill something directly into Fiona's brain. Margaret was right, Fiona grudgingly admitted, but damn if she wasn't draining. The woman had already hit that particular level of intensity that bordered on madness.

❖

Fiona straddled Gordon in the moonlit room, her mind oddly detached. She felt no shame, no guilt. Margaret, who'd lately taken to gin and fire-and-brimstone sermons with equal fervor, wouldn't even consider this a real betrayal. Different perspectives and all that.

Still, Fiona was done with these furtive encounters. A flimsy screen between them and Amelie in this sprawling Victorian felt... wrong. She loved the manor, but this setup had to change.

As Gordon's hips bucked wildly, his fingers digging into Fiona's thighs, she felt him swell inside her. The fullness sent shivers of pleasure radiating through her core. Fiona cupped her firm breasts, offering them to Gordon's hungry gaze. Her wild, thick hair formed a dark halo backlit by the silvery moon streaming through the window.

His face contorted in ecstasy, sweat glistening on his brow. Right as he reached that point of no return, his whole body quivering on the cusp of release, Fiona leaned in close. Her lips brushed his ear as she dropped her bombshell.

"Gordon, I'm pregnant."

He came with a strangled groan, words failing him. If Margaret had been eavesdropping, she might've shed a tear of joy. Or at least relief.

Gordon's mouth worked silently. In the distance, an owl hooted from its perch in the gleaming firs. The words hung in the air between them:

"Gordon, I'm pregnant."

❖

Isobel froze as she entered the living room. On the couch, Sheila lay with her legs spread wide, Phil's head buried between them, sucking on her clitoris. The sight of her father figure in such an intimate position made Isobel's cheeks burn. This was definitely not a "Hey, I'm heading out, need anything?" moment.

Opting for a hasty exit, Isobel slipped out through the kitchen window. She had packed several large garbage bags full of childhood relics - notebooks, posters, photos, stuffed animals, sports gear, girl's magazines, and framed portraits. A lifetime of memories destined for disposal.

She began hauling the bags to the leaf-burning area behind the house. With each trip, Isobel's eyes were drawn to the writhing figures on the couch. Their pale skin gleamed in the dim light, naked bodies shifting into new positions as if on cue.

Try as she might, Isobel couldn't look away. Like a driver rubber-necking at a crash, she found herself stealing glances at the primal scene. The whole situation felt surreal, especially when Phil caught her eye and winked.

❖

Isobel glanced up to see Phil standing at the kitchen window, clad only in briefs. He nibbled delicately on an apple, mindful of his dental issues. Catching her eye, he gestured toward the bags, offering assistance.

"No thanks," Isobel called back. Phil waved, unbothered.

As she prepared the fire, Isobel's thoughts drifted to Sheila. The image of the eighteen-year-old sprawled on the couch, sated and sex-dazed, lingered in her mind. She wondered if men of a certain age possessed secret knowledge about female sexuality, using it to maintain control. The idea was unsettling.

Unbidden, memories of her dentist surfaced. Isobel pushed them away, disgusted with herself for the intrusive thoughts.

Phil's voice cut through her musings. "There's gasoline in the shed if you need it," he called out.

Isobel turned, taking in the sight of this hairy, middle-aged man in tiny briefs. This shameless figure was the man she'd once called father. The realization hit her anew, strange and jarring.

Shaking her head, she returned to her task. The sooner she could burn away the remnants of her old life, the better.

❖

The Aston Martin's engine growled as it carved through the Highland night. Cameron glanced at Rhona, his voice low. "What are your deepest thoughts on this?"

Rhona sighed, her gaze fixed on the dark road ahead. "I wish I knew. It's tormented me for years, but I'm no closer to an answer now than the day she was born. It seems impossible, yet here we are. This mystery feels... imposed on me somehow."

Cameron's hands tightened on the wheel. "If she's my daughter, I'll know soon enough. Remember, I wasn't supposed to feel anything. It'll be like the first time."

"And you'll just feel it? Where I, her mother, have failed for twenty years?"

"Absolutely. I'll know in the first minute."

Rhona began giving directions, a sign they were nearing their destination. The country road wound through fields and woods, the landscape growing wilder. They drove with the windows down, cool air whipping through the car. Despite their attempts at lighthearted banter, tension crackled between them.

Rhona felt a twist in her gut at the thought of bringing Cameron to this place—her old life, shared with another man, where Isobel had grown up. Cameron, for his part, already despised this haven of Rhona's past.

Then Rhona pointed out the path that led to the house in a small clearing.

The Aston Martin slowed, gravel crunching beneath its tires.

❖

As they stepped out of the car, Cameron caught an unexpected scent in the air. The acrid scent of smoke hung in the air. Cameron sniffed, brow furrowing. "Are they grilling sausages?"

Inside, Phil had donned pants and a t-shirt, tidying the living room. "Sheila, for the love of God, put on some underwear before everyone gets here," he pleaded for the umpteenth time. Sheila, sprawled on the couch and spooning ice cream into her mouth, ignored him.

Behind the house, flames leapt high, casting writhing shadows. Isobel paced nervously, watching her past turn to ash. As each memento vanished, she felt increasingly untethered. The enormity of what was happening crashed over her. She cursed, fists clenching.

The fire's heat intensified, sending a shower of sparks skyward. Isobel retreated, leaning against the shed. Impatient to finish, she grabbed a hideous earthenware pitcher – a relic from her pre-high school days – and filled it with gasoline.

It was reckless, idiotic even, and she knew it. A sharp tapping drew her gaze to the window. Phil stood there, his ring creating a staccato rhythm against the glass as he emphatically shook his head 'no.'

Isobel sneered. The last thing they needed was her burning the house down. Though it would certainly give them something to talk about if conversation ran dry.

Somehow, Isobel managed to ignite the very shed she'd sought refuge in—one of those improbable events that pepper existence, defying logic yet undeniably real.

Phil, witnessing it all, later recounted the irresistible chain of events. Isobel, spotting their arrival at the last second, dashed into the shed. In her haste, she broke rule number one: always keep the hose at hand, especially when the blaze roars like a reactor, spitting long, swirling flames.

The roof, a tinderbox of wood and tar, caught fire as if by sorcery. It ignited like paper just as they exited the car. Heat created a vortex, driving flames against the old barn-turned-storage shed—Isobel's last sanctuary. The jerry can exploded, engulfing the structure in a river of fire. Everyone hit the ground as the inferno lit up the countryside.

Isobel cowered beneath the workbench, terror gripping her. Fire invaded through windows and door, molten tar raining from above. Acrid smoke choked the air, filled with a hellish symphony of crackling, roaring, whistling, and creaking. Around her, glass shattered, paint bubbled, metal warped. Tools clattered to the ground as rags became impromptu torches.

Trapped in this nightmare, Isobel cried and coughed, her lungs burning as fiercely as the world around her.

❖

As chaos reigned, fate intervened. Through the hellish tableau, a figure emerged - Cameron, silhouetted against the inferno.

He batted at his smoldering sleeve, flames licking at his skin, eyes watering in the smoke. Dodging a falling beam, forehead blackened, he locked eyes with Isobel. A smile, incongruous yet reassuring, flickered across his face as he spotted her cowering form.

Fear paralyzed Isobel. She trembled, whimpering - more frightened cub than defiant woman. The air around them roared, thick with heat and smoke. In that moment of sheer terror, something primal awoke within her. Bones shifted, skin rippled, and fur sprouted as Isobel experienced her first transformation into a wolf.

For a heartbeat, Cameron stood transfixed, marveling at the unlikely tableau. Then, without hesitation, he scooped her into his arms. No words were needed; Isobel's labored breathing told him all he needed to know.

Cameron began a frantic dance, weaving through flames and dodging embers raining from above. Isobel clung to his neck as he pivoted, grunting with exertion. He aimed for the exit he'd used, but disorientation set in as smoke filled his lungs.

In this crucible of fire, rescuer and rescued moved as one - a strange danse macabre amidst the flames.

Cameron made a split-second decision. Clutching Isobel tightly, he leapt through a window, its charred frame crumbling at their touch. They tumbled through the air, landing with a thud in Phil's carefully tended cannabis patch.

For a moment, Cameron lay on his back, gasping for air. He hadn't loosened his grip on Isobel during their fall, cradling her against his chest like a precious pup. Her breathing came in ragged pants, hot and fast against his neck.

Behind them, the shed's roof groaned, on the verge of collapse. Flames roared skyward, transforming the night into a hellish tableau. The inferno blazed like a fallen star, casting everything in stark relief.

As Cameron caught his breath, a thought flashed through his mind: saving his daughter's life on the day they met - not a bad way to start things off.

It was then that he truly saw Isobel for the first time. In her wolf form, she was breathtaking - coat as black as midnight, pierced by startling neon blue eyes. She was every bit as striking as her mother, a true black wolf of legend.

END OF SEASON ONE

THE CLAN OF BRUCE SAGA WILL RETURN:
THE LAST VAMPIRE FAMILY - SEASON TWO

A FAVOUR BEFORE YOU GO!

As we close the first season of *Clan of Bruce - The Last Vampire Family*, I truly hope you've enjoyed the journey as much as I've loved creating it. Your companionship through these pages has been invaluable.

Now, I have a small but meaningful request. If you found yourself captivated by this story, please consider leaving a review. Whether it's just a few words or a detailed account of your experience, your feedback means the world to authors like me. It also helps other readers discover and join us on this adventure.

You can share your thoughts on the platform where you purchased the book or on your favourite review sites like Amazon, Goodreads, Barnes & Noble, and more.

Thank you for being part of this journey. I can't wait to share more stories with you in the future!

With heartfelt thanks,

Alice Rose McQueen

FEELING SOCIAL?

LET'S KEEP IN TOUCH! CONNECT WITH ME HERE:

www.alicerosebooks.com
Facebook.com/booksbyalicerose
Instagram.com/booksbyalicerose/
Tiktok.com/@booksbyalicerose

About the Author

Alice Rose McQueen is not just an urban fantasy author but also a singer and magician who often spends her time on tour. Her literary adventure began with a tumor she had to tame, which became a persistent companion, bringing good days and bad. The pain often prevents her from functioning normally, and when she has to lie down and stay still, she writes. Convenient, right?

In her daily life, Alice is surrounded by her two feathery and mischievous companions, Jimmy and Jean-Kevin. These two birds, although a bit too noisy and often intrusive, bring a joyful cacophony to her writing days.

In addition to juggling her many passions, Alice is also a young grandmother, having become a mom at a very young age. This adds an extra layer of chaos and happiness to her busy life.

She also has a few little secrets: despite a general indifference to chocolate, she devours impressive quantities of it while writing, even if it means gaining a few pounds per finished book (4 kg on average).

To add a touch of adventure to her already eventful life, Alice has had a near-death experience—an adventure that was strange and almost pleasant, profoundly influencing her perspective on life and death.

Her mantra? "Let's enjoy life before it kills us." Alice Rose lives with resilience and passion, continuing to captivate her readers with magical and deeply human stories.

Printed in Great Britain
by Amazon

54423434R00218